CAN YOU HEAR THE NIGHTBIRD CALL?

ALSO BY ANITA RAU BADAMI

Tamarind Mem
The Hero's Walk

ANITA RAU BADAMI

CAN YOU HEAR
THE NIGHTBIRD
CALL?

 ALFRED A. KNOPF CANADA

This is a work of fiction. All situations, incidents, dialogue and characters, with the exception of some well-known historical and public figures mentioned in this novel, are products of the author's imagination and are not to be construed as real. They are not intended to depict actual events or people or to change the entirely fictional nature of the work. In all other respects, any resemblance to persons living or dead is entirely coincidental.

PUBLISHED BY ALFRED A. KNOPF CANADA

Copyright © 2006 Anita Rau Badami

Published in 2006 by Alfred A. Knopf Canada, a division of Random House of Canada Limited. Distributed by Random House of Canada Limited, Toronto.

Knopf Canada and colophon are trademarks.

www.randomhouse.ca

Library and Archives Canada Cataloguing in Publication

Badami, Anita Rau, 1961–
Can you hear the nightbird call? / Anita Rau Badami.

ISBN-13: 978-0-676-97604-5
ISBN-10: 0-676-97604-2

I. Title.

PS8553.A2845C36 2006   C813'.54   C2005-901791-0

First Edition

Printed and bound in the United States of America

2 4 6 8 9 7 5 3 1

IN MEMORY OF THE MAN ON THE BRIDGE IN
MODINAGAR AND THE VICTIMS OF
AIR INDIA FLIGHT 182.

My memory keeps getting in the way of your history.
—Agha Shahid Ali, "Farewell"

—

"We went to him and said, 'What's this
you've done? You've had all our men killed.
You were known to us.'"
—Nanki Bai's testimony, from
The Delhi Riots: Three Days in the Life of a Nation,
Uma Chakravarti and Nandita Haksar

—

"In one of the worst acts of aviation terrorism, Air-India's
Boeing 747, *Kanishka,* on its way from Toronto to India
via London, was blown up off the Irish coast on
June 23, 1985, killing all the 329 people on board."
—"The *Kanishka* Bombing," www.hindustantimes.com

CONTENTS

PART FOUR – HERE AND THERE

PART FIVE – ENDINGS

CAN YOU HEAR THE NIGHTBIRD CALL?

PART ONE

—

BIBI-JI

ONE

CHILDHOOD

—

Panjaur

1928

Years before she stole her sister Kanwar's fate and sailed across the world from India to Canada, before she became Bibi-ji, she was Sharanjeet Kaur. Her memories began from the time she was a six-year-old living in a village called Panjaur, a dot in that landscape of villages scattered across the fertile plains of West Punjab, alike in their annual yearning for the monsoon rains and a bountiful harvest. The house in which Bibi-ji, or Sharan as her family called her then, lived with her parents and Kanwar was as unassuming as its surroundings. One of a small cluster of Sikh and Hindu houses, it was separated from the Muslim homes by fields of swaying sugar cane. Built of mud and thatch, it was much smaller than the one made of brick and mortar farther down the dusty gulley. That house belonged to Sharan's best friend, Jeeti, and never failed to create a tumultuous envy in her childish heart. Though she was fond of Jeeti, Sharan resented her for having so much—a brick house, servants who did the housework, fine clothes and a father who did not lie inert on a cot all day while his wife and daughters slaved away. But the thing she envied most of all was Jeeti's supply of lavender soap, sent by Sher Singh, her father, all the way from Canada.

Years later, when she possessed enough money to build a house out of soap if she so desired, Sharan could barely recall Jeeti's face or her elaborate home. And since, after Partition, Panjaur itself disappeared into that grey zone between India and Pakistan where floodlights threw every detail into stark contrast, barbed wire bristled and soldiers kept watch year-round, she could not even return to the place of her origins, a necessary thing if memory is to be kept fully alive. Yet some of those days remained in her mind, sharp and clear as shards of glass.

The first of these was the day her father, Harjot Singh, disappeared. It was only the second time in his life that he had left his family, but this time he did not return.

That day Sharan had been woken at five o'clock in the morning by her mother, Gurpreet Kaur. The late September sun was just rising, wreathed in mist. She lay on a mat in the courtyard of the house, her dark eyes squeezed shut, hands pressed tight against her ears to block the sound of her mother's voice cutting through her comfortable blanket of sleep.

"Do I have to do everything in this house?" Gurpreet shouted from the kitchen, where she was already cooking the morning meal though it was barely past dawn. "Look at this princess! Servants she has! Maids and chaprasis! *Sharanjeet*. Wake up this minute, or you will get a bucket of water on your face."

How unfair, Sharan thought. Would she *ever* have the chance to sleep until the sun climbed into the sky? A tear worked its way down her cheek. Another tear joined the first, and soon a storm of weeping shook her small body. "Why do I have to get up?" she sobbed. "I don't *want* to!

"There is no place in this house for wants, memsahib!" Gurpreet called sharply, smacking a ladle hard against the edge of a pot. Her daughter knew how effectively she used her kitchen utensils to indicate various degrees of annoyance, from mild indignation to rage. "Needs, yes, those I can take care of," she continued, "but wants are for rich people! Understand?" Another tap-tap of metal on metal. Sharper, more insistent this time.

A warm hand descended on Sharan's heaving shoulder and shook it gently.

"Wake up, child," said her father. "Amma is calling you."

Sharan sniffed a little louder, removed her hands from her ears and turned over so that her father could see she had been weeping. She opened her eyes dolefully and, pushing out her lower lip, allowed it to tremble, hoping that she looked tragic, that he would take her side, as he so often did. Was she not his favourite daughter? Was she not the only person who listened to his endless stories of a ship called the *Komagata Maru* and a voyage that ended in nothing?

But there was no help. Wake up, wake up. This was her fate, written on her forehead by the gods, she thought unhappily, rolling to a sitting position and wiping her wet face with the end of her faded kameez—it was her *wretched* fate to have to wake up and dip her hands in piles of excrement. Every morning since she was four years old, she had had to start the day by picking up the hot, stinking shit that the family's two cows dropped in the courtyard. Then she had to make balls of the disgusting mess and pat them into circular cakes against the walls of their house. And the smell—how the smell corrupted her waking hours and infected her dreams and ruined even her meals. This was what Sharan resented most of all, for she loved eating. Her joy at the sight of food turned even the simplest combination of rice and dal into a feast, but when she raised a morsel of food to her mouth she could only smell the overpowering odour that had written itself into her skin, instead of the fragrances of turmeric, fresh rice, butter melting on hot phulkas, green chillies frying. She wished then, with all her heart, that she, like the Arabian princess in a tale the wandering storyteller had told her, might wake up and find herself in a different home altogether, carried there by the jinns in the service of a handsome prince.

Later, in Vancouver, when she had lost her past, she would feel shame at her thoughtless girl's wish. She yearned for the return of that time when her family was entire—her mother squatting by the clay stove, the harsh angles and hollows of her exhausted face exaggerated by the glow from the fire, her father with his distant eyes, and most of all Kanwar, her sturdy, loving, lost sister. Lost, because she, Sharanjeet Kaur, had been greedy for something much larger than the world she inhabited.

But on that day in 1928, the six-year-old child thought only of how much she loathed the grating, ever-present irritation in her mother's voice, the heat, the dust, the smallness of Panjaur, the seemingly endless quantities of shit that their bony cows produced morning, noon and night, her two faded salwar kameez suits, Kanwar's silent acceptance of everything that was thrown at her, and most of all the fact that she had no soap with which to wash her hands after working on the dung.

She dragged her feet out into the morning and splashed water from a bucket on her face. Having cleared the sleep from her eyes, she chewed the bitter neem twig that served as a toothbrush and stared out at the fields, which were separated from the house by a dusty lane and a canal of brackish water. She could see small splashes of colour where villagers were working in their fields or crossing them, carrying bundles of laundry, to reach the river. A child screamed from one of the nearby houses. Perhaps it was Jeeti's brother, a spoilt child who howled for any reason and had to be regularly appeased with a treat.

A cool wind blew in from the west and tore through the tall stands of sugar cane, making them bend and shudder in their shadowy depths. Another month and the Diwali festival would be here, Sharan remembered with a spark of pleasure. She ran out of the yard to the edge of the field, where a holy stone, believed by the Hindus of the village to harbour a powerful goddess, reared out of the earth. It was smeared with turmeric and vermilion, and someone had scattered flowers around it. She touched the stone, earnestly whispering a prayer, as she and Jeeti often did together. As a Sikh she already knew she was not supposed to worship idols and stones and pictures, but her mother had said that gods from all religions were holy and it would not hurt to pray to them now and again. Sharan begged the stone for a good harvest so that there would be money left over after paying off the moneylender and she would get a new set of bangles—red with gold stripes—just like Jeeti's. She trailed back into the yard, chewing discontentedly on the neem twig, moments before her mother emerged from the house. Gurpreet stood at the door, arms akimbo, glaring at her younger daughter. "What are you doing for so long? Your teeth will fall out if you rub them so hard!" She pointed her chin at Kanwar, who had also woken before dawn and was now in the yard shaking a soopa of rice to remove the chaff from the grain. "Look at her, how much she helps me! And you . . ."

Kanwar, who never did anything to stir her mother's anger, waited until Gurpreet had retreated into the house before grabbing her sister around the waist and hugging her close. Tall and strong for her fourteen years, she lifted Sharan in the air, swung her around, set her down and tickled her vigorously. "Gudh-gudhee, gudh-gudhee!" she said, using the nonsense words she reserved for Sharan, prodding her waist, her round belly, the hollows under the childish arms. "Let's see a smile! Khillee-khillee!"

Sharan wriggled away, refusing to humour Kanwar although it was hard not to respond to her tickling fingers.

Still, it was necessary to let the world know how resentful she was, so she shrugged out of Kanwar's embrace and, picking up a basket as large as herself, walked off to where the cows were tethered. She scooped the slimy dung into the basket and took it to the side of the house where the sun shone all morning. Her father had already dragged his cot there and lay motionless, ignoring the hubhub around him. Sharan squatted beside the sun-stroked wall of the house and began to slap small balls of the dung against it, quickly patting each into a disc with her fingers.

Soon Gurpreet and Kanwar left the house with a jangle of glass bracelets, each bearing a bundle of laundry on her head. Sharan watched them make their way through the rattling green of the sugar cane fields until they disappeared from sight.

She worked steadily until the wall was covered with even dung pats like so many rough quarter plates. Then she put the basket away in a corner and washed her hands hard, wishing she had something other than wood ash with which to scrub. She longed to run down the road to Jeeti's house and beg for a small smear of that most coveted of belongings—a bar of scented soap. Surely Jeeti would not begrudge her a tiny bubble or two?

Sharan glanced at her father. His eyes were shut, and his breathing had evolved into a series of snores, which meant that he was fast asleep. She could run to Jeeti's place and be back before he had finished a snore. She tiptoed close to the cot and peered at the hairy face with its unkempt beard and moustache, slack mouth, long thin nose and narrow forehead. His hair, which like that of the other Sikh men in the village was long and uncut, was loosely knotted on top of his head. His knobbly hands were clasped on his oil-slicked chest, which rose and fell to the rhythm of his breathing. Sharan wondered why her father slept all day long. As far as she knew, he was not a sick man. He did not constantly cough or wheeze or complain of aches like the grandfathers who gathered like a flock of cadaverous old crows around the banyan tree in the centre of the village every afternoon. Harjot Singh's limbs were intact and he ate like a buffalo. But he rarely spoke, never left the house and always looked lost, as if there was something he had forgotten and he could only lie helplessly on the cot, staring off into the distance, until it to came back to him. Sometimes it seemed to Sharan that her father was not really there at all, that he was just a shadow. It would take many years for her to understand that Harjot Singh was *not* in fact there. In his mind he was continents away, in a green and blue city called Vancouver, which he had once seen from the deck of a ship—a place that had turned him away from its shores as if he were a pariah dog.

Her breath feathered across her father's face and stirred the wispy hairs of his long beard. Harjot Singh opened his eyes and caught Sharan in his gaze. He sat up, yawned mightily and drew her down on his lap.

"Are you done, child?" he asked, one thin hand caressing her head, smoothing the tendrils that had escaped from the thick braids that hung down each side of her face. "Do you want to eat your food now? What has your mother made for us, hmmm?"

Sharan gave him a sideways look, her chocolate eyes calculating. "Bappa, can I go to Jeeti's house? I will come back very quickly. In this many minutes." She held up five small fingers and tilted her head in a way she hoped was disarming.

But Harjot's gaze skimmed past her face, out of the narrow door that framed the stark sky above and the dust-strip of a road below, past the wave of sugar cane and the stretching mustard fields so golden bright it seemed the sun had turned liquid and poured across the earth, across the familiar landscape to that unknown distant land that was lodged within him like a thorn.

Then he said sadly, as if his daughter had not spoken at all, "I was *almost* there, putthar. Like Sher Singh, I could have lived in Canada and become rich." His gaze returned to rest on his daughter's pleading face. "If they had allowed us to stay there, you know what your life would have been like?"

Sharan sighed. "No, Bappa," she said, and resigned herself to listening to the story that had begun years before she was born. She hated this ship that had caused the disappointment clogging her father's heart, that had snatched his dreams away and turned him into a barren-eyed man with no desire to do more than lie on his cot.

"If they had allowed me to get off the *Komagata Maru*, you and your mother and your sister would now be living like queens. We too would have had a pukka house with five rooms, three cows, and twenty chickens . . ."

Six-year-old Sharan looked into his sombre black eyes and listened to his stories of a mighty ocean, of strange fish that flew out of its rolling depths to catch the sun's rays, of dark forests of trees that grew tall and pointed like great arrows. She wondered at his tales of the unimaginably distant lands he had crossed to reach the place he called Canada. She marvelled at the thought of the bullock carts, buses, trains and ships that had carried him there. She had never stepped outside the close circle of her village, did not know what lay beyond the fields spreading out from the dust road outside their home, while her father had been to places like Amritsar, Delhi, Calcutta, Singapore. And Hong Kong! Where on earth was this strange place that sounded like the mournful call of geese flying over fields? She listened open-mouthed even though she had heard the story a hundred times already, her stinking hands a mere memory until, with a jangle of bracelets, her mother returned balancing one bundle of clean laundry on her head and holding another on her hip like a baby. She dropped her load on the ground and looked tiredly at her husband and daughter relaxing in the shade.

"Amma, I finished my work and Bappa was telling me about his dreams," Sharan said quickly, hoping to avert the descent of her mother's hard hand on her legs and back. She thought guiltily of the dirty basket that she should have washed as soon as she was done with the cow dung.

"Dreams?" Gurpreet said sardonically. "How nice it would be if these dreams could be harvested and sold to pay off our debts to that moneylender."

Sometime that night, while the wind hissed through the village and the cane shook its long fingers at the dark sky and a bird called in warning from the tamarind tree, Harjot Singh finally left the safety of his string cot and his home and walked away. His family awaited his return for weeks, unwilling to believe that the man who had been a fixture on that cot was no longer there. No one in the village had seen him go. The pariah dogs that roamed the dusty roads had not warned of his departure with a volley of barks. Not even Dhanna, the halfwit who was in love with the moon and stayed up all night bawling out songs to it, not even he had seen Harjot leave.

When there was no news for a month, rumours began to circulate: Harjot Singh had been carried away by evil spirits; he had run off with the woman who did the juggling act with the travelling nautanki troupe; he had gone to join the struggle against the British, drawn like increasing numbers of young men in villages and towns across India by the insistent drumbeat of the independence movement. This last story was the one that Gurpreet decided to keep. After all, she told her neighbours and her daughters, Harjot Singh *had* been resentful about his treatment at the hands of the goras who ruled the country, he had never understood why he and the other passengers on the *Komagata Maru*, every one of them British citizens, had been refused entry to Canada and the ship turned back. So Gurpreet informed the women at the village well and the other nosy parkers who came with avid eyes and false sympathy to her door that her husband, the man who for years had clung to his cot and to his silence, had been transformed into a fiery revolutionary and was roaming the country. Now, every time news arrived in

13

Panjaur of a railway line that had been blown up or a bridge that had been sabotaged in this or that part of the country, Gurpreet spread the rumour that Harjot was one of the perpetrators. In time, and with frequent telling, everyone, Sharan included, came to believe that he had indeed joined the revolutionaries—a hero if he was alive, a martyr if he had died. She was a pragmatic woman. She had two daughters to marry off, and unsavoury stories about evil spirits or an elopement with nautanki dancers were not needed.

But in the privacy of their home, Gurpreet cursed her husband for leaving so abruptly. She shook her fist at fate for bestowing such a man on her, and at the heavens for not sending enough rain to feed her fields. She yelled at her daughters for everything else. Her deepest ire, however, she reserved for Sher Singh, the man who had introduced the irresponsibility of dreams into Harjot's life.

In 1906, fed up with the capriciousness of the monsoons, Sher Singh had gone in search of wealth to the western shore of Canada. From the letters and money orders he sent every month to his wife, Soniya, the villagers assumed that he was doing very well there. Over the years the number of his cattle increased from one cow to three, his house was rebuilt with brick and mortar instead of mud and had a tin roof instead of thatch, and on festival days the aroma of expensive basmati rice wafted out from his kitchen. Sometimes he sent parcels of strange and wonderful things like soap and chocolate, paper and pencils, and socks that looked small and wrinkled but that stretched like pale skin all the way to Soniya's crotch. She wore these socks even in the middle of summer, rolling her salwar up to her knees so that the other women could see her smooth, peach-coloured legs and die of envy.

Gurpreet's troubles had begun when Sher Singh returned to the village. He showed Harjot Singh an advertisement from a magazine—he even read out the English words, much to Harjot Singh's amazement. There was no doubt that Abroad caused magic to occur: illiterate men came back not only with money but with that other, more powerful thing—knowledge. The advertisement, placed by a logging company in Canada, invited strong men to come and work in the company's forests and mills. It promised that the workers would be well paid and given a place to stay.

"Look at me," Sher Singh had said, waving an expansive arm at his fields, his cows and his brick house. "I have worked hard and made money. Why not you too?"

"Indeed," Harjot told Gurpreet later that day. "Why not me too? Why shouldn't I also go to this place where money seems to grow on trees?" Why not obtain freedom from the endless cycle of uncertain monsoons, the certain arrival of the tax collector with his pursed lips and implacable eyes, and the inevitable journey to the money-lender who waited like a vulture to lay his hands on their meagre land?

Gurpreet had anxiously rattled pots inside the house. Questions such as the one her husband had flung into the air always warned of approaching silliness. The last time he had asked *Why Not,* she had lost her entire battery of hens and found herself the owner of a pig. What were they to do with a pig? They were god-fearing Sikhs, and neither they nor their Mussulman and Hindu neighbours ate the dirty animal. Harjot had muttered something about selling the creature to the English collector sahib, in whose house such creatures were consumed with great relish, and using the money to buy better chickens. The pig just grew fatter and fatter. Harjot could not muster the courage to go to the collector's house to ask if he wanted a pig, and the creature had eventually been sold in the weekly market for half the amount they had spent on it.

Now, less than two months later, the Why Not question had arisen again, and before Gurpreet knew it Harjot had sold her wedding gold and remortgaged their land to the moneylender. He used the money to travel across the country to Calcutta, from where he hoped to catch a ship to Canada. It was a full year before Gurpreet received a letter from Hong Kong, penned by a letter writer on behalf of her husband. *"From Calcutta I have travelled to Singapore and from there to Hong Kong,"* he wrote. *"Here in Hong Kong I have met an old man named Baba Gurdit Singh who is chartering a ship for many of us Indians who desire to sail to Vancouver. The ship will leave in a few months. I have found work as a security guard in a Chinese businessman's house in order to earn the fare. Sikhs are much in demand as guards in this country. We are the tallest people here other than the goras from England and Holland. My employer tells me that the sight of my beard and turban is enough to send any thief running as fast as he can go."*

That was the only news Gurpreet received of her husband until the postman arrived at her door one afternoon in December 1914.

"I have heard from a man who knows these things," he said, looking down at his hands, for he was a sensitive person and did not like to see unhappiness in the faces of the people to whom he carried bad news. "The ship carrying your husband reached Canada. But the people there would not allow the passengers to get off even for food or fresh water. They threatened to shoot them. It is said that they sent a warship and drove them away as if they were criminals!"

"Where is my husband? Is he hurt?"

"The news is that when the men returned to Budge-Budge near Calcutta, the British were waiting for them with guns," the postman said, shifting awkwardly.

"Guns! Why did they have guns? What did our men do?"

"Do the sahibs need an excuse to raise guns to our heads?" the postman asked. "I don't know the details. But there is a war starting in Europe, and it is said the British think the men on the ship were traitors and spies. Many were taken to prison but others ran away. Only two or three died. God willing your husband was not one of them and that he is on his way home."

A month later, just when Gurpreet was beginning to give up hope, Harjot returned to Panjaur. He wasn't sure what had happened to end the voyage so abruptly. It had taken him two years and all the money he possessed to get on board the *Komagata Maru* in Hong Kong. And yet here he was, denied entry into Canada, denied a chance to make a better life and finally accused of treason. Since when, he asked Gurpreet bitterly, since when had it been treasonous to wish for a better life?

The disappointment and the long and fruitless trip had exhausted him, and Harjot Singh could not bring himself to leave the house and the string cot again, not even to work his small fields, until that night in September 1928 when he disappeared.

"Beware of anything that begins with the troublesome question Why Not," Gurpreet would warn her younger daughter after Harjot's disappearance, for she knew Sharan was a girl given to much questioning and curiosity, unlike Kanwar, who questioned little. Over the years the warning became a refrain repeated with increasing bitterness. And, although Gurpreet Kaur did not know it then, ten years later, sixteen-year-old Sharan would stick out her lower lip mutinously, murmur the Why Not question under her breath and change her sister's fortunes and her own as well.

TWO

THEFT

—

Panjaur

1938

"Ah, Amma, that hurts!" Sharan complained, rubbing her head where her mother had just raked a comb roughly through her hair.

She held up the mirror and gazed at herself, pleased at the sight of her oval face framed in the shining glass, her eyes (which one of the village loafers had compared to the night sky with a single star in the centre of each), her full lips and slender nose. She was beautiful and she knew it.

Another sharp tug on her scalp. Her eyes watered with pain and she jerked her head away from her mother's merciless hand. "Why are you combing so hard?" she wailed.

"Oho! Our princess can't take a little pain now?" Gurpreet said, grabbing a handful of thick hair and yanking

Sharan back towards her. It was one of her bad days. She was angry with the world, with Harjot who had left her alone to deal with its vagaries, with Kanwar for being plain as mud and with Sharan who had more than her share of beauty. Kanwar, already twenty-four, was still waiting for a husband. But every man who came to see her wanted sixteen-year-old Sharan instead.

A week had gone by since Kanwar's last prospective groom had come and gone. Like the others, he had changed his mind when he laid his eyes on the younger sister.

"The pretty one," he had sent word through the match-maker early that morning. "The one with skin like a sheet of moonlight, the one with eyes like the night sky, that's the one I will marry."

"It isn't right," Gurpreet brooded as she drew the comb more gently through Sharan's hair.

"What isn't right?" Sharan asked.

"That one should have so much and the other nothing at all," Gurpreet said. "Truly, the ways of the One Up There puzzle me sometimes."

Sharan scowled up at the sun which, grown bolder now, had burned the smoky edges of winter away to reveal a clear morning. "Why are you always so angry with me, Amma? I haven't done anything."

"Haven't *done* anything?" her mother echoed in ascending tones. "Haven't *done* anything? Why, you wretched creature, did you not show your face to that fool who came to see your sister last week? If you hadn't, we might have been celebrating her engagement now! Haven't done anything indeed."

Sharan's eyes filled with tears. She didn't even like any of the men who came—they were all farmers from villages nearby. Was it her fault that Kanwar was without charm? Was it her fault that Kanwar spoke loudly about manly things like the price of wheat and when the sugar cane harvest was due and bored the men who came to see her? Was it her fault that she, Sharanjeet Kaur, was so pretty that even the old half-blind grandpas sitting around the banyan tree turned their heads to peer at her when she walked past? And the women, Sharan knew how they whispered and gossiped behind her back. *Ohhoho,* they went, *look at her strut, what pride, what show, one of these days, yes one of these days she will trip on that long braid and land on her pretty nose and then we shall see.* Sharan didn't care two clicks of her fingers, because she knew that soon, very soon, she would be gone from this speck of dirt called Panjaur. She was meant for better things, and when chance came galloping towards her she would leap on its back and ride like the wind.

"Born greedy," her mother would say sometimes, her voice turning sharp and accusatory. "God will teach you not to be so greedy, I am telling you now!"

As an infant, Sharan had screamed for Gurpreet's breast even after she had been suckled for an hour and her stomach was so round and full that she could barely breathe. When she was older, she would grab the small stones and oddly shaped sticks they used as toys, and take from Kanwar the meagre presents of ribbons and baubles that their mother bought for both of them on market day. But Kanwar, eight years older, uncomplaining, sweet as the sugar that coursed like nectar through the cane that grew in their fields, loved her in spite of these cruelties.

"And my princess," Gurpreet continued, tapping the end of the comb against Sharan's head, making her wince, "you have to come with me to that thieving moneylender Ramchand this afternoon. Don't go away to Jeeti's house, understand?"

"Why do I have to come? Why not Kanwar?"

"Because it is no use if I go," Kanwar replied with not even a twinge of resentment. "I am not as pretty as you. The moneylender will never extend Amma's loan if he sees me." She laughed. "He might raise our rates instead. As if you didn't know that!"

Sharan looked away. She had meant to hurt her sister but ended up feeling small. As her mother so often said, throw a stone in dung and it will only splash up and dirty you.

Gurpreet turned on Kanwar. "This one already believes she is the Queen of Beauties, so why are you adding to her vanity?" She nudged Sharan's head with her knuckles. "I am taking you because your sister has work to finish in the house. I need you to carry water back from the well on the way back. No other reason, understand?"

Sharan rubbed her burning scalp. Yes indeed, she understood. Her mother was angry with her for being good-looking, but when it was time to negotiate with the moneylender for another extension on their mortgage, it was she who had to flirt with the pot-bellied old bandicoot so that he would be charmed into foolishness. And it was she who was expected to flutter her eyelashes at stringy old Banarsi Das when it was necessary

22

to get groceries on tab from his shop. Yes indeed, she understood.

There was a shuffle of feet and Jeeti's mother, Soniya, entered the courtyard. Sharan looked up hoping she had brought her friend, but ever since Jeeti's engagement to a rich shopkeeper in Patiala she hardly left her house, so busy was she getting her skin smooth and fair for her wedding, learning to cook fancy food to please her in-laws and embroidering her wedding dupatta with sequins and seed pearls. Soniya was, as usual, dressed in a new salwar kameez, her stomach pushing and wobbling behind the green material. Around her neck she had a long gold chain, and her earlobes were so stretched with the weight of gold hanging from them that they appeared in danger of tearing. She no longer wore stockings under her salwar, though. In the years since Harjot's disappearance, many other men had left the village for foreign shores and many a package had come back bearing silk stockings for the wives and sisters of Panjaur. It was no longer a thing to inspire envy in anyone's heart.

"Ask why I have come, mother of Kanwar!" she said, sitting down hard on the string cot, unfurling a Japanese paper fan with an ostentatious flick of her plump wrist and churning the air with it. The fan, which had arrived in Sher Singh's most recent parcel along with the usual consignment of chocolate bars and soaps, had replaced the stockings to attract envious stares. Sharan gazed covetously at the pretty black and gold thing fluttering like a trapped butterfly in Soniya's chubby hand.

"Have I lost all manners, that I should start asking these things before I have offered you a glass of lassi?"

Gurpreet asked in her warmest voice, even though she had still not forgiven Sher Singh, and by extension his wife, for pushing Harjot into the realm of useless dreaming. It had left her with nothing, while this fat woman fanning herself with a ridiculous piece of folded paper had everything. "What are you sitting there and staring for?" she reprimanded Sharan. "Go, go, get aunty a big glass of lassi with sugar."

Soniya leaned forward and said in a stage whisper, "Ay-hai! How lovely the girl has grown! What a pity the other one does not even have half of *this* one's looks."

Gurpreet's smile vanished. "Looks are not enough to put food in the belly or harvest the cane, sister," she snipped, waving a flat hand in the air, as if to push away Soniya's comment. "My Kanwar is a good girl. She will make some fortunate man a good wife."

"Yes, sister, I know that," Soniya said. "Why else do you think I am here in the middle of the day when I should be at home chasing after those thieving servants?" She looked expectantly at Gurpreet. "Go on, ask me why."

"How am I to know, sister? It is up to you to tell me," Gurpreet said, swallowing her irritation.

"I have found a gem for our Kanwar, that's why!" Soniya fanned herself hard. "Such a boy you have never seen. Ask me about him. Go on, ask me!"

"What is his name?" Gurpreet asked cautiously. Sharan could almost hear her mother's brain clicking and whirring and thinking: Soniya must surely have a motive for this—when had *she* turned matchmaker? "Where is he from? What family?"

"His name is Khushwant Singh. His parents are dead, and he was brought up by relatives."

"Are you sure he is asking for my Kanwar? What sort of people are his relatives?"

"He is a decent man from a decent family, asking for a good, hard-working girl," Soniya replied peevishly. She snapped her fan shut and open and shut again to emphasize her annoyance. "He lives in Canada. My husband knows of him, and has heard nothing bad. We would have considered him for our Jeeti if we had not already performed her engagement. And I decided to tell you about this proposal because I have known your daughters since they were born, and I cannot bear to see you struggling on your own like this."

"But why my daughter? As you yourself pointed out, my Kanwar is no beauty."

Soniya gave her a sideways look and hesitated.

Gurpreet pounced on the pause like a cat on a dithering mouse. "What?" she demanded. "What is it? He wants money? Gold? What is it?"

"Nothing like that," Soniya assured her. "Just that the boy is blind in one eye. In every other way he is whole and fit."

"How old is he?" Gurpreet asked, still not convinced. Why would a foreign-returned with no family burdens want her Kanwar's hand in marriage? Was he so ancient that he was losing his eyesight? Was this his second marriage? Did he already possess a white wife?

Soniya gave her an exasperated look and, snapping the fan open again, waved it vigorously. "Sister, you question too much! There is *nothing* wrong with him. He is thirty years old and wants a girl from a decent family who will adjust to life in a foreign country. He has lived abroad since he was sixteen and does not care about dowry and all that kind of thing. If you are not interested, tell me right now. There are lines of parents waiting for men such as this one, hanh!"

"No, no, it is not that. You must understand, it is my duty to make sure that my daughter is going to a good man."

"As if I would bring any other kind to your door," Soniya huffed.

Gurpreet soothed her with flattering words so that she left beaming and promising to find a groom just as good for Sharan as well.

"Did you see her gold!" Gurpreet said wistfully as soon as Soniya was safely out of earshot on the dusty path leading to her house. "And her skin. Looks so young and tight. No worries, that's why. What with Jeeti engaged to a fine man, all her responsibilities are done." She turned to Sharan. "A whole month younger than *you*, that friend of yours, and she is already engaged."

As if it is my fault, Sharan wanted to say. If not for Kanwar standing like a rock in her way, by now she would have been married ten times over. But seeing her mother's brooding face she kept her thoughts to herself.

Later that night, however, as the three women lay on mats in the moon-washed courtyard, Gurpreet allowed herself to feel a cautious excitement about Khushwant Singh, the boy from Abroad. "He sounds exactly right for our Kanwar," she said. Sharan heard the smile in her voice. "See, there is a reason that Ooper-Wallah made us wait so long."

"But Amma," Sharan said, sitting up beside her mother's recumbent form. "He is blind in one eye! Who wants to marry a man who can see only half the world?"

"He can turn his head, can't he?" Kanwar asked with surprising asperity. "I don't mind a one-eyed man, so why should *you* care?"

"With a single eye you can see everything you need to." Gurpreet's voice was harsh. "Your father had both eyes but was blind to everything except his dreams."

"Is he good-looking?" Sharan asked. "Is he rich?"

"We will have to wait and see what he looks like," her mother replied. "Soniya said he is not rich, but he has a house, a shop, no debts and is able to look after a wife well. Once our Kanwar joins him, she can help him become rich."

Sharan looked down at her sister's face, transformed by the soft light of the moon and hope into something almost pretty, and was filled with sudden envy. It would be Kanwar, after all, who would go to the country that Sharan had dreamed about ever since she could remember. But Canada, with its lavender soap and chocolate, was *her* fate. *She* was the one who longed for Abroad. She wished that this man who was causing such a flutter in the house was coming for her. *Why,* she thought, *a single look at me and he would demand to marry me like all the other men have.* An idea crept into her mind. *Why not give him the choice, why not let him see both of us sisters and decide?* And this time, if he chose her and if Gurpreet refused to give her hand in marriage, she would run away with the one-eyed suitor. Never mind what the village gossips would have to say about that.

"When is he coming, Amma?" she asked.

"Next week," said Gurpreet. In the darkness, she peered up at Sharan's face. Something in the girl's voice must have alerted her, because she said sharply, "And you are not to show yourself until all the formalities are done, you understand? I don't want this one to go away as well. Remember, if your sister does not marry, neither will you. Do you hear me?"

"Yes, Amma, I hear you," Sharan replied meekly, lying down on the mattress. She felt her mother relax beside her.

"I will ask Soniya to lend us her yellow silk salwar kameez," Gurpreet said. "And maybe she will lend us some jewellery as well. Nothing much, just a chain and two bangles. We don't want to give the boy an idea that we have plenty. Yes, I can feel it in my heart, there will be a wedding this time!"

Yes, there will, Sharan thought, closing her eyes.

The following week, Khushwant Singh arrived in the village to see Kanwar. While Gurpreet fussed around in the front room, anxiously arranging delicacies on plates, Sharan helped Kanwar dress. The sound of chattering and laughter erupted outdoors. Sharan ran to the window and opened the shutters.

"Are they here?" Kanwar asked nervously.

Sharan stuck her head out of the window and watched

a small group of people approach their house. The tall young man with the long beard curling down his chest and the white turban tied in a fancy city style must be Khushwant Singh, she thought. Behind him were Soniya and a few elderly relatives.

"What does he look like?" Kanwar begged, poking her sister's back.

"He's handsome," Sharan replied. She took in the man's wide face and thick eyebrows. He wore black pants and a jacket like the Collector Sahib, and on his feet he had shoes. Real shoes! All the men in Sharan's life so far, including Banarsi Das, the wealthy grocer, went about barefoot, their knobbly feet cracked and ugly and visible to all the world. He walked past the window. Sharan leaned out a bit more and giggled loudly. Khushwant Singh looked up, startled. His expression changed from surprise to pleasure. He grinned, displaying strong white teeth. Sharan still could not make out which eye was blind and was relieved that it was not obvious. She smiled back boldly, allowing him to gaze at her face for a long minute, and then ducked out of sight. She had caught him, she thought smugly, she was sure of that.

Why did Sharan show her face at the window, even though her mother had threatened her with three kinds of beatings if she did? Even though she loved her sister deeply? Even though she knew it was wrong? Perhaps it was the scent of lavender soap haunting her nostrils. Perhaps it was that distant Why Not that had propelled her father into making one journey and likely the next one too. *Why not take a chance?* she had asked herself.

29

After they were married, Khushwant Singh held his sixteen-year-old bride against his body, stroked her skin with a hand scored rough by hard work in the lumber mills of Duncan and Vancouver, and whispered against the delicate curve of her throat how he had fallen in love the second he saw her. He had come to Panjaur expecting a girl who was known more for her virtue and hard work than her looks. He had thought that his bad eye would prevent him from getting anyone better than that. Then he had spotted Sharan, framed in a window, and wondered if she were a figment of his imagination. A pari, an apsara, a goddess, he whispered as he thrust into her virgin body, and she muffled her screams in his shoulder. He was a man given to superlatives. Besides, he had spent all these years in Canadian lumber mills dreaming of lush beauties raised on the water and wheat of his native Punjab. Who could blame his ardour?

When Kanwar and not Sharan had emerged from the kitchen bearing a glass of lassi, Khushwant Singh had been filled with dismay.

"She isn't the one I saw," he blurted out. "Who was the girl at the window? *She* is the one I want to marry."

"That's the younger daughter," Soniya said before Gurpreet could comment. "A nice girl, very talented and beautiful, as you saw for yourself. Sister, where is our Sharanjeet? Why is she hiding? Gurpreet, sister, it is time to celebrate. He has liked your daughter. He wants to marry her!" She clapped her hands and laughed, ignoring Kanwar, who stood in the corner, dressed in borrowed finery, resignation stamped on her face.

Gurpreet was furious with Sharan *and* with this heart-less young man who had humiliated Kanwar. Recklessly she brushed aside Soniya's babblings.

"No, he can't marry Sharanjeet," she said. "Either he marries my older daughter or nobody."

"You are a foolish woman," Soniya hissed to Gurpreet in the privacy of the kitchen, where she had dragged her. "And too proud for your own good. Do you want to die the mother of two unmarried daughters?"

Gurpreet was adamant. After the visitors had gone, she thrashed Sharan hard, without saying a word. Kanwar did not intervene to save her sister from the beating. And Sharan, dodging her mother's hand, wondered how to contact Khushwant Singh and offer to run away with him.

The next morning, to everyone's astonishment, the young man sent word with Soniya. He begged Gurpreet's forgiveness for having hurt Kanwar, but his heart couldn't accept her as his wife. Only one woman would do.

"He says that he wants no dowry," Soniya reported. "He says he will pay for the wedding. I think he is a fool, but who am I to say anything?"

Khushwant Singh also had another groom in mind for Kanwar—a widower cousin with a young son and a few acres of land in a nearby village. In fact, if Gurpreet gave him permission, he would tell his relatives to start the negotiations immediately.

"But all this only if you give him your Sharan," Soniya said, flapping her fan.

Gurpreet gave up. She had no choice. Matches like this arrived only by the greatest grace of God. If it was not

Kanwar's fate to go to the country her father had tried to reach, then it must be Sharan's.

Two months later, Gurpreet celebrated both marriages.

Sharan's new husband left for Canada soon after the wedding, in 1938. World War Two broke out the following year; many Sikh men from the villages of Punjab died fighting for the English in that war, and Sharan was glad that her husband's blind eye prevented him from joining the army. At least she would not become a widow before she had even lived with her husband. But as the war dragged on and Sharan remained in Panjaur, she began to feel as if she was indeed a widow.

Meanwhile Kanwar moved to Dauri Kalan, her husband's village, some distance away from Panjaur. She came home six months later for the birth of her first child, a boy named Gobind. Sharan held the tiny infant in her arms and envied her older sister all over again. She had stolen the man meant for Kanwar, but as time passed, with only letters from her absent husband to mark the passage of time, she began to wonder whether she had done the right thing after all. Was she only going to have a long-distance husband? Would she ever see anything more of him than the lengthy epistles he sent every month and that the postman read out with zest to her and later disseminated to the rest of the village? He always began by telling her how much he missed her, his Baby, his Honey, his Beloved, and assuring her that very soon she would be by his side. This would be followed by a brief report on the state of his health (which was always fine), after which Khushwant

Singh would cover several sheets of paper with impassioned essays on the history of the Sikhs in North America. He seemed to be obsessed with his community, and underlined the richness of Punjabi traditions and culture. Then, in seemingly direct contradiction, he would write that she should learn English ways, should become a modern woman so that she would be able to settle into life in Canada. Sharan was confused—what exactly did he want her to be? A traditional Sikh or an English mem? And how, she wrote back, was she to learn English in a village where nobody other than the postman knew it?

"I have arranged for you to go to Amritsar and stay with my relatives," he replied in his next letter. There she would be tutored in the English language by a gori memsahib named Mrs. Hardy. She would also attend classes at the Golden Temple to learn how to read and write Gurbani.

"It is important to know where you are coming from and where you are going," her husband wrote. *"For this you need both languages, the language of our soul and that of the goras. This way you will be a two-edged sword."*

Sharan was excited at the thought of leaving her mother's house to go and live in Amritsar, Sikhism's most holy city. This would be her first journey away from home. She was determined to become a modern woman with two tongues in her head: one to do business with the goras who ran the distant country that awaited her and the other to deal with her own people.

Every morning for the next several years, Sharan walked through the narrow gullies of Amritsar, past the

Golden Temple, to Mrs. Hardy's home, where she sat before the elderly Englishwoman's sky-blue gaze in a drawing room festooned in lace and learned ABCD and 1234 like a little girl. From one window she watched the gardeners struggle to tend an English garden of roses, delphinium, phlox and lilies that drooped and died under the scorching sun of Amritsar. From the other window she gazed at the dome of the Golden Temple. When she first arrived, determined if often scared and lonely, Sharan would glance out of the window before her lessons for the blessing she believed she would receive from the mere sight of that golden structure rising gracefully into the hot shine of the sky. On Saturdays and Sundays she would go to to the temple to learn a different alphabet at the free school run by the priests, to become the two-edged sword that her husband wanted her to be. Not that she minded the effort all this sudden flood of learning involved. She would tell herself that if it had not been for a husband as enlightened as hers, she might still be an illiterate farmer's daughter, waiting stupidly for her fate to turn. But now she had the opportunity to be something better, and so, not being one to turn up her nose at chance, she applied herself with diligence to her studies.

Twice a year, to celebrate the Baisakhi and Diwali festivals with her mother and sister, she caught the bus back to Panjaur, glad after each visit that she had managed to get away from the smallness of life there. During one of her visits, in 1940, Kanwar gave birth to her second child, a daughter named Nimmo. Sharan cuddled the warm baby

34

and wondered whether she would ever join her husband in Canada. She decided to accompany Kanwar back to Dauri Kalan for a few months and help her with the new infant before returning to Amritsar.

Finally the war was over, and one evening she returned to her relatives' home from her session with Mrs. Hardy to find her immigration papers had arrived. By then she was no longer a villager from a dusty dot on the map but a city girl who knew how to read and write, who had surreptitiously broken the religious rules of god-fearing Sikhs and cut her hair a few inches to even out the ragged ends. She was ready to take her future in her own hands and shape it to her liking.

She paid scant attention to talk of the impending independence of her nation and the division of the subcontinent into India and Pakistan, even when the murmuring turned to a shouting. She had too many things to do in preparation for her departure. And then, in January 1946, waving goodbye to Gurpreet, who had made the trip to the city to help her daughter prepare for the journey, Sharan caught a bus from Amritsar to New Delhi, a train to Calcutta, and from there a ship that sailed via Hong Kong to Vancouver. While Kanwar stayed behind in a land that would soon be split into two nations, Sharan—inheritor of her father's dream and that troublesome question Why Not—was on her way to a new life.

Two months later, when she reached the port of Vancouver and saw the dark trees pointing at the sombre, rain-laden sky of that city, when she heard the cry of the gulls in the harbour, when she finally set foot on the damp earth, Sharanjeet Kaur felt that she had overcome space and time and won the country that had turned her father away all those years ago. Her life, she thought buoyantly, was complete. What more could she ask?

THREE

GUILT

—

Vancouver

1951

Sharan—Bibi-ji, as she was now called—sat at the cashier's desk in the dim interior of East India Foods and Groceries. She tapped out a tuneless tattoo on the wooden surface in front of her with one plump, long-fingered hand. The late autumn sun warmed her gently through the sheet glass window she cleaned every morning so that she could see the world clear and undimmed by yesterday's grease and dust. And, of course, so that the world would see her, Bibi-ji, wife of Khushwant Singh, or Pa-ji, unchallenged owner—no, *proprietor;* that sounded grander—of East India Foods and Groceries, 2034 Main Street. And full owner also of the apartment above the store—the one with two bedrooms, one and a half bathrooms, a living-cum-dining room, and a kitchen with more pots and pans than she knew what to do with.

Yes indeed, Bibi-ji had arrived. Her life was now enriched by all manner of luxuries that an ardent Pa-ji poured into her lap, even though he could not always afford them. Pa-ji was a great giver of presents. He loved the feeling of power that he experienced every time he entered a shop, pulled out his wallet and purchased something for his young wife. He loved spending because he could. There was a time, not so long ago, when he had to count every penny. In most people the experience of extreme poverty inspires extreme parsimony, but Pa-ji was different. He forgot the past by living it up in the present. These gifts to Bibi-ji were apart from the ones he purchased on birthdays, on anniversaries and for every festival he could find in the calendar. He insisted on being multi-denominational as far as festivals went, and celebrated them all—Baisakhi, Diwali, Eid, Hanukkah, Christmas. If there was no reason to buy a present, he discovered one. When Bing Crosby came to the Sunset Community Centre as the star attraction the year Bibi-ji arrived in Vancouver, Pa-ji decided to celebrate the twin arrivals of wife and film star by buying a gramophone player and two Bing Crosby records. The first day of winter was greeted with new toques and matching mitts for both Bibi-ji and himself. The appearance of buds on the cherry trees, the arrival of a pair of blue jays in the garden of the house behind theirs—anything was reason enough. Sometimes Pa-ji made up these occasions. "Business boomed this evening," or "Churchill came to our shop to buy basmati rice," or his favourite—which always drew a laugh from Bibi-ji, no matter how often it was repeated—"I was just elected the Prime Minister-ji of Canada."

Bibi-ji, though, was torn between wanting all the luxuries Pa-ji heaped on her and being appalled by such extravagance. The poverty of her childhood had made her cautious about spending money. She found pleasure in hoarding and counting, in making sure that there was more money rolling in for the future.

"Why are you buying all these things for me?" she demanded of Pa-ji, even while splashing her favourite lavender perfume all over herself, carrying a different handbag to the shop every morning or trying on yet another pair of shoes. "I am not in need of three sets of cutlery, ji. I eat with my hands." But none of her protests had stopped him. What, he had demanded, was the use of having money if not to spend it? And what was the use of having a beloved, *and* beautiful, *and* smart wife, if not to spoil her?

Bibi-ji glanced around the tiny shop. Four rows of shelves loaded from one end to the other with sacks of rice, bags of mung, toor, chana, masoor dal, kidney beans, chick peas, navy beans and spices from India. This is all mine, she thought proudly. What a transformation she had undergone—from a girl named Sharanjeet who had nothing to a woman of substance named Bibi-ji.

It was her husband who was responsible for the new appellation. He had a variety of affectionate nicknames for her—Honey, Rani, Bebby. The last was the one that had stuck. He really meant to say Baby, like the characters in the romantic Hollywood movies he loved to watch, but his Punjabi accent interfered and messed up his English. People in their small Punjabi community, who weren't sure what this word meant, tagged on their own marker of respect and called her Bebby-ji. And soon "Bebby-ji" became a word used so frequently that, like a stone worn small and smooth with caressing, it was turned by the constant touch of many tongues to Bibi-ji. She did not mind the transformation. The term meant Wife, and that was what she was: the respected wife of a respected man. It went well with Pa-ji, which was how Khushwant Singh was addressed by the newly arrived immigrant men over whom he presided like an older brother.

In the thirteen years since she had snared Pa-ji with her fluttering eyelashes and dimpled smile, Bibi-ji had become a handsome young woman of twenty-nine. She had put on weight, and her cheeks were taut and pink with good eating and better living. Her hair was piled fashionably in a bun, with a curl or two escaping artfully to decorate her wide, smooth brow. She applied make-up with an extravagant hand, her special weakness being lipstick in shades of dark red and pink. Her voice too had changed. It had grown deep and resonant as a temple bell, ringing solemnly out of the generous spread of her body.

Smoothing a hand absently down the pink and green kameez that she wore, she wondered what her mother would have made of her new status in life. And what about Mrs. Hardy, to whom Bibi-ji was daily grateful for teaching her the p's and q's and other things about the gora way of life—how to eat food with a knife and fork, how to hold a teacup, how to use a hanky to blow her nose? Mrs. Hardy, who had taught her that it was polite to constantly say sorry and thank you—habits that were dismissed scornfully by Pa-ji, even though he had insisted on Bibi-ji's English education.

"The goras hide behind these politenesses and commit all kinds of sins," he told her. "You should say sorry and thank you only when you feel it from the heart, not every two minutes."

But truth be told, Bibi-ji didn't feel quite as strongly about the goras as he did. In fact, she had a sneaking admiration for these fair-skinned people who had infiltrated every part of the world with their manners and customs and languages, who had managed to make even a refrigerator of a country like Canada a place of comfort and plenty. Unlike the Panjauri villagers who assigned everything to Fate, the goras, Bibi-ji noticed with admiration, wanted to know why and what and when. It was not boats or horses that had transported them to all corners of the world, but their long noses, which quivered with a desire to poke into everything. Their sky-coloured eyes watered with the need to peer under every stone, their white fingers itched to take everything apart until they understood it, learned how it worked, found what they needed to make their own lives better.

"Bibi-ji? What should I do with these two sacks of rice?" It was the lanky Sikh youth, Lalloo, who helped in the shop. He was Pa-ji's protégé, the son of a school friend from Amritsar. Lalloo was only about nineteen, but Bibi-ji was pleased with his bright mind, which soaked up information as rapidly as a sponge, filed it away and used it whenever the opportunity presented itself.

"Put them on a shelf, not on the floor. If there is a flood or something, we will lose it all," she said.

From her apartment upstairs, which had become a stopping place for newcomers who needed a bed and meals until they found their feet, came the muffled sounds of the radio and of people moving around. Pa-ji believed in running an open house. Anyone was welcome: relatives, friends of friends, refugees, children of friends on their way to somewhere else, they were all ushered in. They slept wherever there was space—on the floor in the living and dining rooms, in the landing and in the spare bedroom. Pa-ji, she knew, would be locked in their bedroom, working on his grand book of history as he did whenever he had a spare moment.

She shifted in her chair and reached into her capacious handbag for a letter she had read so often it was beginning to fall apart. It was the last letter she had received from her sister, Kanwar. It had arrived four years ago and was dated February 11, 1947. A few months later, in August, the British had left the Indian subcontinent and Punjab had been divided between two new nations—India and Pakistan.

The Punjabi lettering was neat, written by the schoolteacher in Kanwar's village.

"My dear sister, I have bad news for you. Our mother died suddenly yesterday. It happened in her sleep and without any pain. Only people who are blessed die in this manner. She was

speaking about you a few hours before she fell asleep, my sister, and was sad that you were so far away from us. She missed you and so do I and the children." Tears welled out of Bibi-ji's eyes. She wiped them away with the end of her dupatta. "*Your niece Nimmo, in particular, asks after you often. She is now almost seven years old and talks without stopping. She looks at the letters that you send and asks me what they say. I have to pretend to read them out to her. I feel ashamed sometimes that I do not even know what the pen-marks on the paper mean. I have asked my husband if she can go to school with her brothers so she too will learn to read like her foreign aunt. I am also happy to tell you that I am expecting another child.*"

Bibi-ji remembered guiltily how envious she had been the first time she had read this letter. Now Kanwar was swelling with another baby, she had thought, while her belly, for all of the nightly loving that she and Papa-ji indulged in, remained flat as the Gangetic plain. At first she had told herself that her body needed to adjust to the change in climate. Vancouver was so different from Panjaur. Perhaps all the rain they endured here in this place full of trees was not good for growing babies. The fetus turned to mould like bread left out in the damp. Which would explain why there were hardly any people here. Deep down, Bibi-ji knew such thoughts were ridiculous, but her desperation made her willing to believe almost anything. She wished that her mother was near to give her advice on what she should do about her lazy womb. She had racked her memory for the recipes that the midwife in Panjaur had suggested for barren women. She swallowed concoctions involving turmeric, nettle juice, milk, saffron, almonds given to her by other women in her community. She lay in bed with her thighs crossed tight after Pa-ji had poured his sticky seed into her, and she lay there with a bladder full of urine, refusing to go to the toilet, afraid that it would wash away the fetus that she prayed was forming in her womb.

Nothing had helped.

"The child is due in October and this worries me," Kanwar continued in her letter. *"Ever since it was announced that there will be a division of land between the Hindus and the Mussulmans, there has been unrest everywhere. There are rumours that Punjab will be broken into two pieces—one piece of our heartland to stay in India and the other to go to Pakistan. This is the name that Muhammad Jinnah has chosen for his new country. I do not know which piece we will end up in. Where will my new child be born, I wonder?"*

The door opened, and Bibi-ji looked up from the letter, frowning. A gora came in.

Bibi-ji wiped the frown from her face. "Good morning!" she said cheerfully, just like Mrs. Hardy of Amritsar had taught her. "Howdyoodo?"

The man ignored her and wandered around the shop.

"Are you in need of something in particular, sir?" Bibi-ji called after him, even though he had not responded to her greeting. As if she were invisible. Maybe she was. Maybe when the gora fella looked at her, he saw not Bibi-ji—beautiful and accomplished proprietor and clear owner of this shop and the upstairs apartment, in debt to nobody in the world except God— he saw an insignificant brown foreigner, one of the people

who ran small shops like this one, or worked in the
sawmills, or cleaned up in the posh restaurants, hardly
worthy of notice. Bibi-ji shrugged. It did not hurt her,
this kind of blindness. She knew who she was and she
knew her place in the world.

"You don't keep root beer?" the man asked.

"No sir, but we have many other things."

"How about tuna?"

"No sir, but we have six types of dal. I will show you, if
you wish. And high-quality rice."

The man left without buying anything.

Lalloo's thin, sharp-featured face appeared from behind
a tall shelf. He asked, "No sale, Bibi-ji?"

"No, putthar, the gora wanted tuna and some kind of
beer. Maybe we should keep the things these goras like.
Some root beer, some ice cream, sardines . . ."

"You will need a refrigerator in the store for all that,"
Lalloo pointed out earnestly.

"Mmm, that is true. I will have to think about it a
bit," she said, waving him back to work. Her mind,
though, clicked busily, adding and subtracting, expenses
versus profits, plans and projects for the future. Since
her arrival in Vancouver, Bibi-ji had discovered that she
had a talent for accounting and business. Focusing on
the shop also kept her from worrying about her sister
and her own childless state which, she was certain, was
the Ooper-Wallah's punishment. She had stolen a life
and she would not be allowed to give birth to another.
So she had thrown herself into the business of making
money. To begin with, she had swiftly put an end to

45

Pa-ji's habit of accepting credit notes instead of hard cash for purchases.

"No more credit until arrears are cleared," she told the regulars crisply.

Some of them paid their bills without a murmur. Others did not like it at all—the well-off ones who had no business grumbling about paying two years' worth of debt. One woman whose husband owned acres of vegetable farms in Abbotsford had whined and fussed. "But," she had said, a frown corrugating her high round forehead, "but, but . . ."—like a duck—"I wish to speak to Pa-ji about this. He knows me well. I am not going to run away with the money we owe you, understand?"

"It is his decision to collect all arrears," Bibi-ji had said, staring her down, taking in her gold chains and bangles and thinking, *You are using my money to buy all that jewellery!*

"In that case, sister, I will not be coming to this shop again," the woman had declared.

"Your wish, sister," Bibi-ji had politely replied—wondering briefly if she was ruining the business that her husband had so painstakingly built. "You owe us one hundred and two dollars and five cents."

The woman had slapped the money down on the counter and swept out. A month later she was back for dal and wheat flour, cash in hand, a smile on her face and a gushing invitation to visit her house for an important ceremony.

Bibi-ji had been relieved to see her—and even more pleased that she had, once again, taken a chance and won.

Recently she had set about trying to get rid of the house guests who always filled their apartment.

46

"What is this, ji?" she asked Pa-ji one evening after he had settled in his favourite armchair with a glass of Johnny Walker whisky in hand. "A dharamshaala for every passing person? They are sitting here and eating and sleeping at our expense. At this rate we will be bankrupt."

"Only until they find their feet, my sweet Bebby," Pa-ji said firmly, his good eye fixed on her. "People helped me when I came here, and this is my way of paying back. We are strangers in this land and have nobody but our own community to turn to."

Bibi-ji recognized when not to argue. Pa-ji had said nothing when she stopped taking credit notes, even though she knew that the grumblings and mutterings from the customers had reached him. But on the matter of their house guests she knew he would not budge. However, there were other ways of dealing with the endless train of people wandering through their home; what could not be removed could be used. The women understood this and made themselves useful around the apartment, cooking and cleaning, washing dishes and doing laundry without being asked. It was the men who lounged around, watching television, listening to the radio or discussing the political situation in India. All very well, talking big about distant matters, but what about the here and now? Bibi-ji thought sourly. What about the money that was leaking out of Pa-ji's pockets to feed these people while they sat around talking?

"We are not doing these boys any favours by letting them stare at the walls." She had widened her eyes at her husband in a way that she knew he could not resist, and leaned against him. "They need to keep busy, otherwise God knows what trouble they might get into. They can help in the shop. It will be good Canadian work experience."

Pa-ji looked doubtful. Bibi-ji wriggled her body against his and ran a finger down his cheek.

"Yes my beauty, you are right," Pa-ji sighed and gave up. "It will be good experience for them."

After that, when a grateful newcomer folded his palms and said, "Pa-ji, how can I repay you?" Pa-ji would pat him genially and say, "Pass it on, pass it on. There are certain things that must be passed on, not returned." And in the same breath he would add, "By the way, from tomorrow morning if you could help Bibi-ji in the shop, poor thing, her back is gone lifting those heavy sacks of rice . . ."

Bibi-ji turned to gaze out at the street, her eyes resting momentarily on two small plum trees shorn bare of leaves. A young couple peered into the window of an antique shop across the road, a few yards from the Salvation Army store. Bibi-ji wondered whether there was any money to be made from selling dusty relics from the past. More than her grocery store made? They could become far more prosperous, she was sure of that. Opportunities lay around them like pearls on these streets. But they were visible only to people with sharp eyes.

"What are you looking at, Bibi-ji?" Lalloo asked, coming around to the front with a box full of pickle jars. He lowered it carefully on the floor and stared out the window.

"What am I looking *for*, Lalloo, *for*," Bibi-ji corrected. "I am looking for pearls."

"I don't see anything there, Bibi-ji," Lalloo remarked after a few moments.

She laughed. "Neither do I, but I will. I *know* I will." She continued to appraise the stores across the street—the bakery with the electricals shop on one side of it, and the store selling second-hand clothes, a store, she noted, that was always full of people. The war had left the whole world poorer: why had Pa-ji not thought of opening a used-clothing store instead of this Indian grocery shop? She wondered whether the shop would do better in Abbotsford or in Duncan, where there were more Sikhs than here in Vancouver. But no, she liked being in the city. She had a feeling that it was a city with a future, one in which she would be wise to invest her money and her hard work.

The aroma of cooking drifted down from the upstairs kitchen, and an idea came to her. How about a restaurant? Small, no fuss, just a few things on the menu. She could supervise the kitchen and Pa-ji could handle the cash. But then a real estate agent's sign in a window across the road caught her eye, and the thought of a restaurant slid away. She decided that their future lay in real estate: she would persuade Pa-ji to buy a house and rent out their apartment . . .

She returned to Kanwar's letter. "*Last week there was a big fight between the Mussulmans and the Sikhs in Hazara district in the north-west. My husband's cousin escaped with his life and is here with us now. He spends his days sharpening his kirpan and swearing that he will kill any Mussulman who crosses his path. Across our land, hearts are filling with anger and hate.*

So far there is calm here in Dauri Kalan, but hate is like an infectious disease, it can become a plague very soon if something is not done to stop it. I too am becoming suspicious of every Mussulman in this village. Now I notice there are more of them than of us Sikhs. If there is a fight we will be outnumbered. My husband says I am being foolish and nothing will happen to us. He has known the Mussulmans in our village from the time he was a baby. They are like his family, he says, they will protect us if there is trouble. My husband has lived for ten years longer than I have on this earth, so perhaps he is wiser than I am. But I have a bad feeling about this Partition business. I am afraid."

Bibi-ji had replied promptly, enclosing postcards for her nephew and little niece Nimmo. There had been no answer. She followed up with another letter. Again there was no response. By July, Kanwar's silence began to consume Bibi-ji. The following month, India and Pakistan were due to become independent nations. But the only thing Bibi-ji could think of was the fate of her sister and her family.

That year—her first in Canada—her already crowded apartment became a gathering place for their friends. Every day it was full of people who would huddle around the radio and listen anxiously to the BBC news or discuss rumours of fighting between Hindus and Sikhs on one side and Muslims on the other, of the beatings and rapes and killings occurring daily in the villages near the lines that had been so arbitrarily drawn across the country. An Englishman, Sir Cyril Radcliffe, had been appointed in the days before independence to head a commission that would create two nations in the subcontinent—India, with a Hindu majority, and Pakistan, for the Muslims. Most of West Punjab, with its Muslim majority, would go to Pakistan, as would East Bengal on the other side of India. East Punjab, with its Hindu and Sikh majority, would remain part of India.

The date for Pakistan's independence was set for August 14th and India's the following day. As those dates drew closer, the conversations in Bibi-ji's apartment grew more intense and carried on even later into the night. Bibi-ji listened to the stories with a growing sense of worry and confusion. Even though Kanwar's letters had spoken of premonitions of disaster and rumours of killings and quarrels, Bibi-ji found it hard to believe that people who had lived as neighbours and friends for so many years could suddenly become enemies just because of a line drawn on a paper map in a government office.

August 14th had arrived like a hurricane. Bibi-ji had sat with Pa-ji and listened to the radio as the new Pakistan was born on the stroke of midnight. On the following midnight India assumed its newest incarnation as an independent nation. In the months that followed, stories of the savagery sweeping Punjab in the north-west and Bengal in the northeast trickled steadily into Vancouver. Entire villages—Hindu, Muslim and Sikh—had been burned to the ground. Women had been killed by their men to preserve their honour, for it was feared that if they remained alive they might be abducted or raped. Trains loaded with dead bodies came and went across the newly established border, and ten million people lost their homes, their families, communities and memories. News, both of great escapes and of confirmed deaths, grew. But out of this tumult of information and rumour came not a whisper about Kanwar or her family. A shroud of silence lay over her area. Dauri Kalan appeared to have vanished, leaving no trace. Had it been seized by the Muslims and burned to the ground? Had it been reinvented and turned into a Pakistani village? Was it perhaps in that band of dust that lay between the new countries of India and Pakistan and that had since become a no man's land of mines and soldiers and hot white searchlights? Was it even possible to say where that small collection of homes and families that had been a village might now be found on a map? Bibi-ji clung to Pa-ji, asking him to find answers for her. He contacted relatives and friends in Amritsar and Delhi, Jullundur and Lahore. He knew people everywhere; he would find Kanwar for Bibi-ji, he promised. "Nobody disappears," he said confidently. "These things happen only in the films, only in storybooks."

By January 1948, when there was still no news, Bibi-ji had become frantic. She had insisted on going back to India. It was to be the first of a series of trips that she would make to that newly formed country in search of her sister and family. She contacted government agencies in charge of displaced persons in Pakistan and India. She left word at as many gurudwaras as she could reach, and she wandered around the refugee camps in both countries, asking for anybody from Dauri Kalan village. An old man in Amritsar told her with absolute certainty that Kanwar's entire family had died: he had seen it with his own eyes. But a fifteen-year-old boy with a cracked voice who claimed to be from Dauri Kalan said that he had with his own eyes seen Kanwar's five-year-old daughter Nimmo in the sad procession that had wound its way through the burning fields of Punjab.

The old man had shaken his head at this and said, "Don't listen to him, daughter. He makes up stories. The poor boy has lost his entire family and it has affected his mind. He tells everyone who comes here that he has seen their kin in that kafeela. Yesterday he said that he was from Nandayal village, today he is telling you he is from Dauri Kalan."

"But then how does he know my niece's name?" Bibi-ji asked. She turned to the boy. "You said Nimmo, didn't you?"

"Nimmo, my little Nimmo," repeated the boy obediently. "My sister Nimmo."

Bibi-ji didn't know whether the boy was talking about his own sister or her niece; Nimmo was such a common name. She looked closely at the boy, wondering if he could be Kanwar's older son, but that child would now have been little more than seven years old, whereas this boy looked to be fifteen or sixteen.

Bibi-ji asked him a few more questions, but all he could tell her was that he had seen a girl called Nimmo in the kafeela. She imagined two long caravans of people working their way across the new border, one heading for Pakistan and the other towards India. So many millions leaving their living and their dead without farewell or proper ceremony; perhaps somewhere in their midst was Kanwar's daughter, small, lost, terrified. If she was alive.

—

The clatter of shutters descending from the shop next door alerted Bibi-ji to the fact that it was five o'clock and time to close up. She folded Kanwar's letter carefully, noting that the thin paper was beginning to tear along the folds, that Kanwar's words were disappearing along those same lines. She pressed it to her lips, smelled the faint scent of lavender. How much she had loved that smell once, she remembered. There had been a time, when she arrived in Canada, that her life had been lined with lavender. Inside their home—underlying the strong odours of garlic and turmeric, cumin and coriander—a sensitive nose could catch the determined drift of lavender. Dried lavender lay scattered in her underwear drawers and in her shoes. She was identified not by the sound of her footsteps, but by the fragrance of lavender that preceded her arrival and remained like a memory after her departure. But after Kanwar's disappearance, she had swept all the soaps and perfumes from her cupboards and into the garbage. She shook out the sachets that she had tucked into the folds of sheets and towels and in the drawers. But no matter what she did, the smell of the herb clung to her like guilt.

She slid the letter into its envelope and replaced it in her bag. One day she would find her sister and bring her family to safety in Vancouver. For that search, she would need money; she and Pa-ji must buy, sell and invest to become wealthy. She owed this much to her sister. With that defiant thought, she began to count the cash. Her mind shifted to the possibilities presented by the silent street outside her window. Opportunities like pearls, she reminded herself. It was only a question of spotting them. Perhaps a restaurant. Perhaps they could buy the small house with the For Sale sign that she had passed a few days ago. Then they could rent out the apartment upstairs and have a steady stream of income . . . She emptied the day's takings into a pouch, locked up and, with Lalloo following, climbed the narrow flight of steps up to the apartment.

FOUR

THE DELHI JUNCTION

—

Vancouver

1967

Nineteen sixty-one was a momentous year for the world: the handsome young John F. Kennedy became the first Roman Catholic president of the United States, and a few months later a Russian named Yuri Gagarin became the first man in space. It was also a banner year for Pa-ji and Bibi-ji, who finally opened their restaurant, The Delhi Junction Café—realizing yet another of Bibi-ji's ambitions.

Now here she was, six years later on a busy Saturday afternoon at The Delhi Junction, snapping a rubber band around a box of fresh samosas.

"One dollar, please," she said, pushing the box across the counter to the waiting customer.

Another customer took his place with a request for chholey-bhaturey, followed by a woman who placed a large order for lamb curry. There was a lull in the traffic at the counter after she left. With a sigh of relief, Bibi-ji eased herself on to the bar stool and worked her shoes off her feet, wishing she had not worn the pointed green heels today. If the steady stream of customers was any indication, it would be another busy Saturday and she would be on her feet for a while. Not that she minded. A full restaurant was a good thing—yes, a very good thing indeed. She surveyed with satisfaction the crowded tables and the waiters running in and out of the kitchen carrying loaded trays. Her eyes fell on Colonel Samuel Hunt, ex–British India army, one of the regulars and the only gora in a sea of brown-skinned desis, deliberating over the brief menu before ordering, as always, the same items—mutton curry with naan and a pint of lager to wash it all down. In the six years since the restaurant had opened, Samuel Hunt had become known for his uncomplimentary sentiments towards immigrants who did not share his racial heritage—a fact that used to aggravate Bibi-ji no end, until she came to see him as a sad old man whose eyes and ears were so sealed by his skin that he could neither witness nor understand the changing world. But whatever his feelings towards the desis who gathered at The Delhi Junction, Sam Hunt could not resist their food. After twenty-five years in India, the old man had developed a taste for curries. The taste became a craving once a week, which was when he marched over to The Delhi Junction. There was also, perhaps, an unacknowledged need to mingle with the people who had surrounded him for a quarter of a century, to argue with them, to hear the mixture of languages, to smell familiar smells. In short, Bibi-ji realized with some amusement, Samuel Hunt, the Englishman transplanted to Canada, was doing the splits between two cultures, just like the desis were.

Now she was relieved to see that he was being served by one of her more seasoned waiters, for the old India hand was crusty and reduced the less experienced waiters to nervous wrecks with his demands.

"Hot, hotter, hottest, Colonel-ji?" the waiter asked politely, as he had been taught by Bibi-ji.

Sam Hunt considered the question for a few moments, as if it were the first time he had heard it, and said, "The hotter, I think, or perhaps . . . no, on second thought, the hottest."

Bibi-ji smiled and looked away. Sometimes it was hard to believe that things had turned out exactly the way she had planned. It had started in 1958, when they purchased a small house on 56th Avenue. She and Pa-ji had rented out the apartment above the grocery store and then, in 1961, had leased out the store as well and bought this property on the corner of Main Street and 49th Avenue. It had once been a shop that sold sewing machines and had large display windows on three sides. On the left was a gas station, to the right was Mrs. Wu's vegetable store, and across the road was a row of small shops selling, among other things, fabrics, groceries and baked goods. Not much, she had said to Pa-ji at the time.

"But don't worry," Lalloo had advised in his Punjabi-accented English. "Locationn. Locationn. Locationn. I am telling you, Bibi-ji," he added, as if he, not she, had discovered the place, "you wait and see, in a few more years this area will be booming." Lalloo had evolved from an awkward turbaned youth to a man about town. He had set himself up as an immigration consultant and marriage broker, and dabbled in real estate in addition to carrying on other businesses that bordered on the illegal. Despite Pa-ji's objections, he had cut his long hair and traded his turban for a hat, his pyjamas for a suit and his worn sneakers for a pair of well-shined boots. He was in with the Italians, the Chinese, the Japanese and more than one politician. He knew people in construction and renovation, and within a few months he had these friends turn a bare space into this restaurant.

That was six years ago. Now look at it, never a quiet moment. The Delhi Junction had become a ritual, a necessity, a habit for many of the city's growing population of desis who stopped by for a quick meal or afternoon tea.

Pa-ji had wanted to call the place Apna, a Punjabi word meaning Ours. However, Bibi-ji felt that they needed to have a broader appeal, so they settled on The Delhi Junction Café, hoping the little restaurant would live up to its name and one day host, if not exactly the multitude, then at least a semblance of the crowds that streamed through New Delhi's railway station daily.

Bibi-ji had the walls painted her favourite shade of strawberry pink and asked two of the men who had then been house guests to make wooden tables for the café. An assortment of chairs was acquired from second-hand shops and cheap furniture stores. Another long-term visitor was set to work making table cloths from a roll of blue and pink fabric that Bibi-ji had bought cheap at the fabric store across the road. Over the fabric she put sheets of plastic to minimize laundry costs. A single brass vase bearing a plastic rose adorned each table. Every morning when Bibi-ji came into the restaurant, the first thing she did was sprinkle water on the plastic roses. On one wall she hung lithographic prints of the ten Sikh gurus, a highly coloured painting of the Golden Temple with a garland of flashing bulbs around it, maps of India and Canada, pictures of Nehru, Gandhi, Bhagat Singh, Marilyn Monroe, Meena Kumari, Clark Gable and Dev Anand. On another wall were clocks displaying the time in India, Pakistan (East and West), Vancouver, England, New York, Melbourne and Singapore. The clocks were Pa-ji's favourite items of decoration—at any given moment, he could see the time in the many countries that carried the offspring of Punjab in their bosoms. It pleased him to be reminded that Sikhs were scattered all over the world, like seeds that had exploded from a seed pod.

The clocks were also appreciated by the customers, who imagined a grandmother bending over her work in her yard in Patiala, a mother performing her evening prayers in Lahore or a brother heading for school in Chittagong. It gave them the illusion that they could reach out and touch their distant loved ones.

Bibi-ji had chosen the menu items carefully, making sure that neither beef nor pork were included so as not to offend any religious group. She hired a cook and paid him an excellent salary, aware that the restaurant's success depended on him. She saved on the wages of the waiters by taking advantage of the ready-made, unpaid and therefore floating staff drawn from the people who continued to move through her new home—in even larger numbers now that the Canadian government had opened its doors to immigrants from India. On weekdays, while Pa-ji manned the cash register, Bibi-ji helped with the service. She had a good memory and remembered the names of her customers, their villages, their wives, children, mothers, sisters and brothers. She remembered who liked fresh chillies served on the side with the chholey, and she knew whether they preferred the roti with ghee or well roasted on the fire. Sometimes, to please a regular, she would offer to make puris instead of rotis for a change. To the new arrivals in Canada she handed out advice on visas and immigration procedures, work permits and rents, the best places to buy vegetables and groceries, as well as a free bowl of sugary kheer if this was their first time at The Junction, as the regulars now called it.

Both she and Pa-ji were glad to see the new immigrants. They felt a deep affection for these people, even when they were not from Punjab. Fuelled by frequent infusions of tea, they liked to *discuss* things. They were old hands at gup-shup and welcomed Pa-ji's loud interventions from his station at the cash register.

As for the children—the boys with their little topknots if they were Sikh, and the girls with their swinging braids and ponytails—they were allowed to eat for free. It was not good for business, Bibi-ji knew, but she counted on

The One Up There to witness her act of kindness and grant her a dupattaful of blessings. At one time she had hoped that these blessings would take the form of children of her own.

Then on Saturday last week, she had turned forty-five and finally relinquished hope of ever becoming a mother. She had gone to The Delhi Junction feeling depressed until Pa-ji, on a rare day off, surprised her by showing up in the middle of the morning with Lalloo in tow.

"Come, I have to show you something," he had said mysteriously, his eyes gleaming with excitement.

"What? Now?" Bibi-ji asked, her bad mood compounded by the fact that he was dragging her off somewhere in the middle of a busy working day. "And the restaurant? Who . . ."

"Don't worry, Bibi-ji," Lalloo had said, handing her her purse and pushing her out the door. "I will take care of it. You go."

Bibi-ji had climbed into the car wondering what was going on.

"What's wrong? Where are we going?" she had asked the unusually silent Pa-ji, who was driving as fast as he could without breaking the speed limit.

"Wait and see," he replied mysteriously.

Driving past their own home to a large, newly built white house at the end of the road, they stopped at the ornate wrought-iron gates. With a flourish, Pa-ji opened the passenger door and offered Bibi-ji his hand to step out of the car. With an even greater flourish, he gave her a small box wrapped in gift paper. Inside it was a key.

"Happy birthday, my Bebby," he said. "This is our new home."

Bibi-ji was struck dumb.

"What do you think?" Pa-ji asked. He caught her hand and pulled her towards the wrought-iron gates. "I've named it the Taj Mahal," he said, pointing at a brass plate, inscribed with flowing letters, on the faux-marble gateposts.

"For me? A Taj Mahal?" She was simultaneously thrilled by the size and grandeur of the gift and alarmed at the thought that they must be mortgaged up to their eyeballs for this extravagance. She had never outgrown her childhood hatred of poverty and her suspicion of moneylenders, and the banks, as far as she was concerned, were only suited and booted versions of Ramchand, the dhothi-clad moneylender of Panjaur.

Pa-ji chuckled and pinched her cheek as if she were a little girl. "Why not? If that Shah Jahan could build a palace for his Mumtaz Begum to lie dead in, why can't I build one for my queen to live in?"

Bibi-ji slowly traced the name and number on the brass plate.

"I tried to get those idiots at the municipal office to let me number it 1922, your birth year. But they refused. If this was India, I could have named the entire street Sharanjeet Kaur Avenue if I wanted to!" Pa-ji reached out to open the gates and pulled her after him. "These gates will always remain open," he declared. "For all those who need a place to stay."

"And who is to pay for this?" Bibi-ji demanded as they walked up the long driveway—lined with pine trees and bordered by a garden in which, she noted, her favourite roses had already been planted—to the front door.

"We have the restaurant, the apartment—and now the other house. We will rent that out, just like we did with our apartment. Everything you wanted is coming true, enh, my Bebby?"

She had squeezed his hand and nodded. Yes, everything she had wanted in her life she had found, except for her sister and her family.

The door of The Delhi Junction swung open, letting in a draft of cool spring air and, with it, Hafeez Ali, one of the Saturday regulars, dressed impeccably as always in a beautifully cut achkan, his hair brushed back from his high, bony forehead. Bibi-ji snapped out of her thoughts and slid off her stool to welcome him as he touched a hand to his forehead and offered her the traditional Muslim gesture of greeting: "*Salaam-alai-kum,* Bibi-ji!"

She smiled warmly at him. "*Salaam,* Hafeez Bhai, how are you today? How is your beautiful wife? And the children? I heard that your son won a prize in mathematics at school—clever like his father, eh?"

Hafeez laughed and shook his head. "I don't know about that, Bibi-ji. I am not much good with numbers, you know. It is my wife who is the financial manager at home. Like you, it seems. You women are taking over the world!"

"Yes, and a good thing too!" Bibi-ji remarked. She enjoyed listening to the elegant Urdu that the Pakistani man spoke, more formal than Hindi and richer than the village Punjabi she knew, though occasionally she could not understand some of his words. "And what can I do for you today? The usual? Two tandoori chicken and five naan?"

"Yes, the usual." Hafeez nodded. "And I will be ordering some food to eat here. Alibhai will be joining me. And our families too."

With a wave of her hand, Bibi-ji signalled a waiter to take Hafeez to the table that he and his friend Alibhai usually occupied. It was across the room from the table beside the window closest to the cash counter, which was reserved, on Saturdays, for the Indian regulars—Dr. Majumdar, a tall, suave Bengali with a sardonic face; portly, balding Menon, who spoke English with a heavy Malayali accent; the Gujarati doctor Harish Shah, also rotund and balding; and the new arrival from South India who had shortened his complicated name, which Bibi-ji could never remember, to the more manageable Balu Bhat.

In the early years of the restaurant's life, the Indians and the Pakistanis had sat hunched around the same table, fuelling their conversations with samosas and endless cups of boiling sugary chai tinged with ginger and cardamom, discussing their lives, their families, cricket matches, their work and, most of all, the politics of their country of origin. A taut rope tied them all to "home," whether India or Pakistan. They saw their distant homes as if through a telescope, every small wound or scar or flare back there exaggerated, exciting their imaginations and their emotions, bringing tears to their eyes. They were like obsessed stargazers, whose distance from the thing they observed made it all the brighter, all the more important.

When China invaded India in 1962, not long after the two nations had declared undying friendship, and then India's prime minister, Jawaharlal Nehru, died a year later, The Delhi Junction's regulars were unanimous in their belief that the Chinese invasion had killed him.

"The Chinese *betrayal!*" round-faced Shah had declared, thumping a fist on the table.

"It broke Nehru's heart!" Menon had agreed. And for a few months they all refused to patronize Mrs. Wu's vegetable shop. And when Nehru's daughter Indira Gandhi became prime minister of India in 1964, Bibi-ji marked the day by distributing free sweets to everyone who came to The Delhi Junction, for by now she had decided that her loyalties lay with India, not Pakistan. She was proud of—no, she identified with—this young woman who was almost the same age as her, for having taken on a job of such magnitude. Although she was now only a visitor to that country, Bibi-ji knew that India was no easy nation to manage, that it was not like Canada, so quiet and nice and well behaved, so good about following rules.

Pa-ji contributed to the celebrations by acquiring a framed portrait of the young prime minister. He hung it on the wall of The Delhi Junction, adding a new star to the firmament of heroes and heroines, political and popular. Indira Gandhi, eyebrows sharply angled over heavy-lidded eyes, stared arrogantly out of her frame, and every time she passed the portrait Bibi-ji gave her an affectionate smile.

In 1965, when war broke out between India and Pakistan, the battle came to The Delhi Junction as well. The seating maps altered, and Hafeez and Alibhai moved defensively over to a separate table across the room from the Indian group. The linoleum floor between them turned into the Line of Control—an unseen barrier of barbed wire stretching across it, hot lights blazing warnings as soldiers stood guard with guns cocked. Anger, hurt and loss simmered on both sides. As the war across the world went on and casualties mounted on both sides, conversation between the two factions in The Junction ceased altogether, and when Pa-ji began to vocally support the Indian side, Hafeez and Alibhai stopped coming to the café. But when the war ended a few months later, they reappeared as if nothing had occurred. A good meal, with familiar spices in a foreign country, meant more than the enmities generated by distant homelands.

An elderly customer with a bright yellow turban entered the café. It was one of Pa-ji's friends from his logging days.

"*Sat-Sri Akal,* Bibi-ji!" he said. "I hear that you have a grand new house?"

"Yes, a Taj Mahal, no less." She felt flattered and absurdly spoiled.

"So what are you going to do with your old one? If you are selling, let me know. I am looking for investment property in this area."

"No, we are planning to rent it out for now," Bibi-ji said. "Do you know anyone in need of a place? We are looking for a decent family."

"Decent family for what, Mrs. Singh?" Majumdar came through the door, followed by his friend Menon. He was the only one of her customers who did not call her Bibi-ji. She could set her clock by him, for he always showed up on Saturday mornings at eleven o'clock sharp.

"Your table is waiting for you," Bibi-ji smiled and nodded at the two men. "And we are looking for a decent family to rent our house."

"What about you? Are you moving somewhere? Please don't say you are! What will we do without you and The Junction?" Majumdar, elegant and sardonic, threw up his arms in mock horror.

Bibi-ji laughed. "No, no, we aren't going anywhere! We have a new house, that's all. So if any of you gentlemen know of someone in search of a place to rent . . ."

"Wasn't Balu looking for something? Didn't he say that his family is arriving soon?" Menon asked. He looked at Bibi-ji. "You know our friend, the one who recently arrived from India?"

"The fellow with the name as long as the Fraser River?" Bibi-ji asked. "The one who shakes his head like this, like this, when he talks?" She waggled her head in imitation of Balu Bhat. "Of course I know him, and here he is—in person!"

A short, pleasant-looking man with large, dark eyes entered the café. He called a greeting to his friends, caught Bibi-ji's eye and smiled at her.

"We were just talking about you, Bhat-ji," she said. "Your friends tell me that you are looking for a place to rent?"

Balu wobbled his head to indicate either a yes or a no, Bibi-ji could not tell. "Yes I am, Bibi-ji," he said.

"I have a place, if you are interested."

"Ask her the rent first, Balu," Majumdar interjected.

"Rent is very reasonable and the house comes fully furnished," Bibi-ji said. She studied Balu, wondering whether he would be able to pay even the low amount that she and Pa-ji had settled on. He worked only part-time at a local community college, and she knew that teachers did not make big salaries. "We don't want money, only a good tenant who will take care of our property and pay us on time."

"You don't want money, Bibi-ji?" Menon laughed. He shared with Balu a tendency to rotate his head when he spoke, in that same indeterminate movement, which led Bibi-ji to believe that he too was a South Indian, a breed as foreign to her as the goras, or Mrs. Wu, or Majid the barber. "Then how about free chai and samosas today?" Menon grinned, his moustache moving upwards and touching the tips of his flaring nostrils.

"Why not?" Bibi-ji said, surprising herself by her sudden generosity. Later, when she went over the conversation, she would add this impulsive act to the list of Good Deeds that were earning her a golden star from the Ooper-Wallah, or the Upper-Wallah, as Pa-ji preferred to call him. The One Up There, God, Allah, Krishna, whoever, would be pleased with her. "Now about our house, Bhat-ji. Are you interested?"

"I would like to see it first," Balu said. "I am definitely looking for a place, but my wife, Leela, can be a little fussy, you know. She and the children are arriving in a month, so I don't have much time to look around. Not that she wants a palace, nothing like that, but still it should be a comfortable size. At a reasonable rent, of course. But before I say anything, what I mean is—"

"I understand," Bibi-ji interrupted. "I will call Pa-ji, and you can go and see the house after you have had your chai and samosas."

By the time Balu was done with tea, Pa-ji had arrived at the café to help with the rush of customers. So it was Bibi-ji who took Balu to see the home in which he would live for the next several years. After some haggling over the rent, which Bibi-ji reduced just a bit more (yet another brownie point from God), Balu signed the lease for the two-bedroom house with the oversized couches and bright floral curtains. He would move in the following Saturday, a few weeks before Leela and their children, Preethi and Arjun, arrived.

For years after, Bibi-ji would thank her stars that she had followed her more generous instincts. She would look back to the moment when she had offered the house to Balu Bhat, and she would find herself grateful to The One Up There. But that was before events in distant India poisoned her life, before bitter anger wiped out the gratitude and her friends became her enemies.

"Your wife will be happy with your choice, I hope, Bhat-ji," she said as she handed Balu the keys. She wondered what kind of woman Leela Bhat was. Pretty? Gentle? Bossy and opinionated, like Dr. Majumdar's wife, whom she had only met twice and disliked thoroughly?

"Yes, I hope so too," Balu replied. He smiled and held up his hand with fingers crossed. "I very much hope so."

PART TWO

—

LEELA

FIVE

HALF-AND-HALF

—

Bangalore

1946

There were those who called Leela Bhat a snob, a difficult woman, with a too great sense of her worth in the world. Her cousins Narayana and Vishnu and their spouses were among the people who portrayed her thus. It could be argued that their animosity had deep roots, extending to the time when they were children growing up together in their ancestral home in Balepur, which had now been gobbled up by and assimilated into the super-high-tech city of Bangalore. It could also be argued, as Leela did, that people who said she was difficult and a snob were just plain envious.

To be fair to Leela, it must be acknowledged that her cousins, in particular, could not help feeling peeved whenever they saw her sharp, wheat-complexioned face, with its peppering of dark freckles across the bridge of her nose and cheeks, her grey eyes and her small, bustling person always dressed so well—whether in starched cotton saris, light printed silk ones or the Canjeevarams heavy with gold embroidery, as the occasion demanded—ordering, bossing, arguing, correcting and generally queening it around as Mrs. Bhat, the wife of Balachandra Bhat, daughter-in-law (the only one) of the famous Gundoor Bhats. They found it difficult to forget that she had once been Leela Shastri, the pale-eyed, thin daughter of Hari Shastri and Rosa Schweers, a half-and-half hovering on the outskirts of their family's circle of love. It was a time that Leela herself had shoved to the remotest corner of her mind, although she could never really forget that day in February 1946 when, as a child of eight, she had watched her mother die.

The day had begun well enough. A photographer had arrived to take pictures of the entire extended family that lived in the Shastri home: Akka the matriarch, Hari Shastri, his brothers Cheenu and Rama, and their wives and children. They had all arranged themselves in the sunny central courtyard of the house in various groupings and poses. Only Leela's mother, Rosa Schweers, was not in the picture, for she had refused to come downstairs from her room.

Now the photo session was long done. Leela finished her lunch and washed her hands. She looked over at her cousins Vishnu and Narayana, who still had mounds of rice piled on their plates, and decided she had enough time to go outside the house and see if the custard apples hanging on the tree in the backyard were ready for picking, and get back in before the two boys finished their meal. The house was quiet. Her two uncles had retreated into the cool, shuttered bedrooms surrounding the large courtyard for much-needed rest with their wives.

Leela had left through the back door and wandered around the yard, humming an improvised song to herself, touching the walls, peering into the well, which was covered with a sheet of tin to prevent nosy parkers like her from falling in, gently squeezing a low-hanging custard apple and finding it still too hard to pick. *"This is the house that Rama Shastri built,"* she sang. *"This is the well in the house that Rama Shastri built. This is the tamarind tree by the well in the house . . ."* She felt overwhelmed by a hazy sense of contentment. She *belonged* here. She was part of the family of Well-Known People living inside these walls. All this was hers as much as it was her cousin Vishnu's or Narayana's, no matter what they said.

The thought of her cousins sent her hurtling back into the house, to the central courtyard where her grandmother Akka sat in an easy chair. As soon as Vishnu and Narayana arrived at her side, Akka would, as she did every day, start to tell her grandchildren stories from the *Mahabharata,* the *Ramayana* or the *Panchatantra.* This, she said, was how she taught them what was good and bad and how to live a proper life edged with righteousness and decency and goodness. Leela was determined to get to Akka before her cousins did so that she could sit in the favoured spot, right beside the old lady. This way, she hoped she might get a loving pat on her head the way the boys did, or perhaps some of the sugar beads from a silver box on the table beside Akka.

But it was no use. Moments after she had settled down close to Akka's chair the two boys strolled into the court-yard, emitting little burps in imitation of the men of the house and thumping their fists against their bare chests as if to beat out a frog stuck there. Akka's dark eyes, which were stones whenever they looked on Leela, turned to melted tar. She beamed at her grandsons and crooned as if she had not seen them for a year, "Aha Naani my pet, aha Vishnu my monkey, come, come and sit next to me!"

And somehow, without quite knowing how, Leela discovered that she was no longer right next to her grand-mother but off to one side.

Now Akka began her story: "Many centuries ago, there was a king named Trishanku who wanted to take his body with him to heaven when he died. He went with his absurd request to the great sage Vishwamitra, who agreed to send the king to heaven in his mortal form. He chanted mantras and performed such powerful penances that the three worlds shook with the force of his will. Soon Trishanku began to rise heavenwards. This unnatural occurrence raised such chaos in the three realms that the gods became alarmed and begged Vishwamitra to stop defying the laws of the universe, which decreed that human beings should shed their worldly skin before leav-ing earth. Vishwamitra gave in to their pleas, but because he had promised Trishanku that he would send him to heaven, he stopped the king in the void between heaven and earth and created another heaven around him. And so the poor king was condemned to hang upside down between worlds, unable to do anything other than wait for the universe to end. And so, when somebody is neither here nor there we say that they have attained Trishanku's heaven, not a very pleasant state of being at all!"

Leela waited for Akka to add an example of a real person who resided in this state of perpetual indecision—this was how she ended each of her story sessions. Yesterday, when she had told the story of Lakshmana, the faithful brother of King Rama, who left his wife and a life of comfort to serve his older brother in exile for fourteen years, Akka had pointed at Leela and said, "Your father is a lucky man to have such devoted younger brothers. Why, if not for them, goodness knows what your father would have done in his time of difficulty."

At the mention of her father's "difficulty," Leela had blushed. Was it her fault that her father, Hari Shastri, had strolled down the street in London on which Rosa Schweers had lived? That a potted geranium which she had been watering had fallen off the windowsill and hit Hari on his head? That Rosa had come running down the stairs to help the unfortunate young man get up? That Hari, on opening his eyes, had seen a pair of charming breasts threatening to spill out of a lacy nightgown (Rosa had a weakness for that garment), topped by a pretty, anxious young face and, as her mother had often told Leela, had promptly fallen in love? And, carried by that tide of affection, had married Rosa Schweers, a casteless German woman of no known family? Was it Leela's fault that she was the product of that union? Leela wished that she had the courage to fling these questions at her grandmother. But the old lady terrified her almost as much as she inspired a desperate need for approval in Leela's small heart. Leela wanted more than anything to see a look of pride in Akka's eyes.

Beside her, Narayana nudged Vishnu and whispered something. Vishnu shot Leela a look and giggled.

Her grandmother's dark eyes turned to her favourite child. "What is it, Naani, what are you and your brother laughing about? Let us all hear this joke," she said indulgently, stroking his thick, curly hair.

Narayana wriggled about and shot his brother sly grins but kept his mouth shut. Vishnu, however, could not keep quiet. "He says that our Leela is up-in-the-air like that upside-down king, Akka." He covered his mouth with his hand and giggled again.

"Like Trishanku?" Akka asked. "And why do you say that, Naani, my pet?"

Leela glanced from her cousins to her grandmother, not sure whether she was supposed to feel flattered or upset by the comparison.

"Because she is also half here and half there, that's why," Naani explained. "Like the Anglo-Indians of Cox Town."

Leela felt as if her heart would burst with shame and hurt. To be compared to those people, so reviled by good Hindu families like her own—it was unbearable! Tears burned twin trails down her cheeks as she rose to her feet and ran to the drawing room, where her father usually spent his afternoons, alone, lying on the divan reading law journals or the newspaper, while her mother rested upstairs in her darkened bedroom.

Rosa was always resting; everything made her ill or nervous—the dust, the heat, the food, the old neem tree outside her window, which she had had trimmed so thoroughly that it listed to one side away from the house, as if in weary disgust. Most of all Rosa was sick of the people in this house, particularly her mother-in-law, Akka. Her dislike was reciprocated with much malice. Akka made it clear to all that she thought the foreign daughter-in-law was a disgrace to the family name, a conniving trollop who had snared her innocent son while he was lost in a foreign country without any of his family to guide and advise him properly. She refused to call Rosa by her name or to acknowledge that she was married to Hari Shastri.

During the first few years of her life in the house, Rosa had energetically countered the old woman's nastiness with her own sallies. Her favourite method of annoying her mother-in-law, who maintained a strictly vegetarian household, was to order the servant Savitri to bring her a tiffin-carrier full of mutton curry or a chicken biryani from a Muslim restaurant in the town market. The maid, who loved the dramatic confrontations between Rosa and Akka, would promptly report to the old lady that she was off to get the white wife some food from, of all places, a Muslim restaurant. And Akka would bang the heel of her hand against her forehead, call to her sons and complain, "I am telling you, if dead animals come into this house and are eaten by that woman, your mother will go away. She will leave and *die* on the street."

The maid would be sent back to Rosa, a tennis ball between two strong-armed players. Sometimes Rosa would win the fight and the maid would be successfully dispatched to the restaurant. And Akka would sit in tight-lipped silence, her eyes red from weeping, her suitcase packed and ready beside her so that she could move out of the house and expire as she had threatened, while Leela's uncles would touch her feet and beg her to stay, saying, "Akka, if you go away who will be our mother?"

Venki the cook, whose hatred of Akka predated Rosa's arrival, was the only one who refused to be involved in this family drama. He would stand at the door of the kitchen, in his dhothi, stained with turmeric and oil and other kitchen ingredients, tied high under his chest, leaving much of his spindly, hairless legs bare, and smile cynically at the histrionics in the courtyard.

On days when Rosa lost the battle she would sulk spectacularly in her bedroom upstairs, either shouting abuse—in German, English and the small amount of Kannada that she had managed to acquire—at anyone passing her room, or marching out the front door to the veranda in one of her cotton nighties, the outline of her panties and bra and her shapely legs clearly visible through the thin fabric. She knew her near-nakedness appalled Akka, especially when the bangle seller was at the door.

"Go back!" Akka would hiss when Rosa drifted back into the house, a pleased smile etched across her pretty face, her arms jangling with the fragile bangles. "Go back where you came from, you piece of trash!"

Many times Rosa had considered divorcing her husband and his family and returning to Germany or England, but she had lost contact with her family long ago. Then in 1938 Leela was born, and the following year World War Two broke out. After that, the energy and lively sense of self-preservation that had sustained her for so long seeped out of Rosa. She lost interest in everything, including quarrelling with Akka. She locked herself in her bedroom for long periods of time, ignoring the maid who brought the infant to her to be fed. She grew corpulent on a diet of forbidden meat that she ordered regularly from the Muslim restaurant and on which Akka had ceased to comment. On rare occasions, at dusk, just before the family gathered for dinner, Rosa would wander down the stairs and out, alone, into the backyard.

This was about the time when Hari Shastri left his wife's bed and began sleeping in his library. He too abandoned his daughter to the servants, waking early to leave for work and returning only late in the evenings.

In the end, it was Venki who brought up Leela. Perhaps he did this to spite Akka, who refused to touch the child even while making a great show of cuddling the children of her younger sons. Or perhaps there was something about the frail baby, her eyes grey as the monsoon sky and with her desperate wailing, that tugged at the old cook's heart. Whatever the reason, Leela became Venki's child. She might not even have known that she was related to the pale woman who lived upstairs in a bed shrouded in mosquito netting, and who emerged once in a while at dusk to wander through the thicket of trees and plants in the large backyard, if not for Akka's barbed reminders.

"Half-breed," Akka would mutter out loud. "Worse than an untouchable. At least a toilet cleaner has caste. But this girl, where does she belong? Tell me, somebody, *where?*"

And when she was a little older, the reminders of her mixed origins came from Rosa, who would send the maid to fetch Leela up to her. The little girl would tiptoe into the dark, shuttered room to find her mother lying huge in the centre of the bed, cocooned in the white mosquito netting, the gramophone playing soft western classical music or German songs. Leela would advance reluctantly and stop just outside the netting draped about the bed. Her mother then would hold the net open, and Leela would be obliged to crawl into the stale-smelling space. Rosa would press Leela close to her spongy body and murmur in a mixture of languages that Leela only half understood. "Never forget you are mine. Even though you have their brown skin, you see the world with my grey eyes. They are wicked, filthy creatures, pigs, dirtyevilpigs."

Leela would lie beside her mother, stiff with pity, fear and revulsion, and run back to that other world as soon as she could, though she knew that downstairs—despite the sun and the noise, the colour and the life—she would be just as unhappy, and that everyone there—Akka, her aunts, her uncles and her cousins—would look sideways at her, the half-and-half child of mismatched parents. She would hide away in the gods' room and pray to the silent silver idols there to make her mother disappear, to erase Rosa Schweers as if she had never been, for only then would she, Leela Shastri, begin to exist whole and unblemished. Some days she would clumsily pile bits of her mother's hair or nail clippings or a handkerchief stolen from her room, place half a lemon over the objects, add a sprinkling of vermilion powder and incinerate them with matches and oil stolen from the kitchen, all the while imagining that she was performing black magic spells like Venki sometimes did, cursing whoever had offended him with headaches or diarrhea, or cramping aches in the feet. She would crouch over the smoking debris, mutter her childish incantations and imagine that her mother was disappearing with each charred bit of hair and curved toenail.

After the story session that had ended so disastrously, Leela had gone first to her father, who offered little more than a pat on the back. Unsatisfied, she proceeded to the dark and oily kitchen, where Venki held her quivering little body, stroked her hair with his calloused hand and whispered gently, "Oh-ho, oh-ho, my sweetness, jewel of my eye, why are we so sad now, tell old Venki!"

Leela buried her face in the old cook's chest, inhaling the odours of turmeric, asafetida, mustard, cumin and cardamom that had embedded themselves in his leathery skin. "Narayana said that I was half-and-half, like Trishanku," she sobbed.

Venki reached for the tin in which he kept treats for Leela and fished out a round piece of jaggery. He popped it into her mouth. "So what is wrong with being like Trishanku? Was he not a lucky fellow to have a foot in two worlds? Did he not have a heaven of his own around him? Hanh? Tell me? My chick pea, listen, it can be an advantage to live neither here nor there, like a frog, comfortable in water *and* on land. The thing is to understand how to make use of this ability."

Venki, Leela thought longingly, was neither a frog nor a Trishanku. His entire life had been spent inside this house. His father and his grandfather had cooked here before him. He had grown up in this courtyard and had known Leela's grandmother since the day she had arrived in the house as a bride. He had cooked the auspicious meals when Akka became pregnant with Leela's father, Hari, when she gave birth to him and her other two sons, at their weddings, at the arrival of each new grandchild and, most recently, for Leela's grandfather's death ceremonies. He had his place in the world, and it was in this dark and smoky kitchen.

Beginning his preparations for the evening meal, Venki gave Leela small tasks to distract her from her sorrow. Soon dusk wrapped itself around the old house and long shadows lay in the empty courtyard. A fragrance of incense floated about as Akka and the aunts lighted the lamps for evening prayers in the gods' room. From one of the rooms around the courtyard came the mutter of times tables as Narayana and Vishnu did their homework, which reminded Leela that she had work to finish as well. Venki paused suddenly in his peeling and raised his head.

"What is it?" Leela asked.

"Your mother," the cook said. His sharp ears had caught a whisper slithering like a snake around the house.

And at once Leela too could hear the susurrating voices as Rosa made her slow, bulky way down the stairs: *She is coming down, she is coming down, where is she going, what is she doing, she is coming down.*

She watched from the kitchen door as her mother emerged and waddled out the back door and into the garden, down the narrow path, past the well, past the guava trees, past the mango trees grown especially for use on funeral pyres. With a sudden, intense longing Leela followed her mother, keeping a careful distance but not sure why she did so. She watched Rosa trail her hand against the coarse, dark bark of the trees, brushed her small fingers against the same rough areas and felt her mother's sadness.

Rosa walked until she reached a green, scummy pond at the end of the property. Here the trees ended their shadowy guard and the last of the day's sunshine touched the deep water, making it glitter. White water lilies floated on the surface, and dragonflies hung in glittering concert over the flowers and leaves. The only sounds to be heard were the guttural croaking of frogs and the quieter humming of small insects. Stepping carefully over the moss-covered stones, Rosa reached the edge of the pond, where she stood silently, her entire body relaxing. Leela wondered what her mother saw in this place full of shadows where everything shifted with the movement of the sun. She longed suddenly for the safety of the house behind her, the solidity of its walls, its pillars, its foundations. Inside that house lived respectability and stability; rites and rituals were strictly observed, and festivals and

ceremonies were performed according to the rules laid
down by her Hindu Brahmin forefathers. But she continued to stare at the woman by the edge of the water.

A mosquito landed on Leela's bare arm. Sucking in her
breath, she slapped at it. Her mother, hearing the slap,
whirled around as sharply as her bulk would allow. She
lost her balance and fell, arms flailing, face-first into the
pond. The green water splashed upwards, a swarm of
insects erupted from the surface of the pond, and then
silence, only ripples. Leela waited, poised to run, for her
mother to rise up and call out, to rise up, *to rise up*. But
Rosa lay still, her legs sticking out like fleshy white batons
from the edge of her nightgown, her small feet a cartoon
pink in their bright blue Hawaii chappals.

"Mama?" Leela called softly, hardly able to believe that
the silent, inanimate body lying a few feet away was her
mother. She backed away, then ran panting and terrified
back down the path to the bright, noisy house. No one
noticed her. She sped up the stairs and entered her
mother's room, hoping the event she had just witnessed
was a bad dream, that she would see her mother there in
the gloom, shrouded in mosquito netting. But no one was
in the room, only a lingering odour of old things—clothes,
paper, food. She wondered whether she should tell anyone that her mother was lying face down in the pond.
What if they blamed her? She went back downstairs and
Venki, peering out of his kitchen, beckoned to her.

"Guess what I made for my little pet tonight for dinner?" he asked, smiling.

"My mother is not in her room," Leela said.

"She went out to the back garden, remember? Now, do you want to know what I made for my baby?"

Leela shrugged and looked away. "I saw her go out there." She waved vaguely in the direction of the back-yard. "To the pond. But she hasn't come back yet."

Venki gave her a sharp look. "Didn't you follow her? What happened?"

"She fell in the pond. I don't know what happened to her," Leela whispered.

Later, when Rosa's body had been lifted out of the water and carried back into the house, Leela looked at the heavy, shapeless face of the woman who had once been her mother. *I have killed her,* she thought numbly, twisting the fabric of her long skirt tightly around her fingers. *It was me, I killed her.* She had performed black magic using her mother's nail clippings, she had prayed hard that her mother would vanish, and now her wish had come true. What had she done? But hot on the heels of guilt came a confused relief that finally, *finally,* there would be no white woman to remind people that she, Leela, was a half-and-half.

At that moment, she looked up to catch Akka staring at her, her eyes cold as always, and understood that Rosa Schweers would never fully disappear from her life. Rosa would always be there in the colour of Leela's eyes and, worst of all, in the memories of her family. She also understood that to survive she would have to use what-ever means she had to get away from this house to a place that she could own entirely. She would have to create, like the sage Vishwamitra had done for Trishanku, a heaven for herself. Venki was right: there were two ways of understanding that story. Leela stared back at her grandmother, and finally the old woman looked away.

Twelve years passed. Leela grew from a quick-witted, petite child into a short woman with a sharp, watchful face. She might have been pretty had she smiled more often, but Leela did not think there was much to smile about. She had, however, developed a shrewd confidence in her ability to survive. After Rosa's death, she had reviewed her modest options and decided that she needed another ally besides Venki. The old cook gave her love and food, but she needed someone with more authority in the household. She devoted herself to her father, Hari Shastri, bringing him his slippers when he came home from work, taking his tray of food to him in his room, doing her homework on the floor of that room, asking him to explain this or that to her and generally insinuating herself into his life. She anticipated his wishes—ensuring that his pens were full of ink and that he always had sharpened pencils on his desk, that all his papers were neatly clipped together and filed—and if he needed anything, he only had to say "Leelu" for her to appear at his elbow. Before Akka knew it, the grey-eyed grandchild whom she thoroughly distrusted had somehow taken charge of her son's life. Now that Leela was grown up, Hari Shastri gave his paycheque to his daughter instead of his mother. There was little the old woman could do when Leela bought herself saris with her father's money, purchased gifts for her aunts to keep them happy in case she needed their help and, after high school, decided to continue her studies in university. If she did not get married, she would at least have an education to fall back on. She could find herself a job as a teacher or perhaps study a little longer and become a college lecturer. But she kept these plans to herself and, to avoid offending her grandmother, Leela always made an ostentatious display of placing Hari Shastri's paycheque at the old lady's sharp-edged feet, respectfully touching them with her small hands.

"Akka," she would say, "is there anything you want from the market? I'll get it on my way home from college." But before her grandmother could reach down for the piece of paper, she would whisk it away and tuck it into her blouse, where it stayed securely between her breasts until she deposited it in the joint bank account she maintained with her father.

And whether her grandmother requested anything or not, Leela would return with long strings of jasmine buds strung together, fruits of various kinds—including golden apples from Ooty, an expensive indulgence for Akka, who loved their crisp sweetness—to place in front of the gods. For Leela continued to pray fervently twice a day, her fierce belief in gods that she could neither see nor hear jostling against the empirical truths of the maths and sciences she studied at university. She embraced the erratic gods on one side and rationalism on the other. Half of this and half of that.

Then, in her second year of university, Leela was invited to the wedding of her best friend. She was seated near the aisle in one of a row of seats in the wedding hall, dressed in a pale green sari. On the raised dais at the far end of the hall, her friend circled the sacred fire with her new husband. Leela, feeling a cramp in her leg, stretched it out into the aisle just as a young man walked by. And Balachandra Bhat, cousin to Leela's friend, tripped over her small foot and stumbled to the ground.

"Ay-ay-yo!" exclaimed Leela, leaping out of her seat, embarrassed. "So sorry, hope you are not hurt . . ." She leaned down to give the young man a hand up, unwittingly repeating the actions of her mother so long ago. Coincidence? Perhaps. Chance brings lives together in unexpected ways and breaks them apart with equal randomness.

The young man who was sprawled on the floor rolled over awkwardly and found himself looking into a pair of anxious grey eyes in a freckled brown face. The unusual combination intrigued and charmed him, and by the time he had dusted himself off and accepted Leela's apologies—made in a deep, husky voice oddly at variance with her small figure—Balachandra Bhat, fondly known as Balu by his friends and family, decided he was in love. As he floated home, he recalled and embroidered, in rich detail, the entire encounter with Leela. He thought her eyes were like a grey sky shot through with sunlight. He remembered her smile and the small dimple on the left side of her mouth. He wished he had had time to count the freckles scattered across the bridge of her small nose and high cheekbones. He confided his passions to his mother, who promptly sent a letter to the Shastris asking for Leela's horoscope.

On the outskirts of Bangalore, in the little town of Balepur, Leela set Venki the task of collecting all the information he could gather about the short young man with the prematurely receding hairline who had fallen at her feet. The old cook, a wizened gnome by now, almost blind and deaf, cooking more by instinct than anything else, found out through his network of cooks and maids in various homes that Balachandra Bhat, the only son of the widowed Mrs. Bhat, had a doctorate in chemical engineering from the highly regarded Indian Institute of Science. He had recently found a job in a newly set-up research institute in Bangalore. But although Balu Bhat was an eligible young bachelor, Venki's sources warned, he was difficult to please. He had a fondness for certain modern, western, *strange* notions about divorce and widow remarriage, the education of women and their inheritance rights. And there was another thing about this young man that made him less than desirable. He had the distressing habit of discussing books with his prospective brides. He quizzed them about history and independence and politics and made them feel like foolish students if they did not have the answers to his questions.

Leela wasn't unduly worried. She read the daily papers, she knew what was going on in the world. She asked her father to send her horoscope, as it would have seemed indecent to do so herself, but she wrote the letter that accompanied it; and her father, used to letting her handle all his correspondence, signed it without bothering to read it. If he had, he would have been surprised to see that Leela had not included the usual information about her beauty, the colour of her skin and her talents as a cook. She wrote about her love of books, her interest in current events and her intention to work after she had finished her studies.

Her aunts and her grandmother shook their heads and laughed at the thought that a man from such a well-known family, such a high Brahmin, should wish to marry the little half-and-half. Had they not already gone through a virtual parade of prospective grooms for Leela, all of whom had left without uttering the word that presaged an engagement, the simple "Yes"?

When Balu arrived with his parents to see her, Leela wore a yellow printed silk sari, a string of jasmine in her braid and little jewellery. She had spent the previous two weeks reading books on British-Indian history as well as a novel by Bankim Chandra Chatterjee. In addition, she reread *Macbeth,* which she had first studied in high school. She struggled through the play, reaching the end feeling as if she had been through a dark maze, full of boulders made of words—large, bumpy, strange—which frequently tripped her up. But she intended to capture this Balachandra Bhat, most eligible of bachelors, and what she lacked in understanding Leela made up for with a prodigious memory. And she found she did like Lady Macbeth—she recognized something of herself in her ambitious ways. Still straddling two worlds, she also prayed round the clock and acquired two new amulets from a sadhvi who was known for her ability to resolve matters relating to love, marriage and childbirth. Thus prepared, Leela went to out to meet her future husband.

Balachandra Bhat was thoroughly enchanted. Compared with the numberless overdressed mamas and their eager daughters, Leela did not simper or giggle or flutter her eyes nervously at him. She looked him straight in the eye like a western woman, and when he asked her if she liked reading, she said that she had read *Macbeth*. He had not read it himself and was duly impressed. Then Leela *lectured* him on Lady Macbeth. He didn't agree with her views, thought them a bit gory as a matter of fact, but he considered himself a true Enlightened Indian Male: he was all for free speech and democracy. Everyone had a view. Moreover, everyone had the right to express it. So he uttered the much awaited word, not once but twice.

"Yes," he said. "Yes."

SIX

FALLEN ARCHES

—

Bangalore

1967

Was it the letter from Canada, or the arch that collapsed, that caused Balu to leave everything solid and stable and permanent in their lives and move across the world? Leela was certain that it was both. For almost ten years she had lived the comfortable life of Mrs. Bhat—a full and happy existence, punctuated by weddings, birth and death ceremonies, and the dozens of festivals that marked the Indian calendar. She had borne her husband a son and a daughter, Arjun and Preethi, and had believed him as satisfied with their life as she was.

Balu, however, was looking for more. Perhaps his discontent with Bangalore, with the street on which they lived, with their home, had begun with his friend Venkat Rao's letter from Toronto two and a half years ago. Looking back, Leela had little doubt of it, for there had been not a single mention of travel abroad before that. Every morning Balu had gone willingly to his job as a chemistry lecturer at a college close to their home and had returned at exactly five o'clock, looking just as fresh and good-natured as when he left. He never complained about either his colleagues or his students, or the load of exams and class assignments he had to deal with. But now that she thought about it, Leela recalled that he had become unexpectedly preoccupied soon after reading the letter from his friend. A few photographs were included with the letter—of Venkat and his wife, wrapped up in winter jackets and standing against what looked like a high-school geography textbook illustration of the tundra in winter.

She had laughed then. "You can barely see their faces, poor things!" she said, passing the pictures back across the table to Balu. "Imagine walking everywhere in those thick clothes! Imagine the cold!"

Balu, on the other hand, was entranced by the fairy-tale quality of the frost-edged pine trees in the background. "It looks so soft," he had said, touching the picture wistfully, as if he could feel the snow. "So new and clean. You know, Leela, I have never seen snow!"

The following week, Balu had gone to the railway station to see off a friend who was leaving Bangalore for New Delhi. Later, when he tried to explain to Leela his desire for them to leave the country, he described his feelings as he watched the train steaming away, his nostrils filled with the smell of the dark smoke of departure, of distant places. He too wished he was heading out somewhere into the world, away from the life he had inherited from his ancestors. Filled with this new yearning, surprising even to himself, he had walked slowly towards the great stone arch that led out of the station. The arch had been built by Balu's grandfather and had the family name inscribed on a copper plate embedded in one of its pillars. There was no escaping the family, at least not in this town, he had thought as he passed underneath it, his eyes watering from the sudden brilliance of the sun after the dark of the station. He wondered whether he had the courage to pull up his roots—those deep and tangled roots that reached at least two hundred years into the soil here—and move to a new place.

"And then I heard this enormous roar," he told Leela, and she had shivered.

As if a giant hand had struck him from behind, Balu had fallen flat on his face on the ground. He had lain there stunned, wondering wildly whether this was God's response to his desire to get away from the town of his ancestry. He heard screams and feet stampeding around him. He scrambled up and started to run, stopping only when he was a good distance away from the station, at the outer edge of the taxi stand. When he turned to see the disaster that had occurred behind him, he discovered that the massive arch had collapsed and that two people who had been standing directly beneath it had died. A few seconds earlier, and one of them might have been Balu, killed by his grandfather's grand gesture.

"Maybe this is a sign that God is angry with us for something," Leela said when she heard Balu's story. "Maybe we need to hold a puja." Alarmed by the near-tragedy, she worried the gold and black marriage beads around her neck, sending up a silent prayer of thanks that Balu hadn't been injured in any way, that she hadn't become a widow. "Yes indeed, that is what we will do," she said, feeling her equanimity being restored, as always, by the prospect of working hand in hand with the gods to maintain the Bhat family happiness.

"Of course it is a sign," Balu said, more quickly than was his wont. "Your gods are telling us to leave this place. Go, *go,* they are saying, before the rest of this town buries you as well." He paused and then nodded, as if he had reached a decision. "Yes, it is very clear to me now. We shall go to Canada."

Leela stared at him as if he had lost his mind. "Canada? *Why?*"

"As you yourself pointed out, your gods are sending us a message. And that letter from Venkat—it is as if everyone is sending us a message—don't you see?" He waved his arm to encompass the sunny yard outside the window, the row of coconut palms leaning against the compound wall, the sparrows pecking and chirping in the red dust that turned into a bloody mush when it rained, all that was so familiar and beloved to Leela. "I have been here too long," he said. "Too long."

Leela lay awake for a long while that night. When a potted geranium had fallen on her father's head, he had come home with a white bride who in turn had given birth to a half-and-half child. Why, Leela wondered despondently, did her destiny appear to be linked to things that fell from the air?

Events moved rapidly in the following weeks. Balu travelled to Madras and came back with a file full of information, addresses, phone numbers. He took some money out of their savings account and sent off immigration applications. All their conversations seemed to be about Abroad. He wrote to Venkat. He asked his friend to send him job advertisements from Canada. For three days in a row he took Arjun and Preethi to see old Hollywood movies, as if the films held the key to that distant continent, as if Marilyn Monroe, Grace Kelly and Charlie Chaplin would prepare them for the journey he had planned for them. He bought them ice creams and chocolate bars, an extravagance that delighted the two children, although when they returned home it was to meet Leela's disapproving gaze.

The immigration papers arrived in due course. Balu left first to find a job and now, a year and a half later, Leela was preparing to follow with the children. He hadn't told her much about his job in Vancouver, other than that it was a teaching position at a community college. He had rented a house for them all—a small one, so Leela was not to bring too much. *How small was small?* Their landlord was a Sikh named Pa-ji. His wife, Bibi-ji, had offered to show Leela the ropes when she arrived. *Bibi-ji? What kind of silly name was that?*

As Leela packed the possessions she thought they would need, stuffing things into every crevice of the overloaded suitcases, she was overcome by a sense of betrayal. She had married Balu because of his apparent stability. She loved his ancestors—purebred Hindu Brahmins, untainted either racially or in their religion—whose photographs hung in solemn, garlanded rows on the wall, their glassy foreheads smeared with kumkum and ash, their saintly eyes looking down at the serene, uneventful span of their offsprings' lives. And she loved the living relatives, every single aunt, uncle, cousin and second cousin, all bearing the stamp of unambiguous stolid perfection.

When she met somebody at a wedding or a birth ceremony or at one of the procession of feasts, celebrations and festivals, Leela would introduce herself: "We belong to the Kunjoor Bhat family—you know, the well-known one?" She would end this statement with a satisfied nod of her neat, oiled head, a pursed smile and a quick tug of the end of her silk sari, which she wrapped around both shoulders because it made her feel matronly and responsible and Bhat-ish. There was not a doubt in her mind that the whole world was aware of the existence of this deeply respectable family. In return, the Bhat family repaid Leela's devotion by never referring to her mother, never remarking on the colour of her eyes, never asking her why she did not return home to visit her own family during festivals. As far as they were concerned she was married to Balu, she was one of the Bhats; and that was all that mattered.

On the day they were to leave, Leela wandered slowly around her house, touching every window and door in farewell. She stood for a long time in the airy room that

99

had been her father-in-law's study and was now Balu's. Her father-in-law had died a year after she had come to this house as a bride. She remembered him sitting here quietly day after day, reading books in English, Kannada, Sanskrit, working his way through his library. He was a quiet man, with so many ailments that no one knew which malady needed to be treated first. Every second day the town doctor arrived, checked his vitals, scolded him for not following the prescribed diets and left behind another set of small maroon or dark blue bottles of medicine. The old man rarely opened them.

One day, not long before his death, Leela had come into his study to bring him a tumbler of hot coffee. He was staring intently out the window, and when Leela entered he beckoned her to him, pointed a long, shaky finger out of the window and without turning around, asked, "Can you see him, ma?"

Leela shook her head, "See what, Appa?" she asked.

"There he is, coming to me, I can see him," the old man murmured.

"Who, Appa? I don't see anybody," Leela had said nervously.

"Why, it is my old friend Yama-Raja, girl. He has been waiting a long time for me, and I have been saying, wait, wait, let our doctor try another of his medicines on me, let me finish reading this book and this and this. But he is getting impatient now, he can't wait any longer. And I have finished reading all my books, so perhaps it is time." The old man was silent for a long moment. Then he turned to look at Leela with his faded eyes. "*Now* can you see him? There, that dark fellow riding a buffalo, swinging his lasso. See?"

This time, when Leela had looked out she thought—no, she was certain—that there, behind the mango trees, the neem trees and the coconut trees, ambled a large black buffalo with curving horns, and on his back rode a god with green skin and a curling moustache.

She glanced down at her father-in-law, catching such a look of peace on his face that she wanted to weep. And as if he had read her thoughts, the old man murmured, "What a blessing it is to die in your own bed, under your own roof, with your family surrounding you, full of the knowledge that you have lived as thoroughly as you wanted to."

Yes, the young Leela had thought, yes, she too would like to die in this home that had received her with such love, she too wanted to be heralded out of this world with the chop-chop-chop of mango wood from her own back-yard and the fragrance of a few drops of precious sandal-wood oil.

Finally departure day arrived. Her mother-in-law accompanied Leela, the children and their mound of luggage to the railway station, where they would catch the train to Delhi, spend a day with Vimala—one of Balu's innumerable cousins who were conveniently stationed all over India—and then fly to Vancouver. At the station, Preethi and Arjun leaned down and touched their grandmother's feet. Both children were hugged and wept over in turn. They boarded the train in sorrow, and as it began to pull away, Leela pushed her arm through the window bars and waved to the elderly woman who had become like a mother to her.

"I will go and come back," she shouted tearfully, "I will go and come back." A farewell and a promise repeated for generations.

"Is that true, Amma?" Arjun asked. "Will we really come back?"

And Leela replied firmly, "Yes, of course we will. We will."

"When?" Arjun wanted to know.

"In two years," Leela promised, confident that it would take only that long for Balu to give up on his dream of Canada, for they were after all, the Bhats of Bangalore.

Their brief stay in Delhi with Vimala and her husband passed sooner than anyone had wanted and once again it was time for goodbyes.

Leela looked at the battered black taxi that Balu's cousin had procured to take them to the airport. "Will we all fit in there?" she asked. It didn't seem strong enough to carry its own weight, let alone six people, six suitcases and an assortment of carry-on baggage.

"Don't worry, madam," the tall Sikh driver assured her. He managed to fit one more bag into the trunk, then jammed the lid down as far as it would go, tying it to the fender with a thick rope. "This car can carry ten people, no problem. Believe me, I have taken passengers all the way to Simla and back. What is the airport with a little luggage after that, tell me?" He smiled at her and piled the rest of the suitcases onto the luggage rack on top of the car, tying them down with more rope.

He turned out to be a friendly, chatty sort and gave them a running commentary on tourist spots along the way, though it was too dark to see anything properly. Leela sat between Preethi, who was pressed against the door, her small hands clutching a last-minute present of a book from Vimala, and a silent Arjun. Leela stared out the window wishing it was morning so that she could capture last glimpses of the country of her birth. She had blithely told her son that they would be back in two years, but now doubts were beginning to swarm in.

The driver's voice broke into her reverie. "Where is madam going?"

"To Canada," she replied.

"Ah! Canada!" exclaimed the cabbie. "Many people from our community are in that country. I am told the life there is a good one."

"I don't know. This is my first time." Now Leela wanted to cry.

"Which city you are going to? Trontoo?"

"No. Vancouver."

The driver was silent for a few moments and then turned around to look at Leela without diminishing his speed. "May I ask you a favour, madam?"

"Keep your eyes on the road, ji!" Vimala exclaimed.

"Small favour," the Sikh said. The car had not swerved off its straight path.

"What is it? Tell me and I will see," Leela said reluctantly.

"It is nothing much. My wife has an aunt, her dead mother's sister, somewhere in Canada. My wife does not remember much about her, she was very young during Partition. Only that her name was Sharan, and that she was married to a gentleman from Vancouver. If you meet someone by that name, please, will you give her our address and tell her to write?"

Leela laughed. "There are millions of people in that country. You think I will be able to find your wife's aunt? When I myself know nobody there?"

"Anything is possible in this world, memsahib," said the Sikh. "Without that hope, how can we live? I do this airport route occasionally, and every time I take some-body who is going to Canada or Britain—there are a lot of Sikhs there also, you know—I tell them about my wife's aunt. If Guru-ji wills it, we will find her one day! The world is not such a big place. It is a possibility, is it not?"

"Yes, baba, everything is possible," Leela agreed, think-ing of the coincidences that had propelled her own life forward to this point.

"So madam, will you take my address with you, just in case?" The driver swung into the airport and joined the long line of taxis inching forward into a general chaos of people, baggage and exhaust-belching vehicles.

"All right," Leela relented. "I will take it with me."

After the driver had loaded the bags into a cart that Vimala had managed to commandeer, Leela wrote down the man's wife's name and address on a piece of paper.

Nirmaljeet Kaur, daughter of Kanwar Kaur (sister of Sharan), Dauri Kalan village.

What was the harm, Leela thought as she scribbled, what was the harm in keeping someone's hope alive? For a moment the anxiety, the annoyance with Balu for having ripped them all away from their home soil, the fear and sadness, all of it lifted. Leela wasn't sure why this Sikh taxi driver's request should so lighten her own mood but it did, and when she waved goodbye to Balu's cousin and to India, it was without too much pain. She would be back soon, she thought, and then everything would be all right.

"I will go and come," she said, hugging Vimala.

"Don't forget to write to me as you promised," Vimala insisted, holding her tight.

"And you too. Every bit of news from here, you understand?"

She waved once more, and then she and the children were inside the warm airport.

In the airplane, Arjun covered himself with his blanket and went to sleep. Leela turned to Preethi, who had cornered the window seat and was poring over the book Vimala had given her.

"Amma," she said, leaning against her mother's shoulder, "what does node mean?"

"It means where two or three things cross," said Leela. She examined the book curiously. "What are you reading?"

"About Indra's Net," Preethi said. "Do you know this story, Amma?"

"No, I don't." Leela stroked the child's soft hair. "Why don't you read it to me, very softly, so we don't disturb anyone, hanh?"

"Indra the god of heaven flung a net over the world," read Preethi, with Leela helping her along when she stumbled over the more complex words. "Its shining strands criss-crossed the world from end to end. At each node of this net there hung a gem, so arranged that if you looked at one you saw all the others reflected in it. As each gem reflected every other one, so was every human affected by the miseries and joys of every other human, every other living thing on the planet. When one gem was touched, hundreds of others shimmered or danced in response, and a tear in the net made the whole world tremble."

Preethi stopped reading and looked out the window. Far below, from out of the pitch darkness, a long string of brilliant lights stretched like gems into infinity. The plane was crossing the India–Pakistan border, which was lit up in vigilance, echoing the line that had been drawn on maps in London and Delhi little more than two decades ago to mark the beginning and end of a pair of young nations at war with each other from birth.

"Amma, look, look!" she whispered excitedly. "It's Indra's Net!"

Leela leaned across her daughter to peer out the window. She gazed down at the brilliance scattered across the darkness, imagined the mountains, valleys and plains cut by that rope of light. Perhaps, she thought drowsily, reluctant to dampen her daughter's excitement by telling her the truth, perhaps it was indeed Indra's Net. And their movement, their migration from one world to another, had set it in motion, causing a series of tremors. How it would all end, she did not know.

SEVEN

INDRA'S NET

—

Vancouver

1967

"This," Balu said proudly, waving his arm out the car window as they drove away from the airport, as if he had created it himself, "*this* is Vancouver." He waited expectantly for his family's reaction to the sweet mid-afternoon air, the sun-drenched expanse of land leading, on one side of the road, to a low range of mountains still hazy with cloud cover, and on the other to grassy fields. "Well? Isn't it beautiful?"

"Actually, it smells just like Cubbon Park after the rains," Leela declared.

"But nice, hanh? It smells *nice*?"

"I don't know," Leela said. She would not allow herself to be beguiled. She was feeling the oddest mix of emotions, agitation and anger, for no particular reason. Disappointment, yes, that's what it was. She was *disappointed* that Vancouver was not something she could readily and immediately hate. And it did not smell like Cubbon Park at all. It was different—a wonderful, clean smell of tree resins and new rain. Leela had to admit it, she *liked* the smell.

They passed a wide green field and she said, "See, like our own paddy." She spotted a low arc of mountains beyond the field. "Just like our Western Ghats, only smaller," she remarked.

"Leela, those are the North Shore mountains," Balu said, getting a bit wound up now. "They look nothing like the Western Ghats." He braked ferociously several car lengths behind another vehicle.

"I don't know about North Shore and all." She sounded childish and obstinate, even to herself, but couldn't help it. "Those are the Ghats." And the river that glinted down there through the trees, that was the Cauvery.

Balu clutched the steering wheel, deflated and angry. A silence fell over the family, and the car moved along the roads in spurts and starts, for Balu was an uncertain, nervous driver. A cyclist narrowly missed climbing the pavement as a result of Balu's manoeuvres and stopped to give him a dirty look. A bald man wearing glasses leaned out of a red car that roared alongside theirs after almost rear-ending them, thanks to Balu's abrupt braking, and, sticking his middle finger up in the air, yelled, "Fucking Chinese drivers! Go back where you came from!"

"*What* did he say?" Leela asked, startled out of her silence.

"He called us fucking Chinese drivers," Preethi announced happily.

"What cheek! And you, Preethi, don't use that word again," Leela said, annoyed equally with Balu for inspiring such wrath among so many because of his driving and with the rudeness of the people shouting at them. "Do we *look* Chinese? He is blind, that lout!" She was particularly offended by the Chinese reference. "Because of them poor Jawaharlal had a heart attack!" she muttered.

"What?" Balu was bewildered. "*Who?*"

"Our first prime minister, Jawaharlal Nehru. Killed by the treachery of the Chinese."

"Leela, honestly, for a clever woman you say such rubbishy things sometimes. Nehru died of a heart attack, period!"

Leela fell silent again. It *wasn't* rubbish, she thought mulishly. She had admired Nehru just as much as she now admired his daughter, Indira Gandhi, the current prime minister of India. And the Chinese *had* broken his heart when they invaded India in 1962.

With a final slam of brakes, Balu brought the car to a halt outside a small house. It was white with a blue roof and reminded Leela of the cottages pictured in the English books she used to read to the children. It didn't look very different from the houses on either side: four windows downstairs and four upstairs, and a small lawn on either side of the walk leading up to the front door. It wasn't as *big* as their home in Bangalore had been. She climbed out and breathed in the clear air.

"Well?" Balu asked, coming up to stand beside her.

"Hoonh, it is not bad," she said, unwilling to give too much away. It still rankled that Balu had decided to drag her all the way here without even a proper discussion of the matter.

Balu opened the front door with a flourish and bowed low, pretending to sweep an imaginary hat off his head. "So glad it meets with your approval!" he said.

Leela smiled and shook her head. At least they had all reached this place in one piece. At least their luggage hadn't been misplaced or lost. She composed a letter to her mother-in-law and Vimala. *Vancouver is not a bad place. It looks a lot like our Bangalore with many large trees and clean roads. It is naturally not as big as Delhi and there are very few people. The house is very nice also.* She would never write anything but positive words in her letters. It wouldn't do to let people know that she was in any way dissatisfied.

Preethi ducked past her, ready to charge inside so that she could claim the nicest room, but Leela seized her arm and pulled her back. "Right foot first," she commanded. "Otherwise we will have bad luck."

"Even in Vancouver?" Preethi asked.

"Even here," Leela said. She carefully put her right foot forward and crossed the threshold into the house, her family close behind. "And don't stop in the doorway," she called over her shoulder. "Remember, it's an in-between space. Neither here nor there. It is dangerous."

Doorways between inside and out, sea foam that was neither wet nor dry, dusk, dawn, these were all zones of dis-ease, where wicked spirits lurked waiting to carry you away into sorrow, madness, ill health, death.

Her nose wrinkled slightly at the smell of cleaning fluid and floor polish. She would have to light some incense sticks as soon as possible; that way it would smell more like Home. She would hang up her pictures, she would set up her gods. She would cut this New World into the shape she wished it to be, pull at the edges that didn't match the pattern of her memories and rename it. She would redraw maps and mythologies like the settlers who came before her, those men and women from Europe who had taken a land already scored by earlier populations and marked it with their own symbols and meanings, owned it with their namings and words. Like them, she would make this corner of the world her own until it was time to return home.

Her grey eyes ranged around the drawing-cum-dining area, which, she realized, was stuffed with furniture. There were four bookshelves and two huge sofas—one the colour of mud with orange roses all over it, the other blue with white checks. Accompanying these large pieces were three coffee tables—one with a vase of fresh tulips—and a television on a stand.

"Bibi-ji, our landlady, sent these flowers to say welcome to all of you," Balu said. "From her own garden."

"And all this furniture?" The dining area was even more crowded—with a table that had a wad of newspaper stuffed under one of its legs, and five mismatched chairs, a towering glass-fronted showcase which was empty except for a few books on the bottom shelf, a pot stand with a ragged-looking fern and another small table that didn't seem to have any particular reason for being there.

"My friend Dr. Majumdar gave some of it, and the rest came with the house."

"Why can't we buy our own furniture?" Leela wanted to know.

"Do you know how expensive it will be to get new? And if someone is giving us something for free, why spend money?" Balu replied.

Leela was silent. What had happened to Balu? Where was his pride? Had they become a charity case? Did he not mind that people were giving him things because they thought he couldn't afford them himself, just like she used to give away their old clothes to the servants in Bangalore?

When the Bhats had finished unloading the car, Leela shut the dark blue door behind them. Preethi went down a flight of stairs and discovered the basement. She came running back up. "There is another house downstairs!" she exclaimed breathlessly.

Leela was pleased. This house wasn't so bad after all—it had a ground floor, a first floor *and* an underground floor. She composed more of the letter that she would write tomorrow to her mother-in-law and to Vimala. *We have a three-storey house which is a relief because it is good for each of the children to have a floor to themselves.*

She busied herself in the kitchen, setting up her gods in the space that Balu had arranged for them, allowing a pan of milk to boil over in a ritual meant to ensure that there would be no dearth of food in this household, and that luck, happiness and good health would overflow like the milk frothing over the stove. A few incense sticks and a small prayer to ask the gods to make true all that the boiling milk symbolized, and the formality of entering a new home was done. Leela climbed the stairs to the first floor to begin unpacking.

From the window in the landing she could see the road outside their new home, straight and long, running in both directions past houses that seemed to be about the same size as hers, except for a large white one at the end of the road. A fine drizzle had started and the grey sky poured over the city, dripped down the roof and veiled the tops of a tall fir tree in the front yard so that it loomed like a long-robed old wizard.

How far away were the shops she had noticed while driving home from the airport, she wondered? She climbed the remaining stairs and entered the bedroom claimed by the children. Preethi was stuffing her things haphazardly into a white dresser while Arjun was lying on the bed, staring up at the ceiling. Leela wandered over to the window that overlooked the backyard. In the time that it had taken her to get to this window, the rain had halted and the sun shimmered like a dream behind a haze of cloud. A twisted old tree bearing acid-green leaves grew in the far corner of the backyard, and on the lawn an exotic black bird with a white streak down its chest pulled a worm out of the earth. There was a profusion of flowers in one bed, a circle of rose bushes in the centre and a low hedge separating their property from the neighbours on either side. The yard to the right had a swing hanging from a large tree and a child's bicycle lying on its side. The lawn was worn in patches, showing bare earth. The yard to the left of hers, though, was as beautifully maintained as her own. From where she stood, Leela could see a wedge of her neighbour's lawn; purple and yellow flowers lined it like embroidery. A woman with white hair kneeled in the grass at the edge of the flower bed, digging into the rich black soil. Beyond her, in another yard, Leela spotted a line of clothes, swelling with wind for a few moments before flattening out breathless. The ordinariness of the scene, so like that in her own yard in Bangalore, reassured her.

Then Balu entered the room and said, "Okay Leela, I have to go. I will be back around six or seven o'clock."

"Go? Where are you going?" Leela was hurt. "Can't you take today off?"

"I can't miss my class. I am not permanent at the college yet. If I cut work they might not get a very good impression of me, no? But tomorrow—Saturday—I am not teaching, so we can go out together and see Vancouver if you want. Maybe have lunch at The Delhi Junction. You'll meet my friends there."

She followed him down the stairs and to the front door, watching as he backed out of the driveway, waved and drove off. Beside the door was a thick new telephone directory. She bent down to pick it up. Just as she was turning to go in, she caught sight of the white-haired woman from next door whom she had seen earlier tending her flowers in the backyard. The woman raised a hand in greeting and smiled. Leela returned the smile, vaguely surprised by the friendly gesture. She had heard that white people were very private and kept to themselves, that they did not make friends easily. She must have been misinformed. Or perhaps this woman was an exception. She wondered whether she should go over to the fence and introduce herself. But what would she say? *I am Leela Bhat, of the famous family of Kunjoor Bhats?* Would it mean anything here?

She went back into the house carrying the directory and set it down on the kitchen counter. It was so big—were there really so many people in this city? She had seen hardly anybody on their drive from the airport.

She opened the book at random pages. How strange it was to have a telephone directory that possessed not even one name she knew. How lonely it made her feel! She checked the Bs to see if Bhat was listed and was idiotically gratified to see their name. She held the phone book as if it were a gift. Then, setting it down again, she leafed through it to see if she could find another name she recognized. And there it was, even though she had not met him yet— Alok Majumdar—Balu's friend, the one who had given them the dining table that had to be kept steady with a wad of newspaper folded into a small square. She left the directory on the counter and opened another suitcase. It contained more clothes and a couple of photo albums, which she took to the living room. She placed them on one of the coffee tables wondering drily who had donated that particular piece of furniture to the Bhat charity.

She continued unpacking steadily for the next few hours, exhausted from her journey but too keyed up to sleep. She was busy emptying packets of spices into bottles when the doorbell rang. Leela paused, startled. Could Balu have returned already? What time was it? She went to the door and peered through the spyhole. A tall woman stood there with her finger on the doorbell. Beside her was a smaller, youngish man in a black suit carrying several bags in his hands.

Leela slipped the safety latch into position and opened the door a crack. "Yes?" she said suspiciously. "What do you want?"

"Hooh! Thank the Ooper-Wallah that you have arrived!" exclaimed the woman in a posh BBC accent bizarrely at odds with her flamboyant, heavily made-up, Hindi film star looks. "I knocked a few times on the back door, but no one answered. I was becoming worried, you know! Were you asleep? Can we come in?"

"But who are you?" Leela asked, ready to slam the door shut if necessary.

"Sorry, no introductions, what must you think of me . . ." The woman smiled at her. "I am Bibi-ji, your land-lady. And this is our Lalloo, almost like a son to Pa-ji and me. I brought him along to help with all these heavy bags."

"Oh?" Leela said, still suspicious. She wasn't sure she liked the look of the young man, who had the most bizarre sideburns—long and cut sharply at an angle just below his cheekbones, making him look vaguely like Dracula.

"Balu did not tell you? I said I would come over and say hello. Ah, these men are very forgetful creatures. No sense either. Now, are you going to let me in or what?"

"Yes, of course, come in." Leela stepped aside to let her visitors into the house.

Bibi-ji handed a bag to Leela.

"What is all this?" Leela asked. "You really shouldn't have . . ."

"I have brought thirty parathas." Bibi-ji ignored Leela's protests and waved her hands at the plastic-covered cornucopia that Lalloo had deposited on the kitchen counter. "That should last for two days at least. Balu told us that you have children. They eat all the time, so you will need the lot." She glanced around. "Where are they, anyway?"

"Upstairs, asleep, I think. We've crossed so many time zones . . ."

Bibi-ji nodded. "Yes of course, I'd forgotten how it feels. It's what, three o'clock in the morning India time now?" She settled with a deep sigh on the blue-and-white-checked sofa and passed a critical eye over the rest of the furniture. "You like the furniture? No? Yes? If you wish, we can bring other pieces."

Leela shook her head vehemently, but Bibi-ji was off before she could say anything.

"No, no, don't be formal, don't be shy," the older woman urged. "We have many kinds of sofas, neh Lalloo? Ask him, he knows everything about our house. Lalloo, putthar, tell our Leela how many sofas Pa-ji has put in the Taj Mahal?"

Taj Mahal? Was that the name of the restaurant this Bibi-ji owned? "Would you like some tea?" she asked politely.

"Lalloo can make it. You sit here and tell me how your journey was." Bibi-ji patted a spot beside herself on the sofa.

"No, Lalloo can sit with you," Leela said firmly, trying to regain control. "I will make the tea."

—

When Leela returned bearing a tray with teacups and biscuits, she found Bibi-ji and Lalloo browsing through one of the photo albums. Bibi-ji smiled at Leela. "Your family?" she asked, tapping the album.

"Yes, mostly Balu's relatives. They like taking photographs, his family."

"And these people? Who are they?" Bibi-ji pointed with her plump manicured finger at a black-and-white photograph of Hari Shastri and Rosa Schweers carrying an infant Leela.

Leela's heart clenched painfully. "My parents," she said. It was the only picture she had of herself with them.

"But this woman looks like a gori," Bibi-ji said, bringing the album close to her face and frowning at it. "Your mother is a white woman?"

Leela bit her lip and thought, why should it matter here in this country where I know nobody other than Balu, and now this strange pair in my living room, and nobody knows me? "Yes," she said. "Yes, she was. She died when I was very young."

"Oh, I am sorry to hear that," Bibi-ji said. She stared at the photograph for a bit longer. "I wondered about your eyes, now I see where you got them from." She closed the album and accepted a cup of tea from Leela. "You will fit in without a problem, then, eh Leela? With eyes that see just the way the goras do?"

Leela nodded briskly and tried to steer the talk away

from herself. "And you, Bibi-ji? What about your family? Are they here? Or in India?"

"My mother died soon after I came here, and my father went away when I was six or seven years old." Bibi-ji sipped her tea. "And your father? Is he alive?"

"No," Leela replied. She busied herself with the tea things, rattling the spoon in her cup with more vigour than necessary. She racked her brains for a way to change the topic of conversation.

"How did your mother die? She must have been young, na? Was she sick?" persisted Bibi-ji.

"You could say that," Leela nodded. "Biscuit?"

"They call it cookie here," Bibi-ji said. "You will find many things like that which they say differently. But you will learn. I did, and I was just from a small village." She laughed, displaying perfect white teeth, and not for the first time Leela thought that she was a remarkably handsome woman.

"Do you go home often, then?" Leela asked. "Do you have sisters or brothers or other relatives back there still?"

"My home is here now. Down the road, to be precise! I came before Partition. My village disappeared during that time. It was right on the new border, but God knows where its people are now." Bibi-ji fell into a brooding silence. "I had a sister, but she too . . . I have looked all these years for her and her family, but no luck."

"I am sorry," Leela murmured.

Bibi-ji picked up one of the framed photos Leela had piled haphazardly on the coffee table. "Are those your children?" she asked.

"Yes, that is Preethi, our daughter, and that is Arjun, our son. Do you have any children?"

"No," said Bibi-ji. She did not elaborate. "Lalloo will help you with school admissions and all that sort of thing. I will take you to the shops."

"No, no," Leela replied. "I don't want to bother you."

"No bother. If we desis do not help each other, who will?" She peered at the photographs of the children again. "So sweet, so young. How old is this little girl?"

"Preethi? She is six this year and Arjun is ten."

"My sister's daughter, Nimmo, was the same age as your little girl when I last saw her," Bibi-ji said. "That was the year before Partition. We used to call her Nirmaljeet."

The name seemed oddly familiar to Leela. She struggled to think why but couldn't remember, and a moment later Lalloo's voice distracted her.

"Bibi-ji, it is getting late," Lalloo reminded the older woman. "You have to take over from Pa-ji at the restaurant, remember?" He tapped his large golden watch. "He has a meeting with the temple committee members tonight."

Bibi-ji rose to her feet. "Ever since this new gurudwara was built there are only meetings-meetings-meetings," she remarked. She leaned forward and patted Leela's arm. "Now you listen to me. If you want anything at all, any help, you call me right away. Don't be shy now. Okay? This is my phone number at home, and if I am not there I will be in our restaurant. The Delhi Junction. Balu can bring you there tomorrow for lunch." She searched in her handbag for a pen and scribbled a number inside the telephone directory. "Oh, and by the way," she added as she started moving towards the door, "the rent cheque is due on the first of every month. You can drop it off at our house." Bibi-ji pointed in the direction of the big white house at the end of the road. "That is where I live—the Taj Mahal. That's what we have named it. Come any time you want, it is an open house every day at our place. Even if I am at work there will definitely be somebody there to make you a cup of tea."

Leela looked out at the white house, the "Taj Mahal," shimmering in the early evening light like a frosted cake, and nodded, not quite able to imagine a prolonged friendship with this big, noisy woman, and not sure she wanted it either.

EIGHT

INTRODUCTIONS

—

Vancouver

1967

That Saturday Balu kept his promise and took Leela and the children around the city before bringing them to The Delhi Junction Café for lunch. It was already full when they entered. An elderly white man, seated alone at a table in the middle of the café, was shaking a copy of the *Vancouver Sun* newspaper and making annoyed noises.

"That's Colonel Samuel Hunt," Balu murmured in Leela's ear. "A real character. You will see. Endless stories about native rebellions and British bravery."

"Ridiculous! Intolerable!" the old man spluttered.

From his station behind the cash counter, a large Sikh with a turquoise turban and a grey beard called out,

"What is the matter, Colonel-ji? What is bothering you today?"

"That's Pa-ji, our landlord," Balu informed Leela, leading her and the children to a table beside the cash desk. "And this is my good friend Dr. Alok Majumdar."

A tall, lean man scraped his chair back and rose to his feet. His clothes, Leela noticed, were very elegant. She remembered that Balu had told her that he had never seen Majumdar wear anything other than a suit, a tie and highly polished shoes, and that he couldn't even imagine him in bed wearing anything else.

"And you must be Leela," Majumdar greeted her, smiling and offering his hand.

Leela took it diffidently, unused to touching a strange man's hand.

He patted the children on their heads. "And you are Arjun, and this little one must be Preethi, right? Come, come sit down and join the fun."

"What is our Colonel getting so worked up about?" Balu asked.

"This piece in today's paper," Majumdar said, holding out his copy of the newspaper and pointing to an article. "It's about a young man from East Pakistan." The man, Majumdar said, filling them in quickly, was the second son of a farmer who had tilled his small square of land until there was no life left in it. Finally, unable to bear the annual catastrophes that struck—cyclones, floods, droughts and disease—he had smuggled himself to London, where he had tucked himself into the wheel well of an airplane scheduled to fly to Toronto. While the passengers munched peanuts, while they dozed, drank, played cards and read books, the second son clung to the leg of the giant metal bird, starved of oxygen and frozen to the marrow. He managed to hold on through the long flight across the Atlantic, but as the plane circled the sky above Toronto preparing for landing, his frozen arms released their grip and his long-dead body fell through the frigid night air to hit the tarmac.

"The poor bastard was hungry, so he took a plane across the world to look for food," Majumdar said, raising his voice and looking across at Sam Hunt. "What's wrong with that, Colonel?"

Samuel Hunt, who met every stereotype of the old British India army officer—bottle-brush moustache, staccato speech, stiff-backed gait—glowered back at Majumdar. "Bloody cheek, that's what!" he said. "All these people coming in. Too many of them. Messing up the place. Don't know why we let them in!"

"Yes, of course, Colonel Sahib," soothed Pa-ji, used by now to the contradictions in the old army man's nature—his love of Indian food and his nostalgia for India coexisting with his dislike for Indians. "But we all need a place in this world, don't we? You and me and the cook in the kitchen who makes your curry."

"Without permission! Illegal immigrants, breaking the laws of this land!" huffed Sam Hunt, ignoring Pa-ji's comment.

"Well, Colonel, this *is* a country of immigrants, no?" Pa-ji said. "We are all from elsewhere."

Samuel Hunt gave Pa-ji his most offended look and said, "Yes, but I am *legal*. These are riff-raff thugs who come with no passports, no visas, no papers. And my wife's people came on the first boat that arrived on these shores."

"Ah, so one might say that she is one of those boat people, Colonel? Wouldn't you agree?" Majumdar suggested mischievously.

The old soldier bristled at the implication of the Bengali's words. He didn't approve of Majumdar. The man was too clever by half, had something devilish about him, come to think of it. "No, I *wouldn't* agree!" he snapped, and rustled his paper.

At the till, Pa-ji suppressed a smile.

"Taking away our jobs, taking away our land, taking away the view." Samuel Hunt stabbed at a piece of mutton with his fork.

Majumdar did not rise to the bait. "I must leave now; I've piles of class assignments to correct," he replied.

"What do you teach, Dr. Majumdar?" Leela asked politely.

"Women's studies," Majumdar said. "And do call me Alok—this doctor business sounds too formal."

"I told you, remember?" Balu said. "We teach at the same college. In fact it was Majumdar here who informed me about the vacancy in chemistry."

"I must have forgotten." Leela smiled apologetically at Majumdar. "Balu has told me so many things recently that it is difficult to remember everything, you know."

Majumdar waved his hand. "No problem, it is only natural."

"But I was wondering," Leela continued. "What exactly *is* Women's studies? I mean, *what* do you teach your students?"

"I tell them about the condition of women in Third World countries and all that. They love hearing about dowry deaths and sati and child brides and such things," Majumdar said.

"Sati? Child marriages? Wasn't all that abolished a century ago? These things do not still exist in India, do they? Is this a history course?"

"Everything still exists and coexists in India, don't you think?" Majumdar replied. "And no, I don't teach history, although I used to be a history teacher back home. But when I came here, it turned out that nobody was interested in the history of India. So what to do? I decided to remake myself, create a new-model Majumdar. My dissertation in India was on the role of women in India's independence movement, Sarojini Naidu, Madame Cama, you know . . . I took a few courses here because they said the usual things about my degrees not being as good as the ones they have here, and voila, I am now a teacher of women's studies. The thing is to give them what they want. They need to feel a righteous indignation about heathens. It's their upbringing, you know, Christian, save-the-world, missionary, that sort of thing. I am simply using it to make a living."

Leela wasn't sure whether he was joking.

Majumdar laughed at her expression. "You see, Leela, if I may call you that, here you are on your own—no ma-baba to bail you out or uncle-aunty-friend to pull strings and find you a job. You have to do whatever is necessary. And I am not hurting anyone, am I?"

"Well, your students must have a very odd notion of India and its women," Leela said.

Majumdar shrugged. "Do the women in India care about the opinions of others thousands of miles away? Most of them are more concerned about making sure they have food for their children." He paused and grinned mischievously. "Now, if my students met Mrs. Majumdar, they would all know I am a liar through and through. *There* is an Indian woman for you! She would make most men commit hara-kiri, I can tell you that."

Balu decided to take his family for a drive around the city before heading home. As he drove he told Leela the details of his friendship with Dr. Majumdar, whom he had first met right there in the restaurant. A few months after his arrival, Balu had been wandering around the area, unemployed and beginning to feel that he might never find a job, might never bring his family over, might even have to go back home to India, when he had smelled the delicious and familiar smells of cumin and coriander and cardamom. As if in a trance, he had followed the tantalizing aromas and found himself standing in front of an Indian restaurant. He had gone inside to find Pa-ji perched behind the counter, Bibi-ji ordering two young waiters around, and a dozen Indian men—it was almost always men on weekdays, he discovered—seated at various tables. Majumdar was at his usual seat by the window, and when Balu entered he had given him a curious look, smiled and waved him over to his own table. The friendship had deepened as the year wore on, and when the job became available he had helped Balu to rework his résumé.

"Don't you have any extracurricular interests?" he had asked in irritation when he saw the half-page CV that Balu had typed up. "You need to show them that you are an all-rounder, a well-developed fellow."

"Well," said Balu doubtfully, "I read when I have time."

"So does half the world, Balu. Do you sing, dance, play cricket?"

"I like listening to music. Classical Carnatic, some Hindustani, old Hindi films. I received a prize in high school for the best essay on Gandhi. Nehru gave me my trophy and shook my hand. I have a photo."

"Keep going, all this can be used." Majumdar had taken out his pen, carefully uncapped it and written on a piece of paper: *Interests: Classical music, reading, prose writing. (See list of prizes won.)*

Other qualities: Enthusiastic, quick learner, communicates effectively in written and spoken English. ("They think we Indians don't know any English," Majumdar said with fine scorn. "What did they think we were doing when we were in bed with the likes of Sam Hunt for three hundred years? Playing gilli-danda?")

"Anything else you would like to add?" By now the résumé had expanded satisfyingly to three sheets of paper.

"A photograph, perhaps?" Balu had asked sarcastically.

Majumdar had grinned and capped his pen with satisfaction. "I wouldn't do that if I were you, Balu. You aren't exactly Gregory Peck."

To his surprise, Balu got the job. It was only part-time and his contract had to be renewed every year, but it was a beginning.

"If not for Alok," Balu finished, "I might still be looking for a job, and there is no telling when you would have been able to join me here."

Leela watched the houses stream past, some with the window blinds up or curtains drawn so that she sometimes caught a quick glimpse of the inside of a room. They seemed opaque, these strangers' homes, and she wondered if they would ever fall open and reveal to her the lives, the thoughts, the feelings that occurred inside them. Would she ever understand the people who inhabited them? What made them belong, and what made her a foreigner? How long would she remain foreign? Would she eventually become a woman of meaning here, a person who was a somebody, or would she remain without context, tied to a past that meant nothing to anyone except herself? A past, that would, if they lived here long enough, become irrelevant to her children?

Balu broke into her thoughts. "I wanted to take the scenic route home, but now I think I might be lost. Can you get the map out of the glove compartment and check, Leela?"

Leela removed the map and, unfolding it, turning it this way and that, realized with some embarrassment that she had never before consulted a map to find her way around. She had never needed to. In Bangalore, Balu, who had every street and gully of the city etched into his mind, had been her guide. And before that, in Balepur—her father's town—if you wanted directions you asked the nearest person, and if it wasn't Dodda the madman you would be told, *That way, two furlongs past the neem tree that belongs to Sheshadri Rao,* or, *Left, past the police station, and then right after the dog sleeping in the shade of the dispensary. The black dog, not the white and brown one, mind.*

But this new world they had moved to was different. Here you *needed* maps to find your way. Her eyes wandered over the lines criss-crossing the map, absorbing the details of the colours and the shadings and the words, until the hidden patterns of the city's roads became apparent. She found the road she was looking for and proudly pinned it with a finger before slowly tracing their way back home.

"Take the next left," she told Balu. And then the next right, and a left again. Leela felt absurdly pleased with herself. Soon she might not need any maps at all. Soon Vancouver might become a place as familiar as Bangalore or Balepur.

NINE

COINCIDENCES

—

Vancouver

1967

A week later, Leela walked down the street to the Taj Mahal to return Bibi-ji's food containers. She had filled them with samples of her own cooking: it was rude to return empty boxes, and an admission of poverty. Even though Balu's salary was barely enough, she had discovered, to cover their weekly basic requirements, not to mention the rent on the first of the month, and their savings converted from rupees to dollars amounted to a frighteningly small sum, which was dwindling at an alarming pace, there was no way Leela would either display a lack of manners or admit to a lack of money.

She walked through the open gates of the Taj Mahal, noting the faux-marble lions adorning the gateposts on either side. She thought them a bit over the top. Continuing down the driveway, lined with its twin rows of young pine trees, she cut through a sunny garden full of rose bushes. Between them were tulips and a variety of other flowers that Leela could not identify. Beyond all this was the Taj Mahal.

A Sikh youth opened the carved front door when she rang the bell, and led Leela through a long corridor crowded with a variety of odd objects: an elephant-shaped umbrella stand, two enormous Chinese vases with pink-and-green-and-gold decorations creeping all over them, a photograph of Queen Victoria and several more of people Leela assumed were the Singhs' relatives. She followed the young man through a spacious room where more men sat on opulent couches and armchairs around a television set. She realized that they were giving a soap opera their rapt attention. In one chair lounged Lalloo, the man who had accompanied Bibi-ji to Leela's home a couple of weeks ago. He was wearing a dazzling yellow shirt with black stripes, and a pair of black trousers. He looked, to Leela's eyes, like an exotic insect. He was leaning forward and, she later discovered, providing a running commentary on the soap. When she got to know Bibi-ji better, Leela discovered that it had been Lalloo's idea to plant the young men in front of the television—he believed there was no better way to learn English than by watching the soaps. It was how he had acquired the language himself, spending long hours in Bibi-ji's living room, his eyes fixed on the screen. And nothing, according to him, provided more information about western society than the daytime soaps.

Lalloo waved cordially at her and called, "Halloo, Mrs. Bhat, how you are?"

"I'm fine, thank you," she shouted back, over the din of the television.

They passed through the dining room, which had more of the large, heavily carved furniture the Singhs seemed to favour, and entered the kitchen. The room was crowded with women of all ages, some squatting on the floor rolling out rotis or chopping vegetables, others standing at the stove and stirring vats of food. A cacophony of voices, speaking what Leela assumed was Punjabi, filled the air.

"Leela, come, come, sit down," Bibi-ji said, beaming at her. She sat at a small table surrounded by bills and receipts that she was entering into a ledger.

She pulled out a chair and patted it. "Tea? Coffee? I know you South Indians like coffee. Whenever your Balu comes to The Delhi Junction, he wants coffee and then he complains about it. Says that it is nothing compared to your Mysore coffee, henh?"

"No, it is okay," Leela said. "I just came to return your boxes. And to give you a sample of my cooking."

"Nobody who comes to this house is allowed to leave without at least a cup of tea," declared Bibi-ji. She opened the boxes that Leela had filled with food and smelled them. "Oh! This smells wonderful! I have never tasted South Indian food!"

As if it is from some other country, Leela thought. She had tasted Punjabi food often enough; even the restaurants in her childhood town of Balepur served the mandatory chholey-bhaturey, naan and saag-paneer. But she smiled and said politely, "Hope you like it. But you have so many visitors. I don't want to interrupt . . ."

"No, no, these are not visitors," Bibi-ji exclaimed, catching Leela's arm and pulling her down on the chair beside her. "These are . . ." She paused and crinkled her forehead. "They are not relatives or visitors. Just people who have newly arrived, staying until they find work and a place to live and all that." She leaned forward and whispered sotto voce, "I don't even know some of their names."

Leela looked around in amazement. The Singhs were hosting all these people, at their own expense? They must be rich.

"They made those parathas I brought for you the other day," Bibi-ji said. "Nobody stays here for free. Life is all about give and take, eh, Leela?"

Leela gave Bibi-ji an appraising look and nodded. She was beginning to appreciate this woman with the loud voice and louder clothes.

One of the women brought them cups of tea, thick with milk and sugar. Bibi-ji pushed a tin full of orange jalebis towards Leela. "Take, take, it is very good," she said. "Homemade, fresh and crisp."

Leela picked up one of the sugary concoctions and bit into it, letting loose a thread of sugar that dribbled down her chin. She laughed. Who would have thought she would end up in Canada and find herself in a home called the Taj Mahal, full of Sikhs chattering in Punjabi, sipping milky chai and eating hot jalebis?

"Something is funny?" Bibi-ji asked. In the time it had taken Leela to eat one of the sticky sweets, the older woman had consumed three.

"No, I was just thinking, I might be in a house in Punjab," Leela said, waving her hand around.

"But this *is* Punjab," Bibi-ji pointed out. "Inside my home it will always be Punjab."

Naturally, Bibi-ji had to return to Leela's with another instalment of boxes to show off her culinary range, for how could she allow a small, sparrow-shaped Southie to outdo her in the kitchen? Which meant that Leela had to make another trip to the Taj Mahal. And so they went, back and forth, until the urge to show off their cooking became a simple desire to meet over a cup of chai and chat about this and that and the children and the weather and the strange ways of the pink-skinned goras, whom Bibi-ji had come to understand and often appreciate after twenty-one years of puzzling over them, but who needed to be explained to Leela the new immigrant. They discussed recipes endlessly, each woman reclaiming the place left behind—Home—in the food that she cooked. And so, if one day Bibi-ji chopped onion-ginger-garlic to create a sauce for her famous chholey, leaning over the pot, stirring-stirring-stirring, adding a pinch of this or that and inhaling the aromas until she knew it was just exactly right, the next day saw Leela standing on tiptoe, using a long-handled ladle to draw forward the sealed packet of asafetida from the back of the kitchen cupboard, carried all the way from There to add to the pot of Venki's famous eggplant sambhar. As for the authentic ingredients to create the authentic taste? Well, Bibi-ji knew where everything could be found.

"For dal and rice and cumin and coriander go to JB Foods," she said. "Even your Southie things you will get there. The Korean store for fruit and the Chinese store is where you go for the vegetables."

Chinese? Leela shook her head. No, never.

Bibi-ji was puzzled by her friend's vehement refusal to go to Mrs. Wu's shop, where the whole world—even the goras, who usually shopped in the big chain stores that carried perfectly shaped but soulless vegetables—came for their greens.

"Why?" she wanted to know. Large-hearted Bibi-ji knew little about the irrational angers, carried for years, that created hard calluses in the heart. She did not have Leela's grudge-bearing nature, the kind that did not forgive unloving grandmothers, cousins who humiliated her or the Chinese who had invaded India.

"So now do you see why I cannot go to this Mrs. Wu's shop?" Leela demanded, having also catalogued China's responsibility for Nehru's death. "*Now* do you see, Bibi-ji?"

"Now I see nothing!" snorted Bibi-ji. "Other than that you are a silly-billy, Leela! Was this Nehru your own daddy-ji or what?" Bibi-ji jangled her bracelets, purple and pink to match her dress, at Leela. "Now that you are here, all that old stuff does not matter. What matters is that you want the best beans and cauliflowers at the lowest prices. For that you must go to Mrs. Wu!"

Forgetfulness was good, said Bibi-ji. A bad memory was *necessary* for a person wishing to settle in, to become one

of the crowd, to become an *in*visible minority. This was
the first lesson she imparted to her new friend, although
invisibility was not a lesson that she herself had been able
to practise. "The Chinese, the Japanese, the Italians, that
barber Majid, you and me," Bibi-ji said. "In this country
we are all in the same boat."

"What boat?" Leela asked.

"The Minority Boat," Bibi-ji said darkly. "A leaky
thing—could go down any minute if you don't watch
out." She patted Leela's arm. "Make sure it does not
drown you."

Leela looked at Bibi-ji with some surprise. Somehow
she had never seen this woman as having a history of her
own. She seemed so rooted, so much a part of this world.
How silly I am to have imagined such a thing of anyone,
Leela thought. She wondered about the distances Bibi-ji
had travelled before arriving here at this steadiness. As
for her own layers, how long would it take for this new
life to become a skin over the open wound of departure,
or the older wound of being half-and-half? All week she
brooded over Bibi-ji's remark about minorities. She had
grown to perceive herself as one of the Well-Known Bhats
from Bangalore. It was a nose-cut, a comedown, a hum-
bling thing to realize, that now she was a Minority
lumped together with an assortment of other Minorities.
All in-between people.

Then on the last Saturday of the month, when Leela
went to Bibi-ji's house with the rent cheque, she discovered something else new about her friend, who was
seated, as usual, at the kitchen table, surrounded by the

clatter of voices and utensils. Leela's eyes fell on the stack of envelopes filled with bills and other letters. A number of them were addressed to Khushwant Singh and several others to Sharanjeet Kaur.

"Is this you?" she asked Bibi-ji, picking up an envelope. "Sharanjeet Kaur?"

"Who else?" Bibi-ji said.

"I didn't know," Leela said. "You never told me."

Bibi-ji shrugged. "Everybody calls me Bibi-ji now. To my family I was Sharanjeet. Or Sharan. That's what my older sister, Kanwar, called me."

Leela frowned at the envelope in her hand. "Your name sounds so familiar . . ."

"It is a common name. Half the women in Punjab must have it!"

But Leela wasn't listening. She was scrabbling around in the bottom of her handbag, turning it upside down, emptying its contents on the table before her. "It is *here,* I know it is," she muttered. "I haven't emptied this purse since . . ." She located a scrap of paper and held it up. "Here it is. I knew I had it."

Bibi-ji leaned forward. "What is it?"

"An address. It might mean something to you, it might not, I don't know. I had forgotten all about it. And I am known for my memory, believe it or not! A taxi driver in Delhi gave it to me when I was leaving. Here." Leela unfolded the paper and passed it to Bibi-ji. "This is his wife's name—Nirmaljeet Kaur. She was a child when India and Pakistan were formed. You said you had lost a sister and her family, Bibi-ji. This woman's mother was Kanwar, same as your sister. And her aunt was Sharan. I didn't think of it before. Your name . . . I didn't realize . . ."

Bibi-ji stared at the grubby scrap of paper. "Is such a coincidence possible?" she whispered.

"Yes it is," Leela said firmly. She was an ardent believer in Fate. Look at how an extended foot had brought Balu into her life and how a fallen arch had propelled them across the world to Vancouver. "It surely cannot hurt to write. And who knows, she might be your niece after all." She tapped her fingernail on the paper. "I have a good feeling in my bones about this, Bibi-ji. Believe me."

PART THREE

—

NIMMO

TEN

A BIN OF GRAIN

—

New Delhi

June 1967

Four o'clock in the morning, and already the busy alley was wide awake and humming with life. From the kitchen of her two-room home in the centre of the alley, Nimmo could hear the milkman arguing with Asha, the tailor's wife next door. Nothing unusual about that, she thought, smiling to herself as she moved around softly, boiling some milk in a pan. Asha needed to disagree with the whole world about this, that or the other. She carried on a running battle with each of her neighbours. Last month it was a dispute with Nimmo over the branches of a neem tree that had roots in her compound while most of its branches leaned into Nimmo's.

"What can I do if the tree insists on growing this way, Asha?" Nimmo had asked, half amused by the woman's indignation. "And anyway, I don't take the leaves, so why make such a fuss?"

"*You* don't, but those boys of yours are always pulling down branches, climbing up the tree, making a mess. I am telling you for the last time, sister, this is *my* tree!"

So what if two small boys pulled a few leaves and branches down? It wasn't as if they were killing that wretched tree, Nimmo thought. "In that case, *sister,*" she said, "since it bothers you so much, I'm going to cut down every branch of the tree that is on my side of the wall. Then there will be nothing to fight about."

"That will kill it!" Asha protested. "You can't kill my tree."

"But it is interfering with the air on my side of the wall," replied Nimmo. She had no intention of acting out her threat, but Asha could do with a scare.

After that exchange, Asha had simmered down and started a war with her neighbour on the other side. All of them lived too close to each other, Nimmo thought.

A new sound joined Asha's high-pitched diatribe as Nimmo's other neighbour, Kaushalya, emerged to feed her hens and collect their eggs. The clucking and squabbling of the hens reminded Nimmo that she was out of eggs and would have to buy some later in the day.

A child howled somewhere; vehicles screamed, rattled, honked their way down the narrow gully. Above all this noise a bird sang deliriously, as if determined to drown it out. Perhaps it was the fabled nightbird, so sweet and unearthly was its singing. Nimmo had a vague memory of her mother telling her stories about this bird, whose song was a portent of ill luck. Or was it death? She shook her head to remove the darkness and started to prepare the day's meals.

Her ears caught the sound of her husband's car drawing up on the road outside, the soft thump of the door and the slap of slippers coming towards the house. She opened the door before Satpal could knock. Nimmo didn't want to wake their boys, asleep in the inner room, for another hour at least. She wanted a small wedge of time alone with Satpal before he dropped into bed. When he woke at eight, he would leave again for his day job at the mechanic's shop that he owned with his partner, Mohan Lal. By the time Satpal came home in the evening, Nimmo would be busy with dinner and the children, and then it would be time for his taxi shift again. If not for the single hour they had alone together at this time every day, they might be strangers living in the same house.

"Did you have a good evening?" she asked after he had washed his face and joined her in the kitchen.

"The usual." His voice was tired. As he settled down on the floor, she put a glass of hot milk in front of him. "I don't know whether it is worth going on with this taxi business. There is too much competition, and petrol costs are going higher and higher. Maybe I should sell the car and put all the money in our shop. But then we might have to take out another loan on this house to get by. What do you think?"

Nimmo was silent. She did not like rushing into things. Neither was she particularly happy about mortgaging their house for a second time in three years. What if they were unable to meet their debts? "I don't know," she said finally. "Why can't Mohan Lal find some money to put in this time? He is your partner in the shop, after all."

"He doesn't own his house, Nimmo. You know that," Satpal replied. "So a mortgage is out of the question for him. He has taken two loans from his father-in-law, and they are not exactly rich people themselves. Selling my taxi to repay the loan I took to buy it and remortgaging our house are the only options."

"Maybe you should talk to a few people? Elders at the temple, perhaps?" Nimmo suggested.

Satpal did not say anything, focusing instead on dipping a slice of bread into the tumbler of warm, sweet milk. He slowly ate the soft slice of bread. "We need the money urgently." He looked up at her, and Nimmo saw the lines of worry creasing his forehead.

"How urgently?" she asked, fear knocking at her ribs.

Satpal shrugged, then saw her worry and smiled at her. "We can think about that later. I am too tired now. You tell me, how was your day? Were the boys good? That little one is turning out to be a real devil, isn't he?" There was a tinge of pride in Satpal's voice. "Now that he is in school you will have some time for yourself. Maybe you can do some tailoring work and bring in extra money, hanh?"

"It might not be possible for another three to four years," Nimmo said. She paused. Her news was good, but she knew it would cause anxiety too. "You are going to be a father again."

Satpal stopped fishing bits of soggy bread out of the

milk and looked at her. "Again? Another one? In how many months?"

"Seven, I think. I will go to the doctor today."

"Another one," repeated Satpal.

"How will we manage?" Nimmo asked.

Satpal touched her face gently. "Don't worry, I will think of a way," he said.

But it seemed to Nimmo that the worry lines on his forehead had deepened. Was this the moment to tell him her other news?

"Something else, ji," she said. "There was a letter . . ."

"From whom?" Satpal was surprised. They rarely received letters, not even from his older sisters in Chandigarh and Amritsar. "From my sisters? Not bad news, I hope. Are they well?"

"No, it isn't from them. It's from a woman in Canada who says she might be my aunt."

She rose to her feet and, reaching up to a shelf high on the wall, removed a thick envelope from behind a picture of Guru Nanak. She kept her important papers behind this brightly coloured lithograph of the founder of Sikhism in the belief that no one who looked into his eyes would steal the papers.

Satpal weighed the envelope speculatively in his hands. "When did this arrive?"

"A week ago," Nimmo admitted. "I wanted to think about it before I showed it to you."

"How . . ." Satpal began, and then broke into a delighted grin. "Was it me? Was it one of those people I took to the airport?"

Nimmo, pleased to see the boyish delight on his care-worn face, smiled and nodded.

"Who? The sardar who was going to Toronto? I knew it. I felt it when I gave it to him!" Satpal slapped his thigh and laughed again.

"No, it was not a sardar," Nimmo said. "It was a woman going to Vancouver. She gave this Bibi-ji our address," Nimmo said. "But I am not sure whether I should reply. Suppose she is not my aunt?"

"And suppose she is? Does she mention your parents?"

"Yes, she does. She writes pages describing my mother. But I don't remember anything about her—or about my family, for that matter," Nimmo pointed out.

"What about that postcard you showed me? That is proof, is it not? It has the name of your parents, doesn't it?" Satpal's voice rose with excitement.

Nimmo was silent. She had never told him that the post-card might not be hers, that she might have picked it up on her journey to India during Partition, twenty years ago. When she had showed it to him a few weeks after their marriage, after he had asked if she remembered anything of her family, she had produced the postcard, hoping that he would not ask any more questions. She hated any attempt to dig up the past. Unfortunately he had taken it upon himself to try to find her family, believing—or hoping—it would lift the sorrow that hung over her like a veil.

"Well? Those are your parents' names on that postcard, yes?" Satpal asked, lifting her face by the chin and peering into her secretive eyes.

"Yes," sighed Nimmo. "Yes they are."

148

"Then why don't you write to this Bibi-ji? What is the harm? Even if nothing comes of it, so what? You have me now, you don't need aunts!" With a rough palm he stroked her cheek, lingering on her warm throat. "Now, come to bed," he urged softly.

She caught his hand and held it hard against her body for a moment, tempted to follow him to where she had spread their mats. Then a whimper emerged from the inner room and she moved away reluctantly. "Not now. The boys will be waking up soon," she said.

As if on cue, the younger child, Pappu, drifted out sleepily, rubbing his eyes. He headed for his father's lap, and Satpal sighed. "Okay, not now. Wake me up at seven."

A wave of morning sickness caught Nimmo by surprise and she rushed into the small bathroom, pulling the door shut behind her.

She stood at the sink catching her breath and trying to ignore the scuffle of feet and whispers outside the door. The older boy, Jasbeer, was awake as well. She heard the rumble of Satpal's voice. "Your mother will be out in a moment, putthar. Leave her be."

A moment later Nimmo heard Jasbeer's heavy nasal breathing at the door of the bathroom. She smiled. "Mummy, I *need* to go!" the seven-year-old moaned.

And now Pappu's voice, slightly distorted by the wood. "I need to go too, Mummy."

Nimmo imagined the two small warm bodies on the other side of the door. The older boy standing straight, his legs apart, head flung back in a childish imitation of his father; the younger one, still a baby at five years of age, pressing his mouth against the door. She was responsible for these two young lives, she thought, savouring a last small moment of quiet inside the bathroom before emerging to receive her world. And now she was going to add another creature to her list of responsibilities. Would she be able to bear the weight of their needs? Would she be able to ensure that nothing bad ever happened to them?

A banging of small fists. "Mummy, hurry, hurry, hurry! I need to go!"

"No, me first, I woke up first, Mummeee!" came Pappu's childish treble.

Nimmo rinsed the sourness out of her mouth and came out. "Okay, okay, one at a time now. Let Pappu go first, putthar." She gently restrained her older boy from shoving his way in. "And you hurry up, okay?" she admonished the little one.

Jasbeer moved away sulkily. "He did that on purpose, just because I wanted to go. I hate him."

Nimmo caught him and pulled him to her. "Don't say things like that about your brother." She stroked his hair away from his forehead, gathering the long strands into her hand, marvelling at their softness. The caressing motion removed the sting from her rebuke. "He is a baby." She kissed his cheek and worried about the darkness she sensed in his thin body. Had she passed it on to him with the milk she had fed him when he was an infant?

But Jasbeer slipped out of her arms, his eyes full of resentment. "You are always on his side."

—

By nine o'clock Nimmo was alone. The children had left for school with Pappu clasping Jasbeer's hand tightly, and Satpal had gone to his shop. Nimmo hoped that Jasbeer would remember her stern instructions not to let go of his brother, to stay on the pavement and avoid talking to strangers. She thought about Bibi-ji's letter, resisting the temptation to reread it before she had finished the housework. She moved about quietly, washing the dishes, putting them away, soaking the dirty clothes, sweeping and swabbing the floors. She was rigorous about cleanliness and scrubbed the small house every day, her strong body revelling in the work. The noise in the neighbourhood had also subsided, except for the dull roar of traffic from the nearby highway. Nimmo worked steadily, loving the silence that would be hers until the children returned from school. By eleven o'clock she was done. The house was so neat it looked as if she were the only person living in it. The clothes flapped on the clothesline in the tiny front yard, and the afternoon meal was ready for her sons.

Nimmo wondered whether she should go down to the fruit vendor's stall a block away and pick up some bananas. She decided not to; instead, she unfolded the letter that had arrived from Canada, and began to read it for what seemed like the hundredth time.

You will no doubt be surprised to hear from a stranger living across the seas. My name is Sharanjeet Kaur but these days

*they call me Bibi-ji . . . I got your address from a woman
who was taken to the airport by your husband, Satpal
Singh, and I am writing in the hope that you are related to
my sister, Kanwar Kaur, who was married to Pardeep Singh
of Dauri Kalan village . . .*

Nimmo pressed the letter against her breast and leaned
forward to gaze in the mirror at her long, smooth-skinned
face, secretive eyes and lips that she kept pressed together
as if afraid of what she might let loose. She took a deep,
calming breath, trying to quell those dark memories for
which she could never prepare herself, urged as they were
into life by the most unexpected things. Once it was a
sudden breeze bearing the fragrance of champa flowers in
bloom—that had happened near the flower sellers' stalls in
the market one day. Another time it was a woman calling
for her son. They were like wicked spirits, these memories,
changing, uncertain, leaving her reaching out hungrily.
Which one was true? *A child runs through the rustling shadow
of tall sugar cane, its syrupy smell mingling with the pungent
odour of smoke from burning roof thatch.*

Was that it? Perhaps not. Here was another one. *A five-
year-old sulks near the well, angry because her father would not
take her with him and her brothers to the fields that morning. She
leans over the edge of the well and throws a stone in, waiting to
hear the distant splash. From the echoing darkness a voice comes
wafting upwards: run, run, run.*

Not that one either. Set it aside. Here's one that rings
true. This is it, then: *A small girl plays in the dirt outside a
low-roofed house made of bricks and clay, freshly whitewashed.*

Nimmo was sure of that detail. There on the wall, beside the front door, had been the imprints of three pairs of small hands and, on the other side, two larger sets. She, Nirmaljeet Kaur, had made the smallest pair of handprints. The other two pairs belonged to her older brothers. Sometimes their names teased at the edges of her mind and she would reach out stealthily, across the shadowy landscape of memory, hoping to trap the names of her brothers between her hands. But they were always swifter. Sometimes she wondered whether she had had any brothers at all. She had no trouble recalling her mother's name, Kanwar Kaur, and her father's, Pardeep Singh. Village, Dauri Kalan. At least that's what it said on that postcard from long, long ago, the one from Canada, with the picture of a looming black bear, fuzzy green trees rising behind it. But what proof that Kanwar was indeed her mother and Pardeep her father? There was not a single word in the postcard that proved Nimmo belonged to these two people, *Kanwar Kaur, c/o Pardeep Singh.* And what about the person who had sent the postcard: *Your younger sister, Sharan.* Was this woman really her aunt? Everything about her past confused Nimmo.

She read a little more of Bibi-ji's letter, a sheet covered with neat Punjabi writing from a woman thousands of miles away, and wondered if she had changed in any way since its arrival. She drew out the photograph of Bibi-ji that had come with the letter—the woman was large and smart in a bright yellow salwar kameez, her face made up like the posh women who drove cars and shopped in Khan Market.

Had her own mother looked anything like Bibi-ji? Nimmo couldn't be certain. But she did remember standing with a woman she presumed was her mother at the door of their home, while a man, tall and stooped and with a green turban coiled neatly about his thick knot of hair, and two young boys walked away from them and towards the fields. The boys had turned to wave. Nimmo had felt her mother's tall, solid bulk beside her, comforting in its strength and permanence. She had hugged the long legs, modestly covered in a coarse cotton salwar, and her mother had stroked her head absentmindedly.

The morning had drifted by in silence, a peculiar silence, when Nimmo recalled it from this distance in time—a waiting, shadowy quiet, as if even the birds had a premonition of the horror creeping towards them. Around mid-afternoon, there was a commotion at the far end of the mud lane that crawled past their house and into the heart of the village. Her mother went out of the house to see what was going on, came rushing back inside the house and locked the door. She picked up Nimmo and lowered her gently into the large wooden bharoli of grain that sat in a dark corner of the house.

"Don't make any noise," she said. "Don't even *breathe* loudly. I will come and take you out in a little while."

"Are we playing chuppa-chuppi?" Nimmo had asked, delighted that her mother had finally found the time to play with her.

"No, but you must be as quiet as if we are playing it. Understand?" Her mother lowered the heavy wooden lid of the container, wedging a rolling pin under it to allow for fresh air.

A few minutes later, from her grainy hiding place, Nimmo heard fists pounding on their door.

"Who is it?" her mother asked. Her voice, normally deep and sure and comforting, now had an unfamiliar quiver.

Nimmo wasn't sure what the people outside said in reply, but she did hear her mother unlock the door. The sound of footsteps entering the house and insistent male voices. Her mother's voice grew higher and more angry. It altered and became pleading, and then abruptly she uttered a single scream, which turned into a sound like the one a stray dog had uttered when they found it dying in the gully behind their house. Then it ceased, that quivering animal whimper. A man laughed, and Nimmo heard receding footsteps.

She had stayed in the bin for a long time, waiting for her mother to pull her out. Time lost its shape and meaning as she sat hidden in the grain. She sucked on her fingers, consumed by a terrible thirst. But mindful of her mother's warning not to make a sound, to stay until she was taken out of the bharoli, she crouched there until painful cramps overtook her legs and she changed her position slightly, hoping no one would hear the agitated rustling of the wheat beneath her shifting body. She tried chewing a few grains, but they tasted like chalk and made her even more thirsty. To her shame she felt her bladder open and the warm liquid spread around her bottom. She had fouled her mother's stock of wheat—how could she tell her of this awful thing she had done? Nimmo began to cry softly, less from discomfort than from a fear of what her mother would say.

When her mother eventually opened the lid and lifted her out of the bin, Nimmo hardly recognized the dirty, bleeding woman who held her and rocked her and wept with a soundless, juddering agony.

"Amma, I peed in the bharoli," Nimmo whispered. "I couldn't stop. I didn't know what to do."

Her mother didn't seem to hear her confession. She shushed her, told her to keep quiet while she washed herself with the water stored in pots in the kitchen. She didn't light the lantern though it was pitch dark inside the house. Even the soft splashing of water sounded unnaturally loud. A sweet fragrance came to Nimmo. Her mother, she realized, was using the pale violet-coloured soap that her aunt had sent from somewhere far away and that she used only on special occasions.

Still in the dark, her mother changed Nimmo's soiled clothes and, pushing her into an inner room, drew the door shut. What was her mother doing on the other side? Nimmo had wondered, beginning to panic. She had pressed her ear to the door but heard nothing.

This silence returned to haunt Nimmo again and again. Had she buried another memory under this one? Had her mother really come back to take her out of the bharoli? Or had she crawled out of it herself? If it had indeed been her mother, where did she disappear to after she had washed herself and Nimmo? And where was she when Nimmo cautiously emerged from the dark room into which she had been pushed? She had joined a kafeela heading for the Indian border and had walked for days in that enormous, ragged line of people, begging strangers for food and water, until a couple with two children a little older than Nimmo had taken her under their wing. They had wound their way across fields that hissed in the wind. Every time they heard approaching horsemen or car engines on the dusty road, they had hidden behind shrubbery or lain flat in sugar cane fields that had been burned down to stubble and still smouldered in patches. They heard trains chugging slowly a few miles beyond the fields, saw their dark trail of smoke. A rumour spread that the long metal caterpillars were full of dead bodies—of Hindus and Sikhs if the trains were heading towards India, and Mussulmans if they were going to Pakistan. They passed burning villages and villages that were unnaturally quiet, and sometimes more people joined their kafeela, all heading south, hoping to cross the new boundary line which had appeared like a wickedness in their innocent lives, into India. She saw men weeping for their losses. Bloated corpses floated in the canals that ran along the edges of the fields, and lost-eyed children like herself begged pitifully for food and water.

Her long journey ended in New Delhi, in a vast village of tents and shacks—a refugee camp set up by the government of the newborn India. Weeks, perhaps months later, some well-dressed women in pretty saris, with notebooks and pens in their capable hands, had arrived. They had asked Nimmo questions about her family. She had shaken her head shyly at their questions and sucked her finger. She had called her mother Amma. Her mother had called her father Sardar or ji. She could not remember anything else. She did not show the women her discovery: a postcard picture of a bear she had found tucked into the waist of her salwar. Suppose they took it away from her?

Another month went by, and Nimmo found herself adopted by the Sikh couple who had rescued her in the kafeela. And soon, growing up in a busy city, playing with her adoptive siblings and going to school, Nimmo almost forgot her vanished family. She was eighteen when she married Satpal, and within a year she was pregnant with Jasbeer. Two years later Pappu arrived, and Nimmo found herself settled into an uneventful existence broken by nothing more disturbing than Asha's daily battles.

Yet the chalky taste of fear that had clogged her throat since her mother had thrust her into the wheat bin remained with her even now, when she was a grown woman with a family of her own. Sometimes when she heard water running at night she was reminded of her mother's furious washing, and her nostrils would fill with the smell of the pale violet soap. She hated waking up and not finding her husband's body beside her. How would she live without Satpal's gentleness and strength? How would she sleep without his arms wrapped around her to keep her nightmares at bay?

Her fear was a monstrous, silent thing that often woke her, sweating and shaking, from troubled sleep. It made her suspicious of everyone, even neighbours she had now known for many years, the woman who sold her mangoes in summer and cauliflowers in winter, the milkman, the

owner of the bidi shop, the electrician, the policeman—
every single one of them was a threat to her security, her
peace of mind.

"Sometime in your life you have to let the fear go,
Nimmo," Satpal had once said. "It is not good for your
blood pressure otherwise."

He had read an article in the papers about the dangers
of high blood pressure and for a while found a reason to
work it into everything he said. This gentle, unimagina-
tive person she had married had no idea of the meaning
of terror, Nimmo reflected. His greatest fear was illness
leading to a doctor's visit. How could she explain to him
what it was like to have your life pulled out from under
your feet, to wake up one day and find you have no family or home in the land your people had tilled for a hundred years? How could he understand the pain of not
knowing whether these memories were in fact memories
or only figments of her imagination? Of relying on
unconnected bits and pieces to tell him who he was? Of
knowing only half your story?

She had smiled up at her husband that morning, loving
him for his sunny nature, his certainty that he could protect her. But inside her own heart she carried other, darker
certainties: that she would never be able to rid herself of
the dying-dog sound that a woman had made one night
while a child sat uncomprehending and cramped in a bin
of grain. And much as she tried, Nimmo could not rid
herself of the memory of a pair of feet dangling above a
dusty floor, their clean pink soles smelling delicately of
lavender soap.

I have searched for many years for some trace of Kanwar and her family. But nobody could tell me anything about her. Then by great coincidence, the woman I mentioned earlier, Leela Bhat, recently come from Delhi, gave me your address. I believe in things such as coincidence and chance and therefore I am hoping that you are indeed Kanwar's daughter and my niece.

Nimmo had no idea how long she had stood there, holding the letter pressed against herself. She would reply to this. She would be honest, and she would tell this Bibi-ji that she did not know for sure if her mother's name was Kanwar. She would tell her, "I called my mother Amma, I did not know her name." She would show her the postcard and tell her that she had found the name there but did not know how she came to have it. It had not been much to keep—a pair of names that might or might not have belonged to her parents.

Nimmo took a sheet of paper from her son's notebook and found a pen. In a neat hand, she wrote: *"Respected Bibi-ji, My regards to you and hope you are well. I am writing in response to your letter. I was very surprised to receive it and cautiously happy. I do not know whether we are indeed related, for I was a child when the sorrows occurred and I do not remember much. That my name is Nirmaljeet Kaur is the only thing I know for sure about myself . . ."*

Nimmo wrote slowly, considering each sentence before committing it to paper, her hand cramping from the unaccustomed exercise, her back hurting from sitting hunched over the pad on her lap. She wrote about all the fragments she remembered and the bits she thought were true. She wrote every detail of that last terrifying night in Dauri Kalan, except for her memory of a pair of lavender-fragrant feet suspended above the floor. At last she was done. Bibi-ji might or might not be related to her. It did not matter, really. By the simple act of writing to her, Nimmo realized, she had gathered up those shards of memory and looked straight at them for the first time.

ELEVEN

GIVE-AND-TAKE

—

New Delhi

September 1967

Three months later. The early autumn sunshine fell gently over the city. Asha could be heard arguing with the banana vendor, the chickens in Kaushalya's yard were clucking contentment and, as usual, chaos reigned in Nimmo's home.

"Come on, what are you doing? You want a caning from the headmaster or what?" Jasbeer shouted to his younger brother, who was hurriedly tying his long hair, which his mother had braided, into a topknot. He swung his satchel over his shoulder. "Pappu always makes me late," he grumbled, stalking out of the front door.

"Wait for me!" Pappu yelled, struggling to clamp a rubber band over the white square of cloth he used to cover his topknot. Finally he was done, although it sat slightly askew over the fat ball of hair. He turned to face his mother.

"Is it okay?" he asked anxiously.

"Yes putthar, even *I* couldn't have done it better." Nimmo gazed at him fondly. He insisted on performing this part of his toilette himself, though it would have been faster if his mother had done it for him. In a few more years, he and Jasbeer would be winding turbans around their heads just like their father, Nimmo thought.

She patted Pappu's cheek and pushed him out of the door. He broke into a run to catch up with his brother, who was already marching resolutely ahead. Nimmo watched from the alley until they reached the main road and were swallowed up by the rush of people and vehicles. A small worm of worry crawled through her mind. Jasbeer was too sensitive, he took things too seriously. Perhaps she would make him a treat for dinner tonight, maybe buy him one of those brightly coloured tops that she had seen in the big shop two roads away. Only for him, not for his brother—although she couldn't see how she could get something for one child and not for the other.

The sun threw a slant of light on the tulasi bush that Nimmo had planted in the tiny paved area in front of the house. Her Hindu neighbours believed that the tulasi brought peace and prosperity to the house. She wasn't one to scorn other people's beliefs, so she had taken Kaushalya's advice and planted the bush the year Pappu was born. Her reverie was interrupted when, in the distance, she heard the tragic wail of an ambulance. There had been an accident, her boys were hurt, she thought. For all her memories, how little she had understood of fear until she had given life to these children. The wailing passed, headed in the opposite direction, and her heart stopped its thundering.

Satpal wheeled his bicycle out of the house. He had sold the taxi in an effort to reduce their debts, and no longer worked the night shift.

"You are leaving early?" Nimmo said, surprised to see him heading off so soon.

Satpal avoided her eyes. "Mohan Lal and I have to meet the bank manager."

"Again?" Nimmo exclaimed. "Why?" She had never been inside a bank. All her transactions were in cash. Banks were intimidating places and she felt the people who worked in them were faceless and frightening and could ruin your life.

Satpal grimaced. "I told you months ago we might need to take another mortgage on our house. Besides, I have to ask the bank to extend the deadline on our current loan."

"But I thought after selling the taxi we would be all right."

"That money barely covered the taxi loan," Satpal said.

"If the bank doesn't give, then what do we do?" Nimmo asked.

"I will ask Girish Jain," Satpal said.

"That moneylender? Ji, why? We could pawn my jewellery, no?" Nimmo was ready to weep. Everyone knew that you went to the moneylender only when matters were desperate.

"Your jewellery is for our daughter—if we have one," Satpal said. "Don't worry, it is only until business picks up at the shop. I hear they are building a new housing colony near by. We will have more customers then, I know it. And Mohan Lal might be able to get a bit of money from his wife's brother. Now, enough money talk . . . Do you want me to pick up some vegetables or fruit from the market?"

"No, I can buy some from the fellow near the gurudwara on my way back from the Ram-Leela field."

"Why, what is happening there?" Satpal asked.

"Arrey, ji, how many times do I have to tell you? Our Indira Gandhi is coming to give a speech. Especially for women. All of us are going, Kaushalya, Geetha, Preetam . . ."

"What do you get out of these speeches, enh?" Satpal wanted to know. "Your Indira Gandhi is just a politician like all the others, makes promises to do this and that, but nothing happens."

"It takes time to run a country this big, and she has been in power for just a few months, ji," Nimmo said indignantly. "I am beginning to think that you don't like her because she is a woman!"

"But I love women," Satpal teased, stroking Nimmo's backside.

She tutted and whacked his hand away. "Don't do that! What will our neighbours think?" she said. "I like Indira-ji, she is smart and she gives us women courage. If we have a daughter, I want her to grow up into an Indira Gandhi!"

"Okay, okay, but be careful. In your condition—in a crowd—is that good?"

Nimmo laughed. "You don't worry, I will be fine. Go now, or you will be late for work." She leaned against the faded wooden door frame, her hands linked around her swollen belly.

Satpal paused at the gate to look back at Nimmo as she stood at the door. He did this every morning, paused to glance back to assure himself that the happiness in the tiny house really did exist, that the tall, handsome woman who had borne him two sons really was a part of his life. He was filled with a vaulting ambition to do huge, generous things for her. He thought anxiously of the debts that were piling up, wishing that business in the little mechanic's shop that he co-owned with mild-mannered Mohan Lal would pick up soon. Then he could spoil Nimmo and his children with gifts and clothes, perhaps even add a second floor to the house to accommodate their growing family. He wondered whether she was as happy with him as he was with her. She was not a very demonstrative person, silent and solemn. A taut reluctance to trust anyone tightened the skin around her eyes and mouth. Only with Satpal and the children did she relax completely. Only then did her face dissolve into love and laughter.

Although Nimmo knew that if she didn't go inside and finish her chores she would be late in getting to the maidan, she continued to stand at the door, staring at the day roaring along, colourful and chaotic, on the dusty road in front of her home. There was a slight chill in the air, the sun shone and dew lay heavy on the leaves of the neem tree. Nimmo played languidly with the long braid that fell over her left shoulder, coiling down her old cotton kameez, almost reaching to the middle of her thigh. She thought of the child growing inside her and, for the first time in years, felt an exultation untainted by fear. If there was one thing that had prevented her from fully enjoying her life, it was the fear that always walked beside her, familiar as her own shadow, until this moment, on this sunlit morning, in the city of New Delhi in a country called India which had, by chance, become hers. The letter she had so painstakingly written three months ago to the woman in Canada named Bibi-ji, and now this new child growing inside her, allowed her to believe that at last she could let go of fear. For though she was not a trusting soul, she was, curiously enough, a hopeful one. It was hope that braced her as she walked through life. And so she stood there, this handsome woman of twenty-seven, neither too young nor too old, languid and full of the brilliance of the day, alight with the knowledge of her fecund body.

She stroked her belly. Early next year there would be an infant in the house once again. She knew in some mysterious way that this one would be a daughter. She could feel it in the blood that surged with extra strength through her wide-shouldered body. *I will always look after you,* she murmured to her unborn child, *I will give you everything your heart desires.* And in exchange, this unborn child would be her talisman against fear and sorrow.

She touched the door frame gently and turned to enter. From the corner of her eye, she noticed a taxi approaching slowly and then stopping across the road. She paused, wondering who in the neighbourhood had visitors that could afford to take a taxi from the station or the bus depot.

A heavy woman in a shiny red and white salwar kameez suit emerged from the vehicle, energetically arguing over the fare in ripe Punjabi. Having settled the dispute to her satisfaction and now dragging a bag out after her, the woman walked across the road towards her. As she entered the narrow gate, she saw Nimmo standing at the door and slowed down.

"Nirmaljeet Kaur?" she asked.

"Yes," Nimmo said cautiously.

"I am Sharanjeet Kaur–Bibi-ji–your mother's sister!" said the woman. "I couldn't bear to do this letter-writing business anymore, so I caught a plane and came."

Caught a plane, Nimmo thought in awe. As if she did it every day, like catching a bus. Bibi-ji dropped her bag, clasped her hands to her chest and burst into tears. Nimmo glanced around embarrassed, picked up her visitor's bag and led her into the house before Asha could appear at the wall.

She opened two of the folded wooden easy chairs and gestured to Bibi-ji. "Please sit," she said awkwardly, wishing that Satpal was home to help with the conversation. "I will make some tea."

Dark lines of eye make-up ran with the tears down Bibi-ji's cheeks. "No, no, sit with me and let us talk," she said, mopping her face with a handkerchief she had extracted from the neckline of her kameez. "I have waited so many years, and I don't want to waste another minute." She looked appraisingly at Nimmo. "You have my sister's eyes," she said finally. "And her build. She was a tall woman. I remember when I was a child she used to carry me around so easily." Bibi-ji giggled and pointed at her bulk. "Now it would be impossible, neh?"

Nimmo shifted uneasily. Bibi-ji had clearly decided that she was the lost niece, with no evidence to support her belief. She leaned forward and caught Bibi-ji's hands. "Look," she began, wanting to say, *Let's wait a bit, let's talk this through, I'm not sure I am who you think I am. I'm not sure where I came from, I don't know my mother's name or my father's, I was a small child . . .*

But before she could finish her thought, Bibi-ji pulled her into her own capacious arms as if she were still a child and stroked her head. "No, don't say anything to spoil this moment for me. I know in my heart that you are my Nimmo, my sister's child. My heart is never wrong."

A faint, familiar fragrance filled Nimmo's nostrils. She struggled in the older woman's embrace, wanting to get away from the memory that it evoked. It was the smell of the pale violet soap. It was the smell of death and fear. With a small cry, Nimmo pushed Bibi-ji away and stumbled to her feet.

"What? What is it?" Bibi-ji asked. Seeing the look in Nimmo's panic-stricken face she sighed, "It is okay. I shouldn't have come here like this. You must think, who is this crazy woman? It is okay. You make me some tea, and we will talk about this and that and maybe find a connection."

"The scent you are wearing," Nimmo said. "It seems so familiar. I was surprised, that's all."

"Scent? Oh, my lavender splash," Bibi-ji said. "I used to send lavender soap to my sister. Perhaps you remember that? I loved it as a child. But I hated it after I lost your mother—I stopped having anything to do with lavender. When I found you, I decided to use it again."

Feeling unsettled, Nimmo went into her kitchen to make the tea. Left alone in the living room, Bibi-ji let her eyes wander around the small, neat, sparsely furnished house. She saw how scrubbed and clean it was but noticed the walls that desperately needed painting, the faded and much-darned clothes hanging on the line outside and the cracked floor in the kitchen, and she understood there was not much money here.

Nimmo brought tea to Bibi-ji, and they sat in silence for a few minutes. Then Bibi-ji started to talk about the childhood she had shared with Kanwar, about their father's disappearance, about their mother. She talked about everything except how she had stolen Kanwar's future. She wanted Nimmo to think well of her.

Nimmo had nothing much to say about her own childhood—despite Bibi-ji's gentle prodding, she could still barely recall anything other than the images that haunted her. She had described them all in her letter to Bibi-ji, all except the image of a pair of well-washed feet hanging in the air that she still could not bring herself to share. But Bibi-ji made her tell them again, reliving the sound of her mother's anklets, the handprints on the wall of the house, the smell of wet earth after a monsoon. As for her life with the couple who had adopted her here in Delhi, what could she say, other than that it was happy? And safe—above all, it was safe.

Then she had an idea. "I have a postcard with me," she said. "It might be one that you sent to my mother." She went to the picture of Guru Nanak and reached behind it for the envelope containing the postcard.

The older woman eagerly took it from her. "Yes, I sent this. I remember picking it out because I thought your brothers would enjoy the picture of the bear. Inder and Gobind, do those names strike a bell?"

Nimmo shook her head. "Maybe the second name—Gobind. But I can't say for sure."

"There was another one I sent with this postcard—a picture of whales. Do you remember that?" Again Nimmo shook her head. Bibi-ji turned the card over and tapped at the faded writing. "And see, it's me—Sharan. That's what your mother used to call me, you know."

Taking the card back, Nimmo turned it round and round, trying hard to remember her family the way that Bibi-ji did, and failing. The older woman had claimed the postcard immediately, but was it truly Nimmo's? Had the card belonged to her mother, or had it been given to her by a stranger?

Too honest to keep such doubts to herself, she said, "I could be anybody. Where is the proof that I am the Nirmaljeet Kaur that you held in your arms when I was a child, Bibi-ji?"

"You don't want me as your aunt?" Bibi-ji asked, her face sagging with disappointment. "You don't like me?"

"I do, I do," Nimmo said. "It's just that I don't want to take advantage of your kindness like this. There must be thousands of women my age, from Punjab, who are called Nirmaljeet. Perhaps one of them is your niece. What if I found this card when I was running from my home to join the kafeela?"

Bibi-ji leaned forward and held Nimmo's worn hands in her own soft ones. "I am the one who came looking for you, you did not come to me. But I see my sister when I look at you. I am sure. I am forty-five years old. I have no children of my own. I have no family other than my husband. I have lived in guilt for twenty years. I left the village. I did not help my sister. Now I am sure. This is right."

Nimmo looked at Bibi-ji's face and gave up. She would be this woman's niece. She nodded and pressed Bibi-ji's hands in return. "Tell me more about my mother," she said. "You knew her longer than I did. Tell me about my grandmother and my brothers. Tell me all that you can about me."

"No, I have talked enough for today," said Bibi-ji. "You tell me about your life now. You have children, you said in your letter?"

"Yes, two boys," Nimmo said, exhausted by the tide of memory and emotion that had flooded so unexpectedly through her small home. "And this one is coming soon." She touched her belly.

Bibi-ji felt a sharp jealousy knife through her. "Where are your boys?" she asked.

"School," Nimmo said and looked at the time. She had missed Indira Gandhi's speech. No matter. "They should be back soon. The younger one comes home early some days, but today his older brother will be bringing him home. I was supposed to go out . . ."

Bibi-ji heaved herself to her feet in dismay. "Oh! Because of me . . . What must you think, I just land up like this . . . Oh!"

"No, no, it is only a speech by Indira Gandhi. Nothing so important. Sit. Please sit."

"But I too must go. I am staying with friends in Defence Colony. You know that area?"

Nimmo nodded. Yes, she knew of the area, it was very posh. She had passed it on the bus once or twice and wondered at the cars lined up on the street outside, the servants, the well-dressed people emerging from the houses.

"When did you say the children were coming home? I brought presents for them."

"In a few minutes. They would like to meet their aunty-ji, I am sure." Nimmo smiled with pleasure at the sound of that. A relative from her side at last.

"Great-aunty," Bibi-ji corrected.

As Nimmo had predicted, the door soon flew open and Jasbeer entered, impetuous as ever. "I'm hungry, Mummy," he called. "What is there to eat?" He stopped when he saw the visitor and suddenly became shy. He stood on one foot and stared. They had never had such a finely dressed person in their home. Not even his father's oldest sister, Manpreet, who was richer than the rest of them, had such shiny clothes.

"This is Jasbeer, my older boy," Nimmo said. "And . . . Jassu, where is your brother?"

Jasbeer looked down at his feet and muttered, "I don't know."

"What do you mean you don't know? You were supposed to bring him home from school."

Jasbeer shrugged. "He wasn't there."

Nimmo caught his face in her hand and twisted it up so that he was forced to look at her. "What do you mean he wasn't there?" she demanded, her voice rising. She forgot Bibi-ji sitting there, forgot the hours that had drifted by. "What do you mean? Did you even look for him? You wretched boy! Tell me, tell me the truth!"

Jasbeer burst into tears. "I was only teasing him, I was hiding and then when I came out he had gone somewhere. I didn't mean to . . ."

The door banged again, and Pappu entered crying dramatically. "Mummy, Jassu didn't wait for me. I came with Shaukat and her big brother." He caught sight of his older brother and increased his bawling, rubbing his eyes hard with plump fists.

"Thank God!" Nimmo exclaimed. She pushed Jasbeer away from her with a fierce whisper: "I'll deal with you later." And held out her arms to Pappu. "Come here, putthar, don't cry now. See who is here? A new aunty-ji." She turned to Bibi-ji. "I am sorry for all this confusion. Really, this older child of mine, God only knows what is wrong with him these days!"

"Never mind, Ooper-Wallah be praised that they are both okay," Bibi-ji said. She turned to Jasbeer, who was kicking angrily at the door frame. Vividly aware of his inarticulate hurt, she said, "It's okay, putthar, come here

174

and let me see your face. Do you know who I am? No? I am your mother's aunt, like your grandmother almost." She sat down again. "Come Jasbeer, don't you want to tell me about your school? And your friends?"

"And *my* friends?" Pappu demanded, from the circle of Nimmo's arms. "I have twenty-hundred of them."

Bibi-ji couldn't help laughing at his disarming liveliness. "After I talk to your brother, you little imp!"

She reluctantly left them at six that evening, after giving the boys an assortment of colouring pencils, t-shirts and toys and promising to return early the next day. When Satpal came home, exhausted, at nine o'clock, he found Nimmo excited and surrounded by a sudden wealth of belongings spread out on the floor.

"What is all this? You went shopping?" he yelled. "After I told you that money is short? Are you mad?"

"Shhh! The children are sleeping!" Nimmo said, pointing to the inner room. "And why are you shouting at me? I didn't go anywhere. An amazing thing happened today . . ."

"Good," grunted Satpal, his usual good humour entirely absent. "I hope it was a *nice* amazing thing, because I don't have good news for us. The bank has refused to extend the deadline on the loan repayment. And Girish Jain is willing to give us the money only at an exorbitant rate of interest, and provided we sign this house over to him as surety. But it is already mortgaged twice over to the bank!"

"So what are we to do?" Nimmo asked, her balloon of happiness punctured and forgotten.

Satpal's dejection was complete. "I don't know. I have to think. I'll ask people at the gurudwara on Sunday. Maybe someone will come up with an idea. Or money." Then he forced a smile. "But we will worry about all that tomorrow. Now give me some food and tell me about this amazing thing that happened. Was it because of your Indira Gandhi? How was her speech? Some more tain-tain about removing poverty, eh? How about I ask her for a loan?"

Nimmo went into the kitchen to get Satpal his dinner. What were they going to do without money? And with the new baby arriving soon? How little—she thought suddenly—how little her new aunt, Bibi-ji, must worry about such things!

She brought a plate of food to where Satpal sat examining one of the toys lying beside him. "I didn't go to the speech," she said. "We had a visitor."

In a low voice she described the details of Bibi-ji's arrival, the stories she had told of Nimmo's mother, the presents she had brought for the boys.

"She sounds like a wealthy woman," Satpal mused. He grinned mischievously at Nimmo. "Maybe we should ask her to take us all back to Canada with her!"

Nimmo laughed. "I am sure she would if we asked," she said.

"In that case, maybe you could ask her to save my business for us," Satpal said.

Nimmo laughed again. "Yes, why not?"

After a brief silence Satpal said, "I was serious. Why not ask your rich and generous relative to lend us some money?"

Nimmo gaped at him. She had never thought she would hear this from Satpal. Ask a stranger for money?

"Well? Will you ask her?" Satpal insisted.

"No. No," Nimmo said. "It is indecent! We have just met her—what will she think of us taking advantage of her like this?"

"Okay, okay, don't get angry. It was just a thought." His voice was tired.

He cleared the rest of his dinner off his plate. Silence again, and then Nimmo asked, "But what will we do? Where will you find the money? Will we have to leave this house?"

"I don't know, Nimmo. And I am too tired to think now."

"We will sell my jewellery," Nimmo offered again. "At least we will get a little money for it—not much, though."

This time Satpal did not rush to refuse.

Bibi-ji returned early the next day and the next, and in the following months she became a familiar sight in the gully. All Nimmo's neighbours knew who she was, and some, like Kaushalya next door, rejoiced for Nimmo. Bibi-ji arrived each morning with bags of fruit and other treats for the children. "I am your aunt," she would say firmly, in response to Nimmo's protests, dumping the bags on the floor and kissing the boys, who acted as if they had known her all their lives. "If an aunt cannot bring gifts for her family, then who can?"

On Saturdays she insisted on taking the family with her to see Delhi. Nimmo enjoyed these outings. Although she had spent most of her life in the city, she had neither the leisure nor the means to wander around it like the foreign tourists, who with their baggy clothes, beads, wild hair and

dark glasses had taken to arriving in droves recently. Satpal
never accompanied Nimmo and Bibi-ji on these trips.
Nimmo felt guilty when she found him sprawled in
exhaustion on their bed after returning late from one of her
excursions with Bibi-ji. The food she had cooked would be
untouched, and Satpal morose. She dared not ask him how
the business was doing—it was evident from his mood that
it was not going well. She filed her worry into a corner of
her mind, intent on enjoying the pleasure of having her
unexpected aunt spoil her and her boys. Now that the baby
was almost due, Bibi-ji assumed the role of mother as well,
telling Nimmo what food to eat, arriving early and making
meals for her, insisting on buying her tender coconut every
day for the vitamins it contained and eggs from Kaushalya
for the protein. She forced her to drink large glasses of milk
three times a day and made her rest in the afternoons,
while she took care of the boys when they returned from
school. Accustomed to being the caregiver for so many
years, Nimmo felt spoilt and thoroughly content with the
small luxuries Bibi-ji had introduced into her life.

Her euphoria ended abruptly one evening when she
returned early with Bibi-ji and the children after a day of
wandering in Old Delhi to find Satpal already home, lying
on the charpoy with a damp towel over his face. When he
removed it, Nimmo saw with a shock that his face was
bruised and swollen. He had a black eye and his lip was cut.

"What happened?" she asked in alarm as Bibi-ji rushed
the boys into the small bedroom.

"The moneylender," Satpal mumbled. "Bastard sent his
thugs to threaten us. Wants his money back."

"But I thought you said you would not be borrowing from him," Nimmo said, her voice rising.

"I lied. I didn't want you to worry. With the baby coming and all . . ." Satpal dabbed at his lip, which had opened up and was bleeding again.

"How much?" Nimmo whispered. "How much do we owe him?"

"Ten thousand rupees plus interest, which makes it nearly twelve or thirteen thousand."

"And the bank loan?" Nimmo was feeling sick.

"Six thousand plus interest. That is due in a month."

"Can't your sisters help us?" Nimmo asked desperately. From the other room came the sound of Bibi-ji telling Jasbeer to draw her a car like the fancy one they had seen that afternoon. "Manpreet *jeeji* might be able to help. Have you asked her?"

"Yes," Satpal said. "Her husband has already lent a lot of money to his brother, and he cannot give me more than two or three thousand just now. Maybe in a few months, but there is no guarantee."

She did not ask about his other two sisters. One was married to a farmer and herself struggled to make ends meet. The other was not on good terms with Satpal.

They stared silently at each other. In the other room Jasbeer's voice rose excitedly as he explained some complicated thing he had constructed with building blocks. Bibi-ji made admiring noises.

"I'll ask her," Nimmo said to Satpal in a tiny voice. "But I don't want to. God only knows what she will think of us."

—

The next day it was Bibi-ji who brought it up after all. She waited until she and Nimmo were alone in the house and said, "I couldn't help overhearing some of your conversation yesterday, Nimmo. What is going on? Is Satpal in trouble?"

"Yes," Nimmo blurted out. "I didn't want to tell you, but the shop is not doing well at all. Yesterday the moneylender sent his goondas to beat up Satpal. He was lucky, but his partner, Mohan Lal, has a broken leg. We don't know what to do. I am sorry for telling you all this, but . . ."

Bibi-ji leaned forward and patted Nimmo's knee. "Come, come. I am the oldest member of your family now. You don't need to hide anything from me." She looked reproachfully at Nimmo. "I am your family, remember?" She waited, but Nimmo remained silent. "Can I help in any way?"

Still Nimmo hesitated, feeling humiliated by her need. To take a loan from Satpal's sisters, a good friend, an unknown person in the bank or a moneylender was one thing. But to ask a newly discovered relative was another thing altogether.

"Nimmo, do you want me to lend you money?" Bibi-ji asked gently.

"Just for a short while," Nimmo said, twisting her dupatta hard. Crying softly she said, "We will return it soon. With interest."

"Why are you insulting me like this, Nimmo?" Bibi-ji asked. "I am like your mother now. Can a mother take interest from her daughter? No, no. I will lend you the money, and you return it when you are able to. Now go and make me a cup of chai."

Bibi-ji waited until Satpal had returned the money to the moneylender and agreed on a repayment schedule with the bank. She waited until Nimmo had become comfortable with the idea of being in debt to her. She waited until the moment was propitious and then she said, "Nimmo, my daughter, I have a favour to ask of you."

"Anything Bibi-ji, anything," Nimmo said. "We owe this roof over our heads to you. How can I refuse you anything?"

"You know I want the best for you and your family," Bibi-ji said. "And remember it is only if you *want* to give me this favour. I want no ill will between us."

"How can you think that I will bear anything but affection and gratitude towards you, Bibi-ji?" Nimmo replied warmly. "You have done so much for us. Ask what it is you want. I don't have much, but I will try to do the best I can."

"Let me take one of your boys back with me to Vancouver," Bibi-ji said.

Nimmo could not hide her shock. "You want to take away one of my sons?"

Bibi-ji rushed on. "I know it is a big thing to ask, but he will always be your child. I will merely take care of him for a few years, give him the best education I can afford. You don't have to say anything now. Think about it for as long as you want. You can let me know when you have decided. And remember, if you don't agree, that is still okay. I will not be angry. It is just that Ooper-Wallah has not seen fit to fill my lap with children. I feel an emptiness inside, Nimmo, a vast emptiness even now. You cannot understand the feeling." Bibi-ji's eyes filled with tears. "All I want is to help my family—for you are the only family I have. The child will have opportunities that you cannot give him here, and all our love and care. And remember, if you and Satpal decide to grant me this wish, Pa-ji and I will be the boy's guardians, not his parents. You will not be losing him, only lending him to us for a few years." She finished her tea and rose to leave. "It's a big decision, I know. Take your time. I'm not forcing you. I won't come back until you call me," she added, picking up her handbag.

Nimmo nodded but did not speak. She was too overwhelmed to say anything—she did not know whether she was supposed to feel grateful to Bibi-ji or angry with herself and Satpal for having put themselves in this position. She felt betrayed, and guilty too, for deep inside her, another thought fought for survival. If she did not send one of her sons abroad, was she depriving him of a chance for a better life? He would be well taken care of—of that she had no doubt. Bibi-ji would enrol him in a good school where he would learn to be like those smart boys Nimmo saw in the better parts of New Delhi. He would become a doctor, perhaps an engineer. And once he was making a living he could bring Pappu and, Nimmo hoped, his soon-to-be-born sibling over as well. Then ashamed of how rapidly she had become accustomed to the idea of parting with Jasbeer, how she was already building castles with the idea, she began tidying the house. The frenzied ordering of the furniture, folding of the clothes and reordering of pots and pans relieved some of her tension. Then there was Satpal. What would he think of lending his son to this woman who had suddenly appeared in their lives? Well, if he was angry, Nimmo could always point out it was his financial ineptitude that had led them to this point.

Satpal came home and, to Nimmo's surprise and annoyance, was not as upset as she had imagined he would be. He nodded slowly when she told him of Bibi-ji's request. "It is not a bad idea," he said. "Think about it: so many people pay thousands of rupees and line up in front of the embassy for visas and immigration papers, and here our son is being sponsored like a king."

"But my Pappu is only five and Jasbeer is seven. They are so young. And what do we know of these people? They live so far away, and all we know is what Bibi-ji has told us. Suppose she makes him into a chaprasi in their house instead of this king that you are imagining?"

"We can make inquiries. Lots of people in the gurud-wara know people in Canada."

"But how do we decide which boy to send?" Nimmo cried. "And how can we give away the only thing that is completely our own, not on loan from anybody but God?"

"We are not giving away," Satpal reasoned. "Didn't you say that she will only be a guardian? We will ask her to sign legal papers—I will find out about this matter also at the gurudwara. I know many people who have sent their children abroad with their relatives. It is a common thing."

"But which one of our boys?" Nimmo asked again.

"Pappu is too young, he still needs his mother. Jasbeer can go. We will tell Bibi-ji that she will have to bring him back to us every year. Will that make you happy?"

Two weeks went by. Satpal made inquiries in the local temple about Bibi-ji and Pa-ji and, through a complex string of acquaintances, discovered that they were eminently respectable and well liked in Vancouver's Punjabi community. They were known for their generous hospitality and their heavy involvement with the temple there.

"I told you," Satpal announced as he delivered this information to Nimmo at home. "They are good and decent people. God-fearing too, I understand. And here you are, so suspicious!"

In the days that followed, Satpal was repeatedly able to point out to Nimmo the many people they knew who had allowed their children to be brought up by relatives that were better off, to everyone's advantage. He argued that the boys were his sons too, and surely he had a right to decide what to do with them as well. Not that he did not love them, he insisted—he did, and therefore he was wisely thinking of their best interests.

Finally convinced, Nimmo went over to Asha's house to phone Bibi-ji. Since Asha was in the room eavesdropping shamelessly, Nimmo kept her conversation brief, merely asking Bibi-ji to come over whenever it was convenient. The older woman arrived almost immediately in a flurry of purple clothes and jingling bracelets, her lips outlined in bright pink lipstick. She hugged Nimmo and patted Satpal on the back, deposited another consignment of fruit, sweets and savouries in the kitchen and settled into a chair.

"I was talking to my Pa-ji," she began before anyone else could speak. "I told him about my offer and he scolded me. He said you would think that I wanted to buy the child with our money. He said it was wrong of me, and now I feel ashamed. I only want to do everything I can for you, Nimmo. Everything."

"No, no, don't say that," Satpal said, throwing Nimmo a reproachful glance. "We don't think badly of you, do we, Nimmo? We have decided to send our Jasbeer with you. But you will please promise to bring him back to us every year during school holidays."

"Of course," Bibi-ji said, her face radiant.

"It will be a lot of money for you to spend, Bibi-ji, but I don't know how I could bear to be away from my son . . ." Nimmo said.

"Every year," Bibi-ji promised. "Every year your son will return to you. I will bring him myself."

There was much paperwork to be done: legal sponsorship forms to be filed, a passport for Jasbeer, a visa, all kinds of travel details, but Bibi-ji, in a fever of joyous excitement, had no doubt that it would all be accomplished. Pa-ji's various contacts in government and the bureaucracy were phoned and matters arranged with Bibi-ji energetically directing operations.

In the middle of this flurry of activity Nimmo gave birth to a baby girl, whom she named Kamal Kaur. She was glad that Jasbeer would be able to spend a few months with his sister before leaving for Canada.

One evening Satpal told his older son how his future had abruptly been changed. Nimmo, who regretted her decision a little more each day, kept her eyes fixed on the small face, not sure how Jasbeer would react. To her surprise, at first, Jasbeer was proud that he and not his brother had been chosen. He strutted around the house speaking broken English and ordering an awed Pappu around. Bibi-ji took him out alone—just him, and not his brother—a few times, and he seemed pleased to be the focus of attention, delighted with the treats that his new-found great-aunt bought for him, thrilled with the places she took him.

But as his departure drew near, he began to balk at the thought of leaving his parents and his home. Now, when Bibi-ji sang out his name and asked if he wanted to go to this park or that fair, he shook his head and stuck out his lower lip. No, he did not wish to go anywhere. Because his stomach was aching. Because he had hurt his leg. Just because. And when Nimmo scolded him gently for being so unaccommodating, pushed him into Bibi-ji's extended arms, allowed him to be crushed against her bosom, Jasbeer grew even more fearful and moody.

Then the day arrived when all the paperwork was done. Bibi-ji arrived triumphantly with the visa, passport and tickets for the flight to Vancouver. But after she had left for the night, Jasbeer turned his dark, hurt eyes on

Nimmo. "Why do I have to go?" he asked. Was he being sent away so that his mother could focus on Pappu and the baby? Was she angry with him? "Why me and not Pappu, Mummy?"

Because he is younger, putthar, Nimmo wanted to say to the child standing so stiff and accusing before her. *He needs me more than you do.* But the words would not come. How could she have agreed? Would Jasbeer ever forgive her?

"Because you love him more than me?" Jasbeer asked in a small voice.

"That is not true, putthar," Nimmo said beseechingly. "I love you both equally. Your father and I want you to get the best opportunity in the world, and Bibi-ji will take good care of you." She reached out to hug Jasbeer, but he burst into tears.

"Don't send me away, please, Mummy, please," he cried. "I promise I will be a good boy. I won't fight with Pappu."

Nimmo held her son close. "Don't cry, putthar, it is all for your own good," she consoled, pushing away the doubts that assailed her.

A week later, at the airport, Jasbeer clung to his mother's hand while Bibi-ji checked their luggage. Feeling like a criminal, struggling to control her emotions, Nimmo peeled the boy's small fingers off her own one by one. Wordlessly she kissed his face again and again, and then handed him over to Bibi-ji. She watched Bibi-ji smooth a long strand of hair off Jasbeer's flushed cheek with a tender palm and she saw him walk reluctantly into the passenger lounge, his sturdy body trotting beside

Bibi-ji's large, brightly coloured form. Before he disappeared into the crowd he gave her a forlorn, backward glance that pierced her to the heart.

It's for his own good, she murmured, leaning against Satpal, who stood rigidly beside her. For his own good.

PART FOUR

—

HERE AND THERE

TWELVE

EDUCATING JASBEER

—

Vancouver

January 1971

In the kitchen of her Taj Mahal, Bibi-ji sat at the table, an island of quiet in the sea of sound that filled her home as always. She looked up briefly as Jasbeer stamped into the house and up the stairs.

"Jassu, have you done your homework, putthar?" she called after him. There was no response. She sighed and returned to the letter she had begun more than an hour earlier.

Dear Nimmo, Jasbeer is doing much better at school this term. His best friends are Preethi Bhat, the daughter of the woman who gave me your address, and two other children who live close by. I wanted him to include a letter in his own

hand to you, in English, so you could see how well he writes.
But he says to tell you that he will not write until his hand-
writing is perfect. He says to tell you that his mummy and
daddy deserve only the best.

She paused. It was not easy to fabricate the fiction that
she created every month for Nimmo and Satpal. The
truth was that Jasbeer was not doing well at all. He refused
to write to his parents, rarely mentioned them. When
Bibi-ji tried to read Nimmo's loving, anxious missives out
loud to him, he ran from the room. If she insisted he stay
and listen, he stood stiff and silent. He was an angry child
and a destructive one. He hated his school and inspired
complaining letters from his teachers almost every week.
His only real friend was Preethi Bhat. Bibi-ji was consoled
by the thought of the active, gregarious little girl who had
more or less taken over the business of introducing Jasbeer
to her own friends, translating the English-speaking world
to him when he had first arrived—though she was younger
and just as much a newcomer—and generally watching out
for him.

Bibi-ji had taken Jasbeer back to Delhi a year later, in
1969, as promised, but the visit had not gone well. He
fought constantly with his younger brother, kicked his
mother, refused to go near his baby sister and, on the
sixth day, earned a thrashing from his father. He wanted
to return to Vancouver with Bibi-ji and Pa-ji immediately,
he said, and threw a tantrum when Nimmo insisted tearfully that he was to stay with them for the rest of the holidays as planned.

"You are not my mother," Jasbeer said, his small face intense with spite. "She is." He pointed to Bibi-ji, who wriggled uneasily in her chair.

"No, putthar, I am not your mother," Bibi-ji felt obliged to say, although she was gratified.

"But I love you," Jasbeer said. He gave her a disarming look and hugged her as far as his arms would go around her bulk. "I don't want to stay here with them."

Bibi-ji had left him with his family and returned with Pa-ji to their hotel room.

"Leave him here," Pa-ji had urged. "We made a mistake taking him from his parents, but it is not too late to correct it."

Bibi-ji had maintained an obstinate silence. She didn't think they had made a mistake. It would work out; this child was hers.

A few days later, they received a call from Satpal. "Could you please come over? The boy has not eaten anything since you left."

As Bibi-ji had rattled back to Nimmo's house in a taxi, Pa-ji looking worried and not too pleased beside her, she felt quietly vindicated. She got out of the car in front of the modest house that had become as familiar to her as her own, and hurried inside. An unsmiling Nimmo opened the door to her. No sooner had Bibi-ji entered than Jasbeer ran up to her and cried, "Take me back home. I don't want to stay here."

She had looked helplessly at Nimmo and then at Satpal. Nimmo had avoided her eyes, but Bibi-ji knew she was upset.

"I don't know why he is behaving like this." Bibi-ji had spread out her hands. "He was so happy to get on the plane and come home. He told me so himself. Didn't you, Jassu? And he helped me choose the presents for Pappu, didn't you?" Bibi-ji turned to Jasbeer, who kicked the wall. "Putthar, is this any way to behave?"

Nimmo heard the maternal tone in Bibi-ji's voice and was jealous.

Pa-ji took Bibi-ji's hand in his and squeezed it. "Maybe we should leave him here where he belongs," he said.

"If that is what you wish." Bibi-ji looked steadily at Nimmo. "But think, is that what is best for him? Is that what you really want?"

"What do you expect me to say?" Nimmo demanded, her voice catching.

Bibi-ji said softly, "I was trying to help, that's all. But he is yours, nothing can take that away from you. If you want him here, I won't take him back."

"No!" shouted Jasbeer, gripping Bibi-ji's hand tight. "I want to go with you."

She and Pa-ji had returned to Vancouver with Jasbeer a month earlier than planned, promising a silent, distraught Nimmo that they would bring him back the following year.

But she had not kept her promise. Jasbeer had fallen ill with chickenpox just before they were to leave, so the trip had to be cancelled. She knew she was looking for an excuse she could use this year. She looked down at the letter she had begun writing to Nimmo in response to one that had arrived from her last week.

"*We have not seen our son Jasbeer for over a year now,*" Nimmo had written in her neat Punjabi script. Bibi-ji could hear the stiff indignation behind the words. "*We wish you to bring him home soon. I am also enclosing a draft for some of the money that we owe you. God willing, we will pay off the rest soon. Yours, Nimmo.*"

She used to write *Love, Nimmo* or *Your affectionate niece, Nimmo,* Bibi-ji remembered with a pang.

The enormous colour television in the living room blared to life, startling her. Lallo was changing channels fast and, with a brief pause at the news, he stopped at the soap opera of the day, and then Bibi-ji heard the latest instalment of new immigrant arrivals settling back into the sofas and armchairs with a collective sigh. They would be waiting for Lalloo, their cultural and linguistic interpreter, to begin his translation of the antics unfolding before them on the television.

"The dame in the green nightsuit is in love with the red-haired one's husband, and the golden-haired one is a vamp," she heard Lalloo's voice raised authoritatively. "Like our own Helen-ji. And the other one had a child nobody knows about—an illegitimate child. No, not the blonde, the one with short red hair. And the fat guy is the red-haired dame's lover. Enh Bibi-ji," he called. "Why did the blondie leave the fat guy? I am not remembering her name, Sandy or Cecily or something."

"The one who looks like Helen?" Bibi-ji thought all soap-opera blondes looked like her favourite Hindi film actress.

"No, the one who looks like Marilyn Monroe."

"She fell in love with somebody else, maybe," Bibi-ji said absently. She rarely watched the soaps but always seemed to give the correct replies. She reasoned that sooner or later the women would fall in love with somebody else. Bibi-ji had come to the conclusion that these daytime dramas were simply about women who were either in or out of love with different men. They were slippery creatures, like soap—hold them too tight and they would fly out of your hands. That's why the shows were called soap operas. Nobody could persuade Bibi-ji that her reasoning might be flawed. Soap was the centre of most of the problems of life, as far as she was concerned. Lavender soap in particular. Look at what it had done to her own existence and her sister's.

In the kitchen, three women were busy making stacks of parathas. Bibi-ji watched absent-mindedly as two of them squatted on the floor, their knees bent, their chins resting on their knees, their hands spinning as they rolled out the dough into circles and triangles. A third woman stood at the stove slapping one paratha at a time into a hot pan and frying it rapidly. The smoky odour of cooking flour and oil filled the kitchen. Their movements were mesmerizing, their gold bracelets set up a rhythmic *chink-chink-chink* and gossip bubbled and frothed around the kitchen like a small river.

The mailbox clattered, and Bibi-ji caught sight of the red-haired mailman—Tom or Bob or something—cutting across her carefully tended lawn. She got to her feet as quickly as she could and slapped an imperious palm against the window. He turned around at the sound, and she waved her arms to tell him to get off the lawn. Giving her a cheeky grin, he continued blithely onward, leaping over one of her flowerbeds, his big boots narrowly missing the heads of her beloved pink roses, before squeezing through the cedar hedge into the neighbour's house.

One of the women in the kitchen went out to retrieve the mail and came back with a handful, which she handed to Bibi-ji. She riffled through it quickly, pulled out a letter from among the bills and flyers, and frowned at it. It was from Jasbeer's school. *Again.* She opened it unhappily. It seemed to Bibi-ji that the school principal had nothing better to do than send her a stream of complaining letters every second week. They all said more or less the same thing: *Dear Mr. and Mrs. Singh, we regret to inform you that your son Jasbeer Singh has been indulging in inappropriate behaviour. We would like to set up a meeting with you in order to discuss this."*

She tapped the table with her fingertips. Was there something wrong with the school, or was it the way she and Pa-ji were bringing up this boy? Should she perhaps not have taken him away from his mother? Were they perhaps too old to be taking care of a noisy, wilful, *angry* eleven-year-old boy? Were they too indulgent? Or was there something else: was he teased or bullied at school for the colour of his skin or because he wore his hair in a topknot like all good Sikhs? Should she ask Nimmo whether they could cut his hair—the marker of his Sikh identity—as so many other Sikh parents in their community had done for their sons, so that Jasbeer could blend in?

Perhaps it was because he did *not* have enough of a sense of his cultural roots in this western country. No, that was hardly possible, Bibi-ji thought grimly. It was the other way around, more likely. The boy had too *much* of a sense of history instilled into his head by Pa-ji. Too much of ancient stories of wars and warriors. In her mind's eye, Bibi-ji saw the long rows of photographs that adorned her husband's study, the ones he claimed were all his relatives, and she thought of the number of times she had, at Pa-ji's insistence, told Jasbeer of her own father's aborted journey on the ship called the *Komagata Maru*, turned away by this very city. And each time Pa-ji would comment at length on the injustice of the whole episode. Had they burdened the boy with an impossible load, a feeling of grievances unresolved? In addition to the dark well of anger that he nourished within himself?

Truly, she thought, Jasbeer was proving to be a greater handful than she had imagined. She reread the letter slowly. It was indeed the same as the others that had arrived with monotonous regularity. She smacked it down on the table and yelled, "I'm fed up with this!" It felt good to raise her voice.

In the living room Lalloo leaned over and switched off the television. It wasn't often that Bibi-ji shouted. The young men stopped talking. The women who had taken over the kitchen stopped stirring and fell silent.

"What happened, Bi-ji?" Lalloo called, shortening her name affectionately. "Any service I can do for you?"

"There is a letter," Bibi-ji began. "*Another* one. From Jasbeer's school!"

Lalloo got up and came into the kitchen. He tutted and shook his head. "You should change his school," he declared. "Those people are always picking on our Jas." He had a soft spot for Jasbeer, whose willingness to fling himself into a fight and come out of it bruised and triumphant reminded Lalloo of himself at that age.

"We have already changed two schools, Lalloo! And he is only eleven years old." Bibi-ji frowned again. "I don't know what to do."

"Why is the boy needing to go to school? Henh? What has school done for him? Look at you, me, Pa-ji—no school-vool, teacher-veacher, but full-time success." Lalloo raised a satisfied finger. "The world was my textbook, Bibi-ji. When a man has this world to learn from, why he should sit in the classroom and listen to some boring madam going *a-b-c-d* and *one-two-three-four?* You don't want to listen to Lalloo, then at least listen to Churchill, na. What is it he was saying? Open the quotations: *I never allowed my schooling to be interfering with my education.* Closing the quotations."

Lalloo had a particular genius, Bibi-ji thought wryly, for discovering quotes that supported his efforts to eradicate education from society.

She shook her head in disgust. "If that is the case, why are you sending your own son to school?"

Lalloo shrugged. "It is not my idea, it is my wife's. Sometimes for the sake of homely harmony, one must go against one's principles." Homely harmony was another of Lalloo's pet themes, probably because his wife was known for her ferocious temper, her rich father and her six ruffianly brothers who had warned Lalloo, in a straightforward way, that if their sister was unhappy, it was he who would suffer. Excruciatingly. Lalloo had no difficulty believing them.

Later, when the house was quiet and their many house guests had retired for the night to the bedrooms and the basement, which had been turned into a large living area, and Jasbeer too had fallen asleep, Bibi-ji walked across the corridor from her bedroom to Pa-ji's office to tackle him about the letter. It was a large room lined with bookshelves. In the middle of it was his desk, which had papers stacked so high on, under and around it that sometimes even Pa-ji's bulk was not entirely visible. This was where he conducted his business, sent out petitions to fellow Sikhs for funds for this or that charitable cause and worked on his book, *The Popular and True History of the Sikh Diaspora.*

On one long wall of his office were pictures of Gandhi and Nehru and lithographic prints of the ten gurus of Sikhism. There was an enormous, gaudy painting of Maharaja Ranjit Singh, who had created a united Punjab for the first time in history, in royal regalia. On another wall were a dozen framed photographs of people who Pa-ji claimed, to all those visiting or passing through the house, as his relatives.

"You have so many relatives?" a naïve young Bibi-ji had asked when she had first arrived in Canada and seen this photo gallery on the wall of their old apartment above the grocery shop. She had been deeply impressed by this fine record of her new husband's past, and not a little jealous.

There was no one in her family she could point to and say, "That is my grandmother, famous for her sarson-da-saag," or "This is my grandfather, whose dreams brought me here." It was hard enough that her own father had simply vanished.

Pa-ji had consoled her by pointing to a copy of a picture of about twenty turbaned men standing on the deck of a ship with the name *Komagata Maru* painted on its side. One of those men, he said, would definitely have been Bibi-ji's father. Bibi-ji peered at the photograph often but couldn't see anyone who resembled the man who had slept on a string cot. A few faces were blurred or partially obscured by somebody else's head. Perhaps, Bibi-ji thought, one of those hidden men was her dream-ridden father.

"And now I will tell you a secret," Pa-ji had said, in thrall to her supple youth, her lovely eyes, willing to yield every single bit of himself, warts and secrets and all, to her. "These people are strangers. I don't know even one of them."

"Not even that one?" Bibi-ji looked at her husband with round eyes and pointed to a particularly impressive photograph of a young man in the uniform of the British Sikh Regiment. He looked brave and dignified with his long nose and dark beard, his sharp eyes staring out at posterity while posterity in the shape of the Singhs gazed reverently back. On his head was an enormous striped turban with a circular metal pin on the front, and he wore a uniform decorated with a row of medals. Only the day before, she had heard Pa-ji tell some of their house guests that this was his father, Theka Singh, who had fought valiantly for the British and then just as valiantly fought against them. "Rattray's Regiment," he had said. "And then Rebel Regiment."

Pa-ji had laughed. "No, not even that one," he had said. "I found him in a junk shop in Steveston." Three others had been retrieved from a shop in Petticoat Lane in London when Pa-ji was returning to India in search of a bride. Six had been purchased for a ridiculously low sum of money from an old man in an Amritsari gully, right beside the walls of the Golden Temple.

It was true that Pa-ji's father, Theka Singh, had once been in the British army. But he had not fought in any wars either for them or against them. There were no medals, no tales of heroism, no independence-related heroics: a week after signing on, he had died of jaundice. Pa-ji's mother died soon after, and he was brought up by a distant relative in Amritsar along with a dozen other children, all fighting for a space in the sun. Pa-ji was unhappy, lost in the crowd of children, longing for his dead parents. And he confessed to his lovely young wife that to make himself feel better, he had cooked up an entirely imaginary father who was tall and handsome and alive, a famous soldier who had won many decorations fighting for the British, who would return one day and carry Pa-ji away from his foster home. From a brave soldier who had fought *for* the British, the absent father became one of the heroic men who had fought *against* them for India's independence.

In 1924, sixteen-year-old Pa-ji had run away from his relatives' home and worked his passage on a Norwegian merchant vessel from Calcutta to Vancouver, where he had jumped ship and stayed on as an illegal immigrant, acquiring valid papers only ten years later. He had found refuge in the gurudwara on Second Avenue, where the small local Sikh community gathered to pray and mingle, and soon, through the contacts he made, had found work in a lumber mill in Abbotsford, not far from Vancouver. In the dank, crowded house that he shared with ten men, all of them working long hours in the mills, his imagination embroidered other colourful details about his father: he was much taller than Pa-ji, almost as large as the Swedish sailors who stopped in Vancouver's Gastown to drink their shore leave away; he had a booming laugh and a generous heart. In the blank slate of a foreign country, Pa-ji came to understand, you could scribble the truth any way you wanted. You could build entire families out of thin air, turn strangers into brothers and sisters and aunts and uncles, use new relationships and stories to patch up the holes created by lost and left-behind ones. You could, like Pa-ji, spin history using longing for yarn and imagination for a loom.

Armoured by his fictions against the suspicious glances of the Europeans in the city and the fear that the look in their eyes would turn to violence, against the cold that soaked into his bones, against exhaustion and loneliness in a strange land, young Pa-ji had worked hard and saved his earnings. He had moved to Vancouver and with a friend bought a truck which they used to deliver firewood purchased from the lumber mills in surrounding towns to homes across the city. Soon he had enough money to buy a small property on Kingsway Avenue, which he sold at a

profit a few years later. Next he bought a two-storey building on Main Street, one of the poorer parts of town. He
lived upstairs in one of the rooms, rented the remaining
two to other Sikh men and opened a small grocery shop
downstairs. When he had saved enough to comfortably
support a wife, he had taken himself to India and found
Bibi-ji.

Bibi-ji understood his need to possess a piece of history,
she knew all about keeping dreams alive. What harm, she
thought, could his small private fictions do in a world
where larger truths were reshaped to suit those in power?

When Bibi-ji entered Pa-ji's office to discuss Jasbeer, her
husband was watching the news on his private television.
Beside him on the small table was his favourite double
malt Scotch whisky, which he preferred to drink neat.
This was something that Bibi-ji did not approve of. She
believed that drinking alcohol equalled drunkenness and,
as a practising Sikh, Pa-ji had no business imbibing any
kind of liquor. But Pa-ji had airily pooh-poohed her
doubts and criticisms.

"This is just to loosen me up, my honey, so that I can
be a lion in bed!" he had teased the first time she had
objected, hooking his arm about her waist and pulling her
down on his lap, his alcohol-flavoured breath making
her wrinkle her nose. "I have it in person from the Upper-
Wallah that it is okay to take a peg or two once a day. Do
I get drunk? Have you seen me lose control? No. Then
why are you bothering me about it?" He had cradled his
glass of Johnny Walker against his barrel-chest and

laughed. "This is my friend. It kept me warm for many years before you came into my life, my jewel."

In the end, as a concession to her, Pa-ji gargled heartily and chewed a teaspoon of anise seeds before coming to bed, and she had to be satisfied with that.

Now he looked up, surprised to see her in his office at a time when she preferred to be curled up in bed with a stack of magazines. He patted the spot beside him on the couch and she settled down.

"Listen ji, there is something we need to talk about," she said. "Jasbeer has done some naughtiness at school again. They sent a letter. We have to go and meet that principal person, Longfellow or Longman or something."

"What did he do this time?" Pa-ji asked, his tone indulgent. Like Bibi-ji, he could not easily bring himself to be annoyed with Jasbeer.

"He took a kitchen knife to school. He said he wanted to be like your father."

A guilty look crossed Pa-ji's face. Bibi-ji narrowed her eyes at him and asked in a sharp voice, as if he were Jasbeer, "Does this have something to do with your history business, your pictures-of-ancestors story? What ideas have you been putting into his head?"

Pa-ji looked acutely uncomfortable. "A few days ago he wanted a kirpan, like the one in my father's photograph."

"Your *fake* father's photo," corrected Bibi-ji.

"Yes, madam, if you wish to put it that way," Pa-ji said. "But I told him that it was worn only by baptized Sikhs, that even I did not carry one. I promise, Bibi-ji, I did not encourage him."

For the first time Pa-ji had an inkling of the trouble that he had perhaps started with his youthful fictions. He had believed then, as he did now, that a man needed such a thing as a history. Without history you were nothing, a nobody, one of those fluffy seed-heads floating in the summer breeze, unaware of your origins, careless of your destination. Meaningless, mythless, *shapeless*. He had not thought there could be harm in fostering in this boy who had come into their lives a sense of the people he belonged to, a pride in his Sikh roots, so that he would never feel anything less than a healthy respect for himself. A man who respects himself, Pa-ji believed, is a man who is always respected by others. He spread out his hands helplessly. "I swear on my own head, I told him he could not carry knives and swords at this age."

"You did not say it clearly enough, it seems," Bibi-ji said. "We have an appointment tomorrow. And you will come with me too, if you please."

Pa-ji nodded humbly. He hated going to the school and listening to the principal lecture him about the boy, but he knew the look on Bibi-ji's face; it meant he had no choice.

"I will ask Leela what she does to bring up her children so nicely." Bibi-ji batted away Pa-ji's hands, which were now trying to find their way up under the hemline of her nightdress. They paused briefly at her deeply dimpled knees, before inching upwards towards the velvet crease between her thighs.

"Stop that," Bibi-ji giggled. "I am trying to discuss important things and here you are . . ."

Pa-ji's right hand reached its intended destination and Bibi-ji gave in with a sigh. Tonight was Pa-ji's. Tomorrow she would begin to worry about the child she had stolen.

Getting ready to visit Jasbeer's school the next morning, Bibi-ji wound her heavy sheet of hair into a large bun and screwed a pair of gold earrings into her ears. As she powdered her face, she gave Pa-ji instructions on how to behave with the principal.

"You sit there quietly, you understand?" she said. "*I* will do the talking."

"Why? Have I lost my voice or what?"

"You lose your temper, that's why. And remember, even though Jasbeer has been very naughty, it is our duty to support him." It offended Bibi-ji that she had to explain the boy so frequently—couldn't that gora principal see what a bright child this was? She inspected Pa-ji's clothes and tut-tutted her displeasure. "And please to wear your suit and tie, this shirt pant will not do."

Bibi-ji herself was arrayed in a shiny purple silk salwar kameez that lovingly followed every bulge of her body. The neckline of the kameez was breezy with white lace.

"So if I am to sit there quietly, why do I have to come with you, enh?" Pa-ji asked. He struggled into a cream and brown checked jacket. It clashed with his blue turban. Bibi-ji was tempted to ask him to change one or the other but held her tongue. Enough trouble getting him to wear something formal, enough irritation getting him to accompany her. If he managed to stop himself from being rude and disrespectful to the principal, Bibi-ji would be happy.

"And I will not wear a tie," Pa-ji said rebelliously. "It isn't as if I am going to meet the prime minister!"

They drove in silence, except for the music from the car stereo that Bibi-ji barely heard. She was busy composing the speeches she would deliver to the principal, reprimanding him for not understanding Jasbeer. She would inform him about their martial culture, that although it was indeed wrong of the boy to take a kitchen knife to school, he was merely following the call of his ancestors. He was a warrior at heart. She turned around and gazed fondly at Jasbeer as he sat in the back seat, his face disarmingly innocent.

Jasbeer's class teacher, a young woman with a pleasant smile and a nest of light brown hair, waited for them near the principal's office. She looked apologetic about the whole affair.

"But I couldn't let it go. Jasbeer was very naughty," she said after shaking hands with them.

Bibi-ji smiled sympathetically. She was a good and patient woman, this teacher, she thought, fond of Jasbeer, and she took a lot of nonsense from him. Bibi-ji knew it was Jasbeer who was at fault, picking at trouble as if it were a scab, but it hurt to see him chastened.

The teacher ushered them into the principal's office, where Bibi-ji and Pa-ji wedged themselves gingerly into the spindly legged chairs. In the solemn dullness of the room, Bibi-ji thought, they must look like brightly coloured pictures. She noticed, as she did on every visit, that the principal appeared to have only one tie—a striped navy blue and red one. She also saw that the chair in which she sat had a large tear in its fabric. Would this be a good time to donate a new chair to the school, she wondered, or would it be perceived as a bribe? These goras were strange people, Bibi-ji had discovered in her twenty-five years here: everything had to *mean* something. Although in this case, if she did decide to donate a chair, she would certainly expect the school to stop complaining about Jasbeer. A gift was not something bestowed lightly and without thought; it signalled the beginning of a long and mutually beneficial relationship. Naturally it was expected that the gift would be returned in some way— though not necessarily, of course. But to call it a bribe was to impose western notions of morality on the matter of give-and-take.

"So, Mr. and Mrs. Singh," the principal said. He steepled his fingers and tapped the whole tower against his little pink mouth. "So here we are again!"

Yes indeed, Bibi-ji thought, pursing her lips and look-ing righteous. They had been summoned to this brown and white room so often she had lost track of the number of times. Sometimes it was about unfinished homework, but more often it concerned a fight with another child.

"But *he* started it," Jasbeer would protest when Bibi-ji received one of the principal's loathed letters. "He hit me first!"

"Yes, Jasbeer," Bibi-ji would reply crossly. "But did you have to hit back hard enough to break his nose?"

Jasbeer could not understand why he was always the one in trouble—he was merely following his Uncle Lalloo's instructions: *In a quarrel make sure that the beating you give is worse than the one you receive. That way you will never get beaten by the same idiot again. Don't get angry, get even. If you lose your temper, you have lost the war.*

"Mr. and Mrs. Singh," the principal said sternly, "we do not tolerate violence in this school. It is a firm policy."

"One we approve of very much, very much indeed," Pa-ji replied.

The principal tried again. "I understand that in your part of the world it is okay to carry swords, but—"

"*Our* part of the world?" interrupted Bibi-ji. "No, there you have made a mistake, Mr. Longman."

"Longbottom," the principal corrected her.

"Mr. Longbottom. On Main Street we are *very* law-abiding citizens. Nobody carries weapons. Only religious leaders are permitted to carry the kirpan, and baptized Sikhs. Of course for children it is not allowed."

"No, Mrs. Singh. I don't mean Main Street." The prinicipal sounded weary.

Jasbeer kicked the leg of the principal's table. He recognized that tone of voice. It made him helplessly furious. Too young to know that the word to best describe that tone was patronizing, he was not too young to understand the thread of meaning that ran through it.

"Not Main Street? Then what are you meaning exactly, Mr. Longmantle?"

"Longbottom, Mrs. Singh. Why, the Poonjab, of course," the principal's left eye twitched. "I realize it is part of the

Sikh religion to carry swords—or is it knives—and grow
long hair and . . ."

Bibi-ji watched him discreetly consult a sheet of paper
on his desk. Clearly a man who liked to be well prepared
for his meetings with parents. He checked his notes and
forged on: ". . . wear a steel bracelet and underwear."
Another look at his notes to be sure that it was indeed
underwear—possibly steel underwear—that a true believer
wore.

Bibi-ji glared at the principal. "*Pun*jab," she said. "As in
fun, as in *sun,* as in *bun.*"

She had decided, the very first time she met him, that
this milk-faced man with his prissy mouth and the chin of
a horse was not worth liking, and she realized she had not
been wrong. "I don't know where you obtained such
incorrect information. We are a peace-loving people and
take up our swords only when we have to protect the
weak. In our scriptures, Guru Nanak-ji, our first guru, may
he rest in peace, says, and I will quote first in Gurbani and
then in English for your benefit—"

Longbottom raised his hand. "I believe you, Mrs.
Singh, and I apologize for my misinterpretation. But that
is what Jasbeer led us to understand."

"Jasbeer, putthar, is that true?" Bibi-ji transferred her
glare to her charge.

Jasbeer squirmed. "I was only *pretending* to be Shaheed
Dhyan Singh. Jason said I was a wimp because I wore my
hair in a bun like a lady, so I was showing him how brave
Sikhs are."

"That's not the way to show bravery, young man," the

principal said sternly. "I am sure Mr. Dan Singh would not have used a kitchen knife."

"Not mister," Bibi-ji said. "Martyr."

"I beg your pardon?" Mr. Longbottom was confused.

"Shaheed means martyr," Bibi-ji said. "It was *Martyr* Dhyan Singh, not Mister."

"I see," the principal said although he still looked confused. "In any case, we don't allow knives or any other such implements in the school. And if you, Mr. and Mrs. Singh, could make sure our young brave here does not arm himself for school in the future I will be very grateful. He could have hurt another child, and matters could have become very serious, very serious indeed."

Jasbeer's teacher, still looking uncomfortable, followed them out of the office. "I am so sorry, Mrs. Singh, Mr. Singh. But I *couldn't* allow Jasbeer to bring a weapon into school. I hope you understand." It was clear that the meeting had been an extremely awkward one for her.

"Yes, yes we understand." Bibi-ji smiled wearily.

"He is a bright boy otherwise," she continued. "A very smart boy, with great potential."

"Thank you." Bibi-ji felt a glow of pride, even though she suspected the teacher said this to all the parents. She watched Jasbeer give his teacher a winsome smile, his eyes bright with mischief, and looked at him sternly. But what a handsome ladykiller of a boy he was, this child who had been granted to her by the generosity of Wahe-guru, Ooper-Wallah, The One Who Knew Everything.

Once they were out of the school, Pa-ji loosened his tie and ripped it off. He shrugged out of his jacket. He slapped Jasbeer on the back. "That's my boy," he said. "He is a Punjabi lion all right, he has the right instincts. I hope you showed that Jason or whatever his name was, a lesson, eh? What, putthar? You want to join the army, enh? Like who, tell me?"

"Like Theka Singh, like Udham Singh who taught General Dwyer a lesson, like . . ." Jasbeer shouted, swaggering behind Pa-ji as they walked to the car.

Phat! A large hand landed on his back. It was Bibi-ji, who was bringing up the rear. "Bas, bas, this is not your British-times story, this is Canada! No more of this war nonsense, you understand? And you"–Bibi-ji rolled past Jasbeer and tapped Pa-ji's back a little harder than was comfortable as she waited for him to open the car door and then lowered herself into the front passenger seat– "you stop encouraging the boy with all this nonsense, understand? Keep your soldiers and martyrs inside your stories and books. This boy is going to get an education. I promised his parents that. And he is to become a lawyer. Or a doctor. Maybe an engineer. And you better listen to me, Jasbeer, otherwise you know what will happen?"

"Yes, Bibi-ji." Jasbeer settled into the back of the car fully aware that, whatever their differences, Bibi-ji's anger was a temporary thing and would dissolve like mist in the sunshine of her love for him. "You will beat me until I'm inside out." Jasbeer leaned over and kissed her neck, knowing that she would never lay a hand on him hard enough to really hurt. "So hard that I'll fly to Timbuctu."

"Good, don't forget that for one instant. And your Pa-ji also will get what he deserves if he puts any more of these stupid ideas into your head. Did you hear, Mister Khushwant Singh?"

"Bak-bak-bak, that's all she knows to do." But Pa-ji didn't get any further into the argument—as Lalloo had so often pointed out, in the interests of domestic harmony sometimes it was wise to lose.

As they drove down Main Street, Bibi-ji noticed how much busier it had become since they had moved here all those years ago. Two blocks from their restaurant was Majid the Barber, the red and white striped pole outside his shop glistening with new paint. A jewellery store had opened across the road, and Lalloo had opened a travel agency beside it—a shrewd move, it turned out, as there was never a shortage of desis waiting to buy cheap tickets to India. After much thought he had named it Far Out Travels, and the customers had poured in almost from the first week. Farther on were two new grocery stores competing with Mrs. Wu's, but all three shops appeared to have a healthy flow of customers. Lalloo had been right after all, Bibi-ji reflected—location was everything.

They passed the Bhats' home. Bibi-ji wondered whether she ought to consult Leela on bringing up Jasbeer—Preethi was such a dependable child. Arjun seemed a little moody, but he never got into trouble at school, the way Jas did. The car stopped in their driveway just as the mailman trampled across her lawn and leapt over her prize roses to get to her neighbour's.

"Oy!" she shouted, waving her arm wildly out of the window. After all the trouble she took, feeding her roses with tea, crushed eggshells, manure . . . But the mailman was too quick for her and already two houses down the road by the time she was out of the car.

Grumbling to herself, she pulled a sheaf of envelopes out of the mailbox, shuffled through them and sighed at the sight of a flimsy aerogram, a corner of which was covered with Indian stamps. Nimmo again. Bibi-ji would have to complete that letter soon.

"Can I go over to Preethi's?" Jasbeer asked, seeing that Bibi-ji was distracted.

He felt a clip on his ear. Bibi-ji wasn't that distracted, it appeared. "You are *not* going anywhere, putthar," she said, hauling him into the house. "You are going to write a letter to me—three pages—telling me why it is not a good thing to take weapons to school. In running hand."

"But—"

"No buts. You will go up to your room and write me that letter. Are you listening to me?"

Sulky scuffing of shoes on her favourite carpet. Frothing resentment inside the eleven-year-old breast. "Yes."

"Listening with *both* ears?"

"*Yes!*"

No more indulgence, she reminded herself. And, above all, she would have to keep reminding Pa-ji: no more *history*. She tore open Nimmo's letter, and a photograph fell out. Nimmo and Satpal with their two younger children. "Jasbeer, come here and look at what your mother has sent," Bibi-ji called.

Jasbeer stopped at the foot of the stairs but did not turn around. "What?" he asked sullenly.

"Come and see," Bibi-ji said. "It's a photo of your family."

Without a word, Jasbeer stamped up the stairs. Bibi-ji bit her lip and stared after him. Then she began to read the letter. Nimmo and Satpal yearned to see their son. When would Bibi-ji be able to bring him to India?

Bibi-ji walked into the kitchen and was greeted by the familiar chorus of gossiping voices and blaring television. She settled down at the table to finish the letter she had started writing to Nimmo two days ago. *"We have just returned home from a meeting with Jasbeer's schoolteacher, who says that he is a bright boy with great promise. I know that you will be proud to hear this. But you will see for yourself how smart your son is when we come there in December this year."*

THIRTEEN

THE SMALL JOYS

—

New Delhi

March 1971

A hot morning in March. The gulmohur trees were in full bloom, the flowers like flames against the silver sky. Nimmo stood at the side of the road, as she had done for so many years, and watched Pappu trot down the alley.

"Be careful when you cross the road," she called, and her son, taller and thinner at nine, turned around and waved. Nimmo thought of other mornings when two little boys had made their way to school, and her heart clenched with pain. What was Jasbeer doing at this very moment, she wondered? She wanted to see him so badly. A letter had arrived from Bibi-ji two months ago with news about how well he was doing at school, but there was nothing from the boy. Nimmo suspected that all was not as wonderful as Bibi-ji made it out to be, but was nevertheless pleased to hear that Jasbeer would be home in December.

She continued to watch Pappu until he merged into the many tributaries of people emptying on to the main road. A small truck backed up towards her, and she moved aside hastily. The general election campaign was in full swing, and every day brought another truck with yet another political party's posters and banners. The city's walls were plastered with them. They hung down from trees and were strung across narrow streets from upper-storey window bars. *Garibi Hatao!*—Remove Poverty, urged Indira Gandhi's party banners. *Indira Hatao!* shouted her opponents' banners, urging the public, with equal fervour, to remove Indira instead. Nimmo smiled at the wordplay and returned to her house. There was no doubt in her mind who she would vote for. She loved Mrs. Gandhi for her stubborn strength, her refusal to be pushed aside by all the powerful men who surrounded her in cabinet and in the opposition parties, and for the sense that she gave to women across the country that if she could survive so could they. They could survive anything at all and triumph, it just needed conviction and persistence. Nimmo had already cast her vote.

As she re-entered her home, Satpal emerged from the bedroom carrying their three-year-old daughter, Kamal.

"Here, hold her," he said, handing the child to Nimmo. "She won't let me put her down."

"You've spoilt her by picking her up all the time, and

now it's become a habit." She nuzzled the little girl's face and said, "Your daddy has spoilt you, hasn't he?" She put the child down on the ground and said firmly, "Come, let's have some milk and halwa, okay?"

The child nodded and toddled towards the kitchen, where she settled down on the floor and crossed her plump legs. Nimmo sat in front of her and fed her small balls of sweet semolina halwa, making sure there was a raisin in each mouthful.

Satpal gathered his lunch box and his raincoat. "Will you be at home this afternoon? Or is this the day you teach at the gurudwara?"

Their temple had started a small nursery school and Nimmo volunteered as a teacher there twice a week. She liked the change in her routine, and Kamal enjoyed playing with the other children.

"No, not today," Nimmo said. "Why? Are you coming home for lunch?"

"Perhaps," Satpal replied mysteriously.

"Then why are you taking your lunch box?" Nimmo asked.

"Just in case I can't come home." He grinned, and for a moment Nimmo thought he looked like Jasbeer used to when he was up to mischief.

"Well, I have to go to the Ram-Leela field at five o'clock. If you come home while I am away, get the keys from Kaushalya's house," Nimmo said.

"You are going to listen to your Indira Gandhi again?"

"Yes, today she is giving an election speech. Everyone is going. You should also come to this one."

"Sunny was telling me that she is creating a lot of trouble in Punjab," Satpal said. "People are getting angry there. All these politicians play games with us and we, like fools, keep voting for them again and again. She takes away our river water and gives it to Rajasthan, she cuts up Punjab and creates a Haryana for the Hindus, and now she is planning to give them Chandigarh as well. That city belongs to Punjab. First it was Partition and half our land disappeared. Now our own leaders are chopping it up like a piece of meat. How much more are we supposed to give away? Without Punjab this country would be starving, and look how we are treated—like stepchildren! Is it fair?"

"Oof-oh! Why do you listen to that nephew of yours? Why, even Manpreet said that he is hot-headed, always in trouble these days. Now what mother would malign her son like that unless it was true? He failed his first year of college, you know. And you are a Delhi-wallah, why are you concerned with matters in Punjab? You have never even lived there." Nimmo held a glass of milk against Kamal's lips, urging her to sip at it.

"What are you saying? I could be living on the moon and still Punjab would be my heartland. And should be yours too, more than mine. You were born there."

Nimmo wiped her daughter's mouth with the end of her dupatta and said firmly, "*This* is my heartland. This house, this gully, this city. Nowhere else." She got to her feet. "So do you want me to wait for you this evening?"

"No, yes, I will see. Don't forget to leave the keys with the neighbours, though," Satpal said. "Go and listen to that woman tell her lies! *Garibi Hatao*, she will shout, and we will all cheer and vote for her. And then a week later, poverty will still be found in these gullies, and there will still be no water in the taps or electric current in our homes and it will go on and on. You will see, mark my words!"

That afternoon at around two-thirty, soon after Nimmo had convinced Kamal to take a nap, she heard a hubbub outside. She went to the window to see what was going on. A small tempo-truck was parked on the road, and Satpal was supervising its unloading. Something large—it looked like a cupboard of some sort. Nimmo opened the front door. Ever since the birth of their daughter, Satpal seemed to have thrown caution and thrift to the winds, seemed to have forgotten that they still owed Bibi-ji a large sum of money, still had uneven returns from their mechanic's shop. Last year he had bought a refrigerator that often dripped water on the floor, thanks to the frequent power failures in the summer months. If Satpal had to buy something, why didn't he put down a deposit for a telephone? She didn't like going over to Asha's to receive calls from Bibi-ji or Satpal.

She moved aside as the men staggered in carrying an enormous steel cupboard wrapped loosely in corrugated cardboard and plastic sheeting.

They shouted contradictory orders at each other. "Lower it! Watch the doorway!" "Raise it, mind the floor!" Kamal woke up startled, and Nimmo hurried her out of the way. "Why couldn't you have told me that this was why you were coming home?" she said, annoyed. "I could have gone next door with her."

Satpal grinned unrepentantly, his eyes shining with excitement. "I wanted to surprise you," he said. "Now move, woman, this is going in there."

After the delivery men had gone, Nimmo circled the khakhi green–painted steel almirah, stroking a finger across the manufacturer's name, set in stylishly raised silvery steel lettering across the top corner, and wondered at how smoothly the handle turned down to reveal the enormous inside with its heavy shelves, its small locker right on top, the space for hanging clothes. She had seen advertisements for it in the newspapers—*Buy a Godrej, Feel Safe for Life*—but had not thought she would ever own one. At six feet it was a big cupboard, taller than Satpal, and it covered most of the wall. A person could stand inside it when the shelves were removed. It smelled cold.

"Very secure!" said Satpal, knocking his knuckles against the thick green-painted steel. "Very safe."

"What shall I do with such a big cupboard? How much did it cost?"

"I'll take care of the cost. You can start filling it with things for Kamal's wedding."

"Wedding? Are you mad? She is three! And she gets an education before a husband—you promised me that."

"Then start saving money for her college," said Satpal, a little annoyed by her lack of enthusiasm.

After he had left, Nimmo went outside to bring the laundry in the house before heading to the maidan for the speech. She pretended not to notice Asha, who peered over their shared wall.

"Arrey, Nimmo, you got an almirah today?" Asha asked. As usual, her voice was tinged with envy. One day, Nimmo was sure, Asha's constant envy would puncture the fragile bubble of her happiness.

"Yes Asha, we got an almirah," she said, hiding her annoyance. "But I don't know what I will do with it. As you know, I have nothing to put in a steel cupboard, nothing to hide or protect." *Except my children, my happiness, my life.*

"Everyone has something to hide, Nimmo," Asha replied. "And your husband must be doing well to be able to buy such an expensive thing! So maybe you will have lots of jewellery to put in there soon?"

"I don't have any now, if that is what you are asking, Asha," Nimmo said, her voice sharper than she had intended it to be.

"Baba, why should *I* ask anything? Why should *I* care what you have or don't have? Hunh!" Asha pulled the pallu of her sari over her head with unnecessary violence, her bangles jangling.

"Why speak only of me, Asha?" Nimmo continued. She remembered how superstitious Asha was about her own family. "I hear that your husband is getting very wealthy. I hear that he has many important political friends helping him rise in the world!"

"Wealthy? Us? Never! We barely manage to keep this roof over our heads!" Asha clicked her fingers over herself to ward off evil and disappeared indoors before Nimmo could say anything further about her prosperity and bring down jealous spirits.

Kaushalya's head appeared over the other wall as soon as Asha's had disappeared. "Baap-re-baap, the nosy parker spends the whole day watching who is doing what. When does she do her own work, I wonder?"

Asha's face popped back, like a cuckoo from a clock, ready for an argument. "I heard you, Kaushalya!" she shouted. "Spreading rumours about me, I heard you!"

Nimmo paid the vendor and slipped into the sanctuary of her home. She peeked into the bedroom to make sure that Kamal was not up to any mischief, and then went to the kitchen to start preparations for the evening meal before heading to the maidan to hear the prime minister's speech.

The afternoon sun was beginning to lose its intensity and a welcome breeze dried the sweat on Nimmo's face as she pushed her way through the crowds that had arrived to hear Indira Gandhi. The enormous field was already crammed with bodies, and it was with some difficulty that Nimmo and her companions found a space for themselves. This was largely because Nimmo had insisted on finding a spot near the exit gates, where the policemen were stationed.

"If something happens," she said, preparing as always for every catastrophe imaginable, "we can run out fast and the police will be nearby also."

Kaushalya laughed at her fears. "Nimmo, you are always worrying about something. One day at least leave all your fears at home and relax!"

Nimmo's face tightened stubbornly. "If you want you can go and sit up front. I'm staying here with my daughter," she said firmly, holding Kamal close. All she knew was that they were in the middle of a crowd of about fifty thousand people and that crowds were unpredictable— they could go berserk with joy or anger, it didn't matter which. Look at the tragedy at the Kumbh Mela last year— a million people celebrating a holy event, and for some little thing there was a stampede, killing hundreds. This was a country of excesses, and Nimmo was determined not to be a victim ever again.

She sat there for an hour listening to Mrs. Gandhi's nasal, strident voice echoing and whistling through the loudspeakers set up all over the field, outlining her plans to eradicate poverty, to raise literacy, to improve the lives of the people of the country. She had heard versions of the same speech before and knew there was truth to what Satpal had said about a politician's worthless promises.

And yet, there was something about the tiny figure draped in a sari on that stage, the leader of one of the largest and most confusing countries in the world, that moved Nimmo unutterably. She admired Indira Gandhi, she thought tearfully, she adored her, she would vote for her always. Perhaps someday her Kamal would also become prime minister. At that moment, surrounded as she was by thousands of rapt faces, the lights of the city flickering to life as dusk descended and promises echoing all around, everything seemed possible.

FOURTEEN

INTERLUDE

—

Vancouver

October 1971

October flew in on the back of a cold wind laden with regret for another year's ending. Front yards sprouted scarecrows, bats and ghosts cut out from black and white cardboard, witch's hats were propped up on poles and cobwebs were sprayed on to bushes. Bright orange pumpkins of all sizes sat on doorsteps grinning crookedly, waiting for dusk, when their black eyes would light up with the glow of candles. Trees shook their nude branches at the solemn Vancouver sky, and on the ground leaves rustled and whispered and occasionally lifted and whirled like brightly garbed dervishes. It rained briefly and the leaves settled into heaps of muddled wetness. A puddle glinted like an uneven silver coin on the dark road out-side the house.

Leela stood at the kitchen sink washing dishes. It was a day off from her job at The Bay, where she worked in the shoe department. Her neighbour Elena, the white-haired woman who had smiled at Leela the morning she had first arrived in Vancouver, and with whom she had devel-oped a warm friendship, was a manager at the depart-ment store and had suggested she apply there when a vacancy had come up three years ago. Leela enjoyed the days she worked there, and the company of the other salesgirls, especially Erin, a pretty blonde with large, sad eyes, who wiped the cash desk clean repeatedly with a mixture of vinegar and water. She had long, beautiful hands of which she was very proud and which she kept soft by applying cream from a tube in her purse every hour. Erin had showed Leela around the store, covered up for her when she made mistakes and generally made her feel less of a foreigner and a stranger. In the early days, before Leela learned to deal with rude or demand-ing customers herself, it was Erin who unobtrusively managed the situation.

"She's like One of Us," Leela had told Balu at the end of her first month at work. "Exactly like."

She finished the dishes and moved to the service counter separating the tiny kitchen from the living-cum-dining room, carefully balancing her knife, the cutting board and a bowl of vegetables. From there she had a clear view of Arjun moping on the battered couch in front of the television. Now fourteen years old, he was a lanky boy, with long hair curling around his ears and down his forehead, partially obscuring his thin face.

The front door banged open and Preethi, a small, round and confident ten-year-old, came in, followed by three other children—Matt, who lived next door, Jasbeer and Wendy Wu. Leela looked up from the dishes and smiled at the chorus of greetings—*Hello Mrs. Bhat, Hi Aunty-ji, Hello Mrs. Bhat*—and the thud of feet as the four friends made their way up to Preethi's room. At least *one* of her children appeared to have slipped into life here with wild enthusiasm, Leela thought. She guiltily remembered her initial antagonism towards the Chinese, and now here was Wendy, her daughter's best friend. Preethi had met her in Mrs. Wu's shop the first time Bibi-ji had taken Leela there to buy vegetables. But the two girls had not spoken until school started and they found themselves in the same class. The friendship, Leela discovered from Preethi, had been sealed when Wendy offered Preethi candy from the stash she always carried in her school bag and, in exchange, received a marble that Preethi had stolen from Arjun. Leela and Wendy's mother, Linda Wu, had also established a friendship based on their mutual scorn of the Canadian education system.

"No math, no sentence formation, no spelling, what kind of education?" Leela demanded, as she and Linda waited outside the classroom for their daughters to emerge.

"Only play, play, play," Linda agreed. "No homework. No classwork. Play play play!"

"Phonetic spelling!" Leela said with disgust. "Spell any way, and then learn later how to do it right! What kind of thing is this? When we were children . . ." And so they went, the two women, happily dissecting western ways, agreeing that whether Chinese or Indian, the eastern way was best in the end, worrying about their children's abilities compared with those of the genius kids back home.

And then, in 1968, Jasbeer had joined Preethi's group, a year older than them all, tall, lost, awkward and inarticulate at first, unable to understand anything the three children said to him because the only languages he knew were Hindi and Punjabi. But in the way of children, whose minds and tongues and hearts are malleable, Jasbeer learned swiftly enough, although he still seemed to Leela an intense boy given to dark moods.

She raised her head and listened to the sounds coming from Preethi's room above for a minute or two, and was reassured by the muffled laughter. A little more than four years had passed since she had stepped into this house. The phone book that had seemed such a catalogue of strangers that first day was now crowded with friends and acquaintances: the Singhs of course, the Majumdars, Elena from next door, Matt's parents Brian and Cathy, other Indians scattered around Vancouver, her colleagues at The Bay, Balu's colleagues, Wendy's mother . . . the list went on. The Indians especially were now her family, Leela thought affectionately. As for her children, they must be grateful for the number of Aunties and Uncles they had acquired since their arrival here.

"What are you watching, Arjun?" Leela asked, looking over at her son.

"Nothing."

"What do you mean, *nothing?* Obviously it is something that you are watching. It looks like *The Brady Bunch.* Is it?"

"So if you know what I'm watching, why are you asking me?" Arjun demanded.

"I was just . . . never mind. Did you finish your lunch?" Mundane details were comforting. They could be answered with a simple yes or no, could make Leela feel she was still in control, could still take care of her children. Are you hungry, are you sleepy, did you brush your teeth, do you need money for bus fare? Any other topic took her into the pre-adolescent's territory, a place that seemed to be filled with nebulous, lurking disasters, sourceless anger, confused sadness, all those depthless rivers of emotion that Arjun had to traverse before reaching the larger confusion of adulthood.

"Yes, Amma, I ate my lunch," Arjun replied. "Now will you leave me alone?"

He rarely went out, Leela thought fearfully; he seemed to have no friends. Leela had snooped in his room, checked his schoolbag and his trouser pockets; for traces of what, she wasn't entirely sure. She knew Arjun's unhappiness as soon as it began. But the searching told her little about the reason for his present melancholy.

Her anger with Balu for bringing them here flared—if he hadn't, she would not have had to get a job, she would have been at home round the clock keeping an eye on her children, she would have had her mother-in-law to share her worries. At the thought of the old lady, Leela's mood became even darker. Six months ago, a telegram had arrived from Vimala urging Balu to come home immediately as his mother had suffered a stroke and was not expected to last much longer. Balu had left for Bangalore, reaching the city only a day before the old lady died. It hurt Leela that she and the children had not been able to afford to fly back home to see her one last time.

She set the vegetables to cook on the stove and joined Arjun in front of the television to watch a program about death rituals in ancient civilizations. She felt absurdly happy when she drew him close to her and he made no protest, not even when she stroked the hair off his forehead. Her moment of peace came to an end as three pairs of feet clattered down the stairs and hurried out of the door. A moment later Preethi came down and flung herself on the couch. "What are you watching?" she demanded.

"An educational program," Leela said, thinking that television had some advantages. "About Egyptian death rituals."

"Why did they make such a fuss?" Arjun muttered. He yawned and pretended boredom even though he had been watching intently enough before his sister's arrival. "What does it *matter* what happens to you after you die?"

"Of course it matters!" Leela squeezed her son's bony shoulder gently. "I hope you will do all the correct rituals for me when I die."

"Amma, I don't want you to die," Preethi said, wrapping her arms around her mother's body.

"Everyone has to die *some*time," Leela replied. "But I won't go for a long, long while yet, I promise. Not until you are an old lady yourself." She kissed each forehead and hugged her children closer. "Although, when Yama the Death God comes for me, I want all the ceremonies," she said firmly. "I want to be cremated with wood from the mango trees in the grove behind our house in Bangalore. And don't forget a small piece of sandalwood to scent my journey."

"Like they did for Ajji?" Preethi asked.

"Yes."

"I miss her, Amma."

"So do I, baby," Leela said.

"And what if the Death God cannot find his way to you here in Canada? What if he doesn't have a map of the world?" Arjun joked.

"That's why I'm saying I have to go home to die. No confusion and lost roads for Yama-raja." Leela hugged both her children to her again. She would never let them forget that other place, home. They would soon be returning, and until then it was her duty to keep it alive in their minds. She would show them the photo albums that she had carried away with her and say to them: *This is the house that Rama Bhat built. This is the ghost that lives in the house that Rama Bhat built. This is the swing that hangs from the tree in the house that Rama Bhat built.*

Beside her Preethi sat up excitedly. "Amma, can I go dressed as Yama tonight? Can I, Amma? It'll be so cool!"

"Go? Where?" Leela asked, confused.

"Today's Halloween, remember?" Preethi reminded her. "Everyone's going—Jas and Matt and Wendy. So can I?"

"Yes you can, but not as Yama. It might be an insult to him," Leela said firmly.

"Then what should I wear?" Preethi asked in a resigned voice. She knew that Leela did not believe in wasting money on costumes. One year she had been a monster in a Rajasthani sheet with green elephants running around brown and black lotuses and roses and other flowers—an exotic monster, her mother assured her. The next year she was a garbage-bag monster.

Leela stood up and looked thoughtfully at her diminutive daughter, so like her in build and appearance, but with Balu's brown eyes.

"I know!" she exclaimed. She went to the kitchen, rummaged around in one of the cupboards and emerged triumphantly with a box of aluminum foil. She pushed Preethi into a chair and wrapped some foil around her head. She extended one long piece and twisted a few more bits about it so that it stuck out like the spout of a teapot. Then she went to the shoe cupboard and pulled out an unopened box. It contained a pair of gaudy silver slippers—Bibi-ji would love them, Leela thought—that she had bought for Preethi because they were eighty percent off. Preethi had flatly refused to wear them, and they had lain in the back of the cupboard ever since.

"Here, put these on," Leela said.

"What am I supposed to be?" Preethi asked, surveying herself in the hallway mirror, resigned to her mother's parsimony.

"I don't know. How about a saucepan? Yes, that's it, you are a saucepan. And do you remember the rules?"

"Yes, Amma."

"Tell me?"

"Don't leave the street, don't enter people's houses, don't leave the group, don't eat anything until I come home and show you what I got."

Restricted zones and Lines of Control were applied firmly. It seemed to Leela that the edges of a ten-year-old's life were as fraught with danger as that of a country at war.

"Good girl!" Leela said. "You will be only on this street?"

"Yes, I promise, Amma. Nowhere else."

"Hand on my head? What will happen if you break your promise?"

"You will die and I will be dragged off to hell."

"*I* will die, that's all. This hell-well is Christian business, I don't know all that. *I* will die and you will have to pay for it in your next birth. And most important of all, if someone tries to touch you anywhere at all, scream and run away, understand?" She looked sharply at her daughter.

"Yes, Amma," said Preethi. "Now can I go, *please?*"

At that moment there was a banging on the front door. Leela opened it and walked her saucepan daughter out to meet Bibi-ji with Jas dressed as Frankenstein in tow, and a rather solid Matt as a spaceman.

"And what are you supposed to be, Preethi?" Bibi-ji asked, touching the foil wound around the girl's head.

"My mother says I am a saucepan," Preethi said.

"Oh, I see," Bibi-ji said, suppressing a smile.

"Well, I am not going to waste money on a costume," Leela declared.

"I agree," Bibi-ji replied. "But Pa-ji insists on getting the boy something new every year. He says it is to help him settle in better. I don't understand it, though. Jasbeer has to dress like a monster and go knocking on doors to settle in?"

The three children bunched together to give each other confidence, and clutching their pillowcases they headed next door to Elena's.

"Look at them," Bibi-ji said. "So sweet they look, no, Leela?"

"Yes, they do," Leela agreed, gazing after the children with equal fondness.

"But your Preethi is a good girl. My Jasbeer is always in trouble. I am so tired of seeing that principal, Mr. Longbottom, every other week."

"Passing phase, Bibi-ji. Don't worry," comforted Leela. "He will grow out of it. Arjun is also going through the same thing. Not in trouble at school, but so quiet, no friends, you know?"

"That's what you said last year also, Leela. When is this passing phase going to pass?" Bibi-ji asked plaintively.

"I think part of the problem—and don't mind my saying this, Bibi-ji—is that you spoil him," Leela said, looking severely at her friend. "You buy him too many things—everything he demands—regardless of whether he has been good or not. He does not have a sense that his actions have consequences."

"I know, I know. I can't seem to help it. But the presents, that's Pa-ji's fault. He likes buying things for the people he loves. I have told him a hundred times, but will he listen to me? No, not at all." She jingled her keys and then said, "Perhaps it is inside the boy, something he was born with and that we cannot change."

"His *uyir*," Leela said.

"And what's that?" Bibi-ji asked.

"A Tamil word—it refers to something a person's soul has brought with it from a distant place in the universe— not inherited from the parents, nor acquired from the place, or the food, or air, or earth, or water even. *Uyir* is the mystery in every one of us, the thing that makes us move and grow, the thing that makes us alive. Sometimes this *uyir* is good and sometimes it is made bad. It all depends on the circumstances and the position of the stars at birth. *Maybe*."

Bibi-ji nodded and was silent for a few moments. Then she jingled her keys again and said, "Well then, Leela. I hope and pray that my Jasbeer's *uyir* isn't bad."

"Don't worry, Bibi-ji," Leela said, touching her friend's arm. "He will be fine. Believe me."

She walked Bibi-ji to her car and waved as she drove slowly down the road, looking for the three children. As she did each year, she would follow them to make sure they did not get into any trouble and then drive them home for cake and milk.

Back inside the house Leela descended to the base-ment, her India, where the fragrance of incense lingered in the still air, the water pipes had been camouflaged by a false ceiling and the unfinished walls were draped with an assortment of colourful cotton bedcovers. Her gods were waiting for her there, their silver faces impassive as she rang a small silver bell loudly to catch their attention—to summon Brahma back from wherever he was busy writing fates on newborn foreheads, to wake Vishnu from his eternal slumber, to get Shiva to stop his dallying with Parvathi and listen to her, Leela Bhat, wife of Balachandra Bhat of Bangalore. She offered the obligatory flowers (a couple of clematis blossoms, a blue mop-head hydrangea) and fruit purchased the previous day from Mrs. Wu's shop, lit a fresh stick of incense and went on the offensive. "Why?" she demanded. "Why are you making my son so unhappy? Have I not taken care of you? Have I not prayed to you twice a day every day of my life? And is this how you reward me for my faith?"

She wept some, she grumbled some more, she flattered the movers and shakers of heaven, and earth, and purgatory and all the unseen places between Here and There. Then, satisfied that she had laid her case before them as best she could, she returned up the stairs to the other world, with its battered and borrowed sofas, the chattering television, the print of a Degas dancer hanging lopsided on one wall and the batik print of a busty Bharat Natyam dancer striking a challenging pose on the opposite wall. Arjun was sprawled where she had left him, but it seemed to her that her swift appeal to the gods had wrought a change in his demeanour. He was smiling at the television screen, which cast blue spasms of light on the walls, and Leela was content. The gods were on her side after all.

FIFTEEN

THE WRITING ON THE WALL

—

New Delhi

November 1971

"More refugees from East Pakistan coming into Calcutta," Satpal announced, shaking out his newspaper and folding it in half. He continued to read the news out loud while Nimmo, working in the kitchen, listened with one ear. Earlier that year, in March, after Mrs. Gandhi had swept into power on a thundering majority, East Pakistan had declared itself the independent nation of Bangladesh. Immediately, the animosity that had been simmering between East and West Pakistan exploded into all-out war. For the better part of that year millions of refugees had crossed over from East Pakistan into India.

"Indira Gandhi is ordering Pakistan to stop massacring

its citizens," Satpal said. "Why is she poking her long nose into other peoples' affairs?"

"Arrey, how can any decent human being stand by and watch murders taking place? She is doing the right thing, our Indira-ji," said Nimmo staunchly.

"Even the USA is not saying anything," Satpal replied.

"They never say anything to massacres in other countries, only when it affects their own interests."

Satpal looked up, appreciating his normally quiet wife's shrewd political sense, but shook his head. On this matter he could not agree with her. Indira Gandhi should keep her head down, stay out of this matter, send those Pakistani refugees back where they came from. As if India did not have enough people! As if they did not have urgent needs, more important than war. If there was another war with Pakistan, as the rumours went, black-market profiteering would start, prices of necessary commodities like petrol, kerosene, sugar, rice and wheat would certainly go up and business would come down. "War might be good for your Madam Gandhi's image," he said. "But for people like you and me it is bad. It is always bad."

He shook the newspaper and went into the bedroom to deal with his accounts. In the room he had just left, the children started a quarrel. Busy in the kitchen, Nimmo ignored their shrill bickering until Kamal set up a loud wail. Nimmo could stand it no longer.

"Stop it, both of you!" she yelled, brandishing the rolling pin that had so far yielded a stack of ten parathas. "Pappu, leave your sister alone."

"I'm not doing anything!" grumbled Pappu. "She won't let me do my homework. She took my pencil." He swatted at his sister with a rolled-up notebook, and Kamal screamed louder.

Nimmo called to Satpal, "Ji, what are you doing? Can't you take care of these children?"

Satpal left the pile of bills he had been poring over and, picking up Kamal, gave her a look of mock ferocity. She was his undisputed pet, and he could never scold her. "Why were you bothering your older brother?"

"Daddy, he won't give me a pencil," Kamal complained, making her eyes round and innocent.

"Why didn't you come to me, instead of disturbing Pappu?" Satpal asked. He sat her firmly in one corner with paper and another pencil, and peace was restored in the small house. Nimmo smiled as she spun the rolling pin over the last of the parathas and thought of the letter that had recently arrived from Bibi-ji. Jasbeer continued to do well. He would definitely be here in December, when his school was closed for the Christmas holidays. He had many friends. He missed his parents but had settled into a routine. His teacher at school thought he had the makings of a lawyer, perhaps a doctor. Maybe even an engineer.

Nimmo was torn between pride at her son's accomplishments—unaware that they were mostly the product of Bibi-ji's guilty imagination—and anger with herself for having yielded him to Bibi-ji so quickly. She recalled his one visit home and her pain when he had insisted on returning with Bibi-ji—it had broken her heart, but she told herself again and again that that it was the best thing for him—a solid education, a safe, stable life, none of the distractions that her other children had here, crammed into this tiny house, with power cuts every day, and water problems.

"It is like those rich people who send their children to boarding school so that they can get the best education," Satpal had comforted her. "For us it is even better—he is the only child at your aunt's 'boarding school'!"

But there were many dark moments when Nimmo twisted the knife in her own heart, telling herself she had sold her son, wondering whether Jasbeer was really okay, if he was still angry with her for sending him away.

Her thoughts were rudely interrupted when Pappu let out a triumphant shout: "Mummy, look at what Kamal is doing!"

"Kamal, what are you doing?" Nimmo demanded wearily.

"Nothing," Kamal replied, pressing up against the wall and looking guilty.

"She drew with her pencils on the wall," Pappu said with a virtuous expression.

Nimmo lost her temper then, thoroughly. She pulled Kamal to her feet and smacked her bottom. "You naughty girl!" she yelled. "I clean this house all day long, I try to make it look nice and you behave like a junglee!"

Kamal burst into tears, and the uproar brought Satpal out of the bedroom again. "*Now* what's going on?" he asked.

Nimmo looked fiercely at Satpal. "Look at what this wretched girl has done to the wall!" She pointed an accusing finger at the scribble of stick figures running up the white wall and again whacked Kamal, who dodged neatly away and took shelter behind her father's legs. Nimmo's hand swept through thin air.

Satpal tried not to grin but couldn't help it. He pulled the child to him and said soothingly to Nimmo, "What a big fuss over nothing! All it needs is a bit of choona. We have to whitewash this house anyway . . ."

"And after that, if this nuisance child draws on it again? Still you will pet her and spoil her?" Nimmo was unwilling to give up her anger.

Satpal lifted Kamal and held her so that their eyes were level. "Listen carefully, my princess: one more time I see this drawing business on the wall and I will be very angry also, you understand?"

That night, in bed, after the children had gone to sleep, Satpal said, "I think this house is getting too small for us."

Nimmo was aghast. "I don't want to move," she blurted out. This was home, she felt safe here. In spite of Asha.

"Who said anything about moving? We can't afford a new house. No, I was thinking we could add another room upstairs. For Pappu, and for when Bibi-ji comes again with Jasbeer."

"Oh no!" Nimmo said involuntarily.

"What? You don't want more space?"

"No, I mean yes, I do. It's just that that stupid Asha will go on and on and on about it. She will put the evil eye on us, I know it, with her jealousy."

"Why do you let that woman bother you so much, Nimmo?" Satpal murmured sleepily. "Let her say what she wants. This is our life, we will do what we want."

Yes, brooded Nimmo, gazing at the square of night sky outlined by the window, cut into dark slices by the bars, each with its sprinkling of stars. Yes, it was her life. But there were hundreds of people like Asha out there who were willing to tear it into little bits for no particular reason. She would rather stay in a small, crowded place and attract no comment than invite Asha's jealousy with another room. She feared that envious gaze for who knew what miseries it might invoke.

The following Saturday the children were sent to spend the day at a cousin's house, and Satpal's friend Harnam arrived with pots of whitewash.

"How long is this going to take?" Nimmo asked. She had moved all their belongings to the middle of each room and covered them with sheets of plastic.

"Don't worry, sister," Harnam said. "I will do the outside walls and Satpal will work on the inside. We should be done by evening."

At noon they stopped and Harnam went home for lunch and a brief nap, promising to return in an hour. Satpal continued painting. Nimmo watched his bare back as he worked away at the walls, wishing she hadn't made quite such a fuss over Kamal's drawings. Come to think of it, they were sweet pictures. The child had been drawing her family, and Nimmo had whacked her for it. "Can we leave Kamal's pictures like that?" she asked.

Satpal was astonished. "What? Why am I wasting time painting, then?"

"Did I ask you to paint the walls? You were the one who came up with this idea," Nimmo said defensively.

"You are crazy," Satpal said. "No, I am not leaving that monkey's drawing. And you can help me, instead of standing there and coming up with silly thoughts."

Nimmo giggled. "Me? You want *me* to paint a wall? I don't know how!"

"You know how to read and write and you can't hold a brush and move it on a bare wall? Come, try it!"

Again Nimmo giggled, feeling like a girl. It seemed years since she had had a moment alone with Satpal. It *had* been years! She took the brush from her husband and dabbed the wall ineffectually with it, spattering most of the whitewash on the floor. Satpal came up behind her and gently caught her wrist.

"Like this," he murmured, his breath warm in her ear, teasing the drifts of hair that had worked loose from her braid. He dipped the brush in the can of wash, carefully stroked the excess off on the rim and then, holding her hand still, showed Nimmo how to wield it firmly, smoothly. "Like this, like this," he whispered.

She could smell his sweat; feel the heat of his body against her back, her hips and her thighs. She leaned back slightly, wishing that Harnam would not return. Her heart drummed. With his left hand, Satpal cupped her full breast and teased her nipple through the cloth of her kameez. The brush dropped out of her hand and they both collapsed on the floor, laughing and pulling at each other's clothes.

"I haven't locked the door," Nimmo whispered, pushing Satpal's fumbling hands away from the string of her salwar and undoing it in one quick motion.

"The whole world sleeps in the afternoon," Satpal murmured. He pushed her kameez up and kissed her belly.

"What if Harnam comes back?"

"He must be doing the same thing with his wife," Satpal said. He pushed into her and she spread her hands flat against the wet, newly painted walls, the smell of sex mingling forever in her mind with that of fresh whitewash.

After they had hurriedly cleaned up, only five minutes before Harnam reappeared, Nimmo noticed her handprints on the bottom of the wall—upside down—and beside hers, one of Satpal's as well, right side up.

"Leave it," she said, giving him a shy look when he pointed it out to her with a big grin. "If our children can draw on our walls, why can't we?"

In the following years, the house was whitewashed twice again, but Satpal took care not to erase those handprints; and Nimmo blushed like a bride every time he commented loudly on their existence.

"Look!" he would tell his children. "Look, your poor mother and I had to kneel on the floor and paint the walls. So much trouble!"

And the children would wonder aloud why their mother's handprints were upside down.

And for years, whenever she thought of that day Nimmo felt the same hot rush of desire, the same trembling excitement, followed by a happiness she could barely contain. Even later, the time came when she would sit in the same room, dark and filthy and smelling of death rather than fresh paint, and yet when her eyes landed on those faded handprints, the single large one beside her own two, she would feel a tiny spark of that distant, joyous moment when her husband's body had lain on hers, warm and so very alive.

The Diwali festival came with a flickering of thousands of oil lamps on walls and balconies, verandas and pyols. Although it was a Hindu festival, everyone who lived in the gully celebrated it with equal fervour, forgetting the reason behind it and keeping only the exuberant beauty of it in mind. As she made the sweets for the festival, Nimmo remembered Jasbeer. He used to love letting off the firecrackers in front of their home with dozens of other children from the neighbouring houses.

This year, however, beneath the gaiety, the sombre whisper of war gathered force.

A few months later, on a cold afternoon in early December, the rumours became fact. Satpal returned home bearing rolls of black paper.

"We are at war!" he said with barely suppressed excitement. He had planned to build the extra room for the children that month, but now the city buzzed with talk of war. People huddled together on the streets, blowing into their hands to warm their fingers and fearfully discussing what would be the third war with their neighbour in the twenty-four years since Partition.

"We are at war!" Satpal repeated. He thrust the rolls of paper into Nimmo's startled hands and said, "We must cover

our windows for the blackout. The government has said."
He caught sight of Nimmo's expression. "You are afraid?
No need! We will thrash the Pakistanis, you wait and see!"

Nimmo said nothing. She hated this aspect of his character, his delight in the manly business of war.

Satpal put his fingers to her chin and tilted her face up
as if she were one of the children. "What? Still scared?
I am telling you—"

"I am *not* scared," she said. "I am *angry*. Why do we waste
so much time and money fighting with people? Hanh?"

"But this is a necessary war," Satpal said. He sounded
annoyed by her refusal to join in his excitement. "We are
trying to help those poor Bangladeshis. It is our duty!"

Nimmo turned away, fighting back tears. Silently she
began to cut the black paper to fit the windows. A necessary war, she thought bleakly, snipping hard at the paper.
From whose point of view? she wanted to know. The dead?
The maimed? The orphans and the widows? Another
thought came to her, filling her with disappointment.
Jasbeer would not be able to come home this December
if the war continued for very long. She would write Bibi-ji
an urgent letter advising her to cancel their flight bookings.

That night, as the air-raid sirens screamed, Nimmo went
around the house quickly turning out the electric lights
and lighting the kerosene lanterns. Pappu and Kamal
thought this an exciting game and entertained themselves
by making finger shadows on the freshly whitened walls.
Nimmo reached for Kamal, held her and rocked her gently, thinking, *My children should be spared this adventure.*

"Why don't you read to us from the Guru Granth Sahib?" Satpal asked, his voice strange and loud in the shadowy darkness.

"Yes Mummy, please!" Pappu whispered, bored now of folding his fingers into deer and fox and camel.

Nimmo went to the steel almirah and drew the book from the topmost shelf. She removed the dark blue silk cloth that covered it, kissed it reverently. As she opened it a piece of paper fell from its pages. Pappu reached out and picked up the faded rectangle. It was the postcard from Canada, with Bibi-ji's writing on it.

"What is this, Mummy?" He examined the card. "Is this a picture of a bear? Can I keep it?"

"No!" Nimmo said, louder than she meant to. "No, this is mine."

She slipped the card back into the Guru Granth Sahib. One day she might be able to tell her children about those hidden things inside her head. About a small girl crouching in a barrel of grain and a woman whose dangling feet had smelled of a pale violet soap. She would tell them about fear and hate and loss. In this way she would prepare them for the world and its wickedness. Then they would know what to do if that same world bared its teeth at them.

"It is mine," she repeated. "I have had it since I was a girl, only a little older than Kamal."

SIXTEEN

MAPS, COINS AND FLAGS

—

Vancouver

December 1971

Despite the chill winter drizzle, The Delhi Junction Café was crowded. Not unexpectedly, the talk was about the latest war between India and Pakistan. From his station behind the cash counter, Pa-ji noticed that the two Pakistani regulars, Hafeez and Alibhai, were absent from their usual table. He felt a twinge of regret mixed with anger. Why did they all have to cling so tightly to that other world? Why were they incapable of putting it behind them? Old enmities, ancient sorrows were carried around like the hag who climbed on to the backs of unwary sailors, growing heavier and heavier until the poor sailors, unable to shake her off, dropped dead from exhaustion.

"This is all thanks to the British!" someone shouted from the corner of the room. "They were the ones who divided the Muslims and the Hindus so they could rule, and then left the divisions to destroy both of us—Pakistan and India."

"I don't know why we should give the British credit for everything," Dr. Majumdar grumbled, "from creating wars to creating civilization. Their time in India is ancient history. I think we have a phantom limb problem. We don't have Pakistan as a part of our body anymore but keep feeling the itch and the pain."

"What about Kashmir then?" Harish Shah wanted to know. He mopped his red face, sweating from the many pints of beer he had consumed. "Those Pakistanis are after our Kashmir, na? That's why war after war we are having."

"*This* war isn't about Kashmir," Balu pointed out. "It's about Bangladesh."

"It's about land, it is always about land," said Dr. Majumdar. "As for Kashmir, I agree all our wars always boil down to Kashmir. But I think if we had held a referendum there as promised, things would have been resolved years ago."

"Resolved in *whose* favour?" Shah persisted. "What if the Kashmiris voted to go to Pakistan? What then, Majumdar Sahib? Would you be happy to see the crown of our country lopped off? A headless India?"

The Delhi Junction's front door opened, and Bibi-ji entered to take over the cash counter from Pa-ji. He had to drive to the airport to pick up a Dr. Raghubir Randhawa, who had travelled all the way from Southall, England, and who was reputed to be a Sikh scholar. At the arrival gates, Pa-ji saw that the thin man who emerged through the arrival gates had a cadaverous face, grave, deep-set eyes and a grey beard that cascaded down the front of his white kurta almost to his stomach. His turban, a tall, saffron creation with an ornate steel pin in its front, was different from the smaller ones Pa-ji wore and added to Dr. Randhawa's considerable height. On the drive home, Pa-ji also discovered that his guest had arrived on wings of anger and discontent, for it was promises—broken ones— that had brought him to Vancouver. He had been invited to give a lecture at the Sikh temple, and naturally he was to stay with the Singhs at the Taj Mahal.

But his lecture the following evening was poorly attended; there were only five people in an echoing hall that could accommodate three hundred. Used for weddings and religious ceremonies, the hall featured a low dais at one end, with red drapery hanging on the wall behind it.

Pa-ji and Bibi-ji were there, out of a sense of duty towards their visitor and because Pa-ji considered Dr. Randhawa a fellow historian—and a history lesson was not to be missed. Bibi-ji went out of politeness, although she thought the man a pompous fellow who talked too much. But then, she had a deep-rooted suspicion of anyone who wanted to divide up countries, a theme that seemed to run through everything Raghubir Randhawa said.

Lalloo was present as well, because Pa-ji had forced him to attend. He had brought his six-year-old-son, who spent the hour buzzing about the hall pretending to be a fighter plane. Jasbeer was there for the same reason as Lalloo—Pa-ji had insisted. An old Sikh man, spread out over the last five chairs in the hall, was taking a nap, his snores occasionally rising above Dr. Randhawa's impassioned speech.

The erudite visitor seemed undisturbed by the lack of an audience. Throughout his speech he kept his eyes raised upwards, as if he were appealing directly to the Creator.

"The Sikhs have been betrayed!" he declared in florid Punjabi to the ceiling. "We have been betrayed for two hundred years—first by the British, who stole Punjab that our great Maharaja Ranjit Singh won for us from the Mughals with valour and cunning; then by the Congress Brahmans, who gave the Mussulmans their Pakistan and the Hindus their India but left the Sikhs to die like flies in between; then by Nehru, with the rose in his jacket and his cunning words, who tore our hearts in half by making our Punjab a bilingual state. And now we have been cheated again by the rose-wearing Brahman's daughter, Indira Gandhi, who takes the wheat that we grow on our lands and distributes it to all of Hindustan, who diverts the water from our rivers to neighbouring states and leaves us with empty buckets, who has ordered us to share our capital city, Chandigarh, with the Hindu state of Haryana. We fight their wars for them, give up our young men for the safety of their Hindu lives. *Think* how many soldiers in the Indian army are Sikhs! *Think* how many of us are dying fighting the Pakistanis while the Hindus shiver behind their doors! And then *think* what we Sikhs have got in return for all this endless generosity! A kick, that's all. We have been *betrayed,* I say, and we are fools to sit quietly and take it. We might be in the minority in India, but we have the strength and valour of a majority-sized army! Are we going to continue like this? Are we going to let the Brahman's daughter bleed us to death? Are we lions that roar or mice that hide in holes?" The doctor brought his eyes down from the ceiling to glower at his small audience. "Are we?" he insisted.

"Hear hear!" said Pa-ji, clapping hard.

"Nothing doing!" said Lalloo, who had missed most of the speech because his son had been whispering an elaborate story of planes and ghosts into his left ear.

Jasbeer, on the other hand, listened intently. Dr. Randhawa's diatribe of conquest and betrayal and revenge appealed to him. The older man seemed the epitome of a heroic figure lashing out against greater, darker powers.

"No, indeed, we are not," continued the speaker, satisfied with the feeble response. He lifted his gaze once more to the ceiling. "What we Sikhs must do is press for separation. We demand, at the point of our swords, that the government of India return our Punjab to us, whole and undivided. We demand Khalistan, a land for the Sikhs, the pure and the brave. A country of our own. We demand a return of all that has been taken from us in the past hundred years." His eyes fell on his audience. "And now, if I may, I have some maps of our future country that I wish to display."

At the mention of maps Pa-ji, whose attention had wandered, snapped upright. He loved maps: they were integral to the history of the Sikhs. It was maps that caused countries to exist or expire; maps caused bitter wars, maps erased people and landscapes just as efficiently as they created them. Maps, Pa-ji knew, were a bane *and* a boon. He shook Jasbeer. "Listen, putthar, this is important."

But Jasbeer's eyes were already fixed on the thin figure on the stage, dramatically contrasted with the red drapes behind him.

"This," said Dr. Randhawa, unrolling a map of the kingdom of Punjab under the reign of Maharaja Ranjit Singh, "this is the original land of the Sikhs. It is our body and it has been cut to pieces by everyone—the Mughals, the British, the Mussulmans, the Hindus. We lie bleeding, but we are not dead yet. Arise, warriors, and shout with me, *Our Country or Death!*"

Dr. Randhawa's battle cry was met with uneasy silence, but he was unmoved. He was a politician. Regardless of the reality, he continued to believe every soaring piece of fiction, every half-truth, every fact reconfigured to fit the theories that he conjured up. He placed on top of the map of the kingdom of Punjab another of India and Punjab as they appeared now, and then a third map showing the imagined Independent Country superimposed on the map of India.

Pa-ji stared at this third map. If such a thing happened, there would be many millions more of displaced, misplaced Indians—both Muslims and Hindus would be forced out of the new country. He remembered the conversation at The Delhi Junction earlier that day and

Harish Shah's comment about a headless India. He wondered what the Gujarati doctor would think of Dr. Randhawa's map of India without Punjab, the one that showed Khalistan.

"This will be our country again," Dr. Randhawa was saying, tapping his ruler on the last map. "Mark my words, ladies and gentlemen, one day not so far away from now, this will be our country."

From the back row, a gentle snore emerged from the open mouth of the old Sikh. Bibi-ji too gazed at the maps one on top of another, her thoughts wandering in a different direction from Pa-ji's. Like me, she thought. A series of tracings, a palimpsest of images, the product of so many histories, some true, some imaginary, all valid, but surely not all necessary?

Later, at the Taj Mahal, Dr. Randhawa ranged around Pa-ji's office and looked approvingly at the photographs. He pointed at the painting of Udham Singh and quizzed Jasbeer on that hero's achievements.

"Who is that, son?" Dr. Singh asked.

"Shaheed Udham Singh, Uncle-ji," Jasbeer said, proud that he had been singled out for attention by this fierce hawk of a man.

"And why is he famous?"

"Because he shot Lieutenant-Governor Sir Michael O'Dwyer, Uncle-ji."

"And why did he shoot that gentleman, son?"

"Because O'Dwyer approved of the massacre at Jallianwallah Bagh, conducted by his general in 1919,"

Jasbeer said in one long breath, hoping he had remembered the date correctly. His head was stuffed with hundreds of dates, and he often mixed them up.

Dr. Randhawa patted Jasbeer's back and said, "Good boy. Study hard and be a credit to your community. Read the Guru Granth Sahib every day and do not fall into bad habits such as drinking and smoking. Even in this foreign land full of temptations, resolve to remain true to your ancient culture."

He gave Jasbeer one more pat on his back, and turning to Pa-ji revealed that in addition to his maps, which he had distributed to every government in the world, he had also created his own currency. He gave Jasbeer a coin he had struck in his mint in the cellar of his home in Southall. He had also designed a flag, which would soon be in production.

"I will send you one for a reduced rate of one hundred dollars," he told Pa-ji. "With a proper receipt, of course."

"Of course," Pa-ji said unenthusiastically. His business antennae had gone up at the mention of money. Was this a charlatan or a man of convictions, however bizarre his beliefs? Pa-ji wasn't sure. He was enjoying the man's company for his vast knowledge of Punjabi history, although it seemed one-sided to him. *But show me one history that isn't skewed,* he thought.

Out of politeness, because Dr. Randhawa was, after all, his guest and guests were akin to God above, Pa-ji refrained from disagreeing with him on any point. But his sympathies for the visitor waned rapidly. By the time Dr. Randhawa had been persuaded to go to bed, Pa-ji was very bored and anxious to bring out the Johnny Walker.

That night in bed, he turned to Bibi-ji and murmured sleepily, "So, my queen, what did you think of Dr. Randhawa?"

"Idiot," Bibi-ji said succinctly, pressing into the warmth of his body.

"I don't think much of his notion of a separate country, do you?"

"Mmm. I don't care what he thinks," said Bibi-ji. "Why should we concern ourselves with such matters? We are Canadians now. Also I don't like the idea of more partitions and separations, more fiddling with borders." She snuggled farther down into warmth and comfort.

"Look at the trouble it is causing here in our own backyard, this business of partition!" Pa-ji said.

But there was no response from Bibi-ji, only a small snore.

The following morning there was a small ripple of renewed interest when Dr. Randhawa purchased a copy of *The New York Times* and showed Pa-ji a half-page advertisement he had taken out calling for "Free Countries" everywhere to support "Independence" for the Sikhs.

"That," said Dr. Randhawa, tapping the newspaper with a lean finger, "that is my calling card to the president of the United States of America. Soon my dream will be reality. Soon we will have freedom."

Pa-ji was relieved when his guest left. All the talk of secession made him deeply uneasy. He hoped this was the last he would see of Dr. Randhawa and hear about a free country for the Sikhs. He wished it would all go away.

But he was wrong. Nine years later, Dr. Randhawa would return to Vancouver, and this time he would be greeted by an audience that not only filled the auditorium but flowed out of it as well.

Bibi-ji was not a part of that audience. Deep in mourning, she was locked up inside the large white house, unable to go anywhere, not even to The Delhi Junction. Only twenty-four-year-old Jasbeer attended, his dark eyes full of the same zeal that burned in Dr. Randhawa's.

SEVENTEEN

A Brilliant Day

—

Vancouver

June 27, 1975

Leela clumped down Main Street, her pink and white sari riding over the tops of her running shoes. Fourteen-year-old Preethi, a head taller than her mother, strolled beside her. They were on their way to Mrs. Wu's. Leela had received word that a fresh consignment of lychees had arrived.

The street was full of shoppers, though it was only ten in the morning. Unlike Downtown, where Leela went to work at The Bay four days a week and where tall buildings pierced the sky and swarmed down to Burrard Inlet, where posh women in sleek clothes and high heels, and men in suits and with smart haircuts strolled the streets carrying exotic bags printed with fancy names, here on

Main Street, which had its beginnings in the downscale east end of Downtown, the shops were small and smelled of distant countries. The shoppers' bags were usually made of plain brown paper or tacky plastic. Fabric stores sold embroidered slippers and rainbow-coloured glass bracelets flecked with gold, as well as yards of shining silks and bolts of new cotton smelling of sunnier climes. Fashion Mahal had blonde-haired mannequins dressed in turquoise and pink and gold ghaghra-cholis or saris, their slim plastic arms loaded with bracelets, tiklis hanging down their fair foreheads. There was a new travel agency beside Lalloo's Far Out Travels, the windows almost identically plastered with pictures of colourful Indian destinations featuring palm trees, beaches, bejewelled women in embroidered skirts swaying across desert landscapes and the inevitable Taj Mahal (the original one). Leela had gone into Far Out Travels once or twice to ask about the cost of a ticket to India and had come out disheartened but determined to save the money for a trip the following year—if not for herself, then at least for one of her children.

Tires screamed as a driver accelerated and roared past, reckless as a trucker on the Grand Trunk road in India. A motorist backed into some pedestrians, calling down a hail of curses on his head, and nonchalantly parked under a No Parking sign. Another stopped right in the middle of the road to converse with a friend on the sidewalk, each calling news of family and friends to the other while traffic backed up and irate drivers leaned on their horns.

"God, this could be India, honestly." Preethi laughed. "Like Bangalore maybe."

"Not Bangalore," Leela said firmly. South India was different from North India, the distinctions still alive in her mind. "Delhi, more likely." She swooped towards a pile of eggplant on a shelf strategically placed outside a shop they were passing. Leela checked closely to see if they were gleaming purple, their stems fresh and green, and weighed them in her hand.

"Light ones have fewer seeds," she said, moving away. "These are rock-heavy—no good."

She disappeared into another small, dark shop and emerged a moment later, annoyed. "Why can't they keep our South Indian spices also? Only these Punjabi things, and then they call themselves India Market!"

They took a roundabout route to get to Mrs. Wu's vegetable store so that they could avoid JB Foods. JB was possessive about his customers and would be furious to discover that Leela's first loyalty was to a Chinese store rather than a fellow Indian's.

"If you are wanting to buy there you need not come here!" he had snapped at Leela once when he saw the bags from Wu's Store. Then he had made her wait fifteen minutes, pretending she wasn't in the queue, until Leela finally smacked her palm on the counter, dumped her purchases on the floor and left in a huff. Never mind that she had run out of dal, sooji, jeera, kalaonji, cardamom. There was *no* way she was going to allow a stiff-nosed shopkeeper to act funny with her. And as for his claim to Indianness: "He is not a *real* Indian," Leela had declared huffily.

Not only was this world divided, with the desis ranged on one side against the goras, the Asians, the Africans, the Native Americans, but there was a further distinction to be made. There were the *real* Indians, like the Bhats and the Patels and the Majumdars, those travellers who had come from Bombay or Calcutta or Aurangabad. And then there were others, like JB, who had arrived in Canada from East Africa, traumatized by Idi Amin's decision to confiscate their property and belongings and eject them from Uganda with nothing more than the clothes on their backs. According to Leela their two-hundred-year stopover in East Africa disqualified them from being called Indian: they had forfeited the right to return.

"Well then," Preethi had teased, "your grandchildren will never be real Indians either, will they? Or your great-grandchildren or great-great . . ." She wobbled her head like her father and adopted an exaggerated Indian accent. "We are doomed! We will always swing upside down between worlds like King What's-his-name!"

"Rubbish!" Leela countered, a little less robustly. "A Bhat will always be an Indian. And we aren't staying here that long anyway. We will be going home soon."

"And if I get married to a gora guy and have hybrid kids, then what, Amma?" Preethi had asked, grinning at her mother.

They reached Mrs. Wu's store and Leela eagerly made for the mountain of lychees, ignoring the exorbitant price per pound. This was a once-in-a-year or, if she got lucky and beat her friend Sushma Patel to the store, twice-a-year treat, and Leela wasn't overly concerned about the cost.

Her hands landed on the heap just as another arm, loaded with gold and glass bracelets, reached out.

"Half-and-half?"

Leela whirled around, startled by the phrase that echoed from her childhood.

"We will share it out?" Sushma asked, smiling at her. "You take half and I will take the other half?" She picked a sheaf of lychees, dangling like wrinkled rubies from their long brown stalks, and filled her basket.

Leela laughed. "I can't afford to buy up half the stock at this price, Sushma. I just want a pound or two."

Sushma did not have any such problem. She loaded her basket with lychees as if she were going to feed an army at home. As she moved away she called after Leela, "Don't forget, at our place, a potluck party for Independence Day. I will phone and tell you what to bring, okay? Write it in your calendar."

Leela nodded and smiled. Nobody wanted to miss the Patels' Independence Day party, an annual event to which almost everyone who had roots in India was invited. All her friends were curious to see what new (and often bizarre) decorations Sushma would create using saffron, white and green, the colours of the Indian flag. And of course they would come for the company, the gossip and the food. "Yes, I'll make a note of it, Sushma." Leela spotted a pile of bright green beans farther inside the shop and inched towards it, hoping her friend had not noticed them too.

Leela and Preethi entered The Delhi Junction, which was full to capacity, and found Balu and Arjun already there.

Both looked like shorn chickens. Majid the barber had given each of them such a close cut that Leela was sure she could see their scalps gleaming through. The rest of the café's regulars—Dr. Majumdar, dapper in a white shirt; fleshy-faced, balding Menon, and Harish Shah, rotund and belligerent, his small mouth pursed discontentedly—were discussing something loudly. And of course Pa-ji was at the till, leaning forward, alternately throwing a comment into the general stew of conversation, directing his new crew of waiters and tallying bills for departing customers. Not too far away from this noisy crowd sat Colonel Sam Hunt, reading a newspaper and eating mutton curry with rice, his bald head beaded with sweat from the chilli-hot food. Leela smiled around at everyone and waved to Pa-ji.

"She's declared a state of emergency in the country," Balu exclaimed, getting up to take Leela and Preethi's shopping bags and dumping them on the floor beside the table. "Can you believe it?"

"Who, Appu? What are you going on about?" Preethi asked.

"Indira Gandhi. In India," Balu said.

"When did this happen?" Leela asked.

"What's a state of emergency?" Preethi put in.

"All your democratic rights are suspended, free speech and all," Menon replied. "Like a police state almost. Do you remember when Trudeau invoked the War Measures Act? This is something like that. No habeas corpus, they can throw you into jail without telling you why."

There was a shuffling of chairs, tables were pulled

together and the men crowded at Balu's usual table beside the cash desk made room for Preethi and Leela.

"Why has she done this?" Leela asked.

"Indira Gandhi has lost her marbles, that's why," said a hoary old Sikh at a neighbouring table. Although Leela had seen him at The Delhi Junction before, she did not know his name.

"Because she was found guilty of two counts of campaign malpractice during the elections four years ago," Dr. Majumdar explained. "The law of that land grinds slowly, but grind it does. If she were to be convicted, she'd be barred from holding office or running in elections for another six years. So before they could kick her out, she declared a state of emergency. An extremely rash decision on the lady's part, if I may say."

"You may say whatever you are wanting to, Majumdar," Harish Shah interjected. His tiny, pouting mouth set in his round-cheeked, circular face gave him the look of a spoiled baby. "It is not going to make me change my mind."

"I wasn't trying to," Majumdar said. "Why would you imagine such a thing?"

"Mrs. Gandhi is a woman of wisdom and understanding. She knows what is good for our country, and she is doing what she has to." Shah crumpled his paper napkin. "That is my opinion. Emergency is *good*. In fact I would go a step further and say it is the best thing that has happened to India. Too much disorder, too much gol-maal. This will keep all those Indians out there in order."

"What does it matter whether we agree or do not agree?" said the Sikh from the next table. "We are not Indians anymore, are we? We can only sit here and drink Pa-ji's chai and go jhabbar-jhabbar, that's all."

His comment was ignored by everyone but Pa-ji, who tended to side with the old man. Pa-ji wouldn't deny that he was fond of India, that it was part of his being and was where his memories often turned. But history was a picture hanging on a wall, something of the past to spur the imagination, to write books about. It wouldn't do to let it swallow you whole. Pa-ji had ambitions for the future, plans, a political glint in his eye. At some point, he had recently decided, after his book was completed, he might enter the political arena. With all this multi-culti business gaining strength, Pa-ji had an idea that in the future he had as good a chance at a seat in Parliament as any gora. These days he tipped his turban at Pierre Elliott Trudeau.

He sat silently and listened as the debate raged around him undiminished. The normally mild and slow-talking Menon was shouting about the tyrannies of Indira Gandhi's son Sanjay, his heavy cheeks wobbling. How Sanjay was forcing men to have vasectomies. How he was running around the streets of Delhi with a bulldozer and shovelling the slums off the map of the city, people and all. Was all this possible, Pa-ji wondered?

"His mother's slogan was Remove Poverty, but Sanjay is removing the poor instead!" Menon yelled, thumping his fist on the table and rattling the plates and cups.

"High time somebody did something about that population!" Harish Shah yelled back. "*Bloody* hell! In twenty years we will have a billion people there. I, for one, approve of him."

"You, for one, need your own balls chopped to teach you a lesson!" Menon shouted at him. "Why did you have three children, if you were so concerned about population?"

"But I am not living in India, am I?" Shah's voice was smug. "I am building *Canada's* population. Here we *need* people for the economy to grow."

"That is what I am saying. Not living in India but doing big-time jhabbar-jhabbar about it," the Sikh at the next table interjected in his slow, deep voice. "I say, what is the use?"

"And I say we go home," Leela declared, finishing the last of her rice and curry combination and rising to her feet.

As the Bhats edged towards the door, they heard Samuel Hunt's voice making a surprising concession. "But this is impossible. You can't take things lying down! You need a mutiny, gentlemen, a mutiny!"

And Majumdar muttering, "Indira Gandhi has lost her head, I think. Even the newspapers are not allowed to print what they think. Did you hear, this morning—or was it yesterday?—the *Indian Express* newspaper came out with an absolutely blank front page? Without a word, they said everything!"

EIGHTEEN

A State of Emergency

—

New Delhi

August 1975

The monsoon rain was tapering off when Satpal's sister Manpreet fixed the date for her daughter's wedding. Travelling to attend the occasion in Amritsar, Nimmo and Satpal noticed that, unusually, the trains were both arriving and leaving on time.

"It's because of the Emergency," one of their fellow passengers remarked. "We have been deprived of all our rights, we can be thrown in jail and kept there forever if it pleases Madam Gandhi, but the trains run on time. Isn't this the best thing that has happened to us?"

"Not for the thousands who are sitting in jail, bhai," another passenger replied.

"Thousands in jail!" Satpal said. "For what?"

"For *thinking*. For disagreeing with what Madam has done to this country. For exercising their rights, that's what. And tomorrow, if you go and complain about me I might end up in jail too!"

Nimmo shivered and looked around the crowded compartment to see if anyone was listening to their conversation. What if this man was right? Were there spies everywhere? She found it difficult to believe that the woman whom she so admired, and for whom she had voted in two elections, should impose such a thing as this Emergency without good reason. The country must be in danger.

The following morning, in Amritsar, Satpal, Nimmo and the children, accompanied by Manpreet's oldest son, Sunny—a stocky, bespectacled young man of twenty-two— went early to the Golden Temple to pay their respects to the Almighty in this greatest and most holy of Sikh temples. The taxi dropped them off at the eastern gate of the vast, walled complex of guest houses, dining halls and offices that surrounded the main temple—Harimandir Sahib, as it was better known. They jostled with thousands of other pilgrims and devotees who had also arrived at the break of dawn to avoid the even greater crowds that would pour in as the day wore on.

Nimmo covered her head with her chiffon dupatta and stood in silence with her family for a few moments, gazing at the massive marble Harimandir Sahib. Topped by a golden dome, it seemed to rise weightless as a prayer above the green lake that surrounded it. This sacred lake, supposed to contain the nectar of the gods, gave the city its name—Amritsar—nectar lake. A peace unlike anything she had experienced filled Nimmo, her heart beat a little easier and her doubts, large and small, disappeared.

She had made the pilgrimage to the Golden Temple almost every year since her marriage to offer prayers. When she wanted to thank the Almighty for some particular happiness he had sent her way, she would volunteer to cook in the kitchens of the public dining halls or to scrub the vast marble floor of the Harimandir Sahib, where the sacred book, the Guru Granth Sahib, was kept during the day.

Now, with her family, she made the obligatory circumambulation of the temple, stopping to wash her feet in the lake before crossing the walkway into the calm marbled interior. She remembered the conversation on the train from New Delhi and comforted herself with the thought that no matter what wickedness and violence occurred in the outside world, here at least, within the sacred walls of the Golden Temple and deep inside its heart in the Harimandir Sahib, only peace reigned.

Afterward Satpal took Pappu for a dip in the lake, while Sunny, Nimmo and Kamal strolled out of the temple gates to the market that nuzzled up to the walls of the temple compound, its gullies radiating outwards like an intricate spiderweb. In these narrow streets were hundreds of shops, cheap hotels and homes fitting snugly into and over each other, filled with the clamour of shopkeepers advertising their wares, customers haggling, children wailing, cows lowing, bicycle bells jangling. Here silence was unknown.

Staring at the wares on display in the shops, Nimmo felt as excited as Kamal. There were brightly coloured fabrics and ready-made clothes of every size, jewellery, plastic toys, shoes, religious books, paintings and prints of the Sikh gurus and of the Golden Temple, fruit, vegetables, flowers, amulets, charms, cedar and sandalwood worry beads and gaudily coloured boxes of firecrackers. Although Diwali was three months away, the shops were fully stocked with merchandise for the festival.

"Can we get that? Please, Mummy?" Kamal pointed to a large cardboard box that looked like it might contain a cricket bat but was the repository of something called a zing-zing-dhamaal bomb. On the cover of the box was an illustration of a smiling woman in a bright pink sari, holding the bomb—a lethal-looking rocket-like object in one hand, a lighted sparkler in the other.

"No," said Nimmo, dragging her daughter away. Before long, though, Kamal dug in her heels in front of another store advertising a Whistling Catherine Wheel with six-colour stars at the end. Nimmo refused, but Sunny insisted on buying one for his small cousin.

"Why do you spoil her like this, Sunny?" Nimmo protested mildly when the young man, her favourite nephew, emerged from the shop bearing a large plastic bag.

"It's nothing much," Sunny said, presenting the bag to Kamal with a flourish. "Just a small gift for my littlest sister."

Kamal hung on to her cousin's arm as they walked back to the Temple, giggling as he teased her about something. Nimmo smiled and shook her head, feeling thoroughly relaxed and happy. By now the sun was setting and the evening had turned cool. A fine drizzle misted the air. Satpal and Pappu were waiting for them near the jujube tree, where wishes are said to come true and wispy hopes may turn into realities.

Back at Manpreet's house, they found that other members of the family had gathered and were noisily discussing the Emergency.

"Sometimes it is necessary for a woman to be tough in order to run this unruly country," Satpal's brother-in-law, Balraj, a dignified-looking man in his fifties with a grey and white beard, said as they came in. "It seems to have done some good at least in my office. Everybody arrives on time. It is unbelievable. Even that rogue of an assistant of mine, who always has a sick mother or father or some person dying four days out of five, even he has been arriving exactly at eight-thirty and leaving at four-thirty!"

"But a suspension of all our rights? Spies everywhere?" Satpal said doubtfully. "That can't be very good."

Balraj snorted. "And you believe all that nonsense? Hah! That won't happen here, I assure you."

Sunny had been listening silently to the conversation. Now he spoke softly. "It is not nonsense, Baba. I was interrogated yesterday at the police station. It was not very pleasant, believe me. They came to our college and marched me and my friends into the van without giving any reasons. Fortunately one of the senior officers at that particular station was my classmate's uncle and he had us released. But he did warn us that if we were arrested again he would not be able to help."

"You were arrested?" Balraj asked, his voice rising. "Why?"

"We were at a rally protesting the Emergency," Sunny said.

"Is this why you failed again this year? Because you were protesting instead of studying? And why didn't you tell us about your arrest?"

"What would you have been able to do, Baba? I didn't want to worry you needlessly," Sunny replied. "I should warn you though, tomorrow I am joining a citywide march. Everyone I know is taking part. You should all come too." He looked around the room at the assembled people.

"What if you are arrested again?" Balraj asked. "Why do you need to get involved? It could be dangerous."

Sunny frowned. "It wasn't dangerous before the Emergency to protest against something my government did. This is a democratic country, not some banana republic with an Idi Amin at the head of it, shooting any-one who disagrees with him!"

There was an edge to his voice completely unfamiliar to Nimmo, who had seen him only as an affectionate and mischievous boy, and more recently as an indulgent older cousin to her daughter.

"Well, sometimes I feel this country is a circus of lunatics," said one of the several house guests who had arrived for the wedding. "Now and then it is necessary to take a big stick and beat everyone into shape, and that is what Indira-ji is doing. Look at China, how well everything runs there. And Singapore—did you know, if you spit on the streets in that country, you can get a big fine? I am happy that the trains are finally on time, those clerks and secretaries in the municipal offices are on time, and the whole of India is on time. I'm tired of standing in long queues to pay my water bill or electricity bill, then waiting again when the fool closes his window in my face and goes away for his coffee break and there's nothing I can do about it."

"This is wonderful," Sunny said angrily. "You are all so happy that everything is on time, but don't care that some poor innocents are sitting in jail for reasons not known to them? What if it happens to one of you? Or to your sons or daughters? I got off this time, but I hear that student leaders who are against the Emergency are being rounded up and thrown into jail. Then they simply disappear." He stood up abruptly and walked out of the room.

A long, uneasy silence followed. Finally Manpreet broke it by getting to her feet and asking brightly if anyone was ready for dinner.

The following day, in the excitement of preparing for the wedding—getting the mehendi done for all the women, doing the make-up for the bride and taking care of a thousand other details—all thought of the Emergency that shrouded the country was temporarily forgotten.

But on the train home a few days later, with Sunny's voice echoing in their ears, neither Satpal nor Nimmo said anything to their fellow passengers—two clean-shaven young Hindu Punjabis—who were loudly condemning the Emergency. And they were relieved to return to their home, to Asha's voice haranguing the fruit vendor over a matter of a few paise and the contented clucking of Kaushalya's hens.

Asha stopped arguing with the vendor when she saw them alight from their autorickshaw.

"Did you hear, Nihal Singh bought his wife a gas stove?" she called, her face flushed with importance at being the bearer of this news. "I am thinking, I will ask Him to get one for me too." Asha always referred to her small, rat-like husband as Him with solemn deference, although it was obvious from the screaming that emerged from their home that Asha was in fact the boss. "How about you, Nimmo?"

Nimmo shrugged. She had seen the advertisements for this wonderful object which emitted no fumes or smoke or odours. It would be nice to own one, she thought. But she said, "I don't know, Asha. I hear it costs a lot of money." She went into the house to cut off further conversation.

Satpal entered with their bags and muttered, "Don't talk to that woman about this Emergency, understand? Don't say anything to anyone. You never know."

How quickly fear had sneaked into their small, peaceful world, Nimmo thought. How fragile her safety.

NINETEEN

THE RETURN
OF DR. RANDHAWA

—

Vancouver

April 1980

Bibi-ji sat on the couch in Pa-ji's office, still in her dressing gown, her greying hair woven into two thick braids that curled down her ample bosom, sorting through a packet of recently developed photographs. She found one she had taken of Jasbeer just a week ago in her garden. He had turned twenty that day and Bibi-ji had persuaded him to wear a pale blue turban which she thought suited him better than the black ones he had started to wear a few years ago. He had not known that he was being photographed and looked pensive and happy. Nimmo and Satpal would love this image of their son, Bibi-ji thought, as she slipped the photograph into the envelope bearing her letter, even though they had seen Jasbeer almost every year since he had turned seventeen. He had dropped out of high school that year and Bibi-ji had been relieved to stop pretending to Nimmo that her son was academically gifted.

She remembered how surprised she had been when Jasbeer had asked if he could go and spend a few months in Punjab with relatives of Dr. Randhawas's after visiting his parents in Delhi. He had never showed any desire to go to India before, a fact that had given Bibi-ji a guilty satisfaction.

"But why with these strangers when you have your father's sister Manpreet in Amritsar?" she had asked.

"I want to live in the village," Jasbeer had responded. "I want to see what life there is like."

After that he had gone back almost every year, and even though, in the beginning, Nimmo was upset that he preferred to spend more time with friends in Punjab than with his own family, she learned to be happy with the little she did see of her oldest son.

Bibi-ji shuffled her fingers through the photographs trying to find another one of Jasbeer, when she heard a snort of annoyance from Pa-ji who was at his desk going through his mail. She looked up to see him reading a letter and frowning.

"What is it?" she asked.

"He is coming back," Pa-ji said. "He wants to stay with us again. He is one of the chief guests at this year's Baisakhi festival celebrations. He is bringing his own group of keertan singers, he says."

"Who are you talking about, ji?"

"That wretched preacher fellow—Dr. Raghubir Randhawa. Remember him? He stayed with us about nine years ago? He wanted to sell me maps or coins or something? The Independent-Country-for-Sikhs fellow?"

"That boring man who put us all to sleep? Who does he think he is? King of England?" Bibi-ji exclaimed. She had taken a strong dislike to the man the first time she set eyes on him. "As if our house is his personal dharamshaala! Tell him to go jump in the pond, na! No way is he staying here. No way is he eating my parathas."

"Why does he want to stay with us anyway?" Pa-ji asked, tossing the letter aside. "He hasn't heard? I am allergic to these Khalistani types? These militant fellows? Not interested!"

"He is coming because our house is better than a five-star hotel, that's why," Bibi-ji replied. "And it is free. But if you don't want him to stay here, tell him straight off: we are busy, I am unwell, to please go and stay with somebody else. Why don't you?"

Pa-ji didn't respond. He rubbed his unseeing eye wearily with his knuckles and drew a pad of letter paper towards him. Bibi-ji watched him with resigned affection. He was still fit and energetic, his beard just beginning to show traces of grey even though he was in his early seventies now, and she knew he could never bring himself to refuse a request from a fellow Sikh. She left him alone to his correspondence and made her way down the stairs to the unusually quiet kitchen and living area. She had noticed that in the past year, the number

278

of their guests had dropped significantly. No doubt it had something to do with Pa-ji's loud declarations at temple committee meetings that an independent Punjab was a ridiculous idea. So many people in their community were now arguing for a Sikh homeland apart from India for the Sikhs.

She was startled to find Jasbeer in the living room, sprawled across one of the sofas, reading a pamphlet.

"Arrey, putthar, when did you come home?" she asked. "Why are you wearing that black turban? You look much better in light blue or green ones." She worried about him—he was becoming like one of those strange young men with whom he spent most of his time nowadays. More conservative and religious than their parents, they behaved as if they were God's personal messengers on earth, Bibi-ji felt.

"What are you reading?" she tried again when she got no response to her earlier question.

"Something Dr. Randhawa sent me," Jasbeer said, sitting up straight.

"He has been writing to you?"

"Yes, sometimes," Jasbeer said.

"Did you know he was coming back here? And that he wants to stay with us?"

"Yes, I invited him."

Bibi-ji struggled to hide her astonishment and annoyance and changed the subject. "Leela was telling me that Preethi is going away to Toronto for university. And didn't Wendy get a scholarship to some American college?"

Jasbeer shrugged. "Maybe. I haven't seen them in a while."

"And what are you planning to do, putthar?" Bibi-ji asked, holding on to her temper. "You dropped out of high school . . . I promised your mother that you would get a better education here in this country, but look at you . . ."

"I might go back to India," he said.

"Oh," Bibi-ji replied, trying very hard to sound unsurprised. She gathered herself and continued: "Your parents will be happy to see you home. They would have been even happier if you had finished high school, though."

"I am not going to Delhi," Jasbeer said. "I'm joining the Damdami Taksal in Bhinder for a year or so. Dr. Randhawa said I would do well there."

"But that's a religious school!"

"Yes. So?" Jasbeer gave her a challenging look and rose to his feet.

"And why are you listening to that loud-mouthed fraud?" She could no longer hide her irritation.

"He is a great and good man. I don't think you should speak in that disrespectful way about him," Jasbeer said. He turned and left the room and a few minutes later Bibi-ji heard the front door slam. She stood there for a little longer, wondering whether she ought to tell Pa-ji about Jasbeer's decision now or leave it until later. Not so long ago they had had to drag Jasbeer with them to the gurudwara; now he was planning to go to India and live in a religious school. Was that a good thing or not? She was not sure at all.

—

Dr. Raghubir Randhawa arrived a few weeks later, tall, grave and self-important in a grey pathan suit with a gold Rolex pocket watch. He was less thin than they remembered him; his work as an agitator appeared to suit him well. He had also grown in fame, it seemed, because there was quite a crowd at the airport waiting to greet him with bouquets of flowers. Pa-ji was taken aback by the reception, though he was aware that the mood of the Sikhs in his community had changed considerably in the nine years between Randhawa's last visit and this one. A large number of new immigrants from Punjab had come into Canada, and many nursed a deep grievance against the Indian government, which they believed had reneged on its promises to distribute land and river water equitably among Punjab and its neighbouring states. Rumours flew of disappearances, killings, deaths in police custody and the torture of innocent Sikh men in the villages of Punjab. Pa-ji did not think much of these tales, though it occurred to him that they sounded surprisingly like the ones that had preceded the departure of the British from India. That had been different somehow, he felt—a heroic endeavour to rid the land of foreign occupiers. He had contributed as much as he could to that freedom movement, applauded the men and women who had blown up bridges and trains and buildings and shed blood for what he had considered a worthy cause. But this, this desire to create a separate country within India for the Sikhs, seemed to Pa-ji faintly absurd. Neither could he understand how the temple and its priests could encourage the discontent, fan the simmering anger, urge young men to violence in the name of God. Pa-ji's religion was as simple and straight-eyed as his own nature. There was a Being who had created the universe and granted him, Pa-ji, the privilege of being human for a brief span of time. He could not understand how the Being, who must surely be benign, having created this magnificent planet, could generate hundreds of lunacies, little and large, in a person's heart. How could hate be born of something as private as faith in this unseen God?

Lately it appeared to Pa-ji that there were far more immoderate than moderate people in his community. Not so long ago, he was a pillar of that community; when he said something, people stopped to listen. These days, whenever he opened his mouth to object to the politics of power and violence that seemed to be taking over their temple, he was angrily shouted down. At the temple, a visiting preacher from India had delivered a fiery speech about an independent Sikh state. He had ended his speech by passing around a box for funds to set up this state. When the box came to him, Pa-ji had shaken his head.

"No, I am not giving for this," he had said.

"You do not wish for an independent country for the Sikhs, bhai-saheb?" asked the young man holding the box.

Pa-ji's good eye glared at the boy—a stranger who had arrived with the preacher—at the high black turban worn like a beehive on his head, his flat black eyes and his unkempt beard, and said: "Not a question of my wishing. What I am not wishing to do is interfere in the business of another country. I am Canadian, why I should pay for more partition of India?"

"As a Sikh you are not interested, then?" the man persisted. Now other people were turning around to see what the altercation was about.

Pa-ji got to his feet and said loudly, "As a Sikh I am interested in putting money into *building* things—like schools and hospitals—not for breaking up countries!"

Soon afterward, the attacks had begun. First someone threw a rock at the window of The Delhi Junction. Then Pa-ji's tires were slashed in broad daylight behind the restaurant. When he called the police, two young goras arrived to ask desultory questions. They made flat-footed efforts to find the culprits, mostly interrogating the regulars at The Delhi Junction. The community withdrew into resentful silence at the foreign intrusion. Pa-ji was censured for bringing the police into what was surely a family quarrel, and several of his customers transferred their patronage from The Delhi Junction to a new restaurant a block away.

Pa-ji refused to be cowed. He increased the volume of his protests against the growing mood of violence in the temple. He wrote an article that was published in the local Punjabi-language newspaper, urging moderation and asking his fellow Sikhs not to bow to the wave of fundamentalism. Late the following evening, after locking up the restaurant, he noticed he was being followed. He quickened his pace, but not soon enough. He felt a hard, heavy object crash into his shoulder from behind, and then excruciating, blinding pain. If he had not shouted at the top of his lungs then, attracting passersby, he might have been more badly hurt, perhaps permanently silenced. Again the police came, performed their ineffectual investigations and went away none the wiser.

For the first time the Taj Mahal's enormous wrought-iron gates, which had always remained welcomingly open, were locked at night. Lalloo hired a watchman to stand guard around the clock and insisted on accompanying Pa-ji to and from the restaurant every day before heading off to take care of his many businesses. But even he, it pained Bibi-ji to note, contributed to the funds being collected for a separate Sikh state. And when confronted, he insisted that it was to keep his wife's family happy. His brothers-in-law were all for separation from India, even though his wife wasn't too happy about it.

"For the sake of homely harmony," Lalloo had said, spreading his palms upwards. "What to do? You know my in-laws, they are tough guys . . ."

On the day of Dr. Randhawa's arrival, an entire fleet of cars followed Pa-ji from the airport to the Taj Mahal. It appeared that all Dr. Randhawa's acolytes were to be his guests that afternoon, and Pa-ji dreaded the thought of Bibi-ji's reaction to this unexpected influx of visitors. Especially Dr. Randhawa's admirers.

"So, Khushwant-ji, I believe your son is an active member of the organization," Dr. Randhawa said suddenly. During the entire drive from the airport he had been talking to two other men who had got into the car with him, and Pa-ji had paid little attention to them. For a moment he wondered who his visitor was speaking to.

"You can call me Pa-ji, like everyone else," he said.

"Why has the good Maharaj above given you a name then?" Dr. Randhawa asked in a tone of gentle reproach which made Pa-ji feel like a ten-year-old boy.

"What organization is Jasbeer active in, Dr. Randhawa?" Pa-ji struggled to contain his irritation, though he knew the answer. When he had first discovered Jasbeer's involvement with the youth wing of Dr. Randhawa's group, he had been furious. This boy, whom he and Bibi-ji had brought up like a son, was hanging around with the very thugs who might have attacked him? "He eats the salt in my home with one hand and stabs me with the other!" he had raged to Bibi-ji. He had controlled his anger and spoken to Jasbeer in a reasonable voice, but received only a mute obstinacy in response. He had asked Bibi-ji to intervene, but she too had come away empty-handed, saying anxiously that at least Jasbeer was not taking drugs or alcohol or engaging in goonda-activities.

Dr. Randhawa interrupted his thoughts. "Young Sikhs for a Free Punjab, of course. Very good boy. Knows how to get things done. I have received many respectful letters from him telling us what he is doing here in our outreach wing. Yes, indeed, you must be proud of Jasbeer. We need people like him in our group."

Pa-ji grunted and contained his shock. Jasbeer had been writing to this awful man? Telling him what? "He does not tell us much," he said at last, trying for a light tone. "He is too old for all that."

"A son is never too old for his parents," Dr. Randhawa replied. "My children tell me everything every day. We will speak to your boy and bring him back to the right path."

We, thought Pa-ji. Was Dr. Randhawa referring to himself with the royal "we"? Or did he mean the two of them, he and Pa-ji, together? The rest of the day he brooded over the fact that his foster son had been sleeping with the enemy, so to speak, under his very nose. By evening Pa-ji had worked himself into a fine rage. He pushed aside his manuscript and prowled up and down the floor of his office. In the room below was Jasbeer, fawning over that fool of a man who preached hate and violence. Was it for this that he, Khushwant Singh, Proprietor and Landowner, had humoured his wife and brought in the boy? He poured himself a drink and tossed it down, but didn't feel any less angry.

"Bibi-ji!" he roared, opening the door of his office and leaning out. He knew she was in the bedroom, also unable to be around Dr. Randhawa. "Bibi-ji!"

She emerged from the bedroom. "What? What are you shouting like that for? Am I deaf? You will disturb the guests."

"Where is that boy of yours?" Pa-ji shouted, as if she had not spoken.

"I don't know. He is what—twenty? Old enough to look after himself. Surely I don't need to follow him around everywhere."

"That's why he is going the wrong way, woman, that's why!" Pa-ji said. "It is all your fault for not keeping an eye on him."

"What has he done now?" Bibi-ji asked, pushing her irate husband back into his office and following him in. "Now sit. And tell me, what is making you so angry?"

Pa-ji refused to sit, preferring to pace around instead. He went back to the door of his room. "Jasbeer!" he hollered. "You come up here this instant!"

There was a sudden silence downstairs and then Jasbeer's voice answered, "Yes, Pa-ji, coming."

Pa-ji had arranged himself in his chair, Scotch glass in hand, a scowl on his face, by the time his foster son appeared.

"Yes, Pa-ji?"

"You close that door and come in here, boy," Pa-ji ordered.

Bibi-ji went over and stroked Jasbeer's arm. She knew why Pa-ji was so annoyed but could not bear to see him shout at Jasbeer and tried to slip out of the room. Pa-ji stopped her. "Where are you going? You are responsible for this. You spoiled him."

"Oh?" Bibi-ji crossed her arms across her breasts. "And you did nothing except buy him all that *he* wanted and then some more that *you* wanted him to have, no? Spoiled him, he says! Who did the spoiling, is what I wish to know."

"Okay, okay," said Pa-ji, banging his glass down on the table. "I don't want to argue with you. I want to say a few things to this fellow here. Now Jasbeer, putthar, have we not given you everything you have ever needed?"

"Yes, ji, you have," Jasbeer said.

"Then why you are going after that foolish man who preaches death and destruction?" Pa-ji asked in a pained voice. "What is he giving you that you don't get from us?"

Jasbeer gave the old man a level look. "He is not foolish, and don't insult him like that in front of me."

287

Pa-ji gaped at him. He looked at Bibi-ji. "Did you hear that? He is telling me not to insult that bastard, pardon my French, in my own house! Enh? Did you hear?"

"Don't get so angry, my heart," Bibi-ji soothed, but she felt like weeping, caught between the two people she loved most in the world, unable to help either of them. "Jasbeer, putthar, is that any way to speak to Pa-ji? Apologize at once, if you please."

"For what? *He* is the one using foul language, insulting a great and good man who honours him by staying in his house, he is the one drinking alcohol and disgracing his Sikh name, *he* should perform an act of penance at the gurudwara."

With a roar Pa-ji lunged forward, evading Bibi-ji's arms which tried to restrain him, and slapped his large palm across Jasbeer's face. "Look at this beggar! We bring him here to educate him, and now look at how he repays us!"

Jasbeer touched his face and, without another word, turned and left the room.

Bibi-ji turned on Pa-ji, near tears. "Look what you did! Hitting him like that. And did you see his face? I am warning you, if he decides to leave with that Randhawa, I will never forgive you. Never."

She too marched out of the room, leaving Pa-ji alone. He heard her slam their bedroom door shut and turn the key in the lock. He sighed deeply. He would have to fold his body onto the couch here in his office for the rest of the night. He would find a way to make up with her tomorrow, he told himself. And with Jasbeer for having slapped him.

The next morning Jasbeer appeared in Pa-ji's office,

solemn and respectful. He had traded in his jeans for a pathan suit. Standing before Pa-ji he announced, "I will be leaving with the Doctor-ji's people next month."

"Where are you going, putthar?" Pa-ji asked gently. He regretted his previous night's anger, ready to forgive and be forgiven. He planned to buy Jasbeer a nice watch or dark glasses to make up for slapping him. He had even decided to bite his tongue and offer to host Randhawa for as long as he wanted to stay.

"To join the school in Bhinder, the Damdami Taksal. I wish to immerse myself in our scriptures. I wish to live like a true Sikh."

Pa-ji felt his blood pressure rise. "True Sikh? And who decides that, may I ask?"

Jasbeer looked calmly at him. "That is not for me to say, Pa-ji. All I know is that I have not been following the correct path. I have been living a meaningless life, and now I have found a purpose."

"Have you told Bibi-ji? Or your parents?"

"My parents gave me away and therefore do not need to be told. Bibi-ji knows."

Two days later, Pa-ji drove their visitor to the temple for his talk. This time, the hall was filled to overflowing. Pa-ji was given a seat onstage, joining a row of other important people who sat in a row behind Dr. Randhawa's chair. Bibi-ji had refused to attend, pleading illness.

"Listening to that man going bak-bak the past two days has given me a headache," she told Pa-ji angrily. "Now I have to go listen to him officially also? No thank you!"

Pa-ji noticed groups of young men in black turbans walking through the crowd and collecting money in tins. He thought he saw Jasbeer too, but in the confusion of the crowd he could not be certain. The boy had not spoken to Pa-ji since the morning of his announcement and was hardly seen at home except at mealtimes, when Dr. Randhawa and his acolytes returned for their meals.

Dr. Randhawa began his speech, in Punjabi, without any preliminaries. It wasn't very different from the one he had delivered years ago to a crowd of five, with its demands for an independent Sikh state, the slide show displaying flag, coin and map, and a few archival photos of Maharaja Ranjit Singh. He didn't go on as long this time, to Pa-ji's surprise, and his speech was met with rapturous applause. Now he was holding his hand up for silence. "Ladies and gentlemen," he said in English, although there were few women in the crowd. Then he switched to Punjabi again. "There are some witnesses here, who come straight from the torture chamber of the Hindu Raj. They will give those of you who need to be convinced the proof of what I have just said to you—we need our own country where every individual is treated with respect, where we can practice our religion in peace, where we will not be penalized for it."

A young man sitting in the row of chairs behind him stood up and came slowly to the podium. He was only about twenty years old and had the thin, hunched look of a beaten animal about him. Dr. Randhawa introduced him, and he began to speak.

"My older brother, Lakki, wasn't at home that night,"

he said without any introduction, as if he were already in the middle of a story started long ago. "He was rarely home, and we never mentioned him because he would be in danger if we did.

"But there were others who remembered Lakki's existence. One night they came, the killers. My father opened the door, what else could he do? He was an old man, and the only weapon he had was a rusty scythe. Inside the house, my mother quickly unwound my long hair. She didn't know what sort of men were at the door: these days it is difficult to tell. Sometimes it was the police, at other times it was the extremists."

At that, Dr. Randhawa, who was contemplating his hands, looked up with a slight frown. The witness was here to support him; he did not appreciate the mention of extremists.

"There was a war, we were told. My brother was a soldier in that war. The enemy was everywhere, and people had forgotten what the war was about or whose side they were on. We could hear my father shouting something. My mother took a pair of scissors and hacked off my hair, crying bitterly at the sacrilege that her hands were obliged to commit.

"'If the police catch you,' she whispered, 'they will think you are a Hindu. It is safer to be someone you are not.' She was wearing pink glass bangles, and I can still hear the way they went chhin-chhin.

"'Go, putthar, go quickly,' she whispered to me. 'Get help. Tell them . . . tell them . . . I don't know, but bring back help. Run, run like the wind.'

"I didn't know who I was supposed to call for help, but I did run like the wind. I raced around the village banging on doors. But everybody was too terrified of the knock on the door in the middle of the night to help. I ran to the police chowki, but there was nobody there either. When I came home, my mother and my father were dead."

The young man paused, dry-eyed. He touched his head. No turban, no long hair. "I kept my hair like this to mourn, to remind myself of the last touch of my mother's hand. But every moment I can feel the weight of hair on my scalp."

An uneasy silence had descended over the crowd. Many people cried silently. Pa-ji, too, felt like weeping. Was this Dr. Randhawa right after all? Was the situation for Sikhs in India so wretched? Could yet another division of the country heal the wounds that had been caused by the first one? Pa-ji realized it was difficult, from this distance, to have a proper perspective. But he held on to the flickering idea that somewhere, between the boy's raw story and Dr. Randhawa's posturing, lay the truth.

TWENTY

THE NIGHTBIRD

—

New Delhi

October 1983

The air was clouded with the smell of burning wood, the smoky odour that was peculiarly a part of this time of year, which reminded Nimmo that once again Diwali was around the corner and they still hadn't purchased any firecrackers, clay diyas or even cotton wicks and oil for the diyas. Satpal had been urging her to stop this annual ritual of filling a hundred earthen lamps with oil, rolling the cotton wicks into spires and lighting them all at dusk, and to switch instead to the simplicity of a string of electric lights. But Nimmo wasn't ready for simplicity. She liked those small earthen lamps— filling them with oil, arranging them outside and finally lighting them, so that at night it looked like a hundred twinkling stars had fallen about her house. And she had to admit that the celebrations were more for her and Kamal than for Pappu, who was now a towering young man and no longer as excited as he had once been about festivals. Only Kamal shared her enthusiasm, helped her light up the diyas and place them all over the house. Sweet, good-natured Kamal, how happy Nimmo was that she had this last child, a daughter, to complete her happiness.

She waved to her two children from the head of the alley as they went their separate ways to school and work, and returned to her home. In the kitchen Satpal was lifting lids off the pots to see what there was to eat.

"Anda-bhujiya and parathey," Nimmo said. She went to the refrigerator and removed three eggs and a few green chillies. Her husband loved scrambled eggs with spices and onions and hot parathey. "Can you buy some vegetables on your way back home? Don't bring cauliflower again. We've have had it every single night for the past week. Everybody is sick of it."

"Have you forgotten? I am going to Modinagar today. Have to pick up some parts. I'll be back very late tonight." Satpal glanced quickly at the newspaper as he ate his breakfast.

"Do you have to go? Why not Mohan Lal?"

"He has a prospective groom coming to see his daughter this evening," Satpal said.

"How about Pappu, then? It will be good experience for him."

"No, I have to decide what to buy after I see how much it is going to cost. And that young man has to finish

294

work on Sharma-ji's car." Satpal frowned at the thought of Pappu, who had dropped out of high school and joined the mechanic's shop, but was rarely to be found at work. He preferred to hang around on street corners eyeing the girls. Sometimes Satpal wondered whether Jasbeer, their oldest son, might have become a scholar if they had kept him here in India. He too had not done well at school, it seemed from the letters they received from Bibi-ji, but what was that she had said in the last missive? The boy was showing a deep interest in religion, in fact he was planning to go for a year to the Damdami Taksal in Bhinder to study the scriptures? She had not commented either way on this decision, but it worried Satpal. Like most of his friends, he was God-fearing but not fanatical. Not that a good religious education would turn Jasbeer into a fanatic; but still, had they not sent him abroad so that he could become a doctor or an engineer, and was it not better for the boy to remain abroad instead of entering the violent mess that Punjab was deteriorating into?

"What time will you be back then?" Nimmo asked, stirring the eggs in the pan.

"Why? Aren't you going to be at home?"

Nimmo shrugged. "I was thinking of taking Kamal to the market this evening to buy new clothes. I saw a pretty green salwar kameez set in Jain's store. The last one we bought was for the Baisakhi festival in April. She is growing so fast, everything she owns looks too tight." Nimmo thought pleasurably of spending an evening shopping with her daughter. "What is in the news today? Any strikes or anything? I don't want to go out if there is likely to be trouble."

"No news, except for more deaths in Punjab. More violence, encounters with police, encounters with militants, more widows and orphans on all sides," Satpal said bitterly. "I don't know why the government is sitting on its hands and doing nothing."

"You sound like your nephew Sunny, always talking about killing and war and trouble in Punjab. We live in Delhi. It is not our problem." She handed him his plate of food and set the kettle on the stove for tea.

"How can you say that, Nimmo? We are Sikhs, our relatives live in Punjab, it matters to me what happens there. You lost your family and your property because of what happened in Punjab. Now my family is also getting affected. Manpreet says that because of Sunny's involvement with all these political groups the police are harassing them all the time, and you say it's not our problem?"

Nimmo strained the leaves and stirred milk into her tea, sipping it resolutely. Yes, she cared what happened, and no, she did not want to be involved. All she wanted was to be safe. To live without fear.

Satpal rose to his feet. "I can't understand you. What is happening to you these days?"

"Nothing is happening to me." Nimmo snapped, annoyed with him for infecting her morning with dark fears.

Satpal headed for the door and paused. "Sunny is coming to stay with us for a few days. Okay?"

"Kamal will be having her exams, she has to study. Having people in the house will be disturbing."

Satpal gave her an irritated look. "Every time Manpreet wants to send her son here, one of your children has an exam. I am beginning to think that you don't want him to come at all!"

Nimmo did not respond. She was afraid of the politics that Sunny would drag with him into the house, but you could not refuse to host your own relatives, especially not your older sister's son.

"And when I come back from Modinagar," Satpal said, the irritation still in his voice, "I will get that extra room built on the roof. That way anyone can come and stay, exams or not."

Nimmo handed him one of the lunch boxes and said in a pacifying voice, "Okay, okay. Don't leave the house angry. How many years have you been saying you will build that room, anyway? I will write to your sister and tell her to send Sunny to us. But it will have to be next week, after Kamal's exams. At least allow one child to finish her studies well!"

The rest of the day was tarnished as Nimmo brooded over the prospect of Sunny's visit, which filled her with nameless worries. She wished that Satpal's nephew would stay away. Not that she wasn't fond of him; she had good memories of him. But he had changed in the years since that dreadful Emergency, which, Nimmo had been forced to admit, had been a terrible mistake on the part of Mrs. Gandhi. She had seen Sunny turn from a cheerful, open youth into a secretive, hard-eyed man whom she barely recognized. She worried that he might drag the impressionable young Pappu into the politics of Punjab, fill his head with ideas of fighting to create an independent country called Khalistan.

The last time Sunny had visited them, a few years ago, Nimmo was in the kitchen, cooking dinner. Kamal and Pappu were in the front room with their older cousin. She heard them laughing over something that Sunny had said, and then Kamal's voice, begging Sunny to tell them stories.

At first she hadn't paid attention, assuming they were the same ones he had told before—amusing folklore about animals, or the famous Akbar and Birbal tales that Kamal had loved. Then her daughter's voice pierced through her fog of thoughts.

"I don't like your stories anymore, Bhai-ji," Kamal said. "They are so scary."

Nimmo had started to listen more carefully—he must be telling them those silly ghost stories he was so fond of. Like the one about the four-winged nightbird that made those who heard its song go mad. Only those people who were about to die could hear this deadly bird. She remembered hearing this story as a child and being terrified by it. But now what were these other things Sunny was telling her children?

"The police always burn the bodies," she heard him say. "It is the best way to get rid of them. Sometimes, though, a body part does not burn fully. Perhaps it hasn't been doused properly with kerosene; perhaps the police have run out of firewood, for so many corpses need a lot of wood to roast well. Once my friend found a skull in his field, partially covered in skin and soot. Another time, his dog Blackie brought home somebody's hand."

Kamal had run to Nimmo, covering her ears with her hands, and Nimmo had scolded Sunny for scaring the girl. "Stop filling their heads with rubbish," she had said.

"But it is not rubbish, maami-ji," Sunny protested. "It is all true, every word of it. Everybody should hear about the things that are going on in Punjab. Kamal and Pappu as well."

"No, I don't want them to know." She weighed her next words before uttering them. "Maybe you should go home," she said evenly. "As soon as possible."

Sunny had left the next day, giving a puzzled Satpal an excuse about having to meet someone in Jullundur.

Nimmo hadn't told Satpal about this incident. She was certain he would be annoyed by her rudeness. Sunny hadn't showed up at their door for the next four years. Now, Nimmo was certain, he was coming here to get away from the police, or worse. He was bringing Trouble to her home, and she couldn't think how to stop him.

Part Five

—

Endings

TWENTY-ONE

A SENSE OF BELONGING

—

Vancouver

March 1984

I t was a quiet day at The Bay's shoe department, and Leela spent most of it listening to Erin's woes. In the sixteen years since she had started working at the store, Leela had seen her sales manager through three boyfriends and two marriages. She had often wondered why Erin had decided that she, Leela, married for twenty-six years to a man whom she had met only once before her wedding, should be an authority on affairs of the heart.

"I told him he'd better watch out," she said to Leela, fluffing her already high hair with her red fingernails. She leaned against the countertop. "I am not, I repeat *not*, going to take crap from anybody. You know me, Laila. You know I don't take crap, right?"

Erin persisted in calling her Laila. Once, exasperated, Leela had even written it down in big black letters and waved it in front of Erin's nose—LEE-LA—but to no effect. It wasn't that Erin didn't care for her. She had shown Leela many kindnesses, often going out of her way to drive her home, bringing her small gifts every Christmas and remembering her birthday as well as Preethi's and Arjun's. Leela suspected that she had merely decided that Leela could not possibly be a name because she had never heard of it, while "Laila" was the host of an American television talk show Erin watched faithfully. She was now resigned to being the more dashing Laila at work and mundane wife and mother-of-two Leela at home.

"Yes," Leela said doubtfully. Recently there had been signs that her sales manager's latest relationship was in trouble—Erin came late to work, sighed more than she sold, didn't wear the bright make-up of which she was so fond.

"Would you take crap from your guy, Laila? Tell me honestly, would you, as a self-respecting woman, take any old shit?"

Leela thought about it for a few moments. She wasn't sure what rated as crap in Erin's book. She had met Erin's boyfriend, and he had not seemed the sort to give anyone crap. He was a mild-mannered man with a shy smile and seemed to adore her.

She caught Erin looking anxiously at her through mascara-ringed eyes. "Well, would you? Take crap from your husband? Or would you leave him?"

The thought of leaving Balu had never entered her head, so Leela could only nod and say judiciously, "Well, it depends on the crap. I mean what *kind* of crap is Don giving you?" Hearing herself speak, she marvelled at the variety of tongues she had acquired—one that made her sound just like Erin, another a soothing, in charge-of-things tone for the customers who came to her like helpless children holding out pairs of shoes in confusion, a third for her home, the children, Balu, Bibi-ji and the wide circle of friends and acquaintances she now had. How enormous her world had become that she needed so many languages to negotiate it.

"Laila, are you listening?" Erin tapped her nails on the counter.

Leela widened her eyes at her colleague and nodded. "Yes, I am, Erin."

Erin was looking closely at her. "I just noticed, Laila. Your eyes are the same colour as mine."

"You *just* noticed?" Leela exclaimed. "And how long have we known each other?" She began to laugh.

"What's so funny?" Erin asked, looking puzzled.

"Never mind. It's a long and complicated story," Leela said. She shook her head and chuckled again. "I'll tell you some other time."

It was seven in the evening by the time she finished her shift and took the bus home. She settled into her seat with a sigh, noticing two teenaged girls sitting in the back of the bus. With their copycat hairstyles, dark lipstick, fishnet stockings and short leather skirts, they looked, to Leela, like a new singer called Madonna who appeared on television a lot these days. They were having a conversation that involved the repetition of a favourite word in a variety of tones and volumes.

"Fuck!" said one of them, shaking her head and rolling her eyes.

"Yeah, like *fuck,* man!" said the other, more verbose one.

"So I told him to, like, fuck *off!*"

They got off the bus at the next stop. Watching them as they sashayed down the sidewalk, Leela thought back to the first time she had heard their favourite word. A driver had spat it at them the day they arrived in Vancouver. *Fucking Chinese* was what he had called them. He had pointed his middle finger at the sky and she had wondered what all those words and gestures added up to, afraid of the dislike implicit in them. Now it all seemed so long ago and of little consequence.

Fishing around in her purse, she pulled out a letter that had arrived the previous day from Vimala, Balu's cousin in Delhi. It was full of news and gossip about their relatives. Leela liked rereading her letters until she had memorized them. She would reply in her spare time, writing a few words, a sentence or two, sometimes the entire paragraph between chores and during her lunch breaks at work. Somehow she could think of much more news to put into her missives when she wrote them piecemeal than when she sat down and tried to write about everything at once.

"Dear Leela," wrote Vimala. *"The photos you sent were very nice. How lovely Preethi is. We were glad to hear that she has got*

into a prestigious university for her master's degree. What a clever daughter you have, Leelu! As for Arjun, we were glad to hear he has found a job in Vancouver, this way at least one of your children is close by. He must be much in demand in the marriage market. A number of our acquaintances here are inquiring after him and want to know if he is thinking of marriage. There are lots of eligible girls here." Leela paused at that and wondered what her cousin would say if she knew about Arjun's gori girlfriend, Fern. Leela had just found out herself, and after a night of tossing at the prospect of half-and-half—or indeed one-third—grandchildren, she gave up, defeated by fractions, and shrugged mentally. It had been difficult for her—even painful, she remembered, so painful that she had put away, in some dusty corner of her mind, her memories of her large, sad mother. But it would not be difficult in this world, where change and movement and hybridity were commonplace, for any children that Arjun and Fern chose to have. Not so difficult, anyway.

She continued reading. *"Every letter you tell me that one of your friends is coming to India, but when are you coming? Even your children we have not seen, except in photographs. It is time for you to come home, Leela."*

Her stop arrived and Leela got off the bus. Yes, it had been too long. Somehow, without her noticing it, seventeen years had gone by since they had left Bangalore. The world had come apart since then and had fitted itself together again with altered borders. Old countries had become two or three new ones, walls had gone up and had been torn down, ancient enmities had been buried and then renewed with greater rage. Even the neighbourhood where she had lived for a decade and a half had altered beyond recognition. Mrs. Wu and JB Foods had long ago found themselves in competition with a dozen new stores that sold everything they carried, and then some. Korean, Indian, Sri Lankan, Chinese, Italian, Iranian and Greek grocery stores had sprung up or expanded into mini-supermarkets. Lalloo had sold Far Out Travels and was now in the real estate business. His former company now competed with three new travel agencies, each challenging the others with cut-throat pricing and aggressive customer service, offering cheap fares to India, Pakistan, Bangladesh and the Middle East. In tiny offices over these stores, shady lawyers offered to make recent arrivals' immigrant status legal for two thousand dollars.

Nowadays, goras who came here wandered around with a dazed look in their eyes as if they were foreigners in their own country. Landscapes had moved across oceans and superimposed themselves on this corner of the western world. Populations had shifted and created new understandings, belief systems and tensions. Old enmities were forgotten and new ones established. Abroad had turned into Home, and time had turned desis into strangers to their own past.

The real India had overtaken Leela's memories of it. The news she saw in the two-week-old Indian magazines that Balu brought home sometimes seemed to belong to a country she didn't know at all. Even the pictures of men and women in the advertisements astonished Leela—it was as if these people's bone structure had altered. They looked like her children—Indian, but with a subtle glossy western-ness coating their brown bodies.

She was suddenly overcome with an urgent desire to go back There and see if the India she had left behind had really changed so much. For many years she had pushed the idea of returning to the back of her mind, mostly because she could not afford to go. Next year, she would promise herself, next year. And each time the money was used for something else—school trips, music lessons, a new car.

Then, last year, just when she thought she had enough for three tickets, Balu had started talking about buying a place of their own. They had sat in front of the bank manager, a man they'd never met, and given him their pay stubs, income tax statements and other scraps of paper that proved they were capable of repaying a loan. Then they had talked about interest rates and other matters and signed more pieces of paper. As if in a dream, they had driven around the city looking at homes, alarmed at the difference between the prices and what they could afford. Yet, miraculously, they had found one. Several blocks away from the small house they had rented from the Singhs for so many years, this one was even smaller, with a handkerchief-sized yard, but it was theirs—theirs in a way the ancestral Bhat home or even Leela's father's house could never be. They had not inherited it; they had bought it themselves. With her typical generosity, Bibi-ji had insisted they take with them all the furniture that was in their old home, and then sent another truckload of tables and bookshelves and yet another couch over.

The thought of Bibi-ji filled Leela with guilt. After moving into their new home she had held a housewarming party—the last time she had seen Bibi-ji in several months. The children had left home and headed off in different directions—Jasbeer was somewhere in India and Preethi had flown to Toronto—so the young people had not provided an excuse to meet. Once or twice Bibi-ji phoned Leela to worry aloud about Jasbeer. He had not got in touch with his parents in New Delhi. And in the four years since he had left for the school in Bhinder, he had written in his letters to Bibi-ji only of wars and causes but nothing about the school or his studies. So vague were his letters that Bibi-ji had begun to wonder whether he was still at the school, and when she heard from Nimmo that he had not visited them even once in those four years, her nebulous uneasiness solidified into a certainty that her foster son was up to no good.

"Leela, what would you do if you woke up and discovered that Arjun was involved with religious extremists and guerrilla fighters in a country far away?" she had asked.

"I don't know, Bibi-ji. I really don't." Leela silently thanked her gods that her children had not given her and Balu any real cause for concern.

It was May before she phoned Bibi-ji, who was by then busy with her own preparations to leave for India.

"But it is the middle of summer—why are you going now?" Leela asked. "Why not December, like you always do?"

"This June is the hundredth anniversary celebration of the martyrdom of Guru Arjun Dev. I want to be there then.

It is an auspicious time. And I have to ask forgiveness for many sins." Bibi-ji would go despite the heat, despite the crowds, so that she could do penance for having taken a woman's son, promising to take care of him and then losing him. She would go down on her arthritic knees in the Harimandir Sahib, and she would wash the temple's vast marble floors. She would roll out five hundred rotis in the kitchens. She would clean the shoes left at the temple doors by the thousands of pilgrims. "And on our way back, we will visit Nimmo and Satpal and beg their forgiveness for losing their son instead of taking care of him as we promised we would do."

Hearing the weariness in Bibi-ji's voice, Leela offered, "Bibi-ji, why don't you come over for lunch before you leave? I'll make you your favourite masala dosais."

"I have much to do before I leave," Bibi-ji said. "The day after I return, Leela, you can feed Pa-ji and me those delicious dosais. Make sure you have plenty available, hanh? Now, what can I bring back for you from India? Do you want me to take anything to mail to your relatives there?"

"No, Bibi-ji, don't bother. Next year we are thinking of going ourselves."

"You have been saying that every year, my dear. Next year is a long way off. But if you remember anything you want, phone, you hear me? I am leaving on the twenty-ninth of May, so there is still time."

A car slowed down beside Leela. The driver, a woman with a glossy swing of auburn hair and bright green eyes, leaned out the window and said, "Excuse me."

Leela paused and smiled at the woman. "Yes?"

"I seem to be lost. I'm looking for this address"—the woman held out a slip of paper and a street map—"I wonder if you could help me."

And Leela provided the directions: *left at the street corner, drive two blocks, look for . . .* After the woman had driven away, she remained standing near the curb. She felt idiotically pleased. A stranger had stopped *her,* Leela Bhat, originally from Bangalore, India, for directions. She had taken the woman's map from her hands and without hesitating for even a moment had traced the route for her with a red pen. And in the woman's eyes she had seen, not an awareness of her alienness, but a recognition of one who belonged, one who needed no maps to find her way.

By the time she reached her home, she was smiling broadly. She stood for a few moments at the gate and savoured the sight of the house—the sloping roof with cedar shingles, the large windows on either side of the wide chocolate-brown door, the shiny brass knocker on the door. With a swing to her step she walked up the path, inserted the key in the door and let herself in.

She told Balu about the incident at the dinner table as she served him a ladle full of gojju made from raw mangoes. "For a change," she said, vigorously squeezing the rice and gojju in her own plate into a gruel, adding more of one or the other until she had the right consistency, "I was the one who belonged, and the gori woman was the stranger." She laughed like a girl. "And I want to go to India next year. Can we manage that? It has been too long."

"We'll see." Balu reached across to pat her hand. "God willing, and if our finances allow it, next summer we'll go home and eat ripe mangoes instead of these green ones."

TWENTY-TWO

GOLDEN TEMPLE

—

Amritsar

May 31–June 3, 1984

The journey to Amritsar was long but uneventful. After resting a day in a small hotel in New Delhi, Bibi-ji and Pa-ji caught the train to Amritsar, arriving at seven o'clock in the evening. Satpal's sister Manpreet and her husband, Balraj, met them at the station. They would spend the day together before moving to the guest house in the Golden Temple complex. Manpreet was upset by their decision to stay at a guest house.

"When *we* are here, why do you need to stay *there?*" she demanded in a hurt voice. "Besides, I've heard rumours of trouble. They say that Sant Bhindranwale is holed up in the temple complex with his followers and the government is out to get him. I've heard they have been stockpiling arms in there for months—in various buildings, even in underground storage rooms. It is not very safe. I am telling you, Pa-ji, better you stay here at home with us."

Pa-ji had heard of the deeply conservative preacher named Bhindranwale, whose pungent diatribes against the government of India were earning him an ever grow- ing following among the Sikhs. He had heard stories that it was Indira Gandhi who had promoted Bhindranwale for political reasons and now he had fallen into disfavour with her. But he could not really believe that a village preacher, however charismatic, could have the power to create the kind of violence that Manpreet seemed to be hinting at, and so he brushed her fears away. "How can your home be safer than a place of God, sister? We will be all right, don't worry. If things look bad we can always phone, and you can come and pick us up."

"It isn't that easy," Balraj warned. "In this country, a breeze can change into a storm before you end a sneeze! You might not have time to phone. Besides, if there is a curfew we will not be able to come and get you. Manpreet is right. The temple is an arsenal and the situa- tion is very unstable. You really should stay with us for a few days and then . . ."

Bibi-ji shook her head. There was always something going on in this city, in this contradictory country—agita- tions, festivals, processions, celebrations, explosions—it was a part of the daily, occasionally hazardous, business of living here. Religion and politics were always causing some conflagration or other. It had never affected them on previous trips, and she didn't think it would this time either.

But the following afternoon, on the way to the temple, Bibi-ji wondered about their decision to stay there. The evening before, driving through the city from the station to Manpreet's home, what she and Pa-ji had failed to notice in the dark were the soldiers in the streets. Now she spotted them everywhere, standing in clusters, guns drooping from their shoulders, their faces sharp with suspicion. She saw a vehicle being stopped by two soldiers and the passengers being pulled out roughly. And a little later, as they approached their destination, she saw Jeeps, manned by heavily armed policemen, blocking some of the narrow gullies that radiated outwards from the walls of the Golden Temple. This was where she loved to shop for bargains whenever she came to Amritsar, but the market, which should have been full of pilgrims, appeared empty. Instead, soldiers leaned against the doorways, and Bibi-ji glimpsed them on the flat rooftops that abutted or overlooked the walled temple complex. Her unease grew, but she said nothing.

"Did you see that?" Pa-ji remarked, as if reading her thoughts. "It looks like a war zone!"

"It is not *we* who are at war," Balraj remarked bitterly. Overriding their protests, he had accompanied them to the temple guest house. "It is our government, headed by the Pandit's daughter, Indira Gandhi, who is at war with us!"

They fell silent. After what seemed an inordinately long drive, which involved reversing several times to avoid roadblocks, they arrived at the temple gates. Here too soldiers stood around in small groups, carrying guns as casually as cricket bats, a sight that offered a disturbing contrast to the churn of colourfully dressed pilgrims. Bibi-ji shivered slightly, feeling deeply unnerved by the juxtaposition of the carnival atmosphere within the temple gates and the grim-eyed soldiers loitering just outside. From where she stood, she could see the buildings of the complex surrounding the central shrine, the Harimandir Sahib, its milk-white marble walls suffused with the light of day. Great carved doors opened on its four sides, she knew, so that men and women of all castes might enter. A memory came to Bibi-ji of an afternoon many decades ago when, as a young woman, just married, she had arrived in Amritsar. Standing in the living room of Mrs. Hardy, her English teacher, she had been looking out at the golden dome that beckoned in the distance.

The elderly lady had come up to the window and remarked, "Isn't that beautiful?"

"Yes, Mrs. Hardy, it is," Bibi-ji had said shyly, still in awe of this gori woman with her clear blue eyes, who taught her the English language and was fluent in Hindi and Punjabi as well.

"My late husband used to love going there, you know. He was an archaeologist, and the temples in this country fascinated him. He told me that the Harimandir Sahib is built on a level lower than the surrounding land. Did you know that?"

"Yes," Bibi-ji had nodded. When she visited it with Pa-ji's relatives on Sunday mornings, she always climbed down a flight of steps to the level of the water in the lake before crossing the walkway to enter the temple.

"But do you know why that is so?"

"No, Mrs. Hardy," Bibi-ji had replied. She had always been so awestruck by the temple, by the sense that she was in the holiest place in the Sikh world, that she had never questioned the structure of it.

"It is symbolic of your faith, in which everyone is equal. Caste or class does not matter. Every caste is required to go down a step in order to enter the house of God. I think that is a beautiful lesson in humility. Don't you?"

A lesson that had obviously been forgotten, Bibi-ji thought wryly, in this battle between prime minister and preacher.

She and Pa-ji were taken to a bare room in one of the three guest houses within the temple complex—their home for the next few days. They stretched out on hard mattresses on the narrow cots, the only pieces of furniture in the room other than a stiff-backed chair and a table that swayed uncertainly on its legs. Bibi-ji, who had grown used to the comforts of her Hollywood-style bedroom in distant Vancouver, tried not to mind the sparseness of the furnishings, the darkness or the mosquitoes that managed to find her plump body even through the shroud of netting draped over the bed. To live in the hermit-like simplicity of this room, she lectured herself sternly as she turned again on the mattress, trying to adjust her bulk to its narrowness, was part of her worship. She listened to the sly scuttle of cockroaches across the

bare floors, held her breath when she entered the bathroom, which had a faint smell of sewage overlaid with
that of phenol solution, and reminded herself that here
she was not Bibi-ji, wife of the wealthy Sikh gentleman
Khushwant Singh alias Pa-ji, of 212 East 56th, Vancouver,
but a humble petitioner in the court of the Almighty, the
Great Guru, the One Up There.

A tide of delayed jet lag and travel exhaustion knocked
them both into a deep, dreamless sleep that lasted the
entire day. They slept unaware through the citywide curfew imposed at nine o'clock that night, and didn't notice
the power supply had been cut off until Bibi-ji sat up suddenly, wide awake, bathed in sweat, her throat parched,
wondering why the fan was not operating. It was not yet
dawn and Pa-ji was still asleep, sprawled across his cot.
His white hair lay unbound about his wide, still-muscled
back, his breath whistled out of his nostrils and his arm
hung over the side of the bed, outside the mosquito netting. His wrist was red with bites. Bibi-ji gently lifted the
arm and put it back inside the netting. She looked with
deep love at the man she had stolen from her sister so
long ago. He had given her everything, forgiven all her
foolish obstinacies, indulged her whims even when he
had misgivings about them. When she had telephoned
him from Delhi to tell him she wanted to bring Jasbeer
back with her to Vancouver, he had first scolded her:
"It might not be good for the child. You must think carefully about this, my Bebby. It is a human life for which
you are assuming responsibility, not a doll or a pet. Do you
understand that?"

Yes, Bibi-ji had said, impatient with his lecturing, certain of the rightness of her good deed, yes, I know. But she had not known, not really. She had treated Jasbeer just as she would a toy or a pet, indulging his whims, ignoring his faults. And while she had played at being a mother, the boy had drifted far away from her.

Her watch told Bibi-ji that it was three o'clock in the morning but already, in the corridors of the guest house and outside her window, she could hear people move about. There was the sound of water running and the murmur of voices. The pilgrims were getting ready to visit the Harimandir Sahib before the heat made it impossible to walk barefoot on the marble walkway leading up to it. She looked out the window, filled with a childlike excitement. Somewhere out there the sun waited to explode into the sky. In another hour, the holy book would be carried from its resting place in the Akal Takht building, a plain structure that housed the temple offices, across the causeway and over the sacred waters of the lake surrounding the Harimandir Sahib, and finally through the great rosewood and silver doors to the spot where it would stay until nine that evening, when it would be borne back, the way it had arrived, to the Akal Takht.

Bibi-ji had no desire to miss this most beloved of rituals. She scrambled out of bed calling for Pa-ji to wake up as well, shaking him by his shoulder. "I'll have my bath and then you get ready, okay?" She stroked a long strand of loose hair away from his sweating face. It grieved her that members of the community whom Pa-ji had known for so many years, some of whom had stayed at their home as new immigrants, should boycott their restaurant so resolutely. It made her angry that his generosity was being repaid with such ill will. She had been frightened in the past few months by the attacks on Pa-ji, and was glad that he was away from all that—for a few weeks, at least.

"I don't want to miss the Sawari ceremony, so make sure you are up by the time I finish my bath," Bibi-ji said, touching Pa-ji's shoulder again. He stirred and sat up, rubbing his eyes with his knuckles, and after she had made sure that he was not going to slip back into sleep, Bibi-ji headed for the bath.

Day was breaking when they crossed the courtyard separating the living quarters from the temple, and already the plaza around the Harimandir Sahib was packed with worshippers. The dawn singers had started to recite the Asa di War, the first song of the morning, preparing for the arrival of the holy book. Bibi-ji caught Pa-ji's hand and pushed her way through the crowd, pulling him behind her and ignoring his murmured protests that he was content to stay where they were, until they were near the Akal Takht building, directly across from the shrine. The priests would emerge from this building bearing the book on its cushion of tasseled silks, carried in its ceremonial palanquin of gold.

A tall, turbaned Sikh moved into Bibi-ji's line of view. She wondered whether God would mind if she shoved the man aside and planted herself in front of him. No, she decided, God would consider it an act of devotion. Using her plump shoulders as a wedge, artfully placing her bare feet on other, less wary, feet and dextrously manoeuvring both her elbows, Bibi-ji carved a triumphant passage for herself and Pa-ji to the front of the crowd. Just in time, for at that moment the musicians set up a resonant thudding beat on the nigaras. The priests emerged from the Akal Takht building, ceremoniously bearing the Guru Granth Sahib. There was a concerted rush of bodies to touch the sacred book, the cushion and the palanquin, to throw rose petals, to be a part of the ritual. Bibi-ji planted her legs wide and firmly refused to let the rushing crowd dislodge her from her position at the head of the marble steps that descended to the causeway. The priests made their way across the lake in a flurry of tassled fans, rose petals and perfumed water, and as they reached the Harimandir Sahib the singers' voices peaked in a joyous crescendo. As if in response, the sun rose and set ablaze the golden dome and spires of the Harimandir Sahib. Below it, the silent lake caught and cradled the glowing reflection in its calm depths. Bibi-ji held Pa-ji's hand and wept quietly. In the enchantment of the moment, she forgot the armed men outside the temple and the disquiet she had sensed on the streets the previous afternoon.

They spent the morning in the cool of the Harimandir Sahib, listening to the soothing chant of the singers. At one o'clock they joined the other worshippers in the dining hall for lunch. Later they ambled around, stopping occasionally to chat with strangers, for in this place of God they all became kin. Later still, suffused with a feeling of well-being, they sat in companionable silence in the shade of one of the buildings and watched the crush of pilgrims who had arrived for the martyrdom anniversary celebrations. A child ran past squealing with excitement, trailing a bright yellow balloon. In the lake people dipped and bobbed and rose, their clothes drying in the hot sun minutes after they emerged. Women stood chattering in groups. It all seemed so normal to Bibi-ji, like any other festival day, that she began to wonder whether the rumours of armed men hiding inside the temple were exaggerated. Were the soldiers she had seen patrolling the streets figments of her imagination?

But that evening, as they wandered through the strangely silent marketplace outside the temple walls, they could not miss the palpable tension in the air. Shops were shuttered tight, even though the area swarmed with pilgrims and business would have been good. And yes, there were the ubiquitous soldiers, standing silently in the doorways of cheap hotels and at the ends of the dark streets.

"I think we should go back," Pa-ji said, looking around uneasily. "I am not sure what it is, but I can sense that something is wrong."

"Yes." Bibi-ji knew what he meant. They had grown accustomed to the flow of other waters. Here they no longer recognized the changes in current and tide until it was too late.

They returned to the Golden Temple and once again Bibi-ji felt heartened by the serene structure, now gleaming in its tranquil lake in the rays of the setting sun. Pilgrims continued to wander around it, not wanting to break the spell by leaving the sacred place. Bibi-ji looked up at the water tower that soared behind the guest houses and noticed two men wearing tall, bright orange turbans wound like Dr. Randhawa's. Were they carrying guns? She shaded her eyes with a hand and gazed up, but the men were no longer visible.

"Did you see that?" she asked Pa-ji. "Men with guns? Not soldiers."

"Where?"

"Never mind. I must have imagined them. It's nothing."

They had a quiet dinner and sat at the edge of the lake again, watching the sun dip below the horizon and listening to the evening singers' mesmeric chanting. They would stay until the night singers arrived to chant the Rahras and the last hymns of the day before the holy book was returned to the Akal Takht, and the great silver and rosewood doors of the Harimandir Sahib were shut for the ritual cleansing of the shrine. Tomorrow, Bibi-ji promised herself, she would participate in that ritual.

By eight o'clock it was dark but for the stars in the sky and the lights glimmering in the surrounding buildings. The singing in the temple was occasionally drowned out by distorted sounds from loudspeakers making announcements in the streets outside the temple, but Bibi-ji could not understand what was being said. The announcements first increased in volume and then faded away as the vehicles carrying the announcers drove on.

Pa-ji leaned across to one of two middle-aged woman seated beside him. She was watching over six boys aged seven or eight, urging them to sit quietly and listen to the chanting.

324

"Sister, what are they saying out there?" he asked. "It is hard to understand."

"They are announcing a curfew. There was one last night also."

Then the lights died. The power had gone off not only in the temple, Bibi-ji soon realized, but all over the city. For a few moments, until her eyes adjusted to the intense blackness of the night and she began to make out the shapes of people and buildings, Bibi-ji was frightened, feeling as if she had suddenly lost her vision. Moments later, large bonfires flared up in various corners of the temple complex, throwing sharp-edged shadows on the walls. One of the teachers pointed towards the eastern gate of the temple and said, "Look, soldiers are coming in."

"Where?" asked her companion, peering in the direction of her pointing finger. "I don't see anything."

"And there too, can you see now?" The first woman pointed at the opposite gate, and Bibi-ji, squinting into the darkness, dimly saw a group of men running into the complex.

The woman beside her fished around in a large cloth bag and brought out an electric torch. She shone it around, counting the boys. "All of you sit close to Kashmir Miss and me," she said, reaching across to grab a boy who was particularly fidgety. "If you get lost we will not be able to find you, do you hear?"

"Yes Rani Miss," chorused the boys, squatting on the ground. The other woman, who Bibi-ji assumed was Kashmir, took some snacks from her bag and handed them around to her charges.

"Are you here alone with these boys?" Bibi-ji asked the women curiously. "Are these all your children?"

"No, they are from the school in our town," one of the women said. "Kashmir and I brought them here for the celebrations." She waved a hand around. "How were we to know that there would be trouble here? All those men with guns and bombs all over, is this any way to treat a place of worship?"

"It is the government, Rani," whispered Kashmir. "That Indira Gandhi. *She* is the one who has no respect for our faith. *She* is the one who has sent the army into this sacred place."

"But what about the extremists who have been hiding here all these months with their weapons?" Rani's voice was bitter in the darkness. "How are they any different from the government?"

"Extremists? They are freedom fighters. My brother knows them well. Fighting for us. It is the *government* that is against us."

There was an anguished pause. Then Kashmir turned to Bibi-ji. "And you, which town are you from?"

"We are not from here. We came from Canada for the celebrations. To offer seva. We did not know there would be trouble."

"Didn't know?" Rani was suddenly angry. "How could you *not* know? It is people like you sitting in foreign countries, far away from everything, nice and safe, who *create* trouble. *You* are the ones who give money to these terrorists, and we are the ones who suffer!"

Bibi-ji was silenced. Pa-ji was quiet too. Behind them,

the singing intensified, rising and falling as the holy book was borne out of the temple and across the lake and returned to the Akal Takht building.

"Let's go back to our room," Bibi-ji said, suddenly feeling tired.

Pa-ji rose to his feet. "I can barely see anything," he muttered.

"I have my torch," Rani offered. Her voice was conciliatory and friendly again. "Why don't we go together? It will be a big help to us if you could hold some of these children by their hands so they don't get lost."

They made their way hand in hand, the children quiet in the darkness. When they reached the guest house Rani shone the torch in Bibi-ji's bag so that she could search for the keys to their room. The boys, safe again, began chattering and laughing.

"You should ask someone at the reception desk to send you a bucket of water for the bathroom, and some drinking water," Rani advised. "Now that the electricity has gone, who knows? The water might stop too."

"I'll go and ask," Pa-ji said. He waved to the teachers as they led their excitable young charges through the corridor and up the stairs to their room on the floor above.

The reception desk was illuminated with a petromax lantern. "*Sat Sri Akal,* ji," the young man at the desk greeted him.

"*Sat Sri Akal,*" Pa-ji responded. "How long is this curfew going to continue, putthar?"

"I don't know. But it is not a good idea even to leave this building. The army has entered the compound and

I hear there might be trouble. Have you seen them? How hard they walk on this sacred ground. Even God must be terrified!" He lowered his voice. "And it is not just soldiers who desecrate with guns and bombs. Over our heads, on the roofs and under our feet in the storage rooms, our own brothers and sons and fathers, armed too, stamp as hard as demons."

Pa-ji cleared his throat and the young man became businesslike. "But is there something I can do for you?"

"We wanted some water—to drink and to wash, just in case," Pa-ji said apologetically. "But if it is too much trouble . . ."

"No trouble, I will organize it."

"Can we have a few candles also?" Bibi-ji asked. "We will pay for them, of course."

Back in their room, Pa-ji tiredly changed into his pyjamas and lay down with a sigh on the narrow bed. Bibi-ji lit one of the candles and stuck it on the rickety table. She moved around silently, performing her nightly rituals of brushing her teeth, washing and creaming her face and brushing her hair, all of which she had neglected the previous night in her exhaustion. The grooming soothed her tired mind as much as it did her scalp and skin. She felt Pa-ji's eyes on her in the candlelit darkness.

"You are beautiful, my Bebby," he murmured.

She moved over to his cot and leaned forward to place a kiss on the top of his head. She noticed that his once-thick, long hair had grown sparse; she could see his scalp gleaming through. She stroked his face. "Sleep, Pa-ji, sleep. Tomorrow we will ask Balraj to come and take us to his house if the curfew has lifted. I was a foolish woman to insist on staying here."

"You are never foolish, my Bebby," Pa-ji said. He caught her hand and carried it to his mouth. His moustache tickled the skin and she laughed softly. Pa-ji lay back and was soon asleep, his snores reverberating around the room in a rhythm that had long become familiar to Bibi-ji.

She could not sleep, so she sat on the hard chair by the window, the candle flickering beside her, wondering what the day would bring. Out in the temple courtyard that surrounded the shrine and the dark lake, in the low light from dying bonfires, she could see groups of men gathering near various buildings and hear the sounds of running. Occasionally she heard a sharp command in the darkness. She fell asleep on the chair, her head uncomfortably wedged between the window frame and the wall.

A series of sounds, like those of a backfiring car, woke her abruptly. Pa-ji too was startled awake. He sat up and said blearily, "Bebby? What happened?"

"I don't know. Something is going on outside," Bibi-ji replied. She looked out again and was nearly blinded by a floodlight. A loudspeaker stuttered to life and a staccato voice announced, first in Punjabi and then in Hindi, that pilgrims inside the buildings were to come out immediately. They would be escorted off the temple premises by the army. Then there was silence.

"Where do they expect us to go in the middle of the night?" Pa-ji said, getting out of bed and joining Bibi-ji by the window.

"What should we do?" Bibi-ji asked. The candle had guttered away into a blob. She lit another one and squinted in the dim light at her watch. It was four o'clock, an hour before dawn. A crow cawed urgently in the distance, awakened by the bright floodlight, and soon other birds joined in a pre-dawn chorus. Another sound rose above the outcry—that of the morning raagis coming faintly from the direction of the shrine, beginning their chant to a new day. But their song was interrupted by the sound of a helicopter chopping through the dark air, brutish and ugly. Looking out of her window, Bibi-ji saw a circle of light beaming down from it and landing on one of the buildings beyond their own. The loudspeaker crackled again, and the disembodied voice asked women, children and the aged to come out. She saw a small group emerge from the guest house beside theirs and heard the thud of army boots as a group of soldiers sprinted across the expanse of marble floor to provide the promised escort. The group started moving towards the gate closest to the guest houses. The morning singers had entered the Harimandir Sahib, and their singing, fainter now, continued to thread its way into the cacophony—soldiers' boots, the rumble of a tank entering the sacred space, men shouting indistinctly, the buzz of static from the army loudspeaker and the clatter of helicopters above it all.

Pa-ji moved to the door of their room. Opening it slightly, he peered into the corridor. "Better get dressed," he said pulling his head back in and latching the door. "We will have to get out of here. I will see if it is possible to phone Balraj."

"Perhaps we can take a tonga or a taxi or something?" Bibi-ji said, clamping a lid on her rising panic. A moment later she remembered that a curfew had been imposed—they would not be able to find any transportation. Nothing in her previous experience had prepared her for a moment like this. "What kind of government would send an army inside a temple, Pa-ji? Is this Mrs. Gandhi truly mad?"

Pa-ji pulled on his trousers and shrugged quickly into a shirt. "We don't know what is happening. There are extremists here too, it seems, inside their own sacred temple, defiling it with guns and bombs. It is better not to judge anybody yet."

They left their suitcases in the room, locked the door behind them and joined the growing crowd of people that was emerging from other rooms and pooling near the reception desk. Bibi-ji spotted the two schoolteachers, Rani and Kashmir, holding some of the small boys by the hand and sharply instructing the others to stay close. "Hold on to my dupatta, hold my kameez," they took turns repeating to the boys. "Whatever happens, don't let go."

Bibi-ji pushed through the crowd towards the two women while Pa-ji headed for the reception desk, which was already surrounded by people, to ask for a phone. "Wait for me at the door," he said before leaving her side. "I don't want you to go out there alone."

She nodded and continued towards the teachers. "Do you want some help?" she asked.

The women nodded gratefully, and Bibi-ji took the small cold hands of two of the boys.

331

"What is happening?" she asked. "Is it safe to leave? Did you hear those helicopters?"

"Yes, we heard. It was impossible to sleep," said Rani. "If we stick close to the soldiers, they say we will be safe. They will put us on buses and we can go home."

"The curfew has been lifted, then?" Bibi-ji asked with relief.

"No, no, the curfew is still on. But the army wants to evacuate the pilgrims—the women and children and old people. I hear that they are detaining all the men in case there are terrorists among them."

"But these buses will take us wherever we want to go?" Bibi-ji asked doubtfully. "So many of us?"

A short man beside them turned and said, "You are right, they won't take us where we wish to go. Why should they? We will be driven to police stations and kept there until the end of curfew. Then we will be allowed to catch the bus or take a rickshaw home. But I don't know what out-of-towners will do. The borders of Amritsar are sealed. No traffic in or out. Not even the trains are running. We are all trapped here."

Kashmir looked fearfully at her companion. "Rani, I am not leaving this place. Where are we to go with these children if we cannot catch a bus back to the village?"

"She is right," Rani sighed. She took the two little boys from Bibi-ji. "You carry on, sister. We will have to see what is possible for us."

Bibi-ji nodded and pushed her way through the crowd towards the reception desk and Pa-ji. "Did you phone Balraj?" she asked hopefully.

"The phone lines have been cut," Pa-ji said.

"Then what will we do out there? Nothing is open. How will we manage?"

"Just like all these other people," Pa-ji replied. He held her hand in his, warm and firm, and they made their way out of the guest house to a small gathering of pilgrims. They seemed to be the only people outside the dark buildings, Bibi-ji noticed. "Where is everyone? Where are the soldiers?" she whispered to Pa-ji. "I thought you said there would be soldiers to protect us."

Pa-ji shook his head. "I don't know. Maybe we should go back inside."

Bibi-ji looked at her watch. It was five o'clock. She could not see the helicopter any longer. Now the sound of birds could barely be heard over the buzz of voices around her.

Suddenly a sharp sound rang out and a woman in the front of the crowd fell to her knees. Another woman bent down to help her and began to scream. Something was very wrong. An elderly man beside Bibi-ji was the first to realize what was happening. He turned back towards the guest house, pulling two small girls after him.

"Inside!" he shouted as he pushed past Bibi-ji. "They're shooting! Get back inside!"

Someone else took up his cry. "They are shooting, Oh God, they are shooting us!"

People churned around, trying to run this way or that. Who was shooting whom? No one seemed to know. Bibi-ji felt someone shove her hard from behind, someone in a desperate rush to get back inside the guest house. She staggered and felt her hand being wrenched away from Pa-ji's.

"Pa-ji?" She stopped abruptly, turned and shouted. "Pa-ji!"

She struggled to reach Pa-ji, who had been dragged away from her, away from the guest house, by the panicked movement of the crowd. She spotted his tall frame, his dark blue turban, impeccably wound as always, despite the fact that the only light in their room had been from the candle. He turned and waved to her urgently. Go in, his hand said, go in.

Another shot rang out. Bibi-ji saw her husband fall forward as if someone had slammed him hard from behind. She waited for him to rise. She no longer saw the crowd or heard the woman screaming beside the other fallen body. She was aware only of herself standing there and Pa-ji lying on the ground a few steps away. Reaching him, she knelt down slowly, her dupatta settling around his still body.

"Pa-ji?" she said, in the tone she always used to wake him for his morning tea. "Come, Pa-ji. It is not safe here."

TWENTY-THREE

WHISPERS IN THE WIND

—

Vancouver

August 1984

A knife in the heart. A dagger in the back. An insult. An outrage. Shock, then anger, spread across the world like acid, burning into the soul of every Sikh, turning even moderate, temple once-in-a-while worshippers into true believers. Their most holy place had been desecrated by the Indian government. Tanks had rolled across delicate marble floors, crushing ancient inlay. The library had been consumed by flames; centuries-old sacred manuscripts had been destroyed. Pilgrims had been killed. Nobody was sure how many—some claimed that it was two thousand people and others insisted that it was much higher. Humiliation, indignity, death.

The Delhi Junction was closed indefinitely. At the Taj Mahal, Bibi-ji slept in the spare bedroom, unable to use the pink and gold room she had shared with Pa-ji. When she looked in the mirror now, she found that she had grown old. All these years she had seen herself through her husband's eyes—a beautiful woman who never aged. But he was no longer here to look at her, and she crumbled, an old woman alone.

She could not remember much of what had happened after Pa-ji caught the bullet in his chest on that morning two months ago. She carried in her head nothing but the song of the raagis and the wail of a woman. Someone, she did not know who, had carried Pa-ji into the guest house. She must somehow have contacted Balraj and Manpreet, but she did not remember doing so. A funeral had been arranged for Pa-ji, but again she had little recollection of any of this.

Balraj had accompanied her to Delhi a month later when the statewide travel ban was lifted, and she had stayed with Nimmo for a few days before flying back to Vancouver. Mixed with her grief was her shame at having truly lost Nimmo's son. Jasbeer had disappeared. All of Balraj's efforts to locate him through contacts in the police services had yielded nothing. He had left the Damdami Taksal two years ago, Balraj was told. With some other students. But they did not know where he had gone.

Back in Vancouver, her friends arrived, offering words of sympathy. Leela and Balu, the Majumdars and all those—so many—whose lives had crossed hers and Pa-ji's. But each time she accepted their words of condolence, she felt that in acknowledging Pa-ji's death she was in fact causing it.

"How could this have happened in a *temple?*" she asked Lalloo, who had moved temporarily into the Taj Mahal. Leela had offered to come and stay with her, but Bibi-ji found that in this time of mourning she preferred her own people: she found comfort in hearing the sound of her mother tongue all around her. Then there were the inevitable house guests, those she would not turn away even now, for Pa-ji's sake, whose voices she heard at night in the living room in front of the big television screen, rising as one in anger.

Lalloo's voice was often the loudest, bitter in its pain. "They have no respect for us Sikhs," she heard him cry one night. "That's why they could go in like that and trample on our beliefs. I am beginning to like the idea of a divorce from India."

"Yes, Khalistan is what we need!" This was a voice she did not recognize, a young man recently arrived from India. "They forget we are Sikhs, the lions who protected them from the Mussulman invaders, and now they treat us like this?"

"Blood for blood!" shouted another young man. "For every dead Sikh, a hundred Hindus."

Bibi-ji listened, silent, dazed.

"We should hold protest marches every day in front of the Indian High Commission," Lalloo said. "With the biggest rally on August 15th—India's Independence Day."

"I wish to join the rally too," Bibi-ji said to Lalloo the next morning, surprising herself. She had never been one for protest marches and processions. But this year she needed to do something symbolic, for Pa-ji's sake. Instead of celebrating Independence Day at the Patels' as she had done for so many years, she would march in anger.

On the morning of August 15th she combed her long grey hair into a high bun, wore the red salwar kameez that Pa-ji had particularly liked on her, put on all her matching bangles and joined the protesters. "Indira Gandhi, down, down!" they shouted. "Khalistan forever!" "Blood in return for blood!" By the time she returned home, she was hoarse from shouting. And she was as hard-eyed in her rage against the Indian government and Hindus as the young men who surrounded her had been. That night, for the first time since Pa-ji's death, she fell into a deep and dreamless sleep.

In early September The Delhi Junction reopened, with Lalloo at the cashier's desk. Grim and unsmiling, he had abandoned the natty suit he usually wore for a plain white pathan outfit, had replaced his hat with a turban and had allowed his beard and moustache to grow. He had temporarily taken over the running of the restaurant. Bibi-ji had not come in since her return from India; she knew she would only see Pa-ji sitting at the till or leaning over the tables to talk to his customers, and would hear his bellowing laugh and cheerful voice.

By midday, the café was full of Pa-ji's friends; even some of those who had shouted him down at the gurudwara committee meetings came to share their grief. And that old quartet of friends—Balu, Majumdar, Shah and Menon—were there too, sitting at their usual table.

"I still can't believe it," Balu murmured, looking at the counter, which seemed empty despite Lalloo's presence. "What a horrible thing."

Majumdar nodded but said nothing. He had taken Pa-ji's death hard, for he had known the old Sikh for many years.

"We're going to miss him," Menon said. "Have you seen Bibi-ji since she came home?"

Balu nodded. "Leela and I went over to her house. She looked terrible. *Terrible*. Poor thing."

An altercation broke out at a neighbouring table between an elderly Sikh and two younger men. "Are you saying that it was okay for the Indian army to invade our temple? What kind of talk is that?" one of the younger men shouted.

The older man held up his hand. "All I am saying is that there were militants and snipers from our own community hiding in every corner of the temple complex as well. They too had stockpiled arms, they too committed sacrilege by turning our temple into a war zone. How do we know it was not their bullet that killed our Pa-ji?"

Harish Shah, who had been quiet until then, leaned over and said in a low voice to his friends, "He is right, you know. What was Bhindranwale doing inside the Golden Temple? A preacher with guns and bombs? It is okay for him to start a war inside his own temple, but it was wrong of Indira Gandhi to send in the troops to stop it? What else could she have done?"

"I agree that it was wrong of Bhindranwale to turn the temple into an arsenal, Shah," Majumdar said. "But Mrs. G could have used different tactics to deal with the situation."

"You cannot destroy a nest of vipers by stroking them with your hand, Majumdar," Shah replied, raising his voice. "What different tactics are you suggesting, may I ask?"

"She could have cut off water and electricity and waited until the food supplies had run out as well. That would have smoked them all out soon enough. And it would have avoided unnecessary bloodshed and destruction, not to mention further stoking of resentment."

One of the young men at the neighbouring table scraped his chair back hard, glared at Balu's table, and said something in Punjabi. The elderly Sikh caught him by the wrist and murmured placatingly. But the young man continued to glower at Balu and his friends before adding in English, "Bastard Hindus, you will pay for this."

Shah looked belligerent, but before he could say something to exacerbate the tension building between the two tables, Lalloo came over, unasked, with their bill. "Maybe you should leave, my friends," he suggested. "It might be better."

"What if we don't wish to leave?" Shah was irate. "I would like another tea, if you please."

But his friends had risen to their feet. Majumdar paid the bill and urged Shah out of his chair and through the door. "Sorry, Lalloo," he said as they left the restaurant. "Everyone is feeling emotional about Pa-ji. Shah didn't mean anything."

Outside, as they made their way to their cars, Shah turned on Majumdar. "I don't bloody need you to apologize for me. I meant every word I said. And what do you mean by dragging me out like this? I wanted to tell that turbaned thug a thing or two. Didn't you hear? He called us 'Bastard Hindus'!"

"Why don't we go to my place and talk there instead of shouting on the street like this?" Balu suggested. A group of young Sikh men brushed past on their way into The Delhi Junction, and he looked nervously at them.

"No, I have to go home," Menon said. "But you know, Shah, I heard from some friends in India that it is even more tense in Punjab now. Anyone with a beard and a turban is suspect. The army and the police are dragging people out of their houses in the middle of the night and taking them away."

"To be tortured, the rumours go," Majumdar added. "People disappear without trace."

A starched, sharp-edged silence followed. Shah shook his head and laughed. "Really, where do you get all this information? Or should I call it *mis*information?"

"Well, I heard it some months ago from a young man who had been tortured," Majumdar said. "Pa-ji brought him to meet me. He wanted some advice on how the poor fellow could enrol in a course at our college."

"Nonsense. He must have made it up." Shah laughed again. "And I have decided not to go to The Delhi Junction anymore. Not that I have anything against Bibi-ji, but I don't trust her waiters—or Lalloo, for that matter. Did you see the look in his eyes when he brought us the bill? Those bastards are so angry with us, I wouldn't be surprised if they spit in our food before serving it."

Us and Them, Balu thought uneasily. When did we split into these groups? The Singhs were family. How could

Shah, who had known them even longer than he had, abandon the friendship so abruptly and without a second thought?

Two weeks later. All day Bibi-ji had been trying to clear out Pa-ji's papers, but she had got nowhere; she had wept over every one. She could not bear to move a single page of his manuscript, which he had left spread out on his desk, or to straighten his chair. Abandoning the attempt to do anything in the room, she instead wandered around it, touching the rows of memorabilia on his bookshelves that were fighting for space with his books. From the walls, the photographs of his "relatives" gazed back at her, meaningless now without Pa-ji to give them life with his stories.

She looked out the window to see the view her husband had enjoyed when he stood in this spot and noticed a man coming up the driveway, a backpack slung over one shoulder, wearing a black turban, walking with a loping stride, his beard unruly and longer than she remembered it. The familiar figure was unmistakeable. She hurried out of the room and down the stairs.

"Jassu is home," she called to the young men sitting in the living room. "Jasbeer is back," she called to the women, who were busy—as if they had never stopped—making food in the kitchen. She opened the door and held out her arms. "I haven't lost you, I haven't lost you," she whispered.

Jasbeer hugged her close. "I heard," he said. "I just heard, Bibi-ji."

He led her back into the house. Gently, he sat her down on the couch. "Tell me what happened," he said.

—

Another week, and Dr. Randhawa arrived again at the Taj Mahal. He was as tall and grey as ever, and accompanied by an even larger entourage. This time Bibi-ji prepared a lavish welcome for him, cooking a variety of dishes with her own hands and insisting that his acolytes stay in the house with him as long as they wished. She suppressed her dislike of his pomposity, his arrogance. He had been right after all, she told herself. The Indians had humiliated the Sikhs and they had killed her Pa-ji. It was now a question of defending the faith, the thing that gave them, as a tribe, a face and a distinction.

Now large meetings were held at the Taj Mahal every day. Bibi-ji did not know many of the people who attended, and after a while she stopped trying to remember their names. Talk of revenge and of Khalistan whipped around like a bitter wind, fuelled by the arrival of yet more people from Punjab. Their stories were of more brutality, murders, disappearances, torture, humiliation. Jasbeer told Bibi-ji how dangerous it was to be a turbaned Sikh man in Punjab, how you could be picked up by the police or the army, thrown into jail or shot dead in fake "encounters." She was tempted to ask him what he had been doing during his long absence, how he came to know such things, but realized that she was afraid to find out.

October arrived in a flurry of red and gold leaves. Bibi-ji still moved mechanically—she could not believe that so many months of her life had gone by without Pa-ji beside her. One day, as she sat at her old spot in the kitchen—at the table, sorting out the mail—she saw a flimsy envelope from Delhi and noticed the familiar looping, careful handwriting. With a pang of pleasure or grief—she was not sure which—she picked up the envelope, tore it open and skimmed through it.

We cannot stop thinking about Pa-ji and how you must feel without him. This is a time for you to be with us, your family. Let me spoil you as a niece should, Bibi-ji. You have not allowed me the pleasure of this small task. How is our Jasbeer? I was so glad to hear from you that he is staying at home instead of wandering around Punjab in these terrible times. Our young men are hot-headed and jump into trouble without any regard for their safety or the safety of others. Pappu too has taken to saying uncomplimentary things about Indira Gandhi at the top of his voice. I keep begging him to keep his thoughts to himself since these are not good times for us Sikhs, and who knows what might be waiting for us round the corner? But he won't listen to me. He says this is a democracy and we all have the right to speak our minds.

Bibi-ji, I went with Satpal to do seva at the Golden Temple, to join with thousands of other Sikhs who come daily to build our sacred place. I saw for the first time the bullet holes in the walls of the shrine and I cried with hurt and with fear. And anger—with the government for sending tanks into our temple. Are we the enemy, or are we citizens of this country?

I am not the only one who feels this way. Indira-ji may have withdrawn the army from the Golden Temple, but she has left a sea of anger behind. I hope we don't all drown in it.

TWENTY-FOUR

THEY

—

New Delhi

October 31, 1984

A crow cawed insistently on the lawn of Indira Gandhi's residence and a flock of mynah birds quarrelled and twittered nearby. The roses, which had been plump and in full bloom only a week ago, had dropped most of their petals.

Indira Gandhi hurriedly finished breakfast with her family. She was in a rush to meet filmmaker Peter Ustinov, who was making a documentary on her for BBC television. Wearing her favourite orange cotton sari, she cut across the compound to an opening in the hedge separating her home from the gardens of her office. Behind her petite, bustling figure hurried a police constable carrying an umbrella, trying to shade her from the sun. But Indira

Gandhi walked much faster than he did, and he could barely keep up. A train of other people from her office followed her like ducklings. For a woman of sixty-seven, the prime minister was remarkably brisk.

She reached the opening in the hedge, barely noticing the armed guard who stood at attention there. Beside him was the security booth in which another guard waited with a Sten gun in his hands. As she approached the booth, the first guard drew his revolver and emptied it into Indira Gandhi's stomach and chest. At the same moment, the other one emerged from his booth and fired several rounds into her. By the time the turbaned guards had completed their task, twenty-two bullets were embedded in the prime minister's small body. Indira Gandhi died at 9:15 a.m.

Also at a quarter past nine that morning, the bus carrying Satpal to Modinagar left New Delhi's interstate terminus.

The news of the killing did not filter out until late in the afternoon. Even then, it was only a rumour of injury rather than death. All India Radio interrupted its regular programming to broadcast only music, which was limited to mournful songs played over and over again. In Delhi, busy with her class of children at the local gurudwara, Nimmo had no inkling that anything had happened to shatter the beauty of the day until the lunch break, when the head priest called them all together and told them the news. Indira Gandhi had been shot. By her own guards, both of whom were Sikhs.

"I think everybody should go home and stay there," the head priest said anxiously. He pointed to his turban. "It is not difficult to spot one of us, and anyone looking for a fight would have an easy target. If the prime minister really is dead and if the killers were Sikhs, I am afraid there may be trouble."

Nimmo hurried home wishing there was a way to contact Satpal, who must have reached Modinagar by now. Had he heard about the killing? Was he safe? And her children? Her daughter had gone to school as usual, and Pappu was at work. She could do nothing but wait for them.

She had barely entered her house and not yet shut the door when she heard Asha call her curtly from across the wall. "There is a phone call for you."

Nimmo slid her feet into her slippers and hurried to Asha's house. Not for the first time, she wished they had a phone of their own.

Asha waited in her front room, clearly irritated, and continued to stand there, arms akimbo, while Nimmo talked. It was Satpal, his voice distorted by static even though he was only three hours away from Delhi. "Listen, I heard the news. It is terrible. I will try to come home by the night bus, but if I can't then I will catch the early morning one. I will be home by lunchtime. And don't go out of the house. All of you, stay at home and lock the doors."

"I was getting worried. I didn't know where—" Nimmo's words tumbled out.

"And tell Pappu not to air his views on anything to anybody. It is not a good time for us."

Nimmo looked quickly at Asha, hoping she had not heard Satpal's loud voice—he tended to shout as if doing so would lessen the distance. She replaced the receiver slowly.

"Are you done?" Asha asked brusquely. Was there a change of attitude in her voice, Nimmo wondered? Was Asha more unfriendly than usual? She decided to confront it.

"Yes, thank you," she said. "It was my husband, to tell me he will be coming home at lunchtime tomorrow. But he will try to catch the night bus, in case there is trouble." She paused, then ploughed on awkwardly, feeling ridiculously guilty, as if she were implicated in the murder merely by being a Sikh. "Wasn't it terrible, how Indira-ji was killed?"

Asha gave her a veiled look and nodded. "Yes, that was no way for a person to die. Twenty-two bullets those crazy sardars pumped into her. An unarmed woman too. What is this world coming to?"

"I know," agreed Nimmo, grateful that Asha had not lost her temper. "Crazy people with God only knows what wickedness in their hearts."

"But your husband did not like her, did he?" Asha said suddenly, catching Nimmo off guard. "He never did, I know. And you were also angry when she sent the army into your temple! So why are you pretending to feel sad?"

"She was a defenceless woman," Nimmo stammered, unnerved by the spite in Asha's voice. "I always voted for her, you know that. I was upset about the army operation, but that doesn't mean . . ."

Asha's husband, a small man with a large paunch, entered the room, picking something out of his teeth with a fingernail. He gave Nimmo an empty glance, as if she were a stranger. To Asha he said, "If she needs to use the phone, why can't she get her own line? Or use the public booth, na? Always making use of other people, and then stabbing them in the back. And you, what are you standing here and doing bak-bak for? Is my lunch ready or not?" He turned to stare at Nimmo.

She mumbled her thanks, left five rupees on the table, as she always did, and hurried out of Asha's house. Her prime minister had been killed by men who were strangers to her, so why was *she* feeling so frightened? A group of young men drifted past and Nimmo shifted to the side. They turned to stare at her and then turned back with a laugh. One said something that made the rest burst into crude laughter. They were talking about her, about Sikhs, she was positive. Nimmo rushed into her house, the black dog of fear that had stayed low for so long rearing up again, full-grown and monstrous.

Kamal was there, in the kitchen, making a cup of tea and rummaging through the shelves. She turned in alarm when her mother rushed in. "Mummy, is there anything to eat in the house? I am so hungry. And did you hear? Indira Gandhi was shot! Twenty-two bullets! Everyone in the bus was talking about it."

Nimmo slapped her hard on her back.

"*Ow!* What did I do? Why are you hitting me?" Kamal wailed, trying to soothe the spot where her mother's hand had landed.

"Why do you leave the door open?" shouted Nimmo. "Any goonda, thug or murderer can walk right in and there you are, memsahib, making chai without a thought in your head. Stupid, stupid girl."

"The door is always open, Mummy," Kamal protested. "You left it open just now. Where were you? Why are you so angry?"

Nimmo took a deep breath to calm herself. "I was in that Asha's house. I wish we had our own phone. That was your father calling from Modinagar." She looked at her daughter and was filled with a surge of tenderness. "Kamal, why don't you stay at home tomorrow, putthar?" she said in a gentler voice.

"Okay, if you want."

"You are sure?" Nimmo asked anxiously. "Your teacher won't be angry with you?"

Kamal laughed. "Mummy, make up your mind, na? You want me to stay at home or not? Besides, there are a hundred students in my class. The teachers don't care whether we are dead or alive. They don't even know our names!"

"I wish your brother would come home soon," muttered Nimmo, glancing anxiously at the clock.

Kamal returned to the kitchen, emerging a few moments later with Nimmo's tea. "Calm down, Mummy. If there is trouble he will just stay where he is, won't he? You worry for nothing. What can happen?"

What can happen? What can happen? Nimmo wanted to cry: *You can lose everything in one single day, your past, your present and your future.* But she controlled her agitation and sipped the tea her daughter handed her. Then she checked the containers of rice and dal and flour to make sure there was enough food to last for a few days if necessary. There were two cauliflowers in the refrigerator and a few potatoes.

"Listen," she said. "We need some kerosene for the lanterns in case the lights go out, and some onions. I will go to the shop round the corner, okay? And you stay inside here, did you hear me? Hanh? *Inside,* not even an eyelash out the window. And I will lock the door from outside and go, so people will think nobody is at home."

"Mummy, why are you saying these things? You are scaring me. What will happen to us? Why should anything happen? We didn't do anything wrong."

Nimmo stroked her daughter's hair away from her face. "No we didn't do anything wrong. And nothing will happen, don't worry. I am just being careful. At times like this, in a big city like Delhi, there are always people wanting to create trouble."

"I want to come with you."

"No, you stay here and be very quiet. I'll be back soon."

Half an hour later Nimmo returned, lugging a can of kerosene, a bag of potatoes, onions and a few other vegetables. She was ashamed that two men from her community had murdered an unarmed old woman and was convinced that every single person she had encountered on her brief journey had looked at her in anger, as if they knew she was a Sikh, a killer of Mrs. Gandhi. She worried about how that spark of anger could become a fire without warning.

A few minutes after she entered the house, to her great relief Pappu returned. He had more news. "They beat up some Sikhs near the hospital where Indira Gandhi's body was taken," he said.

"I knew this would happen," Nimmo said. "Pappu, your father phoned this afternoon. He said you should keep your opinions to yourself. Don't say foolish things. You never know how people will react in such times. I wish it was anybody but a Sikh that had killed Indira Gandhi."

"There was a good reason, Mummy," Pappu replied angrily. "Look at how she insulted us."

"There is never a good reason to kill an unarmed old woman." Nimmo glared at her son. "And I am hearing stories that you are involved with those Khalistani boys. Is this true? Haven't I told you to stay out of all that nonsense? Listen with both ears open, Pappu. Some of those men are violent, and violence does nothing but breed more violence."

"What about violence to get justice, Mummy? Look at what happened to those pilgrims at the temple. The talk is that more than two or three thousand died. And Pa-ji. What did *he* do to deserve death? He was unarmed and peaceful. Who will bring him justice? Hanh? Tell me!"

"And you think *you* will? Do you know the meaning of justice?"

Pappu set down his teacup angrily. "She got what she deserved." He aimed at the air and said, "Phfff!"

Nimmo leaned over and slapped her son hard on his cheek. "Dirty boy, you need to have your mouth washed out with soap! How can you say such things in this house?" But her slap had stunned her as much as it did Pappu.

He rubbed his burning cheek. "Well, *she* didn't have

any problems killing people, did she? Hundreds of them, thousands. And nobody even knows where some of the bodies are. The people who vanished. And what do you mean, talk like this in this house? What do you think Daddy-ji's friends talk about all the time? Everybody is angry. You must be the only one saying peace this and peace that."

"It has nothing to do with us," Nimmo insisted.

Pappu stood up. He towered over his mother. "You don't understand anything," he said. "You never will."

"You are the one who does not understand," Nimmo replied sadly. "Have you forgotten that life is a rare privilege God has granted us? You have no right to say that it is good to take away a life, no reason in the world can justify murder."

"What right did your Indira Gandhi have to take away lives, then? Is she a goddess?" Pappu argued.

"I don't want to talk to you anymore." Nimmo pursed her lips and turned away.

She would write to Bibi-ji tomorrow, she promised herself. She would ask her to take Pappu as well, far away from this fear and the temptation to do violence. She did not agree with Satpal that he was as safe here as anywhere, that no corner of the world was free from hate and fear. He had scoffed at her fears. "You think it is bad here? At least this is our own country. We have had a good life so far. Over there, in that gora country, he will not be hated for his religion maybe, but for the colour of his skin, for looking different. If you want to be safe, you have to *look* like everyone else, you have to hide yourself."

"What are you saying? Unless you both cut your hair and beards and become munda Sikhs, you will never look like everybody else here either, will you?" Nimmo had said with unaccustomed asperity. She wondered at Satpal's naïveté. In order to disappear in this country they called their own, they would have to sacrifice a part of who they were. Like the tiger in a story she had heard as a child, Satpal and her son would have to burn their hides to rid themselves of their stripes. She could only imagine the pain that would involve.

The day after Mrs. Gandhi's death, the national television and radio networks confirmed the news of her murder. Nimmo stayed awake all night expecting violence to erupt out of the darkness. She could sense it lurking out there in the silent streets, in the narrow gullies, in her neighbour's yard. But when morning arrived the city was calm.

Pappu decided to go to the shop as usual.

"Why can't you stay home?" Nimmo appealed to him. "It is too quiet out there. Your father hasn't come home yet, and I am not sure—"

"Nothing will happen, Mummy. Don't worry. Besides, there is a scooter that has to be finished today, we are already a week behind on the repairs and the customer is threatening to not pay us."

He wrapped his arm around his mother's shoulders and pecked her on the top of her head. Then he turned to Kamal, who was piling some books neatly on a shelf. He picked up her long braid and flicked it down on her back, and she responded with a mock frown. With Nimmo at his heels, Pappu headed for the gate, where he turned around, as Satpal did every day, and looked at his mother leaning against the doorway.

"What is it?" she asked. "Why are you looking at me like that?" She wished she could tie her son up and keep him home.

"I'm just looking, that's all." Pappu grinned at her. He was wearing a pale blue turban that matched his shirt—a colour that Nimmo thought made him look particularly handsome.

"Be careful," she said, following him to the road, watching after him the way she had done for as long as he could remember. "When you are crossing the road, especially!" *Wahe-guru, keep them safe, please keep them safe,* she muttered under her breath.

From next door came the reassuring cluck of Kaushalya's hens. Her friend looked over the wall and said in a low, urgent voice, "Nimmo, listen. My husband said to tell you that he was at the ration store yesterday and heard some men asking for the list of people in this area. He thinks they are getting the addresses of the Sikh homes here."

"What should I do?" Nimmo asked, trying unsuccessfully to keep the trembling from her voice.

"You can come here, to our house. We can hide you," Kaushalya suggested. She did not sound very sure of herself.

Nimmo shook her head. She knew the strengths and weaknesses of her own home. She knew how to take care of herself and her daughter. She would be prepared.

"I will stay at home," she said finally.

"Lock every door and window," Kaushalya warned.

Nimmo re-entered her home, shut the door and locked it securely behind her. She surveyed it thoughtfully and then, dragging the heavy wooden cot from the inner room, pushed it against the door. *The back door,* she thought, *the back door.* She rushed there as well and shot the flimsy metal bolt into place. Then the windows; she was grateful there were iron bars on them already, and wished that the front door had a crossbar to drop into place.

"Mummy, stop locking everything like that. You are making me very frightened!" Kamal followed Nimmo around the house, biting her thumb and looking very small. "Nothing will happen!"

"Don't keep saying that! Stupid girl, inviting evil into our house!" snapped Nimmo.

The hours ticked away. Why had she let her son leave the house? She should have insisted on keeping him here. *Foolish woman what have you done?* And Satpal, where was he? Why hadn't he phoned? Perhaps he had, and that Asha hadn't bothered to call her. Should she go over and find out? Nimmo peered out of a chink in the window and saw nothing.

It seemed to her that there was a waiting stillness on the normally busy street. She came away from the window and busied herself with hemming a pair of trousers. Kamal bent over her schoolbooks, working on some sums. *If only I had a bharoli to keep her safe,* Nimmo thought, a bharoli of corn in a corner, just like the one her mother had.

Kamal looked on with wide, startled eyes as her mother dashed into the inner room and furiously started to empty all their clothes from the steel cupboard, throwing them in a corner on the floor. Then she removed the shelves and panting from the weight, piled them on top of the cot blocking the front door.

She turned to Kamal. "If they come, you go inside there, understand? And don't make a sound until I open the door. Do you understand?"

"Yes, Mummy." Kamal's voice was very small. *They?* she thought nervously. Who was her mother referring to?

It was late in the evening and Nimmo was just beginning to relax her guard when she heard the sound of scuffling feet outside, some yelling and then a knock on the door. She dropped her sewing and sat still. *They were here.* She had always known they would come one day, those men from her village who had made her mother moan like an animal in pain. She glanced across at Kamal, who looked petrified, and placed a finger on her lips. *Shhh!* She rose to her feet and pulled the girl after her to the inner room and the steel cupboard.

"Get inside," she whispered. "Don't make a noise."

Kamal entered the cold metal cupboard reluctantly and sat down. Despite its size it was a tight space, and she had to make herself thin in order to fit in.

"Stay there till I come for you," Nimmo whispered. She shut the door and locked it. She stuffed the key into a bowl full of other keys, coins and odds and ends. They would not think of looking for it there. Let them kill her if they wanted, but they would never get her daughter. She slipped into the kitchen and grabbed a heavy iron poker. Unlike her mother, she was prepared.

The banging on the door became louder and more insistent. There was the sound of glass breaking. The windowpane. Thank goodness for the iron grill. More banging, and then the door burst open, flinging the cot away and scattering the steel shelves ranged on it.

Nimmo glared at the intruders. She recognized some of them—there was the fellow from the ration shop who always cheated her on her sugar rations, there was that Doctor Jaikishen who prayed forty times a day and sold medicines made of sugar and wheat flour to his poor patients. And behind them all, hiding like the coward that he was, was Asha's husband.

"What do you want?" Nimmo asked, holding the iron rod firmly in her hands.

"Where are your men?" one of the men asked.

Nimmo looked at Asha's husband. "Why are you here, brother?" she asked.

He shifted his eyes away from her straight gaze. "You better tell them what they want to know. Otherwise I can't say what will happen," he mumbled.

"You have known us for twenty, twenty-five years, brother. Why didn't you tell them that my men are never here at this time of the day?" Nimmo said. "Satpal is in Modinagar, he called at your house, you know that. You were there, and Asha—you heard me talking to him."

"Enough talking," shouted one of the other men. There were only men in the group, Nimmo noticed. "Search the house. Tear it down till you find the rats who killed our Madam-ji!"

"I said they are not here, didn't you hear me?" Nimmo

screamed. She swung the rod around. "Set one foot inside this house and see what happens!" She was not her mother.

She heard a woman shouting outside the house. It was Kaushalya, her neighbour, owner of the chickens.

"What is going on here?" she called. "Nimmo, is everything all right?"

Nimmo shouted back, "Call the police, Kaushalya!"

The men advanced into the house and Nimmo lifted the rod high over her head before bringing it down hard on the nearest shoulder. The man she had attacked screamed obscenities at her. Somebody else grabbed her around her waist and prised the rod out of her hand.

"Help me!" shouted Nimmo. "Kaushalya, call the police!"

It was too late, of course. The men flooded through the house. One of them entered the bedroom and banged on the steel cupboard in the corner.

"What's inside here?" he demanded.

"Nothing," Nimmo said sullenly. She turned again to Asha's husband, who was standing near the front door staring at the mess with a slightly shocked expression on his face, as if he had not really expected it. "Brother, why are you doing this to us?" she said to him. "We have been neighbours for so many years, tell these people we have nothing to hide, tell them. Please."

Asha's husband looked away uneasily. "Just tell them where Satpal and your son are and they will go away," he said.

"They are not here," Nimmo said. "Why don't you believe me?"

"Open this cupboard," said one of the men. He kicked at the door.

Nimmo glared at him. "I don't have the keys," she said. "What is in here?"

"Just some clothes, that's all. We are not rich people," Nimmo said.

The man banged the cupboard hard so that it rocked slightly. "Is somebody inside?"

Perhaps it was Nimmo's guarded expression, perhaps it was just an instinct. The man looked around the room and his eyes fell on the clothes that were heaped on the floor. "I asked, is there somebody hiding in here?" he asked again.

Nimmo shook her head. "I told you, my husband and my son are not here. I am telling you the truth. They are in Modinagar."

Without another word the man picked up a sheet from the ground and started to tear it into strips. He jerked his head towards Nimmo and said gruffly to the other men, "Take her outside."

"Why? What are you doing? I told you there is nobody here," Nimmo shouted as she was hustled outdoors and to the front yard. "What kind of people are you? Have you no shame? No conscience?"

A moment later, their leader came out of the house and left with the other men. Nimmo looked after them, bewildered and relieved that she and Kamal were still alive and unhurt. Then, from the window of the bedroom, a spire of smoke emerged. Choked by dread, Nimmo ran back inside and saw that the man had lit a bonfire with the bedsheets, her children's textbooks, clothes and anything else that would burn. A strong smell of kerosene filled the room mixed with the odour of smoke. In the centre of the fire stood the steel cupboard. Nimmo heard herself screaming, a high-pitched stream of sound that seemed to belong to somebody else. *Nononono!* She tried to bat the fire down with her bare hands. *Kamal, I am coming.* She ran to the kitchen and rushed back with a bucket of water. Then another and another. Blankets, towels, anything. And screaming all the while, *Kamal Kamal Kamal.* She raced to and fro, her hair wild about her face. The fire wasn't dying down. It licked the steel cupboard into a white heat, the green paint curling away, and was that her daughter shouting from inside? *It was the last safe place in the world, that bin of grain, stay there my daughter, stay there, you will be safe. Don't make a noise or they will get you.* She ran madly back and forth and tried to enter the flames, which leapt about the room making everything blood-red and smoke-black. *Where are the keys? Where is the bowl with the keys? Must get to Kamal.* Nimmo crawled around the room, along the edges of the fire, looking for the key in the mess of things on the floor. *The bastards have stolen the keys. The murderers, the bastard murderers.*

Strong arms dragged her out of the room. Kaushalya's husband. Kaushalya stood behind him in the room that was not burning and clucked like one of her chickens: "Nimmo, let it be, let it be. You will get hurt. Those are only things that are burning, Nimmo. Let it be. The police said they will come as soon as possible. I told them what happened. They said you must come and file a report. Nimmo, come out!"

Nimmo fought to get back to the room where the cupboard held her daughter. *Kamal I am coming.*

The hen again: "Cluck, cluck, cluck, it's okay, it's okay!"

"No, it is not okay," Nimmo panted, still tearing at the arms around her waist. "My Kamal is inside!"

Dawning realization in the hen's eyes. "In the room? Where is she? I didn't see her."

"Inside the steel cupboard, the safest place—she is there, my little daughter," wailed Nimmo. "Nobody can touch her there."

Across the city, Pappu searched for a new set of tires for the scooter that needed repairs. When he reached the supplier's shop, it was shuttered and the normally busy street was deserted. A tea-shop owner, seeing Pappu standing uncertainly on the sidewalk, shouted at him to go home and stay inside.

"They are beating up the sardars all over the city. Better go home, son," said the wizened old man. He too was busy pulling the shutters down on his tiny shop.

By the time Pappu returned empty-handed to his father's shop, the busy street there had been shuttered as well, and a dense silence had descended. Mohan Lal, his father's partner for the past twenty-five years, waited anxiously outside the closed shop for him.

"Son, I decided to close the shop. Everybody is advising this," Mohan Lal said as soon as he saw Pappu.

Pappu looked uncertainly at the grey-haired man,

stooped from years of hunching over machine parts. "So should I go home?" he asked.

"No, no, my house is closer. You are too conspicuous with that turban and beard, especially today, son, especially today. I live a few minutes away, and you will be safe in a Hindu home—they won't look for you there."

Pappu followed him down the narrow gully, a familiar path that he had taken often enough to celebrate many festivals and family occasions with this elderly man who had been a part of his life since his birth. There was the tiny temple dedicated to Shiva, there the quilter's shop, the drain outside thick with floating puffs of escaped silk-cotton, the chatai-maker's warehouse, all shuttered and watchful somehow. Pappu was uneasily aware of eyes following the two of them.

As if sensing the young man's feelings, Mohan Lal said in reassuring tones, "Don't worry, I know all these people. They are harmless."

Finally, after a walk that seemed far longer than the ten minutes it actually took, they reached a small house at the end of the lane. Mohan Lal's wife, Shanti, cautiously opened the door and ushered them in.

"I will phone your mother and tell her that you are here with us," Mohan Lal said. "If the phone booth is open, that is." He turned to his wife. "Don't open the door to anyone, you hear?"

"I know, I know. *You* be careful also," she warned before shutting the door.

She turned to Pappu and said kindly, "Sit, sit. I will get you some tea."

Pappu sat on the charpoy Shanti had unrolled in one corner of the room that served as both living area and kitchen. He had come to this house many times when he was a boy, but his visits became less frequent as he grew older, largely because Mohan Lal's daughters were also grown up and it would not look right for an unmarried man to visit a home with young women in it.

"It is very kind of you to help me like this, Chaachi-ji," Pappu said shyly.

"My child, where is the kindness in taking care of one of our own? These are difficult times for you, and it is our duty to help. Your father would do the same for us, I know that." The thin, grey-haired woman, squatting before the gas stove that sat on a raised platform constructed of bricks and a wooden plank, waited patiently for the water to boil. If she was unhappy about allowing danger into the fragile safety of her home, she showed no sign of it.

She handed Pappu a glass tumbler of boiling tea and settled down to chop vegetables for the day's meal. The silence was broken by the sound of a child screaming in one of the neighbouring houses, and then suddenly there was a knock on the door, tentative at first and then more authoritative. She looked up and whispered to Pappu, "They are here. What to do?"

"I'll go outside, Chaachi-ji. I don't want to cause trouble," Pappu replied softly. He could handle this; what could they do to him?

Shanti shook her head. "No, son, no, you are not causing trouble," she said. "And my husband would never forgive me if something happened to you out there."

There was more banging on the door and several voices shouted at Shanti to open the door.

"I'm coming, wait," she called back. "I am in the bathroom! What is the hurry?"

She pushed Pappu ahead of her and into the tiny bath. "Stay here. Maybe they will go away."

Pappu crouched in the damp, narrow space and waited fearfully. "Who's there?" he heard Shanti asking.

A male voice ordered, "Open the door. We need to talk to your husband."

"He isn't here," she said.

"We want to see for ourselves, open the door," the voice demanded.

"I told you he is not here." Shanti's voice held a tremor of fear.

A steady banging started up. "Open up," an implacable voice said. "Otherwise we will break this door down."

Pappu heard the door open. He glanced around the tiny bathroom thinking there was nowhere to hide, no exit other than that flimsy wooden door, rotting and ragged around the bottom edge where the water touched it constantly.

"What is the matter with you people? Hanh? I told you my husband is not at home. Is this any way to behave with a woman?" scolded Shanti.

"Where is the sardar?" a voice asked—the same one that had threatened to break the door.

Looking around in a panic, Pappu spotted Mohan Lal's old-fashioned razor on the sink and grabbed it. He removed his turban and unbound his hair. Gripping the razor, he started sawing clumps of hair, cursing at its thickness.

Shanti shouted, "Ask anyone, this is a Hindu home! There are no sardars here. I will call the neighbours if you don't leave right now."

Someone laughed. "Arrey, Aunty, one of your neighbours told us that you had a sardar hiding here like a rat. We don't like rats, so we are here to catch him."

The man who had spoken first said in that same quiet monotone, "Is that the bathroom where you were just now? Why is the door closed? Who is in there?"

Pappu caught sight of himself in the flecked and spotted mirror above the sink. He had not even managed to get through half the hair. And his face, there was all that hair on his face. What was he to do with so much hair? And so little time? *God*, he prayed, *send me a miracle. I will do any seva for you, I will wash the floors of every temple in this country for a year, for two years, I will dedicate my life to the poor, oh God send me a miracle.* He attacked his face, scraping away at his beard and moustache, cutting himself all over in his haste. Blood flowered against his skin and flowed down his neck. *Never mind,* he thought, *never mind.*

"In the bathroom?" Shanti's voice was etched with tension. Pappu could hear it. He grabbed a bunch of his beard and pulled it hard, trying to wrench it out by the roots, his eyes filling with tears at the shooting pain. "My daughter is in there now. Who else would be there?"

"Your daughter? All of you are going into the bathroom one after another? Something you ate, hanh? Ask her to come out then. We don't want to hurt innocent people, Aunty-ji," said the quiet man.

"Yes, I will do that, but if she is bathing, it might take a few minutes."

"Who takes a bath this late in the morning?" one of the men wanted to know.

"We poor people have to bathe whenever there is water in the taps," Shanti said bravely. "Six o'clock, ten o'clock, who knows? This is the way in this part of the world! But I will tell her to hurry up. You can wait outside."

"Oh no, Aunty-ji, it is cold outside. We will wait here, and you can make us some tea while your charming daughter is bathing," the quiet man said.

Pappu heard Shanti approach the bathroom door and shout, "Daughter, these men want to make sure that there are no men in there. Finish your bath quickly and come out properly dressed."

The bathroom floor was covered in hair. Pappu didn't know what he was supposed to do. Turn into a woman? He looked at his square-jawed face in the mirror, half-shaved, bristly and bleeding where the razor had cut through skin, swollen where he had tried to tear the hair off his face, his long tresses unevenly butchered. And he gave up. It was no use, they would get him anyway. There was to be no miracle for him today, he knew that now. With a steady hand, he finished shaving his face, trying not to think of the sacrilege he was committing. Then he gathered his remaining hair into a ponytail. He pushed the mess on the floor to a corner, and emerged from the bathroom.

A silence met him as he stepped out followed by a crack of laughter. "Arrey, Aunty, look at what that bath did to your daughter! She has turned into a man! Is there a demon in there doing magic?"

Laughing, they dragged Pappu out into the silent gully. One of the men jammed a car tire down over his body, pinning his arms to his sides, poured kerosene over him and flicked a match, setting him alight.

At the Modinagar terminus, the driver refused to let Satpal into his vehicle.

"Isn't my money good enough for you?" Satpal demanded. He was tired and irritable. The previous evening, a passerby in the market where he had gone to eat his dinner had spat at him and shouted, "Murdering whore-son!" And when he had whirled around to confront the man, he had been surrounded by a group of men armed with crowbars and sticks. If some people on the street had not intervened, he knew he could have been seriously hurt. The incident had left him shaken and anxious to get home to Delhi as soon as possible. Indira Gandhi's death had unsettled people everywhere, he told himself, and there were always thugs and malcontents willing to use the prevailing mood of anxiety for their own ends. He realized that his turban and beard made him a clear target.

He had reached the terminus as early as possible to catch the first bus. But now the idiot of a driver wouldn't let him climb in.

"It's not your money, Sardar-ji," the driver said apologetically. "I don't want any trouble. I hear there are people looking for turbans. You should go home!"

"But that's why I am trying to get into your bus, sahib," protested Satpal. "I live in Delhi. How else will I get there?"

"For your own sake I am saying no," the driver replied. "I can't guarantee that you will be safe on this bus. Find a hotel and stay inside. That is my advice, take it or leave it."

Satpal turned away, angry and helpless. He waited for the next bus, and again wasn't allowed to get on. A taxi would be horribly expensive, and if the road to Delhi was as unsafe as the first driver had indicated, perhaps it wouldn't be a good idea either. Satpal left the terminus and started walking towards the market, hoping to find an inexpensive hotel room, when the first blow landed on his back. He turned around and found himself face to face with a gang of men, their faces filled with hatred.

"Killer!" they shouted. "Fucking murderer! We'll teach you to kill helpless women."

Satpal backed away only to find his path blocked by more men. He lowered his head and ran into one of them, taking him by surprise. He raced through the gap that opened up and across the road to a shuttered café where he had earlier noticed two policemen.

"Help!" he shouted, waving his arms to attract their attention. They did not seem to notice him. He reached them and grabbed one by his arm. "Help me," he pleaded. "Those men are going to kill me."

He looked over his shoulder. The group was strolling towards him. "Please, help!" he begged again.

The policeman he had grabbed gave him a considering look. "I have no orders to help," he said.

"What?" Satpal cried, incredulous.

"I am not in charge of crime, Sardar-ji," he sneered. "I am only here to direct traffic. For crime report you have to go to the police station. I am not authorized."

The other policeman shrugged. "I am on duty only from ten o'clock." And he turned away.

Satpal started to run. Not a single shop on the street was open. A few had been vandalized. He turned into a gully and knew instantly that he had made a mistake. There was nobody on the narrow street that ran between stinking drains and the backs of buildings, the walls dirty with graffiti and film posters. And there was no exit.

He turned to face the men. "I have children, I have a wife," he pleaded, looking at the blank, implacable faces of his attackers. "I voted for Indira-ji. Please." He folded his palms and fell to his knees. "I didn't do anything, brothers, I didn't do anything."

A middle-aged man in a pale green kurta laughed. "Hey, look at this brave lady-killer on his knees! And these bastards call themselves lions! Does a lion grovel like this?"

"Let's see what he keeps inside his turban. Definitely not brains!" remarked another of them. "Hello, Sardar-ji, remove your pagdi!"

"Please let me go. You can take all the money I have if you want," Satpal begged. He scrabbled inside the pocket of his trousers and drew out a roll of notes. "Here, here."

"The bastard is paying us bribes," the first man said indignantly. He took the money and pocketed it. He grinned. "Evidence of bribery." He turned earnestly to the others. "Do you think Indira-ji had time to bribe those fuckers before they shot her? Hanh? Hanh?" He jammed the iron rod under Satpal's turban and flipped it back hard, dislodging the carefully coiled blue cloth to reveal the knot of grey hair neatly braided and bunched with a rubber band. "Open your hair, sardar-ji!" He shoved the rod against Satpal's chest, forcing Satpal to fall back onto his heels. "Let's see how long you have grown it, eating the salt of this country."

Silently Satpal uncoiled his hair and waited trembling to see what further indignities they would inflict on him before they killed him. He wished he had had the time to phone Nimmo again. He thought of her as he had last seen her, standing in the sunlight, leaning against the door of their home. He thought of the red parandhi she wore at the end of her braid when she wanted to dress up. He remembered the handprints on the wall of their little house, the ones she would never let him paint over.

He knelt while one of the men poured kerosene over his head, the acrid smell making him dizzy and nauseous. One man dropped a car tire over his head and jammed it about his shoulders, immobilizing his arms. Another lit a match to his streaming hair, wet with kerosene. The flames ate into his scalp, crept like a dreadful river down his face, licked at his eyebrows, his eyelashes. The heat burned his eyes and his last thought was that he could not even weep. He could not even weep.

TWENTY-FIVE

BIBI-JI

—

Vancouver

November 1984

On Main Street, there was no other news that mattered for weeks. Not the fact that a lantern-jawed man named Brian Mulroney had replaced the suave Pierre Trudeau as Canada's prime minister, not the fact that in the United States Ronald Reagan had just won a second term as president, not even the latest tragedy in India—where disaster seemed to have become a habit—that a deadly gas leak from a chemical factory in Bhopal had killed thousands of unwary people as they slept.

All that occupied the Indian community in Vancouver was the assassination of Indira Gandhi and the resulting murders of innocent Sikhs. Horror piled on horror.

On November 10th, the phone rang in the Taj Mahal and Bibi-ji answered. It was Leela. "Is Jasbeer's family okay?" she asked. "Your niece Nimmo? I heard of the terrible things that happened in Delhi, Bibi-ji. Monstrous. I've been worrying."

"No news, Leela." And Bibi-ji hung up. Over the next few days, she was increasingly conscious that the tension between the Sikhs and the rest of the Indian community, already high after the invasion of the Golden Temple, was now close to exploding. There were insults traded by both sides, subtle and overt. Fireworks were let off and sweets distributed on Main Street to celebrate the death of Mrs. Gandhi. Crowds of Sikhs disrupted traffic in the downtown area in front of the Indian High Commission on Howe Street, screaming fury at the massacre of their people in Delhi. Mrs. Patel's car windows were smashed and the windows of The Delhi Junction spray-painted in retaliation. A Sikh lawyer's head was bashed in with an iron rod because he protested Canadian immigration policies that, he claimed, allowed secessionists and extremists from Punjab safe haven in Canada. And the non-Sikhs in the desi community murmured that it served the bastards right, the turbaned hooligans who wanted to split an already-torn country once again. They deserved the army's attack on the Golden Temple, they deserved what they got after Indira Gandhi's death.

And finally one day came news of Nimmo from Delhi. Terrible news. Her brother-in-law Balraj called to say that Kamal and Pappu were dead. They did not know what had happened to Satpal. They were still hoping to find

him, but the chances were not very good. Balraj and
Manpreet were trying to get Nimmo to move to their
home in Amritsar, but she refused to leave Delhi. She
didn't want anyone to stay with her either. "Bibi-ji, she is
in a bad state," Balraj said. "We don't want to leave her
alone here, but she won't listen to anyone. I think Jasbeer
should come back to his mother. She needs him."

How much more do we have to bear? Bibi-ji thought, sitting beside Jasbeer in a house silent with grief once again.
How many more deaths? "I'll come with you, putthar," she
said, reaching out for Jasbeer's hand, pressing it between
her palms, glad to feel their living warmth.

"No, I want to see her first," Jasbeer said. "She is my
mother. I should have gone sooner."

Bibi-ji was silent.

Lalloo oversaw the arrangements, as usual, contacting
his travel agent friends to book a flight for Jasbeer. "Not
Air India," he said decisively. "There is talk that flights on
that airline will be sabotaged."

"What do you mean?" Jasbeer asked. "Sabotaged? How?"

Lalloo shrugged. "I don't know. These are the rumours
I have heard. There is something bad going down soon.
Maybe just a boycott—symbolic because it is India's
national airline. In any case, I would feel better if you
travelled on some other flight."

But Jasbeer never reached Nimmo. The last Bibi-ji
heard of him—only a rumour—was that he had been
arrested at Delhi airport. She heard other rumours, wispy
and uncertain, that something was about to happen to
avenge the invasion of the Golden Temple and the killing

of Sikhs in Delhi. She felt as if the world that she had known for so long, the stable, safe world, had been blown apart, leaving only smoky puffs of whispering, poisonous rumours.

TWENTY-SIX

THE SAFEST PLACE

—

New Delhi

December 30, 1984

The room was dark, even though it was a brilliant morning outside. Her windows still shut, Nimmo lay on her bed unable to bear the thought of another day. She glanced at the clock; it ticked the passing hours relentlessly, uselessly, reminding her that it was eight o'clock, time to pack her husband's lunch box, nine o'clock, time for her daughter to leave for school, twelve o'clock, time for her son to arrive home for lunch.

But there was no one to wait for. Pappu was dead—dragged out of Mohan Lal's house and burned on the street. And Kamal . . .

And Jasbeer and Satpal, they too were dead, she knew it, for otherwise why would they not come home to her? If she listened carefully, she could hear them both crying from the skies for their last rites. But how could she perform the required oblations when she had no bodies? How could she recite the Sohila, the last hymn of night to lull their spirits to sleep, or the Sukhmani, the psalm of peace for their eternal silence, without their bodies to pray over?

She roamed the house, touching this and that. Although Manpreet and Kaushalya had cleaned the house for her, she was sure that she could see the bloodstains from the man she had struck with the iron poker. And there, clinging to the broken chair like a ghost, was the long pale yellow dupatta worn by Kamal that day. She noticed, once again, the imprints of two pairs of hands low down on a wall—blue hands on a white wall. She recalled the happy origin of those prints.

A few pots and pans lay outside, in the open washing area behind the kitchen, and she sat down to wash them. Ever since Manpreet and Balraj had left a week ago, her neighbour Kaushalya had made it her duty to bring hot meals twice a day. Nimmo barely touched the food. Every time she brought a morsel of it to her lips, she remembered that Pappu had not eaten anything before leaving home that day. Her boy had died on an empty stomach. *Oh Wahe-guru,* Nimmo murmured as she scrubbed the dishes harder and harder, *oh beloved all-seeing God, why did you do this to them? And why have you done this to me?* She rocked on her heels, wiping her streaming eyes with wet fists, weeping like a baby.

A cold breeze started up when she was halfway through the pile of dishes. She sniffed the air with a faint stirring of pleasure, of half-remembered joy. She sucked in her breath, clung to the memory that had surfaced.

A small naked child, gleaming with oil recently applied, dashed out of her arms into the front yard, laughing, leaping up and down in the wintry morning, ecstatic to be alive.

It was the child of her heart, her Kamal, her third and last one—a daughter at last. Every mother has one child she favours if only a little more than the others, and this was the one Nimmo held closest. Was that why she had been so punished? For the sin of loving one more than the rest? It had only been a little more; after all, a daughter was a visitor in her parents' home, soon to be sent away with tears and sweets to her husband's. *The child, naked as the sky, leapt to catch the sun, slipped and fell, scrambled up and raced towards her, weeping from the insult of mud on her small knees.* The mother held out her arms and gathered air.

Dishes done, Nimmo washed the clothes and went out in the front yard to dry them. Asha's barbed-wire voice, which had earlier torn open the day, could now be heard haranguing someone inside her home. On the other side, Kaushalya called to her children. The sound of traffic, which had started at daybreak, had become a uniform roar punctuated by horns and beeps and clanging rickshaw bells.

Nimmo scrubbed the kitchen, the front and back rooms, the bath, the upstairs room. By late afternoon all her work was done and the house was spotless once more. She bathed and wore her best salwar suit, a dark pink silk, which had burn marks all over it. It now hung loosely on her frame.

She combed her thick hair and braided it carefully. She discovered, beneath the cot, a pair of embroidered slippers that her mother-in-law had had made especially for her wedding and that Satpal had removed with great tenderness before he kissed her feet, her ankles, her calves, his hot mouth working its way up, up, up. And she, lying there in a tumult of shyness, had stifled her giggles from the tickling of her new husband's moustache on her young skin.

She shut the front door, which was still weak from the battering it had received two months ago, and retreated into the inner room she had shared with Satpal Singh, owner of a mechanic's shop, for twenty-seven years. She lowered her tall body, once lush with happiness and health, onto the bed, directly onto its ripped and charred mattress, for the murderers had used her sheets as wicks to burn her life down. She lay there supine in her best clothes and poured a bottle of yellow pills in her mouth. She swallowed with difficulty, gagging, but persisted. There was no safe place left in the world, she knew that now. Not a cupboard, not even a bharoli of grain.

She felt her breathing slow, grow quiet.

Brisk footsteps came to the front door. "Nimmo? Nimmo? Are you there?"

Her ears were clogged with silence but she could hear the thin, caring voice. *Kaushalya.*

"Nimmo?" sharper this time. "Nimmo?" A hammering on the door. Then a crash as it was pushed open. "Where are you?" Closer it came, that voice, closer and closer. Who would reach her first? Kaushalya or Yamraj the king of death? A hand on her shoulder, pushing hard. So far away that voice, *Nimmo, wake up, what have you done, Nimmo?*

She was dragged upright. Kaushalya was trying to pull her off the bed. "Walk!" she said. "Nimmo, move your legs. Help me. Walk, walk." *But I don't want to walk, I want to sleep, I want to go where my children are. I want to see my Kamal again, and my sons, like pillars on either side of me, and my Satpal who has left nothing but his handprint on the walls of this house. I want to go to them.*

A great heave of nausea. "Walk, Nimmo, walk." A hand forcing Nimmo's mouth open, fingers pushed inside, tickling the back of her throat, a thin trail of sour vomit. Again and again. The endless walking, dragging along, draped over the tiny Kaushalya, to the kitchen, where she glimpsed the clean pots and pans ranged shining bright along the walls. Opened her mouth again to swallow a glassful of salt water. In the backyard a spray of vomit this time, salt and sour.

Another voice now. It was Kamal, her daughter. *Mummy wake up, Mummy, I am here. Wake up.*

And Kaushalya saying, "Go quickly, get a taxi, we have to take her to the hospital. Hurry, hurry!" *I am to live after all.* She touched Kaushalya's hand. "My child," she said. "I am the one who put her in there. It was me, I know she will be safe."

Kaushalya stroked her hair away from her worn face gently, as if she, Nimmo, were the child. "You did the best you could, Nimmo. It isn't your fault."

Nimmo was puzzled. *What isn't my fault?*

"Those men were responsible for Kamal's death, not you," Kaushalya said, still stroking the hair.

Nimmo shook her head, no, no, Kaushalya did not understand. It was all a mistake. *Kamal is at home, in the safest place of all.*

TWENTY-SEVEN

SILENCES

—

Vancouver

June 1985

In the middle of June, Leela called Bibi-ji again, persistent as a fly. "Bibi-ji, listen, we go back way too long," she said. "Don't put the phone down, please."

Silence from Bibi-ji, but at least she did not hang up. "I am so terribly sorry about what happened to your niece's family. Balu got the news from Lalloo. I wish I could say something other than sorry. Really."

Silence.

"Bibi-ji, how is Jas taking it? Preethi was asking about him."

"He has gone back." Silence again.

"Oh, I see," Leela said, feeling uncomfortable about the long pauses. "I just wanted to tell you, Balu and I are going to India. Is there anything you would like me to bring to Nimmo?" There was no response, and Leela rushed to bridge the silence. "It was very difficult to get seats, but Lalloo's friend who owns one of those travel agencies on Main Street managed to get me a seat on the twenty-second of this month and Balu one on the next day. He was very helpful, Bibi-ji. I am so excited. It has been eighteen years."

"To India?" Bibi-ji asked, her voice sharp. "On which flight?"

"Air India for me and Air France the next day for Balu. Via Toronto and Montreal. Look, Bibi-ji, why don't you and I get together for chai like we used to? Come here. I will make you masala-dosai and we can talk."

"There is nothing to talk about," Bibi-ji said gently. She hung up the telephone and leaned her head against the wall. But Lalloo had said that it was not safe to fly Air India—economic boycott, his friend, the travel agent, had said. Perhaps sabotage. But what did Lalloo's friend, the one who had sold Leela the tickets, know? And what did Lalloo know? He would have said something to the Bhats if there was anything to worry about, wouldn't he? Perhaps she, Bibi-ji, should have said something to Leela. But it was none of her business what happened to them. No, it was not her business at all.

TWENTY-EIGHT

AIR INDIA FLIGHT 182

—

Vancouver

June 22, 1985

The night before she was to leave for India, Leela dreamed that she was in a plane, cutting through the infinity of space towards an unknown destination. Thousands of feet below, the ocean undulated silently. She could not see it but she knew that it was there. It was dark inside the plane and all around her she could hear the sussuration of her fellow passengers breathing.

Leela too shut her eyes but was woken a moment later by the sound of someone approaching. She saw, coming down the cramped aisle of the plane towards her, Yama the god of death.

"Leela Bhat, are you ready?" Yama asked, his deep voice resonating through her body.

"No," she whispered. "No, I am not. Can you not wait until I get home?"

"Your time has come, Leela Bhat," Yama said gently. "I am merely the collector of souls."

"Just another day or two?" Leela gazed up at him with an enormous confused sadness. But his lasso swung over her head and she reached out for it. A wind touched her skin, her eyes clouded and her voice tore out of her in a mournful ululation that climbed higher and higher into the thin air.

She woke up startled, her face wet with tears.

"It's okay, it's okay," said a voice close to her ear. Balu's familiar warmth seeped through her cotton nightdress. His stubbled face rubbed against her smooth one, the rasping sharpness dragging her out of her dream. "Leela, wake up. Just a dream, ma, don't cry."

She swam to the surface of sleep, awake now, aware of some unpleasantness left behind.

"I had an awful dream, Balu," she said.

"It was just a dream, don't worry," Balu murmured. "Now go to sleep, you still have a couple of hours left."

Leela slid back into an uneasy sleep and when the alarm rang at four o'clock she was bleary-eyed and tense with fatigue.

There was already a long queue in the terminal at the airport. "The travel agent was right," Leela observed. "My flight is packed."

"They might not all be connecting with the Air India flight, Amma," Preethi said, noticing her mother's consternation. She was home for the summer.

"Yes, Leela, people *do* travel to Toronto for reasons other than a connecting flight to India, you know!" Balu chimed in.

Not *these* people, Leela thought wryly, taking in the line-up of mostly brown-skinned passengers, the sari-clad women, the children in bright clothes, the enormous piles of luggage accompanying each one of them. These people were *all* headed for India, she had no doubt about it.

She spotted Arjun approaching with his fiancée, Fern. "Hello, Amma. Ready to leave?" he said, giving her a hug.

"Here, Leela. These are for you." Fern added a plastic bag full of magazines to the bags on the cart.

The girl was wearing a sari, Leela noted. The light blue one that Leela had given her as an engagement present last month.

"You look great, Fern," Preethi said. "Doesn't she, Amma?" She shot Leela a meaningful glance, which Leela ignored. What has the world come to, she thought indignantly, that my *daughter* has to tell me what to say or not to say?

Arjun gave her bags a dubious look. "Are you allowed so much luggage?"

"Three check-in and one carry-on," Leela said defensively. "I am slightly over the limit. Look at all those other people. I have *nothing* by comparison!"

Arjun rolled his eyes. "*Slightly* over the limit?! You are allowed only *two* check-in bags, not three. And those bags are the size of rooms. Bet you you're going to have to pay extra for them."

"Why should I pay extra? As if my ticket was cheap! We will see who makes me pay!"

Then Fern and Arjun wandered away to find coffee, and Preethi turned on her mother. "Amma, why are you always so mean?"

Leela widened her eyes artlessly. "What did I do? I didn't say a thing!"

"Precisely. You could have told Fern she looked nice in that sari, couldn't you? She bends over backwards to fit into our family and you bend over backwards to keep her out!"

"Why does she need to wear a sari to fit in? I didn't ask her to. *You* wear trousers and miniskirts, and you fit in okay." But her tone was mild. She was determined not to be drawn into a quarrel with her daughter just before departure. It would be inauspicious. A quarrel invited the wicked spirits in, opened doors for them.

There was a small commotion farther up the line. Two passengers ahead of Leela, a man wearing a grey turban was arguing vigorously with the check-in clerk about his baggage.

"What's going on there?" Leela asked Balu. He strolled ahead to find out.

"He wants his bags checked right through to Delhi," he said when he returned, shaking his head impatiently. "Some of these people, really!"

"Why what's wrong with that? It is allowed, no?"

"Not if you do not have a confirmation on the connecting flight," Balu replied. "Suppose he does not get a seat from Toronto on that Air India flight? His baggage will still be on it, and *he* won't. Creates unnecessary confusion, that's all."

"Not to mention security problems," commented the passenger in front of them. "I doubt they'll allow it."

Leela smiled at him. He was dressed in a nice suit and looked well off, Leela thought, like One of Us.

"What is going on there?" the woman behind her asked, craning to look over her shoulder. "We will miss our connection. What nonsense!" She smelled of sweat and heavy perfume. Definitely *not* One of Us.

Leela watched closely as the turbaned man leaned forward and continued to argue with the check-in clerk. If he was getting all sorts of concessions regarding baggage, she would insist on getting the same treatment.

"Look, I assure you I have a confirmed ticket for the onward journey." The man's voice was suddenly raised. "On business class, as you can see. My brother has it with him—he is flying on another plane to Toronto and then we will travel together from there. If you wish I can go find him and bring the ticket. It won't take long."

The clerk considered his suggestion for a moment and then said, "No, no. There are all these other people waiting. Sorry sir, I can't allow this."

The man wouldn't budge. Now he accused her of being bureaucratic. She looked worriedly over his shoulder at the long, restive queue and gave up. The baggage was checked through. The obstreperous passenger went his way and a sigh rippled through the crowd.

Finally it was Leela's turn. The clerk, now in a thoroughly bad mood, charged her for the extra baggage, refusing to give in to any argument. Leela paid angrily and moved out of the line.

"What cheek!" she exclaimed to Arjun. "That man wanted his bags booked all the way to India without having a seat, and the woman allowed it. The other woman had twice the number of bags I did, and no problem. But me! I had to pay excess baggage for those tiny suitcases. They aren't excess, I know. I weighed them at home and they were within limits. These people will make money any way they can!"

"Leelu, you did have three *huge* suitcases to check in," Balu pointed out.

"Yes, I know all that. But they should have some consideration for people who are going back after so many years, no? I can't go empty-handed. What will all our relatives think?"

With a twinge of guilt she remembered the wild shopping sprees she had indulged in this last month—recklessly buying presents for Balu's aunts, uncles, cousins near and far, their children and grandchildren, friends, aged servants, their children and then some extras, just in case. She wanted to spoil them now that she could afford it. And it was also necessary to show that she was settled into life, prosperous, able to afford such extravagances. In addition there were the things her friends had asked her to take back for their families; these were requests she could not refuse. After all, for so many years, they too had carried things to and fro for her. Now, finally, she could repay all those kindnesses. Mrs. Shah had given her two Teflon-coated frying pans for a newly married niece.

Mrs. Menon had sent a parcel of old clothes for her family-servant's grandchildren. Cashews and black pepper for Mrs. Patel's sisters—both of these items had arrived in Canada from India, but, said Mrs. Patel, they export the best to the West and our own people are left with the poor-quality stuff. Besides, it was cheaper here than in India.

"Amma, we wanted to tell you. Fern and I, we're planning a fall wedding," said Arjun suddenly.

"What? Just like that? I thought you said you had not decided. And what a time to tell me, just before I am leaving! We have to talk about this. Is this fall date auspicious?"

"Auspicious? Who cares? All that stuff doesn't matter here, Amma. When you come back we can pick the actual date. We were thinking sometime in September—it is still nice then."

Leela looked at Balu, who seemed pleased. "Did you know about this? So suddenly these children—"

"No, I didn't," Balu said. "But look, I think you should be heading for the security check now." He propelled her gently forward.

"Arjun, Fern," Leela said over her shoulder. "Phone me when I reach Delhi and we will talk about this. Okay?"

"Yes Amma, we'll call."

Balu patted his wife on her back. "I'll see you in Delhi day after tomorrow."

"Here, don't forget your food bag," Preethi said. She hugged her mother hard. "And be good."

Leela took the large tapestry handbag, which was Arjun's present for her journey. Inside were several Ziploc bags of idlis, parathas, tomato sandwiches. Everyone knew how terrible airplane food was. No spice, no flavour, only that awful freezer smell. She adjusted the pleats of her dark green silk sari so that they hung down at the right height above the stylish green and gold slippers Balu had purchased for a ridiculous price on Main Street.

"Okay, I will go and come, hanh?" *Go and come.* The traditional goodbye, a farewell and a promise of return. For a traveller's journey is never complete until she returns, until a circle has been described, until the people she has left behind are before her once more. *I will go and come.*

Ahead of her, striding confidently through the terminal, was the man who had managed to get his bags checked right through to India. Some people, Leela thought indignantly, some people had all the luck. She quickened her steps to catch up with him and throw him a dirty look, but he walked faster and was soon lost in the crowd of people heading towards the security gates.

The wait in Toronto was longer than expected. There was a problem with one of the engines. Leela struck up a friendship with two teenaged girls going home to their grandparents for the summer holidays and spent a pleasant couple of hours chatting with them, barely noticing the delay until it was time to board the Air India flight to Delhi.

She settled herself in the humming plane, packed with people, leaned back in her seat and thought, *I am going home.* A doubt crept into her mind unbidden. Where *was* home exactly? Back in Vancouver or ahead of her in India? She had forgotten, lost her bearings. *This is the house that Rama Shastri built. This is the well in the house that Rama*

Shastri built. This is the tamarind tree by the well in the house . . .
The ditty she used to sing so long ago, as a child who
wanted so badly to belong to a family that did not love
her. Heard Akka, her grandmother, saying, "Nothing
worse than to be a dangling person, a foot here and a foot
there and a great gap in between. Imagine how painful it is
to stay stretched like that forever." Like King Trishanku, a
floating, rootless, accursed creature, up-in-the-air.

The words shifted, changed. *This is the house that we
bought. This is the house with pine trees and hydrangeas, roses
and clematis.* When her back was turned, while she slum-
bered at night, her life had been usurped by another
country; her thoughts, her memories changed or
replaced. She had tried so hard to appropriate the world
around her by renaming everything so that it would feel
the same as Back Home. She had tried very hard to dislike
Vancouver, to keep it at arm's length. And now, at this
moment, inside the airplane, up in the sky, thirty-five
thousand feet above sea level, she discovered that the city
had stealthily insinuated itself in her mind and her heart.
It had become home just as surely as Bangalore became
home the day she entered it as a bride all those years ago.

Leela glanced at her watch. They were one and a half
hours away from Heathrow airport. Right now, she was
literally between two worlds. She yawned, pulled her
blanket over her legs, and fell into a deep sleep.

Across the ocean, across a continent, the telephone rang
in the Bhat household. Balu struggled out of his sleep,
wondering who would call this early in the morning. It

was Majumdar, who had never learned to sleep, staying up all night, listening to radio broadcasts from all over the planet.

"Balu, listen. Did Leela board that flight to India?"

"Yes," Balu mumbled. "She got lucky."

"Oh no," Majumdar moaned. "Oh God, *no*."

EPILOGUE
JUNE 1986

—

BIBI-JI

The house is hollow with silence—the house guests have gone, hardly anyone comes here anymore. Now there are many other homes that have open doors and the money to afford kindness. Bibi-ji stands before her dressing table crowded with bottles and jars of creams and powders, the trays of lipsticks she has not touched since Pa-ji's death, the silver-backed comb and brush set that was his last gift to her. She looks at herself in the mirror suspended over the dressing table and sees her mother staring accusingly back at her.

"Greedy girl, Sharanjeet Kaur," Gurpreet says, shaking a thin finger at Bibi-ji. "One day you will pay for all that you have stolen from others. You will pay."

"I have, Amma," Bibi-ji whispers. "I have." Not once, but twice. She has learned that for everything you gain, you lose an equal amount. She had grabbed her sister's fate, and Fate had turned around and taken that sister away. Then she had taken Nimmo's son, and he had so warped her sense of right and wrong that she had sacrificed her friend Leela to the gods.

Now Bibi-ji is an old woman living in a dead house on 56th Avenue in Vancouver, on the western edge of the world, with neither husband nor child nor friend, only ghosts and guilt for company. She gazes at her mother's face, reflected beside hers in the mirror.

"Amma, you were right," she whispers. "I have paid dearly."

She pulls open a drawer and removes a letter that arrived from Jasbeer a week ago.

"Dear Bibi-ji, just to let you know. I am out of prison and will be home soon."

Home? She thinks. Her heart flutters with hope for a moment. *But which one?*

PREETHI

Jericho Beach. A beautiful morning just like the one on which Leela had died, falling, falling thirty-five thousand feet into the Atlantic Ocean far from home. Either home, neither home.

Preethi stares out at the flat grey water. At this time last year, they had all come here for a picnic. They talked and joked and laughed. Preethi and Arjun had teased their mother about the things she was taking back with her as presents: umbrellas—six of them—for each of Balu's aunts, bottles of Oil of Olay for favourite nieces, watches for nephews, two transparent negligees without matching robes that she had found in a sale bin and planned to give to a relative who was getting married soon, egg beaters to whip buttermilk into a froth, sheets of stickers for the children in the family. Leela had shaken her head at her critics and defended her purchases stoutly. Balu had presented her with a pair of gaudy green and gold slippers that he had bought from Bela's Boutique as a surprise pre-departure gift. "You can't arrive in India wearing a sari and those running shoes, Leela," he had laughed. "What will our relatives think?"

Preethi worries about her father. He has quit his job and spends his time travelling between their home in Vancouver and the family home in Bangalore that Leela had loved so much. He blames himself for her death. "She never wanted to come here," he had said when Preethi asked him how he could have foreseen or prevented the disaster. "I was the one who insisted. If we hadn't left Bangalore . . ."

She thinks of that terrible morning when Alok Majumdar had phoned them with the news. They had gone to Ireland to identify Leela's body, but nothing had been found of her. Only the tapestry handbag that Arjun had given her as a farewell gift, with the freezer bags of food inside still intact.

She thinks about Brian Mulroney's gaffe, calling India's prime minister, Rajiv Gandhi, to offer his condolences when it was a planeload of mostly Canadian citizens who had died. How would Leela have felt? Preethi wonders. Even in death, neither country claimed her poor mother as its own. A Trishanku for all eternity, Leela used to say.

She glances at her watch. Her father will be here soon with Arjun and Fern, and together they will remember Leela.

The sun beats down on her back. Fishing around in her bag for a bottle of water, her fingers find an envelope. She draws it out and looks at it for a long moment. It is from Jasbeer, and had surprised her when it arrived in August last year. Even now, she is not entirely sure why he wrote to her after such a long silence—or why she has kept the letter. He had written it while he was in prison in India and, as he put it, "had plenty of time to think about my sins." She opens it and reads a random passage. *Do you remember how we used to go from house to house on Halloween saying Trick or Treat and expecting nothing more terrifying than a handful of candy? We were dressed as monsters but we were only children. Now I am no longer a child but in the last few years I had become a monster. I didn't bother to hide myself behind a disguise. I went around the villages of Punjab, banging on doors, holding out a cloth bag. The door would open and a frightened face would peer out. I didn't need to say anything. They knew I was there to collect money. Trick or Treat, I wanted to say, Trick or Treat. Not that the person who opened the door had a choice. I expected a gift of money or gold. Both would be used to buy us food and more guns and grenades. This was how we found the means to fight for a free country. After a while I didn't know what that meant anymore, really. Free country. Every single time I saw a frightened face putting the*

last of their savings—perhaps a gold chain bought for a daugh-
ter's dowry, perhaps money kept aside to thatch a roof or feed
the family for a month—into my bag, I felt more wretched and
unsure. These people were giving me their last pennies because
they were terrified of me. All they wanted was to be left alone to
live their lives. And all I wanted was to go home. I was sick of
the violence and the killing." And then, on a single sheet of
paper: *"Preethi, I read about the Air India flight in the papers.*
I saw your mother's name. I am so sorry."

She can read it no more. She begins to tear up the page,
into tiny pieces. Then, page by page, she tears up the
remainder of the letter and finally the envelope. She gets
to her feet, walks over to the edge of the sea and tosses in
a handful of torn paper.

The tide has retreated. She watches two children
crouched on the sand flats intently poking at something
in the wet mush with their fingers. She smiles as another
memory, more pleasant than the last, of a different day
on the beach, surfaces. Four children on the wet sand,
their heads close together as they pushed a twig down
into a geoduck.

There is a scuffle of feet approaching, and Arjun drops
down beside her. "What are you thinking about, Pree?"

"Something that happened long ago," she says. "Nothing important."

NIMMO
As soon as she comes home, Nimmo collects Satpal's
turban cloths, which she had starched that morning and

hung out to dry—long strips of colour fluttering in the sun, reminding her of him, standing before the small mirror in the front room, winding his turban about his head, catching her eye as she watched, smiling at her. She carries the armload inside, folds them and puts them away. Then she begins to clean the already-spotless house for the second time that day. This is now her daily routine. Get out of bed in the morning after a sleepless night, clean the house of all the evil that she can still smell in it, go to the temple to help with the children in the nursery, visit the market to buy fresh vegetables for her family, clean the house again in case the wickedness has crept back in during her absence, cook for Satpal and Jasbeer, Pappu and her little Kamal, and wait for them to tell her how much they miss her. Then they will drift away, leaving her to another night of sleepless tossing.

The door creaks open and Kaushalya enters the house, her sari rustling. "Why is the door open, Nimmo?" she says. "It is not safe. How many times do I have to tell you?"

"What is there left to take from here?" Nimmo mutters. Why does Kaushalya keep repeating things? As if Nimmo does not know the difference between safe and unsafe. But she does not say anything. Her neighbour has gone beyond the call of friendship, beyond kindness. She has borne witness, talked to the social workers, the politicians, the newspapers and the useless policemen on Nimmo's behalf, and now she comes because she cares for her, Nirmaljeet Kaur, a woman damaged in places too private to see.

"And don't tell me you are cleaning again," Kaushalya says. "Come here and sit down for a few minutes. I'll make us some tea." She goes into the kitchen, and soon Nimmo hears the clatter of kettle and tumblers. At one time she would have felt ashamed of her own lack of hospitality. She would never have allowed a guest to make tea for herself.

"They mentioned that plane in the news again today," Kaushalya says, bringing in the tea and sitting down beside Nimmo. "The one that crashed last year. So sad, no? They still haven't caught the people who did it. Do you remember hearing about it?"

Yes, Nimmo thinks, *I remember.* A plane exploded out of the sky and plunged into the sea. Everyone on board died. Three-hundred-and-twenty-nine people. The plane was flying from Canada to India—from the place to which she had sent her oldest son, Jasbeer. For a few days, until the names were released, Nimmo was afraid that the child she gave away into Bibi-ji's care was one of the dead. But his name was not there. She has no idea where he is or what he is doing, but until she hears otherwise, she knows that she has one living child. And two dead.

Rumours had immediately circulated that it was her people, Sikhs, who had done this deed: put a bomb in the plane and killed all those men, women and children. But why should she, Nirmaljeet Kaur, care? The world is full of news. She too was news in November 1984.

"What a tragedy," Kaushalya says. "So many innocent lives." She finishes her tea and rises to leave. She looks closely at Nimmo. "Do you want me to stay here with you tonight? Are you all right?"

Nimmo nods briskly. "Yes, don't worry about me. I have lots to do." She waits until her friend has left before beginning her preparations for the evening meal. She has planned an elaborate menu. But she will have to hurry, she thinks, chopping the bunch of fragrant coriander that she purchased on her way back from the temple. They will all be back anytime now. They always come without warning and it upsets her no end. *Give me some time to get ready,* she has said to them so many times, but no, does anyone ever listen to her? The onions sizzle in the hot oil, then the spinach and the paneer bits she had fried earlier. This is for Satpal, he loves her spinach paneer with hot parathey. And here is Kamal's favourite, kheer studded heavily with raisins and cashews. It is expensive to put so many dried fruits in a single dish, but her daughter deserves everything she can make for her. Back to the kitchen to heat the oil for Pappu's puris.

She turns on all the lights in the tiny house and lays out the plates, the bowls and the mats for her family to sit on, and waits. They will come back, she knows. She cannot possibly have lost her family for the second time in her life. Oh no, she is a careful woman, a fearful one, who is prepared for trouble. Not like her foolish mother, who left nothing behind except a small, frightened child and the smell of lavender soap. Nimmo lays out her banquet and opens the doors, and opens the windows, and waits in the stillness of the night. *They will come.*

A tall man with a grey beard and a light blue turban walks slowly down the dark gully. The streetlights throw long shadows of houses, shops and shrines, people and cows. The man walks past small stands selling cigarettes and bananas, Glucose biscuits and Monaco crackers, stopping now and again to peer at the house numbers, hoping that things have not changed too much in his absence. He shifts his backpack from one shoulder to another and passes a shop that he remembers visiting when he was a child. His heart beats faster. He is nearly home.

Vancouver—In a stunning conclusion to a case that spanned 20 years, two Canadians were found not guilty on first-degree murder charges in the bombing of Air-India Flight 182 that killed 329 people.
—*The Globe and Mail* (Canada), March 16, 2005

New Delhi—More than two decades later, the Justice Nanavati Commission report has revealed that only one police official . . . was convicted in the 1984 anti-Sikh riots in which more than 3,000 Sikhs were killed in Delhi alone. . . . Interestingly, cases against 14 police officials could not be proceeded with as "files were untraced." Besides these, in cases against two officers "no chargesheet (was) filed" due to lack of evidence. Five others were "acquitted." Against one "no evidence" was reported.
—*The Tribune* (India), August 9, 2005

The history of Punjab that forms the background to this novel is a long and complex one. The following note, a brief summary of that history, may assist some readers in entering into the story.

Punjab, situated in northwestern India, is watered by four rivers, making it one of the most fertile and prosperous states in the country. From around the seventh century, however, because of its strategic location as the gateway into India, Punjab was also fated to be a battleground between foreign invaders, who swept in through the mountain passes of Afghanistan, and local kings.

During the fifteenth century, a particularly violent period in Punjab, the Sikh religion was founded by Guru Nanak Dev and further shaped by the nine gurus who succeeded him over the next two politically turbulent centuries. It was the tenth and last guru, Gobind Singh, who gave Sikhism its present form by formally baptizing five men who would be the nucleus of a casteless, egalitarian community of people. This community came to be known as the Khalsa, or the pure. Men who were baptized gave up their names for the single family name of "Singh," which meant "lion" and symbolized their willingness to bravely fight all injustice. Women took the surname "Kaur," meaning princess or lioness. Five emblems marked the baptized men: long hair and unshaven beard, a comb to maintain the hair, knee-length breeches, a steel bracelet on the right wrist and a kirpan or sword at the waist. Together these articles symbolized the soldier-saint who would wield arms only for a righteous cause.

Until the early eighteenth century Punjab was a scattered jigsaw puzzle of small kingdoms constantly at war with each other or with larger powers such as the Marathas, the Rajputs, the Mughals and the British. Then, in 1801, an ambitious young man named Ranjit Singh conquered these fractured kingdoms and forged a unified nation out of them, thus fostering, for the first time, a sense of Punjabi identity that embraced equally the Hindu, Muslim and Sikh people. Over the next three decades or so he continued to expand his kingdom, making it one of the most powerful in Asia. Following his death in 1839, however, the kingdom began to disintegrate, prey once more to warring factions. Enter the British, who were by then deeply entrenched in India both politically and commercially, and who behind their façade of neutrality had long nurtured plans to take over the wealthy, strategically located Punjab.

The following century and a half saw the region in a state of constant turmoil until 1947, when the British finally pulled out of India, arbitrarily drawing a line across the land, creating two new nations—India, with its Hindu majority, and Pakistan, with its largely Muslim population. Punjab was cut into two bits, with the western half going to Pakistan. This division, and the great relocation of people that followed, caused massive loss of life, ancestral land, history and memory; it created wounds and resentments that festered and grew until the early 1980s when, partly due to differences between the Indian government and the Sikhs over land and water rights, the Punjab was transformed from the granary of the country into a fractured battleground. Between 1983 and 1993, acts of brutality and terrorism—both by the Indian government and by militant groups demanding a separate homeland for the Sikhs—became daily occurrences.

The violence escalated until June 1984, when Indira Gandhi, then prime minister of India, ordered the army into the Golden Temple, the holiest of Sikh shrines, in an attempt to rid it of groups of armed militants who had fortified themselves within the complex of buildings surrounding the shrine. In the ensuing battle the temple was damaged and many of the militants, soldiers and several hundreds of pilgrims (up to two thousand, according to some estimates) were killed.

The anger generated by the invasion of the temple resulted in the assassination of Indira Gandhi by two of her Sikh bodyguards in October 1984. This in turn precipitated the systematic "revenge" killings of innocent Sikhs throughout India; thousands were murdered in Delhi alone. Twenty-two years and nine inquiry commissions later, only one of the perpetrators has been brought to justice, even though many of them were identified.

Less than a year after the invasion of the Golden Temple, in June 1985, Air India Flight 182, en route from Canada to India via London, exploded over the Atlantic Ocean, off the coast of Ireland, killing all 329 people on board. Fifteen years later, in October 2000, two Canadian Sikhs were finally charged with having planted the bomb. Both men were acquitted in March 2005 for lack of sufficient evidence.

The violence in Punjab died down abruptly around 1995, but the chain of tragic events that destroyed many innocent lives continues to scar memories.

Although these well-known historical events form the backdrop for my novel, I would like to emphasize that this story is fiction and that all the characters and their actions, thoughts and feelings are entirely fictional and not intended to represent or portray any actual people.

ACKNOWLEDGMENTS

I owe an enormous debt of gratitude to the following
people:

Dr. Harinder Singh Marjara and Eisha Marjara for sharing
their lives, their family photographs, their feelings with me.

Sushma Datt of Rimjhim Radio Vancouver for long
conversations, Hindi music and loans of cassette tapes
of programs recorded soon after Indira Gandhi's
assassination.

Nsibe Puri for graciously giving me stories of her life as
a Punjabi girl growing up in British Columbia.

Veena Das for her thoughts on the anti-Sikh riots in
Delhi.

Louise Dennys for her patience while this book went
through several avatars, her perceptive comments on all
aspects of story and character, and above all, for the
"eh?" question.

Denise Bukowski for her faith in me even when I was
beginning to lose it.

Kendall Anderson for her editorial honesty, and John
Eerkes-Medrano for his sharp eye for dates and details.

Mini Menon and Yasmin Ladha for being such good
friends and hearing me out every time I came up with a
new version of this story.

Madhav and Aditya for their constant love.

Thanks are also due to the Canada Council for the Arts for financial support in the earliest stages of this book.

In addition, these books were particularly important and useful to me in my research: *A History of the Sikhs, Volumes I and II*, by Khushwant Singh; *The Sikhs*, by Patwant Singh; *The Sorrow and the Terror: The Haunting Legacy of the Air India Tragedy*, by Clark Blaise and Bharati Mukherjee; *The Death of Air India Flight 182*, by Salim Jiwa; *Fighting for Faith and Nation: Dialogues with Sikh Militants*, by Cynthia Keppley Mahmood; *Who Are the Guilty? Report of a Joint Inquiry into the Causes and Impacts of the Riots in Delhi from 31 October to 10 November*, by People's Union for Democratic Rights/People's Union for Civil Liberties, *1984*; *The Delhi Riots: Three Days in the Life of a Nation*, by Uma Chakravarti and Nandita Haksar; *The Other Side of Silence: Voices from the Partition of India*, by Urvashi Butalia; *The Voyage of the Komagata Maru: The Sikh Challenge to Canada's Colour Bar*, by Hugh Johnston.

The following articles from *Communities, Riots and Survivors in South Asia*, edited by Veena Das, were also helpful: "The Survivor in the Study of Violence" by Amrit Srinivasan; "Our Work to Cry: Your Work to Listen" by Veena Das.

The poem "Farewell" by Agha Shahid Ali, from which I have quoted a line as an epigraph to the novel, can be found in his collection *The Country Without a Post Office: Poems*.

ANITA RAU BADAMI's first novel was the hugely successful bestseller *Tamarind Mem.* Her bestselling second novel, *The Hero's Walk,* won the Regional Commonwealth Writers' Prize, Italy's Premio Berto Award and was also named a *Washington Post* Best Book of 2001. It was also on the longlist for the International IMPAC Dublin Literary Prize and the Orange Prize for Fiction, and the shortlist for the Kiriyama Prize. Both novels have been published in many countries throughout the world. The recipient of the Marian Engel Award for a woman writer in mid-career, Badami currently resides in Montreal.

A NOTE ABOUT THE TYPE

Can You Hear the Nightbird Call? has been set in a digitized form of Garamond. This modern version is based on types first cut by Claude Garamond (c.1480-1561). Garamond is believed to have followed classic Venetian type models, although he did introduce a number of important differences, and it is to him that we owe the letterforms we now know as "old style." Garamond gave his characters a sense of movement and elegance that ultimately won him an international reputation and the patronage of Frances I of France.

BOOK DESIGN BY CS RICHARDSON